Women, Science and Fiction

The *Frankenstein* Inheritance

Debra Benita Shaw

First published 2000 by
PALGRAVE
Houndmills, Basingstoke, Hampshire RG21 6XS and
175 Fifth Avenue, New York, N. Y. 10010
Companies and representatives throughout the world

PALGRAVE is the new global academic imprint of
St. Martin's Press LLC Scholarly and Reference Division and
Palgrave Publishers Ltd (formerly Macmillan Press Ltd).

Outside North America
ISBN 0–333–74158–7 hardback

In North America
ISBN 0–312–23605–0 hardback

A catalogue record for this book is available from the British Library.

Library of Congress Cataloging-in-Publication Data
Shaw, Debra Benita
    Women, science, and fiction : the Frankenstein inheritance / Debra Benita Shaw.
        p. cm.
    Enlargement of author's thesis (doctoral)—University of East Anglia.
    Includes bibliographical references (p.) and index.
    ISBN 0–312–23605–0
    1. Science fiction, American—Women authors—History and criticism. 2. Science fiction, English—Women authors—History and criticism. 3. Shelley, Mary Wollstonecraft, 1797–1851. Frankenstein. 4. Shelley, Mary Wollstonecraft, 1797–1851—Influence. 5. Literature and science—United States—History. 6. Literature and science—Great Britain—History. 7. Women and literature—United States—History. 8. Women and literature—Great Britain—History. I. Title.

PS374.S35 S48 2000
813'.08762099287—dc21
                                                            00–034518

10 9 8 7 6 5 4 3 2 1
09 08 07 06 05 04 03 02 01 00

Printed in Great Britain by Antony Rowe Ltd, Chippenham, Wiltshire

For Patricia Jackson

Contents

Acknowledgements

This book started life as a doctoral thesis at the University of East Anglia, Norwich (UK), under the excellent supervision of Mr Jon Cook, to whom I should like to extend my most sincere thanks. Thanks also to my friends and colleagues Drs Megan Stern and Patricia Murray for help, advice and intellectual stimulation, and also for taking the time to read and discuss my final two chapters. Three people whom I have never met in person but whose correspondence proved invaluable in consolidating my ideas should also be mentioned: Sarah Lefanu for helping me to sort out exactly what science fiction *is*; Professor Daphne Patai for some helpful comments regarding the historical connections between writers; and Mrs Isobel Allan-Burns whose reply to my letter requesting information about her close friend Katharine Burdekin helped me to understand the personality behind the writing. In similar vein, I would like to express my gratitude to Caroline Forbes who was kind enough to talk at length to me about her influences and motivations. Thanks also to the librarians at the Science Fiction Foundation at the University of East London (now at Liverpool University) and to my students at the University of North London: in particular, Gareth Parry, Zandra Kuren, Annette Corbett, Ruth Sharman and Carlotta Kaufmann, whose excellent work helped to sustain my own enthusiasm for the subject. Finally, I would like to extend heartfelt thanks to Mrs Patricia Jackson, without whom (as they say) none of this would have been possible.

1
Introduction: Women, Science and Fiction

> Most major scientific theories rebuff common sense. They call on evidence beyond the reach of our senses and overturn the observable world. They disturb assumed relationships and shift what has been substantial into metaphor.... When it is first advanced, theory is at its most fictive. The awkwardness of fit between the natural world as it is currently perceived and as it is hypothetically imagined holds the theory itself for a time within a provisional scope akin to that of fiction.
>
> Gillian Beer, *Darwin's Plots*[1]

> SF is a territory of contested cultural reproduction in high-technology worlds. Placing the narratives of scientific fact within the heterogeneous space of SF produces a transformed field. The transformed field sets up resonances among all of its regions and components. No region or component is 'reduced' to any other, but reading and writing practices respond to each other across a structured space. Speculative fiction has different tensions when its field also contains the inscription practices that constitute scientific fact.
>
> Donna J. Haraway, *Primate Visions*[2]

Both Gillian Beer and Donna Haraway are interested in scientific theory as text: as itself a type of fiction which can be deconstructed to show the ideology at work in its production. This book will explore the 'different tensions' that Haraway refers to in the work of women writers of science fiction (sf), where 'scientific fact' (or, at least, the theories presented as such) can be located as a sub-text informing the style and construction of the work. Taking a diverse sampling of women's sf, from the turn of the century to the mid-1990s, I will demonstrate how these texts respond to an analysis which looks for a critique of scientific ideology: an exposure of the way in which gender is constructed in scientific thought.

While Beer and Haraway are acute contemporary analysts of science as ideology, it is my belief that women writers have, throughout this century, consciously or unconsciously, utilised the freedoms offered by the forms of sf to similarly expose the gender-biased ideology which informs what counts as scientific knowledge and to offer surprising and often revolutionary alternatives to the future visions of their male counterparts. My project will be to examine how specific scientific theories, current at the time of writing, have motivated women to imagine new female identities and social orders which present a re-evaluation of the place of science in women's lives.

What follows from this is a claim that sf can have a socially or politically critical purpose and indeed, as Patrick Parrinder has written, '[a]dmirers of science fiction have always pointed to its role in questioning social assumptions, and today there is widespread recognition of this'.[3] However, as he points out, '[i]n modern literature the terms "social fable" and "moral fable" may be applied to almost any fiction in which the author's didactic intentions override his [sic] impulses towards artistic ... detachment'.[4] Where sf differs is that it is concerned with imagining how scientific theory, if that theory is applied and assimilated into society, may affect the future development of that society. It is fiction 'concerned with the impact of contemporary knowledge and its extension into the future on human behaviour'.[5]

What John Griffiths is referring to here is the technique of 'extrapolation', which describes the way in which sf narratives develop their themes by projecting onto a future, or other, world a scenario that can plausibly be imagined, given that a current scientific theory, or discovery, is provided as the basis. But, unlike Griffiths, I do not want to take issue with 'the extrapolists' over whether this term merely 'equate[s] SF with no more than technological forecasting'[6] but rather make clear my intention to use the term to describe the way in which sf offers potential futures whose most important function is to distance the reader from, and thus offer a critical perspective on, her present. The scientific sub-text thus roots the text in the time and place of its production, while the extrapolation is not so much a forecast of the future but rather a statement about the political implications of scientific theories and new technologies. Writers are free to imagine worlds other than our own, with different historical and biological evolutions, different geographies and hence radically different forms of social relations. This, I would argue, has been the particular appeal of sf[7] for feminists. As Jen Green and Sarah Lefanu put it:

> Science fiction . . . allows us to take the present position of women and use the metaphors of science fiction to illuminate it. We may be writing *about* the future, but we are writing *in* the present.[8]

But what is now recognised as feminist sf is a relatively recent phenomenon, a phenomenon consolidated by Sarah Lefanu in her authoritative overview of the genre *In the Chinks of the World Machine* (1988). For Lefanu, 'Feminist SF . . . is part of science fiction while struggling against it',[9] and she states her intention to 'chart that extraordinary relationship between feminism and science fiction that flowered in the 1970s and that continues to the present day'.[10]

However, the particular nature of the genre makes it difficult to ascertain by precisely what conventions the site of struggle is marked. Since Hugo Gernsback first named sf in 1929, a succession of struggles over what exactly its form might be has ensured a plethora of sub-genres and re-definitions. As Patrick Parrinder has pointed out, 'Definitions of science fiction are not so much a series of logical approximations to an elusive ideal, as a small, parasitic sub-genre in themselves',[11] and, since the growth of academic interest in sf, the net has widened to include earlier works that fall within the terms of various definitions that have been offered to distinguish 'true' sf from fantasy or space opera.[12] So it is perhaps more accurate to suggest, as Jenny Wolmark has done, that, since the 1970s, 'Feminist science fiction has brought the politics of feminism into a genre with a solid tradition of ignoring or excluding women writers'.[13] However, I would disagree with Lefanu's assertion that the 'struggle' necessarily began in the 1970s. The next five chapters of this book present novels and short stories, written by women, and published between 1914 and 1969, which demonstrate an engagement with the genre in a way which clearly recognises its radical potential. What is needed, and what this book will provide, is an analysis of these texts as salient interventions in this 'solid tradition'.

Serious critical analysis of sf, along with its inclusion in university English Literature courses, can probably be traced to the first publication of the critical journal *Extrapolation* in 1959. Two years later, as Parrinder writes, 'Kingsley Amis's widely-read and controversial survey *New Maps of Hell* (1961) did much to make SF intellectually fashionable'.[14] Since this time, Mary Shelley's *Frankenstein* (1818) has been acknowledged as the first sf novel, and H. G. Wells and Jules Verne have been drawn into the net along with individual novels by such writers as Aldous Huxley (*Brave New World*, 1932) and George Orwell (*Nineteen Eighty-Four*, 1949). Brian Aldiss and David Wingrove's comprehensive history of the genre, *Trillion Year Spree* (1988), also includes, among others, Edgar Allan Poe. Despite the proliferation of definitions, conditions for inclusion in this new literary canon generally required the presence of a plausible extrapolation and what Darko Suvin has called 'estrangement and cognition'.[15] The familiar is de-familiarised to facilitate a critical reflection on the writers' and readers' perceived reality.

Although Shelley is the acknowledged 'mother' of the genre, most historical analyses do not dwell at any length on a single woman writer until the publication, in 1969, of Ursula Le Guin's *The Left Hand of Darkness*. As Patricia Monk points out, women in the intervening years have often written 'under the cover of initials or ambisexual pseudonyms' so that 'women writers of science fiction have often tended to be invisible, even when they did exist'.[16] Monk has identified what she calls the 'androcentric mystique' of sf, 'a literary mystique characterised by gadgetry, adventure and androcentric thinking', and finds it unsurprising that 'women writers who have broken into the genre have, on finding it dominated by this androcentric mystique, shown a tendency to succumb and to incorporate the mystique into their own writing'.[17] I would argue here that, in the very macho early days of magazine sf, it would have been virtually impossible for a woman who did not appear to succumb to find publication. These women were engaged in a struggle of their own. What, then, made the likes of Katharine Burdekin, Judith Merril, C. L. Moore, Catherine Maclean, Margaret St Clair, Leigh Brackett, C. J. Cherryh and Marion Zimmer Bradley, among others, wish to involve themselves in the androcentric mystique? I believe this is an important question which can be answered by returning to Suvin's definition of the genre as requiring the presence of 'estrangement and cognition'.

Recent discussions of sf in the context of postmodernism have emphasised the way in which extrapolation has now necessarily become disconnected from what it attempts to refer to. Jean Baudrillard, for instance, considers sf to be now less concerned with presenting potential futures than with attempting to represent what Istvan Csicsery-Ronay Jr has called 'the problematic autonomy of reality'.[18] In other words, the imaginary space that was once held to exist between the extrapolation and its origin has collapsed amid postmodern uncertainty about the concept of originality.

As Baudrillard has (now famously) claimed, 'SF . . . is no longer an elsewhere, it is an everywhere'. 'Classic SF',[19] according to Baudrillard, concerned with colonisation dreams and the conquest of space, was able to function in the imaginary space opened up by the concept of progress. It has, in this sense, a historical specificity and is no longer relevant to a world where, as he says, 'the map covers all the territory':

> the projection, the extrapolation, this sort of pantographic exuberance which made up the charm of SF are now no longer possible. It is now no longer possible to manufacture the unreal from the real, to create the imaginary from the data of reality. The process will be rather the reverse: to put in place 'decentered' situations, models of simulation, and then to strive to give them the colours of the real, the banal, the lived; to reinvent the real as fiction, precisely because the real has disappeared from our lives.[20]

So, as Jenny Wolmark explains it, 'it becomes the task of contemporary SF to present us with the fiction that is our own world'.[21]

But, if sf *is* lived reality, estrangement can no longer function as a distancing technique. Science fiction can only function as a long series of re-presentations in which the pleasure is, perhaps, one of re-cognition. And, if this is the case, what happens to the socially critical function of sf, and of feminist sf in particular? As Wolmark has pointed out, 'as the specificity of human experience is displaced by simulation, then the lived realities of oppression and subordination experienced by women have no way of being expressed'.[22] To return to the allure of the 'androcentric mystique', I think it is clear that the 'decentred situations' that Baudrillard prescribes for contemporary sf were always to be found among the fictions of women writers for whom centrality was never a position that they themselves could claim. We need, perhaps, to return to the days of 'classic' sf in order to discover a continuity in women's sf writing that can re-establish the connection between gender conditioning and the practice and application of science, a connection that much postmodern theory has too readily effaced in favour of the claim that all categories of the 'human' are de-centred in the postmodernist scenario. The (female) scientist, Alice Sheldon, posing as the (male) sf writer, James Tiptree Jr and taking part in a symposium on feminist sf[23] is, for me, a suitably ironic 'fiction' with which to illustrate this point. It is my belief that the appeal of sf for women has always been that it allows opportunities both to express and explore alienation as well as to offer a fictional description of the kind of world that a gender-free or differently gendered science might produce.

I do not, then, want to differentiate between 'feminist' sf and sf that happens to be written by women. Although some of the works that I will be discussing nail their political colours very firmly to the mast, others do not. I am primarily interested in discovering how the writers have responded to the cultural and scientific milieu in which each text was produced and what this can reveal about women's particular relationship to science and technology. How have succeeding developments in evolutionary theory, psychoanalysis, cybernetics, sociobiology, ecology and 1980s/90s technoscience influenced the politics of women's engagement with the genre?

Applied science and feminist fictions

As Evelyn Fox Keller has pointed out, 'the breach which separates women from science is very deep'.[24] The mythology which surrounds the practice and application of science is, as Keller reminds us, inseparable from the cultural construction of gender. The frame of mind thought necessary to the production of scientific research, uninfected with affective bias, is thus thought impossible for women, who are invested with the emotional and affective qualities not permitted to the masculine type. The practice of science can be seen as confirming masculinity and thus jealously guarded as a panacea to male gender insecurity. The problem for feminists in attacking this ground is that science comes to be regarded as monolithic; as so essentially a male invention that nothing less than the stripping away of the entire cultural tradition of scientific practice and technological production will do.

The eco-feminist stance, which promotes the identification of women with a deified nature, has the effect of locating them in the realm assigned to them by the split that associates men with culture and production and women with nature and reproduction. Women are thus excluded, not only from the discourse of science itself but also from the discussions of how scientific discoveries and technological advances may affect our daily lives. As Gillian Beer has pointed out:

> The identification of women with nature has had the effect of prolonging the notion of separate spheres and making women the objects of inquiry rather than its initiators.[25]

In other words, those feminists who would want to exclude women from science altogether, on the grounds that all scientific practice is injurious, risk perpetuating the myth of woman as inadequate to compass the type of consciousness thought necessary to scientific study.

Another school of feminist thought criticises male dominance in scientific institutions and presses for funding and resources to be made available so that women may take an equal place in the scientific community. But, as Laurie Smith Keller points out, 'There is some anecdotal evidence that, even in modern engineering and computing, women bring a different perspective to the work', leading to the assumption that women's particular approach is 'inferior rather than merely different'.[26] And Gillian Beer asks why Eve is not included in 'the list of heroic seekers after knowledge'. Traditionally 'the *nature* of her desire is ignored: it is presented only as appetite. . . . Like Pandora, her inquiry is trivialised as curiosity'.[27] Discussions of women and science are thus perpetually plagued by the twin spectres of essentialism and the hierarchisation of approaches.

What I believe is needed is a more comprehensive understanding of how women perceive themselves in relation to scientific knowledge and the use of technology. In other words, as Sandra Harding says, it is imperative that any dialogue should be informed 'by the voices of the majority of the world's women who are not involved in criticising the sciences at all, but simply in surviving'.[28] If we recognise that science is determined by its social context and that women provide part of that context, whether as consumers of technological products, production line workers affected by science-based working practices, users (not always willingly) of reproductive and medical technology, or simply as excluded from the knowledge that allows individual autonomy in a technological world, then we must also acknowledge a hidden social and philosophical history which can be revealed by the study of women's forays into a literature that explicitly engages with science, its products and producers.

In selecting texts for analysis, I have therefore been guided by those novels and short stories produced by women which show a response to the scientific theories which had a cultural impact at the time that the work was produced. I have also been motivated, as a long-term sf reader who also happens to be a woman, by stories that have affected me personally and by a desire to rescue from obscurity some writers who have received little or no recognition (and, in the case of James Tiptree Jr, an early story that has seemed to perplex some feminist critics but, for me, begs an analysis that recognises that Alice Sheldon herself was, in fact, a scientist). My aim will be to demonstrate how sf can provide a potent mythology for women to recognise themselves as intimate with, rather than separate from, the discourse of science and as agents for change rather than passive victims of the change that new developments impose.

Beginning at the turn of the century, Charlotte Perkins Gilman's *Herland* (1914) was produced in the era of the suffragists and marks a specific response to Social Darwinism and the question of women's role in a society that was beginning to respond to new knowledge about genetic and social inheritance. Gilman herself was an outspoken feminist and is best known for *The Yellow Wallpaper* (1892), a semi-autobiographical novel charting the descent into madness of a woman denied her desire to write. Ignoring the advice of her doctors, Gilman prescribed for herself a rigorous routine of lecturing, writing and vigorous exercise. Remarkably for that time, she gave her daughter into the care of her ex-husband and his new wife so that she could travel the length and breadth of America, often penniless and suffering from acute bouts of depression, to lecture on socialism and feminism. Her Herlanders are the fictional expression of the strong, independent and resourceful woman that she believed to be the only fit mother for the survival of the race.

In Chapter 3, I turn to an analysis of Katharine Burdekin's *Swastika Night*, originally published in 1937, which since its re-publication in 1985 has received scant attention. It has been compared to George Orwell's *Nineteen Eighty-Four*, and certainly the two novels have elements in common, but for me what is most striking is the way in which it actively engages with psychoanalysis[29] in such a way as to suggest that we look for the roots of women's oppression in an analysis of the psychic orientation of the soldier, the extreme type of the 'masculine' male which demands a complementary extreme in the 'feminine' opposite. Burdekin herself is a mystery about whom little is known other than that she published some of her work (including *Swastika Night* and an earlier novel, *Proud Man*) under the male pseudonym 'Murray Constantine', but there are striking similarities between her fictional exposition of male and female psychic development and the theories of the post-Freudian psychoanalysts Karen Horney and Melanie Klein. My reading will assess *Swastika Night* as a document arguing for a feminist politics which looks to psychoanalytic theory to support a claim that gender differences are socially constructed rather than psychogenetically inherent. I will show how Burdekin's work stands as an early formulation of the arguments that have informed contemporary feminist ideology.

Chapters 4 and 5 deal with the so called 'Golden Age' of the 1940s and 1950s when science fiction grew both in popularity and prestige and male pseudonyms (or the ambiguous use of initials) were almost obligatory for those women attempting to find publication in a very male dominated genre. One of these, C. L. Moore, has received some attention for her first story, 'Shambleau', and more recent criticism has recognised 'No Woman Born' for its subversion of the Frankenstein myth to challenge notions of female powerlessness. However, Sarah Gamble finds the story unsatisfying for a feminist reader because the central character achieves her strength through a fusion with technology which cannot be repeated; the story thus 'emphasises her unnaturalness'.[30] I want to offer an alternative reading of the story, based on its engagement with Cybernetics, which looks at the creation of a female cyborg as a metaphor for the empowering potential of women's interaction with technology.

Similarly drawing on the implications of the theory of Cybernetics, Margaret St Clair's 'Short In The Chest', a skilful satire on the human/machine relationship, uses language to set up a sophisticated network of allusions which demonstrate a response to the political situation in the US during the 1950s as well as problematising the sense in which we understand communication. St Clair challenges the notion that we can clearly or immediately distinguish between functional machine output and output that appears in accordance with a machine's function but is, in fact, the result of interference or a fault in the mechanism. My reading of the story will reveal how a simple narrative of patient/therapist interaction can be structured to incorporate a satirical critique of social theories that privilege the *modus operandi* of machine technology in determining human behaviour and, in particular, female sexual behaviour.

In Chapter 6, I examine Tiptree's 'Your Haploid Heart' against a background of the radical politics of the late 1960s and the re-emergence of the women's movement. The 'pulp' tradition was still very strong during this period although, in the UK, *New Worlds* magazine claimed to break new ground by introducing sex and psychedelia into sf.[31] Later stories by Tiptree established her as a feminist writer but I have chosen 'Your Haploid Heart' because I believe that the confusion it has caused some feminist critics, who try to place it within the context of her later writings, can be clarified by understanding the story as a critique of theories of genetic predetermination that were a subject of debate at the time, as well as a response to the debates that had arisen as a result of the growth of the youth counter-culture which challenged the monolithic status of science and the objective frame of mind. My reading will draw on the work of the French language theorist Julia Kristeva, to explore how the text reflects patterns of gendered discourse.

In Chapter 7, I move forward to the mid-1980s when, in Britain, the Women's Press launched their sf list and feminist sf became an acknowledged phenomenon. The lesbian separatist utopias are perhaps its most radical form and generally reflect the growing concern with the environmental effects of the use of technology, which in these texts is identified with masculine power. In this chapter, I offer a comparison between Sally Miller Gearhart's *The Wanderground* and Caroline Forbes's 'London Fields' with a view to examining how stories that imagine a world without men can provide the basis for a discussion of how female knowledge of the world is to be recognised and how this may structure our approaches to scientific knowledge in the future.

Finally, Chapter 8 presents Marge Piercy's cyberpunk novel *Body of Glass* as a radical argument for a technoscientific re-working of gender identities. Acknowledging a debt to Haraway's 'Cyborg Manifesto', Piercy plays with the idea of technological/biological fusion and the limitless imaginary potential of cyberspace to suggest a near future in which redefinition of the self through technology offers dramatic possibilities for revolution. Through an analysis of Piercy's novel as an imaginative flight from contemporary experience which nevertheless poses uncomfortable questions about the postmodern condition, I will demonstrate how a deliberate literary foray into the realm of social theory can raise contentious issues for its application to lived social reality.

The nearly silent listener

In her introduction to the 1831 edition of *Frankenstein*, Mary Shelley described how she was motivated to write the novel. In the summer of 1816, she and Shelley 'visited Switzerland, and became the neighbours of Lord Byron'.[32] Also present was Byron's secretary, Polidari. The weather being particularly bad, they spent much of their time reading ghost stories and agreed that each would attempt a story of their own. Mary was lost for ideas until a particular night when a discussion between Byron and Shelley fired her imagination:

> Many and long were the conversations between Lord Byron and Shelley, to which I was a devout but nearly silent, listener. During one of these, various philosophical doctrines were discussed and among others the nature of the principle of life, and whether there

was any possibility of its ever being discovered and communicated. They talked of the experiments of Dr [Erasmus] Darwin ... who preserved a piece of vermicelli in a glass case, till by some extraordinary means it began to move with voluntary motion. Not thus, after all, would life be given. Perhaps a corpse would be re-animated; galvanism had given token of such things; perhaps the component parts of a creature might be manufactured, brought together and endued with vital warmth.[33]

Shelley then goes on to describe how, once in bed, she 'did not sleep, nor could I be said to think. My imagination, unbidden, possessed and guided me, gifting the successive images that arose in my mind with a vividness far beyond the normal bounds of reverie'.[34]

This, for me, is a potent description of the feminist imagination at work in creating sf. The 'nearly silent' listener, excluded from, but affected by, scientific discourse, finds a voice through an imaginative medium in which she can express her own hopes and fears about the potential for science to transform her life. In the following chapters, I will argue that attention to that voice can reveal a powerful and insistent dialogue which argues for a recognition of women's unique relationship to how knowledge of the world and ourselves is understood.

2
Herland: Charlotte Perkins Gilman and the Literature of the Beehive

If the beehive produced literature, the bee's fiction would be rich and broad, full of the complex tasks of comb-building and filling, the care and feeding of the young, the guardian-service of the queen; and far beyond that it would spread to the blue glory of the summer sky, the fresh winds, the endless beauty and sweetness of a thousand thousand flowers. It would treat of the vast fecundity of motherhood, the educative and selective processes of the group-mothers, and the passion of loyalty, of social service, which holds the hive together.

But if the drones wrote fiction it would have no subject matter save the feasting of many, and the nuptial flight, of one.

Charlotte Perkins Gilman on 'Masculine Literature'[1]

Charlotte Perkins Gilman was perhaps best known in her own time for *Women and Economics*, published originally in 1898, which, according to Sheila Rowbotham, 'pioneered a critique of conventional, male-dominated, economics for ignoring the contribution of women to wealth through domestic labour'.[2] She wrote at a time when the ideas of Darwin were giving rise to much discussion – 'feeding an extraordinary range of disciplines beyond its own biological field'.[3] Gilman, as both a socialist and a feminist, was committed to the belief that evolutionary theory indicated the need for social evolution to be planned in accordance with ideals that would ensure 'improvement' for the human race. What she saw as the prime directive in establishing a more evolutionarily viable society (and she believed the current state of the society in which she lived to be indicative of a morbid degeneration of the species) was the role of the mother in educating her children, a role that she believed the women of her time were poorly adapted to fulfil.

Gilman was supremely aware of the masculine bias of fiction and was concerned that women, 'new to the field, and following masculine canons because all the canons were masculine',[4] should grasp the opportunity presented by a burgeoning women's movement to stake a claim for a literature of their own which would reflect the new freedoms that she saw as offered by a rapidly changing social environment. Against the 'preferred subject matter of fiction ... the Story of Adventure, and the Love Story' which 'do not touch on human processes, social processes ... but on the special field of predatory excitement so long the sole province of men',[5] she proposed a new literature that would give a 'true picture of woman's life'[6] – the life that she believed women would evolve, once released from their economic dependence on men. *Herland* is her attempt to write the new literature; to show how the conventions of the Story of Adventure and the Love Story must necessarily be subverted by the introduction of themes which derive their emotional impact from a conception of motherhood which sees mother love as the primary force in life and the role of the mother as the determining influence on the future, rather than from 'the emotions of an assistant in the preliminary stages'.[7]

This chapter will explore the 'literature of the beehive', Gilman's attempt to popularise these ideas and present an alternative to what she called 'the Adventures of Him in Pursuit of Her:

> and it stops when he gets her. Story after story, age after age, over and over, this ceaseless repetition of the Preliminaries.[8]

Herland was first serialised in Gilman's own fortnightly magazine *The Forerunner*, which she published between 1909 and 1916, writing every word herself, including the advertisements, as a direct response to the reluctance of the publishing paternity to accept her more radical work. In her own words:

> Social philosophy, however ingeniously presented, does not command wide popular interest. ... If one wants to express important truths, needed yet unpopular, the market is necessarily limited.
>
> As all my principal topics were in direct contravention of established views, beliefs and emotions, it is a wonder that so many editors took so much of my work for so long.[9]

Herland was not published independently until 1979, when it was bought by Pantheon Books in New York and, in the same year, by the

Women's Press in London as part of their new and highly successful science fiction series. Although I agree with Dale Spender that 'of all the women writing and lecturing about women's position and the problem of men at the beginning of the twentieth century...Gilman...comes closest to sharing the assumptions and aims of the contemporary women's movement',[10] *Herland*, like all sf writing, is a product of its time, conditioned by prevailing trends in both scientific and social development, and should, I think, be read as such. Gilman's 'social philosophy' needs to be understood as a reaction to, and a consequence of, the paradoxes that Darwinism presented to nineteenth-century intellectuals as it was absorbed into ever more varied disciplines.

Once the theory was reconciled with the religious viewpoint, so another argument would be advanced to prove the laws of nature independent from divine intervention. The essentially theistic view that evolution was merely the playing out of a pre-designed course initiated by a divine creator could answer the question of how a benevolent God could allow suffering by pointing to the fact that the laws of nature had been designed to weed out the 'unfit' so that the divine purpose would be seen to unfold along the lines of Darwin's 'survival of the fittest'. Nevertheless, evolutionary theory, which proved the earth to be much older than could be calculated from the story of Genesis and which denied the separate creation of species, could not be reconciled with a fundamentalist reading of the Bible. Similarly, the planned evolution debate promoted 'negative eugenics' (first put forward by Darwin's cousin, Francis Galton, who believed that the 'worst elements of the poorer classes, those presumed to have subnormal mentalities, would have to be physically prevented from passing on their infirmities', that is, prevented from having children) on the one hand and co-operative effort to raise all members of a society to the level of 'the fit' on the other.[11] Brian Easlea reports[12] that Darwin himself vacillated between a fascistic disclaiming of the value of social support for the weaker members of a society and an exhortation that all members of a society should feel compassion and sympathy towards 'the unfit'. Indeed, the American John Fiske, believed altruism to be 'the guiding feature of human evolution',[13] whereas William Graham Sumner's philosophy was summed up in his own words as 'root, hog, or die'.[14] But in all these arguments, the fundamental question remains that, if natural selection favours only the fittest, then by what criteria do we determine fitness?

Early thinkers influenced by Darwinism were easily able to offer the tenets of evolutionary theory as a justification for *laissez-faire* ideals. Accordingly, 'the survival of the fittest' was interpreted to legitimate the *laissez-faire* economy. Natural selection supposedly favoured the 'captains of industry' with power naturally accruing to moneyed families who instructed their children correctly in the management and maintenance of wealth – progress being commensurate with economic prudence and privileging those who engaged all their energies in the competitive process. In the words of Sumner, a leading proponent of this system of thought, 'millionaires are a product of natural selection, acting on the whole body of men to pick out those who can meet the requirements of certain work to be done'.[15] In this sense, Darwinism could be said to defend an emerging capitalism such as existed in 19th century America, despite the fact that 'these principles of social evolution negated the traditional American ideology of equality and natural rights'.[16] Sumner led the voices against conscious reform and his ideology was widely accepted.

Similarly, the fear of degeneration went hand in hand with the assumption that natural selection necessarily tended toward progress, despite the fact that 'in a truly Darwinian universe there was no guarantee of progress'[17] and that the operation of progress was claimed to be apparent in the distinction between the less technologically advanced and socially sophisticated races and the so called 'civilised' and 'superior' white, industrialised races. Bowler reports that it was 'even suggested that women represented a stage of growth lower than that of men'[18] – a suggestion that, at least in Gilman's view, represented as much a threat to the race as the notion that the 'lower' races could, through immigration and inbreeding, eventually cause the stock to degenerate'.[19]

The appeal to natural selection in re-emphasising the *status quo* necessarily had implications for the status of women at a time when the women's movement was gaining ground and patriarchal ideology was being brought into question. Gilman is an inheritor of the system of thought instigated by the publication, in 1792 in London, of Mary Wollstonecraft's *Vindication of the Rights of Women*, which 'argued for reason as the basis for women's equal part in society and politics',[20] although, like Wollstonecraft, Gilman is 'inclined to be complacent about the inherent progress and superiority of Western civilisation',[21] The collectivity which she advocates and the socialist utopianism upon which *Herland* is based were recurrent themes in the feminism of the period, and a number of thinkers believed domestic reform to be a necessary step in the move towards a more egalitarian society. Gilman's radicalism echoes that of other social reformers like Marie Stevens Howland who 'became convinced that not only should housekeeping be cooperative but that children should be brought up communally',[22] but she was primarily a eugenicist who believed in these changes as a way of influencing the course of evolution.

When Gilman published *Women and Economics*, with its strong bias toward planned evolution in freeing women from 'pitiful dependence',[23] Lester Frank Ward, whose gynaeococentric theory of evolution she called 'the most important single percept in the history of thought',[24] had yet to publish *Pure Sociology* (1903), in which the theory was fully expounded, and his first book, *Dynamic Sociology* (1883), was as yet largely ignored.[25] Ward 'was the first and most formidable of a number of thinkers who attacked the unitary assumptions of social Darwinism and natural-law *laissez-faire* individualism ... he replaced an older passive determinism with a positive body of social theory adaptable to the uses of reform'.[26] His response to the theory of evolution was to argue that human evolution should be brought under conscious control. Like most post-Darwinist social scientists, Ward makes use of analogies from the animal kingdom to give a biological basis to his social theory, and it is this that informs his arguments for a gynaeococentric basis for evolution. Gilman's own work is largely an extension of this theory, relevant as it is to the status of women.

Ward's theory has as its premise that sexual reproduction is the next evolutionary stage to parthenogenesis, which 'is not usually classed as another step in the series but rather as a backward step from a more advanced form':[27]

> The female is the fertile sex, and whatever is fertile is looked upon as female.... It therefore does no violence to language or to science to say that life begins with the female organism and is carried on a long distance by means of females alone. In all the different forms of æsexual reproduction, from fission to parthenogenesis, the female may in this sense be said to exist alone and perform all the functions of life including reproduction. In a word, life begins as female.[28]

The development of sexual reproduction he saw as necessary to facilitate adaptation of the species to a changing environment, but the male, in its first evolution as a separate organism, was merely a fertilising agent and had no life function other than this. However, the female, having the power of selection, would choose to benefit her offspring, favouring the largest and strongest of the available males with the result that the male evolved proportionately in strength and size. Or, as Gilman herself depicts the scenario, early males were 'very tiny, transient, and inferior devices at first, but gradually developed into fuller and fuller equality with the female'.[29] The result, according to Ward, was what he called 'male efflorescence':

> The time came in the development of the race when brute force began to give way to sagacity, and the first use to which this growing power was put was that of circumventing rivals for female favour. Brain grew with effort, and like the other organs that are so strangely developed through this cause, it began to be more especially characteristic of the sex. The weaker sex[30] admired success then as now, and the bright-witted became the successful ones, while the dull witted failed to transmit the dullness. There was a survival of the cunning.[31]

So the human female is the victim of an evolutionary irony. She has been displaced in her 'natural' function as selector of the most suitable mate to benefit her offspring in the race for survival, simply by selecting too well.

Ward and Gilman seem almost to compete in their condemnation of the male. What for Gilman was an 'inferior device', for Ward was 'a mere afterthought of nature',[32] and bees and spiders are frequently brought into the argument to 'prove' the natural position of the male to be one of inferiority. The 'tiny male' of the common spider, who tremblingly achieves his one brief purpose and is then eaten up by his mate,[33] is Gilman's example of a well-adapted sexual relationship, and both she and Ward were delighted to find parthenogenesis among certain varieties of plant lice,[34] although Gilman points out that 'when conditions grow hard, males are developed, and the dual method of reproduction is introduced'.[35] As Mary A. Hill points out, Ward provided the 'kind of intellectual ammunition' that 'many suffragists thought they needed',[36] and what may seem to the modern reader like an argument for reducing the male to a kind of ambulant germ-cell or disposing of him entirely after a 'short period of functional use'[37] was, for Gilman and her contemporaries, authoritative scientific support for metaphorically, rather than literally, cutting him down to size.

It is central to Gilman's argument that women have become slaves to their secondary sexual characteristics, 'those modifications of structure and function which subserve the uses of reproduction ultimately, but are not directly essential'.[38] In other words, the physical characteristics which women have developed, in the course of evolution, to sexually attract the male of the species, have taken precedence over other faculties due to the fact that the female must ensure, by her sexual attractiveness, that the male will also be inclined to feed and clothe her. This is what

Gilman calls the 'sexuo-economic relation',[39] the condition of marriage in her time which dictated that the female develop only those 'faculties required to secure and obtain a hold on [the male]',[40] so that she becomes little more than a decorative domestic servant, performing only those duties necessary for her husband's comfort and thus being ignorant of the 'knowledge of the world',[41] knowledge which he jealously guards lest she become dissatisfied with her position. She has thus developed, not as the best kind of mother, but merely as the best kind of mate for the male – 'over sexed',[42] economically dependent and a threat to the continued development of the species:

> The female segregated to the uses of sex alone naturally deteriorates in racial development, and naturally transmits that deterioration to her offspring.[43]

Therefore, in order to assist evolution effectively, woman must be freed from her 'artificial position'[44] in which she merely competes for male attention and is debarred from cooperative effort as the man is debarred by 'the increasing weight of economic cares. . . . [C]hildren come to be looked upon as a burden, and are dreaded instead of desired by the hard-worked father'.[45]

Although it seems that both Ward and Gilman are arguing for a parthenogenetic world, neither would dispute that evolution has, of necessity, provided for dual parentage, and at one point Gilman stresses that the 'sexuo-economic relation'

> was necessary to raise and broaden, to deepen and sweeten, to make more feminine, and so more human, the male of the human race. If the female had remained in full personal freedom and activity, she would have remained superior to him, and both would have remained stationary. Since the female had not the tendency to vary which distinguishes the male, it was essential that the expansive forces of masculine energy be combined with the preservative and constructive forces of feminine energy'.[46]

So what went wrong? Gilman's argument rests on the proposition that evolutionary adaptation can have negative as well as positive possibilities. We should not assume that evolution is, in itself, a guarantee of survival but should be aware that we have evolved the faculty of reason precisely for the purpose of assessing our chances for survival and directing our social evolution accordingly. But she also believed the growth of 'the "women's movement" and the "labor movement"'[47] in her own time to be indicative of 'a sharp personal consciousness of the evils of a situation hitherto little felt'[48] but was nevertheless despairing of the greater mass of women who did not recognise their duty to 'develope [sic] a newer, better form of sex-relation and of economic relation therewith, and so grasp the fruits of all previous civilizations, and grow on to the beautiful results of higher ones':[49]

> This is the woman's century, the first chance for the mother of the world to rise to her full place, her transcendent power to remake humanity, to rebuild the suffering world – and the world waits while she powders her nose.[50]

Both genders then are handicapped by the 'sexuo-economic relation'[51] and its attendant specialisation of function. Female passivity inheres in a social order which privileges the male as the active sex only because of his biological adaptation, through natural selection, to the tasks that he has appropriated as 'masculine', following the demands of 'male efflorescence' and effectively reducing the demands of motherhood to an inferior position.

In *Women and Economics*, Gilman explores the paradox inherent in the attitude that women should necessarily be dependent for the sake of their progenitive role:

> In spite of her supposed segregation to maternal duties, the human female, the world over, works at extra-marital duties for hours enough to provide her with an independent living, and then is denied independence on the grounds that motherhood prevents her working![52]

Hence, in compiling the literature of the beehive, Gilman was committed to revealing the absurdity of a social order that could support such a paradox while also demonstrating the value, in terms of evolutionary development, of motherhood released from the restrictions of the sexuo-economic relation. *Herland* offers the proposition that, without the presence of men to hinder their development, women will evolve a social structure that privileges the needs of children – a form of co-operative motherhood where the needs of the community become those of the individual and 'conscious improvement'[53] is the driving force behind their development. But, unlike more recent all-women, feminist utopias, *Herland* does not propose the elimination of men as a necessary step in removing all destructive influence from the world.[54] The 2000 years of

Herland's isolation and the reversion to parthenogenesis can be seen instead as a narrative device to demonstrate to both genders the operation of reason, what Gilman called 'the least used of our faculties, the most difficult – even painful',[55] in planning for social evolution – a faculty that she saw as impoverished by the sexuo-economic relation. *Herland* does not propose life without men as the ideal for women but instead makes the argument that men who allow themselves to be directed by reason will themselves see the value of a society organised around motherhood, as will women who allow themselves to think beyond the terms of the romantic ideal. So *Herland* provides a scenario which allows Gilman, as Frances Bartkowski puts it, 'a great deal of space in which to play';[56] to invent a society that ridicules the 'man-made world' while offering a formula for change.

The narrative begins with three male explorers discovering clues to the existence of Herland on an expedition to explore and document the surrounding country and, in a spirit of adventure, returning to the scene in the hope of realising their dream of a country full of willing virgins who would welcome their 'civilising' influence. The reality, of course, is quite different and as Bartkowski comments, '*Herland* maintains its humour through the constant and repeated exposure of the men's preconceptions about what a world of women would or could be'.[57]

The three explorers are representative of three specific male attitudes. Terry O. Nicholson is described as 'a man's man'[58] who believed there to be only two types of women, 'those he wanted and those he didn't'.[59] Jeff Margrave is a romantic who 'idealize[s] women, and [is] always looking for a chance to 'protect' or 'serve' them',[60] while the central protagonist and narrator, Vandyck Jennings, was more than likely intended to represent Lester Frank Ward himself, for whom, as Mary A. Hill writes, Gilman held 'a lifelong hero-worshipping respect'.[61]

Bartkowski believes that Gilman's choice of a male narrator 'is one which might make male readers of *The Forerunner* more comfortable by giving them the privileged place of observer or storyteller'[62], but, while this may be true, a female narrator would not have allowed her to demonstrate that men also have the potential to evolve. As Dale Spender points out, she refused to describe herself as a feminist (a term which she interpreted as representing the 'other' side of masculinist values), preferring instead to claim 'humanity for herself'[63], and believed in 'the full social combination of individuals in collective industry' which would lead to 'a union between man and woman such as the world has long dreamed of in vain'.[64]

I believe it is essential to Gilman's purpose that we recognise *Herland* as a frozen moment in a potential evolutionary history, a moment in which, as the female regains the power of selection, the 'man's man' and the 'romantic' become redundant. For Gilman, Jennings represents the future when 'men and women, eternally drawn together by the deepest force in nature, will be able at last to meet on a plane of pure and perfect love'.[65] For this reason, it is Jennings and his Herland 'wife', Ellador, who are selected to spread the message to the wider world and who continue their adventures in a sequel (*With Her In Ourland*). Nicholson is banished, having attempted to rape his 'wife', Alima, and Margrave is similarly 'written out' by being left behind in Herland. The purpose of *Herland*, then, is to instruct, rather than to confirm the assumed ideals of the readership. While the later lesbian/ feminist utopias propose parthenogenesis as a device to demonstrate the liberation of women from all male influence and to depict the future of cultural development in female terms alone, in *Herland* it allows Gilman to rewrite evolutionary history, as both she and Ward saw it, to eliminate the 'mistake' of male efflorescence.

The arrival of the three men finds Herland quietly prosperous, well organised and abundantly fruitful, with the women 'tall, strong, healthy and beautiful'.[66] In response to questioning, the women reveal that their land was originally populated by both sexes and was much larger, extending from the plateau where they now dwell to the sea. But a series of wars had greatly reduced the male population, to the extent that, when a volcanic eruption effectively blocked the pass from the mountains, the only inhabitants of the plateau had been women and slaves, while the fighting force, comprising all the remaining young men, had been left stranded on the other side of the pass. The slaves had risen in revolt and killed the few remaining men and boys but the women, whom Jennings describes as 'infuriated virgins',[67] finding that they outnumbered their would-be new masters, 'rose in desperation and slew their brutal conquerors'.[68] There then follows an account of the rebuilding of Herland, how the women worked together to feed and clothe themselves and take care of one another until 'the miracle happened – one of these young women bore a child'.[69] The first virgin birth heralded also the beginnings of a new religion – the deification of Motherhood. The supreme purpose of their lives now being to bear and raise children, the Herlanders developed a social organisation which allowed them to work efficiently for their own comfort and survival while raising their children under the best possible conditions.

What Terry Nicholson's Herland teacher, Moadine, calls 'Human Motherhood – in full working use',[70] Gilman saw as primarily educative in function, but *Herland* makes it clear that the term also encompasses the particular type of social organisation which she believed best suited to facilitate that function – as Jennings explains it, 'that limitless feeling of sisterhood, that wide unity in service which was so difficult for us to grasp'.[71] In *Women and Economics* she writes:

> The education of the young is a tremendous factor in human reproduction. A right motherhood should be able to fulfill this great function perfectly.[72]

'Right motherhood' is what she later terms 'wider maternity',[73] which she contrasts to 'the feverish personality of the isolated one-baby household'.[74] Children reared communally, she believed, 'would unconsciously absorb the knowledge that "we" were humanity, that "we" were creatures to be...fed...watched...laid to sleep...kissed and cuddled', fostering an immediate identification of the individual with the wider community and giving the mother 'certain free hours as a human being, as a member of a civilized community, as an economic producer, as a growing, self-realizing individual'.[75]

Gilman's argument, then, is primarily against the patriarchal family, which, while enslaving women, breeds an 'inordinate self-interest'[76] in the next generation, thus creating women who live vicariously through their husbands and children and men who demand domestic service from their wives, who are thus cut off from the means to fulfil themselves both as women and as mothers:

> The human mother does less for her young, both absolutely and proportionately, than any kind of mother on earth. She does not obtain food for them, nor covering, nor shelter, nor protection, nor defense. She does not educate them beyond the personal habits required in the family circle and in her limited range of social life. The necessary knowledge of the world, so indispensable to every human being, she cannot give, because she does not possess it.[77]

Full possession of knowledge, in the *Herland* sense, has been regained through parturition as a motive force, rather than as a condition of dependence. The operation of reason in determining the function of motherhood gives precedence to altruistic concerns. Motherhood, when raised to the status of a religion, dictates moral values centred on social as opposed to personal duty. Gilman believed that:

> To the death-based religion the main question is, 'What is going to happen to me after I am dead?' – a posthumous egotism.
> To the birth-based religion the main question is, 'What must be done for the child who is born?' – an immediate altruism. . . . The first is something to be believed. The second is something to be done.[78]

Jennings explains how the first parthenogenetic mother of Herland had been placed in 'the Temple of Maaia – their Goddess of Motherhood':[79]

> The religion they had to begin with was much like that of old Greece – a number of gods and goddesses; but they lost all interest in deities of war and plunder, and gradually centered on their Mother Goddess altogether.[80]

The women thus have no understanding either of Christianity or of the family, or of the economic principles of capitalism, allowing the narrative to present numerous ironies as the men attempt to instruct them as to the value of their 'civilisation'. The question of surnames raises some confusion, with the women puzzled as to why they should need to 'sign' their children,[81] and they are rather less than honoured by the men's desire to bestow their surnames on the Herland women that they 'marry', a custom that Alima pronounces to be merely 'unpleasant'.[82]

While being forced to account for the apparent inadequacies of their system, the men are brought to question their own role, with the result that, as the narrative develops, Nicholson's defensive and therefore resistant stance is brought into increasingly sharp contrast with Jennings' developing sympathy and admiration. The third man of the party, Jeff Margrave, described as having 'a poetic imagination',[83] displays a subjective reverence for the women which again is contrasted with Jennings' considered, objective viewpoint, mediated by his 'scientific imagination', which, he flatters himself, is 'the highest sort'.[84]

The first chapter, 'A Not Unnatural Enterprise', reveals their disparate personalities as they consider a country of only women. Even Jennings' 'scientific imagination' can see no further than the survival of a 'primeval' matriarchy while Jeff, 'a tender soul', imagines 'roses and babies and canaries and tidies, and all that sort of thing' and Nicholson, 'in his secret heart, had visions of a sort of sublimated summer resort – just Girls and Girls and Girls'.[85] All three imagine a form of conquest to be the outcome of the 'enterprise', and so the easy acceptance of their arrival and the casual use of chloroform to restrain them puts them at an immediate psychological disadvantage. Margrave is prompted to comment, 'It's as if our being men were a minor incident',[86] and Jennings observes that 'such instant recognition of our difficulties, and readiness to meet them, were a constant surprise to us'.[87] It is this lack of alienation on the part of the women that provides the basis for insecurity in the men, leading, initially, to the enjoyably funny 'escape' and, finally, to acute divisions between them – the absence of tension becoming, itself, a form of tension.

The Herland women, secure in their own autonomy, present a psychological challenge to the three men and, through them, to the reader. The challenge is threefold. Assumptions regarding the role and character of women are held up to question and ridicule, the accepted structure of family life is questioned with regard to its effectiveness for the continued growth of society, and the concept of love between the sexes is brought into conflict, as an ideal, against the absorbing passion of the Herland women for cooperative motherhood. Furthermore, the growing divisions between the men can be read as a conflict between potential narratives: narratives that present, on the one hand, distinct responses to evolutionary theory and, on the other, the attempt to write a masculine ending against a conclusion which would deny that such an ending is inevitable.

Newbolt man meets his match

Writing in *Play Up and Play The Game: the Heroes of Popular Fiction*, Patrick Howarth discusses a figure who '[c]ast in the role of hero ... dominated a large area of English literature, which may be loosely described as popular fiction, for about a century'.[88] Howarth's title is telling, in that the adventure stories that he describes appear to derive their narrative from the game of cricket, the hero being the ultimate sportsman and notions of 'fair play' informing the outcome of the adventure. The title is, in fact, from a poem by Sir Henry Newbolt, a poet of dubious talent but extraordinary popularity who wrote at the turn of the century and whom Howarth believes to be the blueprint for what he terms 'Newbolt Man', the archetypal hero whose childhood he discovers in *Tom Brown's School Days*, and whose growth he traces through adolescence in the stories of Henry Rider Haggard and his contemporaries to adulthood as Sapper's *Bulldog Drummond*. Newbolt Man was bold, brave and not particularly bright:

> His philistinism served to widen a largely unnecessary gulf between athlete and aesthete, manliness and art, and so impoverish life. His attitude to women was a curious compound of fear and self-distrust, causing him at one moment to elevate women on to a rather chilling pedestal, at the next to regard them as a kind of permanent second eleven, one or two of whom might in an emergency be allowed to field as substitutes.[89]

The evidence for Terry Nicholson as a parody of Newbolt Man is persuasive. 'Fear and self-distrust' are obvious in his treatment of the Herlanders, and his apparent inability to relinquish values that he believes incontestable is tantamount to Newbolt Man's insistence on bringing the values of the cricket field to a variety of diverse situations in which he is commonly shown to triumph. The world of Newbolt Man is fraught with adventure and physically challenging situations, but, immured within the rules of 'the game', he is able to create a narrative in which he is indestructible. It is a narrative of Christian values, white imperialism and male, upper middle class supremacy in which a mystery must always be solved by the hero. It is just such a narrative that Terry Nicholson tries desperately to create. Indeed, in the opening chapter, all the elements for 'a ripping adventure yarn' are present – secrecy, a mystery to be solved and three potential heroes with the social status and material means to deliver them safely into the plot.

Newbolt Man at his best is an amateur who, invested with wealth and an unswerving devotion to 'fair play', is seen to win out over 'established authority', his attitude towards which is 'governed by a healthy scepticism'.[90] It would seem that Gilman had her tongue firmly in her cheek when she called the opening chapter of *Herland* 'A Not Unnatural Enterprise', and Terry's language throughout is redolent of Newbolt Man of the 'Boy's Own' era. Such exclamations as, 'Come on! Oh, come on! Here goes for Herland!'[91] echoes the captain of the first eleven spurring his team to greater effort for the glory of the school, and it can be no accident that the game of skill which has the men at such a disadvantage in Chapter 4 involves a construction remarkably like the bails and stumps of the wicket.

Nicholson differs from Newbolt Man in that, for him, women are the prizes in the game rather than merely peripheral players, but there is nevertheless a sense in which he attempts to adhere to the Newbolt

Man scenario by requiring them to play by the rules. This is illustrated by the scene in which, announcing that he has come 'prepared', he produces 'a necklace of big varicolored stones' which he intends to use as 'bait'[92] but remains undeterred when his quarry refuses to be 'caught', confidently announcing that 'They expected it. Women like to be run after'.[93] This then is 'fair play' as far as he is concerned. It is not the reticence of the women that has him at a disadvantage but the non-appearance of the opposing team. When, after they have given up chasing the women through the forest, he observes, with obvious delight, 'The men of this country must be good sprinters!',[94] he is clearly anticipating the appearance of worthy opponents. It is when the worthy opponents turn out to be women that his confidence begins to suffer.

At the start of the journey he boasts, 'I'll get solid with them all – and play one bunch against another. I'll get myself elected king in no time. . . . '.[95] And Jennings reports that, initially, '[w]e seemed to think that if there were men we could fight them, and if there were only women – why, there would be no obstacles at all'.[96] Later, when his companions show signs of being won over, having learned the history of Herland, Nicholson attempts to engage their complicity in opposition:

> It's likely women – just a pack of women – would have hung together like that! We all know women can't organize – that they scrap like anything – are frightfully jealous.[97]

Here, he invokes the safe stereotypes that have structured the men's experiences in their home culture in an attempt to rally his flagging team.

Terry's denial is based on fear. The loss of self esteem inherent in his embracing a value system which has no use for a 'man's man' is based on the threat that the Herland women pose to his identity formed, as it is, in opposition to an objectified ideal of woman. When his stated goal of becoming 'king of Ladyland'[98] is thwarted, his frustration manifests itself as anger and he is openly abusive, declaring, 'They aren't human' and 'The whole thing's deuced unnatural'.[99] His anger provides the motivational drive to reassert his 'superiority' in a manner unacceptable to the Herlanders although, as Jennings points out, 'in our country he would have been held quite "within his rights"', as Alima's 'husband':

> Terry put into practice his pet conviction that a woman loves to be mastered, and by sheer brute force, in all the pride and passion of his intense masculinity, he tried to master this woman.[100]

Nicholson's desire to 'conquer' Herland can be seen to parallel his need to prove his manhood by taking Alima by force. In the closing pages, when he is asked to promise not to betray the location of the country on his return to America, he responds: 'Indeed I won't. . . . The first thing I'll do is to get an expedition fixed up to force an entrance into Ma-land'.[101] The penetrative metaphor is doubly symbolic here, as is the fact that he is subdued by the threat of confinement and anaesthesia, a punishment already proven effective directly following his attempted rape of Alima, which is itself symbolic in that it represents both the violent and fragile nature of 'intense masculinity'. Remembering that, for Gilman, 'intense masculinity' is the natural counterpart of the intense femininity which she found so abhorrent and reductive for the cause of planned evolution – the result of 'male efflorescence' – Nicholson and all that he represents are proposed as outcasts in the millennium. With the female regaining the power of selection, 'brute force' is replaced by reason, which is shown to win out even against the threat of violence.

In Chapter 3, I will examine in some detail the fragile construction of the male ego and how object-relations theory can explain the threat of female autonomy to masculine identity (with all that this implies for the potential of violence). However, for now it will be sufficient to bear in mind that Nicholson's fear of castration (for that is what his response implies) also, from a contemporary perspective, gains significance as a metaphor both for the insecurity expressed in nineteenth century 'social imperialism, a policy explicitly designed to unite men of all classes in hatred of the foreigner and to keep women in their subordinate (although important) place as sustainers of warriors and producers of future ones',[102] and for the attitude implicit in the seventeenth-century view of the scientific enterprise.

The all important need for control of the environment through de-mystification of natural processes was, as Brian Easlea reports, the overriding concern of the 'natural philosophers':

> It is very difficult to avoid the conclusion that many seventeenth-century natural philosophers . . . viewed the scientific quest as a masculine penetration into a female nature basically deprived of maternal status (and certainly of the possibility of any dangerous 'sexual' response). They saw nature as a woman passively awaiting the display of male virility and the subsequent birth of a race of machines that would in [Francis] Bacon's words, not merely exert a 'gentle guidance over nature's course' but would 'conquer and subdue her'.[103]

It is hardly surprising then that the 'race of machines' born to the Western, 'civilised' nations ('If they've got motors, they *are* civilized'[104]) gave them cause to consider themselves in pride of place in the evolutionary hierarchy and to fear any regression to prior states of pastoral harmony or animalistic sensuality.

Theories were already in place to support the Social Darwinist notion that a society organised around commerce should be the end result of continuation and progress. Ronald L. Meek (1976) discusses the development of the so-called 'four stages theory' in the latter part of the eighteenth century which, in 'its most specific form ... was that society "naturally" or "normally" progressed over time through four more or less distinct and consecutive stages, each corresponding to a different mode of subsistence, these stages being defined as hunting, pasturage, agriculture and commerce'.[105] European white imperialism could point to the fact that natural selection appeared to favour those races whose achievement had been to reach the fourth stage without dying out from lack of resources or remaining at an earlier stage through lack of control over their environment.

It seems that Gilman is suggesting an alternative 'fourth stage', retaining the equality of the 'primitive' state, while progressing in agriculture and technology. The removal of men from Herland dispenses with the effects of 'male efflorescence' so that the role of nature as 'the great mother' is retained and revered and the need to dominate replaced with active co-operation – 'life [is], to them, just the long cycle of motherhood'.[106]

In this sense, the women display a return to Rousseau's 'state of nature', the supposed primitive state before private ownership and industry led to the present 'state of society'.[107] As Meek points out, 'Rousseau goes out of his way (during the *Discourse on the Origin of Inequality*) on a number of occasions to emphasise the advantages of [this] situation relative to that in which modern "civilised" man finds himself', maintaining that in this 'supposed primitive state' the inequality of mankind 'is hardly felt, and ... its influence is next to nothing'.[108]

Later feminist utopias have developed this idea in response to the concern with ecology that has characterised scientific thinking in recent decades. The presentation of Nicholson's character has much in common with the later versions of the insensitive, male chauvinist archetype, such as the city-men in Sally Miller Gearhart's *The Wanderground*,[109] whose function in the narrative is similar. The women's country presents a challenge – it is 'virgin' territory into which they must 'force an entrance' in a quest for masculine self confirmation.

While it is quite possible that Gilman was familiar with the Newbolt Man style of hero, it is also true that he only functions adequately in the context of British upper class culture. Gilman was an American, writing for an American audience where, traditionally, the frontier provided the necessary challenge for a hero to prove himself. So, if Terry Nicholson can be read as Newbolt Man, urgently trying to forge his identity through a narrative that refuses to adhere to 'the rules', then the 'Not Unnatural Enterprise' is a similar archetype identified by, among others, Nina Baym, in her essay 'Melodramas of Beset Manhood' (1986), as a myth associated specifically with American literature. In essence, Nicholson is Newbolt Man liberated from the mores of British culture and let loose in 'the wilderness'. The wilderness represents the pioneering spirit which fosters individuality while, at the same time, revealing a cultural specific posited as peculiarly American and, as Baym would have it, peculiarly male:

> the essential quality of America comes to reside in its unsettled wilderness and the opportunities that such a wilderness offers to the individual as the medium on which he may inscribe, unhindered, his own destiny and his own nature.[110]

Discussing 'the entramelling society' and 'the promising landscape', Baym finds them to be a constant source of tension in American literature, while both being 'depicted in unmistakably feminine terms':[111]

> the encroaching, constricting, destroying society is represented with particular urgency in the figure of one or more women. There are several possible reasons why this might be so. It would seem to be a fact of life that we all – women and men alike – experience social conventions and responsibilities and obligations first in the persons of women, since women are entrusted by society with the task of rearing young children. Not until he reaches mid-adolescence does the male connect up with other males whose primary task is socialization; but at about this time – if he is heterosexual – his lovers and spouses become the agents of a permanent socialization and domestication. Thus, although women are not the source of social power, they are experienced as such. And although not all women are engaged in socializing the young, the young do not encounter women who are not. So from the point of view of the young man, the only kind of women who exist are entrappers and domesticators.[112]

But the wilderness, by its very nature, embodies the mystery of female creativity. To return to the penetrative metaphor which Brian Easlea finds informing the language of scientific discovery, it would seem that the quest is imbued with similar connotations. Furthermore, although Howarth does not explore the point, I would suggest that Newbolt Man's 'fear and self-distrust' arises from precisely the same rejection of socialisation. If Newbolt Man is the archetypal hero, trammelled by conventions and social taboos, then the American hero is his counterpart in the wilderness, struggling to forge his identity and produce a similarly triumphant narrative.

In proposing a country of only women, Gilman suggests the promise of the wilderness:

> the deeply romantic one that in this new land, untrammeled by history and social accident, a person will be able to achieve complete self-definition. Behind this promise is the assurance that individuals come before society, that they exist in some meaningful sense prior to, and apart from, societies in which they happen to find themselves.[113]

In Baym's terms, the opposition between female society and male individuality is revealing for a criticism of *Herland* which posits the discovery of a wholly female co-operative society as the object of the quest. In The Adventures of Newbolt Man women either do not appear at all, appear as prizes for the 'victor' or exist 'between the lines' as necessary but dispensable (in terms of narrative) vessels of genealogy. Similarly, in the American stories of escape into the wilderness, 'the role of entrapper and impediment in the melodrama of beset manhood is reserved for women'.[114] In both cases, women are merely marginal to the text or represented as obstructions. The quest for self-definition involves an escape from 'entramelling history' into a new history that the hero may write for himself. Whether, within the narrative, women represent a threat or a promise, they as individuals do not write history. They are important only insofar as they represent what the hero must either escape, conquer or win in order that the writing of history may proceed. Nina Baym suggests for consideration Annette Kolodny's theory that

> the hero, fleeing a society that has been imagined as feminine, then imposes on nature some ideas of women which, no longer subject to the correcting influence of real-life experience, become more and more fantastic. The fantasies are infantile, concerned with power, mastery, and total gratification.[115]

The 'mythic landscape' of Herland as the subject of such fantasies is suggested by Jennings when he explains, 'There was something attractive to a bunch of unattached young men in finding an undiscovered country of a strictly Amazonian nature',[116] and the *tabula rasa* promise of the 'feminine' wilderness is perhaps echoed in Nicholson's assertion that '[t]hey would fight among themselves. Women always do. We mustn't look to find any sort of order or organization'.[117] That the intention is to impose 'order and organization' where they expect to find none is obvious as is the desire for mastery and the expectation of submission, all of which combined would satisfy the need for Newbolt Man's predictable narrative while also allowing for the pioneering spirit to triumph. But the playing out of Nicholson's fantasy narrative is thwarted by the power of Herstory and it is the acknowledgement of this power that allows Vandyck Jennings to emerge as an alternative 'hero'. Nicholson's attempt to enforce 'the rules' as laid down by his own culture result in his narrative being inconclusive – he is Newbolt Man in the wrong 'adventure' and, as Jennings comments, 'here he was all out of drawing'.[118] In terms of 'the quest' he is a failure.

Furthermore, I would suggest that what Newbolt Man and the American Hero also have in common is a need to adhere to what Patrick Howarth calls 'Muscular Christianity',[119] confirmation of which is offered by Nicholson's remark to his companions that he would show them 'how a Christian meets his death',[120] as he leads their escape attempt by abseiling down a vertical wall. Committed as she was to the ideal of a religion which recognises 'that life inheres in the race, which is undying, rather than in the individual, which dies',[121] Gilman undoubtedly intended to demonstrate the link between muscular Christianity and male efflorescence. It is perhaps this fact, more than any other, which Jennings is seen to recognise and which allows him a valuable place in the final narrative that stands in stark opposition to the playing out of 'manly' and 'Christian' values which Nicholson seeks to inscribe on the venture into Herland.

Romance and the scientific imagination

If Nicholson represents the mores of the adventure story, the narrative in general can, perhaps more importantly, be read as a love story. *Herland* is a text which is informed by the conventions of romance – romance enacted under the sign of evolutionary theory – an issue discussed in relation to other nineteenth century novels by Gillian Beer in *Darwin's Plots*. To illustrate the importance of sexual selection for the

Darwinian polemic, Beer quotes from *The Descent of Man*, in which Darwin cites the German philosopher Schopenhauer's remark that 'the final aim of all love intrigues, be they comic or tragic, is really of more importance than all other ends in human life'.[122] As she says, 'The idea of sexual selection made for a complex confusion of biological and social determinants in descent, transmission, and sex-roles'.[123] She argues that the crucial significance of 'love-intrigues and the marriage market' for 'the future of the human race' must necessarily inform the fiction of the period, providing 'an imaginative resource extraordinarily rich in tragic potential'.[124] Beer sees the influence of Darwinism on 'topics traditional to the novel – courtship, sensibility, the making of matches, women's beauty, men's dominance, inheritance in all its forms' to be 'charged with new difficulty'.[125] For Gilman, the difficulty was in writing the literature of the beehive in such a way as to offer tensions and resolutions that would satisfy a readership versed in the conventions of popular romance.

However, scientific rationalism and the language of sociology does not readily generate a narrative meeting the requirements of popular fiction. I have already discussed how one form of narrative tension is produced by the Herland women's unexpected acceptance of their visitors' gender and refusal to acknowledge their difference as a threat – this, in large part, being due to a collective autonomy which does not separate woman from woman as rivals for male affection. As Ann Palmeri points out in her essay on Gilman (1983), a crucial factor in her vision of emancipation was a commitment to promoting a form of androgyny as the next step in social evolution, which, 'for her, means a *lessening* of the sexual differences that are culturally reinforced, a lessening of sexual attraction based on physical allurement'.[126] So the Herlanders are 'strikingly deficient in ... "femininity"',[127] 'all [wear] short hair', run 'like marathon winners'[128] and are 'not provocative',[129] and 'their only perception of the value of a male creature as such [is] for Fatherhood'.[130]

In relation to the question of romantic narrative, Brian Easlea believes that:

> If Gilman had been able to write the story in the 1970s she surely could have safely included lesbian loving between the sisters of Herland without compromising the affection and solidarity felt between all the sisters, and made the presence of the three male explorers – who constantly thought in their return of 'penetrating those vast forests and civilizing – or exterminating – the dangerous savages' – as unambiguously unwelcome as it was menacing.[131]

But this, I think, is to miss the point. Lesbian love could only have been included as part of the phase of transition that Herland represents rather than as a political statement (as is the case with the later utopias).[132] For Gilman, it was necessary that the far more important issue of effective motherhood and planned evolution should not be eclipsed by attention to what she would have considered to be superfluous details. So, as Jennings reports, the Herlanders, 'hadn't the faintest idea of love – sex-love that is'.[133] Instead, the men present them with the possibility of 'making the Great Change ... of reverting to their earlier bi-sexual order of nature'.[134] What Gilman wants to stress is that the evolution of the male is not a 'mistake' but a successful adaptation, nurtured through its early stages by the sexuo-economic relation but now in need of a new direction in order to be a continuing success. The men are welcome in Herland because it is for just such an intervention that the women have been preparing.

This, as I have indicated, requires a new form of love story – a narrative which derives tension not from the vicissitudes of a patriarchal economy with woman as the spoils of victory but rather from the endeavours of a unified social organism striving for mutual benefit. But, in demonstrating how the literature of the beehive might be shaped, Gilman needed to acknowledge accepted narrative forms and, indeed, needed to subvert them in order to demonstrate the value of her thesis in fictional form. Her awareness of this need is aptly summed up by Jennings, who, in discussing the drama of Herland, comments that it was

> to our taste – rather flat. You see, they lacked the sex motive and, with it, jealousy. They had no interplay of warring nations, no aristocracy and its ambitions, no wealth and poverty opposition.[135]

Without these oppositions, there is no place for the traditional characters of fiction, still less for the style of narrative which produces popular heroes or romantic heroines.

But Jennings' lack of appreciation can be read as a remaining resistance to the idea of embracing fully the implications of Gilman's belief that if 'love' is to be selected as the most important thing in life to write about, then the mother's love should be the principal subject,[136] reinforcing the sense in which *Herland* can be read as representing a phase of transition, rather than a fully accomplished utopia. Their arts and religion are, after all, a celebration of Motherhood, and Jennings, although of the three men having the most potential as a 'new father', is not yet subjectively involved. The difficulty that he has in appreciating the creative concepts of Herland points up the difficulty that Gilman herself faced in creating a romantic fiction around her 'principal subject'.

The emotive force which characterises the traditional love story is here abrogated by the lack of overt sexual polarity as well as by the criteria which determine the basis for sexual selection. Selection on the basis of individual choice with standards dictated by social position is replaced by considerations as to how the race may benefit and is a matter for community decision. The sisterhood takes the place of the individual so that the men's relationships with the individual women are presented as insignificant in comparison to the wider issue of 'bi-sexual' generation, which concerns the whole society. Hence, the emotional emphasis and the true 'love story' of *Herland* is based on an examination of the values accruing from collective effort and public 'service'. This, and the absence of cultural artefacts associated with courtship, places the men at a disadvantage from which Jennings is forced to re-evaluate his views on the status of women and the status of the men as potential suitors:

> You see, if a man loves a girl who is in the first place young and inex-
> perienced; who in the second place is educated with a background
> of caveman tradition, a middle-ground of poetry and romance, and a
> foreground of unspoken hope and interest all centering upon the
> one Event; and who has, furthermore, absolutely no other hope or
> interest worthy of the name – why, it is a comparatively easy matter
> to sweep her off her feet with a dashing attack. Terry was a past
> master in this process. He tried it here, and Alima was so affronted,
> so repelled, that it was weeks before he got near enough to try
> again.[137]

Gilman's oblique references to sexuality are at times, for a modern reader, difficult to decipher, but it becomes clear that she intends her readers to understand that Alima does not find the idea of sex itself to be repellent but is rather affronted by Nicholson's assumption that she is ready to succumb whenever he demands. Jennings and Elladur talk 'it all out together' so that they have 'an easier experience' during 'the real miracle time'.[138]

Gilman's strategically vague references to sexual intercourse here make for a rather confused reading. While a modern reader may initially con-strue the 'miracle time' to be Jennings' initiation into a sexual relation-ship with a woman who knows what she wants and insists that her sexual needs are satisfied, later revelations make it clear that the 'miracle' is Jennings' ability to accept what Ellador most definitely does *not* want. As Frances Bartkowski notes, 'Gilman's late Victorian sexual ethics are apparent in all her writings',[139] so it is with difficulty that we appreciate her insistence on sex as an activity to be restricted to reproduction and Ellador's surprise that 'when people marry, they go right on doing this in season and out of season, with no thought of children at all'.[140] But while she 'has not come to grips with speaking of sexual pleasure',[141] she makes clear her belief, as she states it in *His Religion and Hers*, that '[i]n normal motherhood, sex use will be measured by its service to the young, not its enjoyment by the individual'.[142] Sexual pleasure, then, is deferred in favour of work and 'social service' as the Herland women 'voluntarily defer' motherhood by deflecting the 'deep inner demand for a child' into 'the most active work, physical and mental'[143] on such occasions as the potential overpopulation of the country demands it.[144] Here, sublimation of instinctual drives is, for the Herlanders, a positive indication of the use of reason in directing social evolution. This is not repression in the Freudian sense[145] but a conscious postponement of individual desires for the greater good of the community. However, despite the difficult (and, frankly, comical) discourse on sexual relationships, what is clearly established is that it is the women who exercise control and the men who submit (Nicholson, of course, is denied the relationship altogether) and Jennings finds that 'an apparently imperative demand had disappeared without my noticing it'.[146]

In Bartkowski's view, 'Gilman replaces religion with sacred motherhood and eliminates sexuality',[147] but I think it is more accurate to say that she eliminates sexuality as a constant factor in male/female relationships, replacing the sex drive, and its attendant spur to creativity, with desire directed towards co-operative effort in 'service to the young'. Hence, the Herlanders' 'drama ... dance, music, religion and education were all very close together'[148] and all prompted by allegiance to an ideal of motherhood, replacing 'the sweet intense joy of married lovers' as the 'higher stimulus to all creative work'.[149] It is thus Gilman's intention to demonstrate the untapped creative potential that she believed would accompany the evolution of human beings from sex-driven individuality (the Preliminaries), to propagation-driven co-operation. Nevertheless, Gilman must retain the sex drive in order to bring her three pairs of lovers together, and it is here that she encounters some difficulty.

While the women of Herland display none of the overt sex-distinctions of their American sisters, Jennings is moved to speculate as to their capacity for sex attraction:

Two thousand years' disuse had left very little of the instinct; also we must remember that those who had at times manifested it as atavistic exceptions were often, by that very fact, denied motherhood.

Yet while the mother process remains, the inherent ground for sex-distinction remains also; and who shall say what long-forgotten feeling, vague and nameless, was stirred in some of these mother hearts by our arrival?[150]

The arrival of the men thus effectively produces an evolutionary regression which is difficult to justify in the terms that Gilman proposes. She reveals the contemporary fascination with 'the natural' in postulating the psychological reawakening of sexual desire in the women to emulate the seasonal mating habits of species unaffected by the sexuo-economic relation – a selective atavism operating to exclude the women's more recent 'harem-bred'[151] racial memories.

The idea of atavism becomes highly problematic in the context of a narrative that is concerned to present what Gilman called 'the attitude of the full-grown woman, who faces the demands of love with the high standards of conscious motherhood'.[152] As Beer writes, the 'quality of latency in the experience of physical growth makes it a possible metaphor for all invisible process[es]':[153]

The particular organisation implied by evolutionary theory and determinism borrows the idea of irreversible onward sequence from the experience of growth. It can't run backwards, though it may include equally convergence and branching. Nor can it stay still. Recrudescence is also not a concept easily assimilable to evolutionary ideas.[154]

Similarly, to the nineteenth-century mind, atavism spoke clearly of degeneration and as Beer documents the attendant assumptions:

The idea of development harboured a paternalistic assumption once it was transferred exclusively to human beings, since it was presumed that the observer was at the summit of development, looking back over a past struggling to reach the present high moment. The European was taken as the type of achieved developmental pre-eminence, and other races studied were seen as further back on the chart of growth. The image of growth was again misplaced from the single life cycle, so that whole races were seen as being part of 'the childhood of man', to be protected, led and corrected like children.[155]

There is nothing to suggest that Gilman resisted these assumptions. The Herland women have developed their 'anthropology' partly on the basis of 'the knowledge of the savagery of the occupants of those dim forests below'[156] with whom, as Jennings reports later, 'they had no contact',[157] making for a high level of assumption in the use of the word 'savage'.

And, during a conversation in which Terry is at pains to point out the virtue of decoration in a woman's dress, he makes a distinction between 'men' and 'Indians . . . Savages, you know',[158] who, it is clearly implied, are to be considered as demonstrably inferior by the fact that they, unlike 'civilised' men (but like their women), find it necessary to wear feathers.

So if the Herlanders are 'full-grown', the three women singled out to become lovers to the three men are, by implication, less highly developed than their sisters. This, in the context of Jennings' remark that 'atavistic exceptions' were 'denied motherhood', makes for an awkward fit between the Herlanders' project of 'race improvement' and the romantic narrative which brings the three couples together. If the arrival of the three men has caused three of the women to respond with atavistic desires, then the advantage gained by curtailing the reproduction of such traits must surely be threatened. There is thus a conflict which is not easily resolved between Gilman's attempt to write the literature of the beehive and her need to re-introduce heterosexual love in order to project her evolutionary narrative beyond the time and place of Herland. The introduction of a recrudescent theme does damage to the project of demonstrating the Herlanders' achievements in terms of growth towards a higher form of civilisation. We are left to wonder whether the 'full-grown' woman should have need of the male at all and, indeed, if the literature of the beehive can be written in a heterosexual world.

It would seem that the scientific imagination is not easily reconciled with romance, and I would suggest that Gilman's problem lies primarily in the absence of social conditions that lend tension to the traditional love story. A. O. J. Cockshut, in *Man and Woman* (1977), discusses the nature of love as expressed in the novel and in the romantic poem. Love 'as traditionally conceived by poets, is private, intimate, intense, even ecstatic',[159] but, in the novel, private feelings are necessarily brought into conflict with the public sphere. The novelist 'writes of love in terms of time and society'.[160] In other words, the 'intense moments' of private love must be presented in the context of their relation to 'religion, to duty, to society or to work, money, recreation and friendship',[161] and tension is produced primarily by the interaction between the demands of (private) love and the equally insistent demands of convention in the public world of cultural norms. But the Herlanders live primarily within the public sphere, and Gilman's concern was to show the smooth integration of personal love with the Herlanders' social duties, rather than to show the two in conflict. Jennings explains that they had 'not the faintest idea of that *solitude à deux* we are so fond of',[162] and Somel tells him, 'this new wonderful love between you. The whole country is interested'.[163] Thus heterosexual love in terms of the Herland society takes on the character of a general election. The 'limitations of a wholly personal life' being 'inconceivable'[164] to the Herlanders therefore makes for an absence of tension, and because tensions and satisfactions normally associated with the love story are missing, so too is the necessary involvement of the reader. The three relationships seem, at least, improbable, and Celis' pregnancy remarkably so.

Nevertheless, at least one traditional character of romantic fiction is brought in to emphasise the lack of equality in the traditional ritual. Most obviously this is Terry Nicholson, as the unsuitable suitor, who must be rejected in favour of a more appropriate match, but the excessively chivalric Jeff Margrave, in terms of nineteenth century morals a more 'suitable' replacement, is here upstaged by the 'new man', Vandyck Jennings, whom Somel describes as 'more like People . . . more like us'.[165] By contrasting the two, Gilman is able to present her ideal of androgyny. Margrave is progressively 'feminised' as the novel proceeds in that in his 'exalted gallantry'[166] he displays a passivity which is brought into increasing contrast with Jennings' developing conscious appreciation of the Herlanders' achievements.

For Jennings, Nicholson is 'a stray male in an ant-hill' while Margrave is 'a stray man among angels'[167] – a relevant metaphor in an age when the ideal woman was an 'Angel in the House, contentedly submissive to men, but strong in her inner purity and religiosity, queen in her own realm of the Home'.[168] In the sphere of the home, she was the keeper of men's morals, the earthly representative of Christian ideals and the social representative of her husband's status. A 'fallen' woman relinquished her angelic status and became unmarriageable. As Jennings reports, Margrave 'accepted the angel theory, swallowed it whole',[169] the implication being that, lacking Jennings' rational curiosity, he is happy to accept the apparent perfection of Herland as the natural result of a land inhabited by angels, rather than the achievement of social planning.

In light of Cockshut's observations on the private nature of the language of romantic love, Margrave's 'poetic imagination' can be read as inadequate to compass the Herlanders' social collectivity as well as their sense of time, which, conditioned by their awareness of planned evolution, must necessarily range well into the future. Love poetry encodes a denial of time, and even 'when there is talk of love as a permanent state, this state may often be conceived of as an eternising of the moment, as if the mutabilities of time were, in this unique case, simply inapplicable'.[170] If *Herland* is read as a frozen moment in evolutionary history which, itself, projects a paradigm for the future then Margrave's remaining happily in this 'eternised' moment, rather than, like Jennings, proceeding beyond the narrative, marks him, like Nicholson, as redundant in terms of the continuing evolutionary narrative. However, this is to reckon without Celis' pregnancy, which marks him also as a seed of change within Herland itself. But this, of course, serves to highlight the fact that Ellador and Jennings must forego procreation in order to pursue their mission, confirming Gilman's dictum that postponement of desire is, ultimately, to the greater good of humanity. There is also a sense in which the environment of Herland can be equated with the home, a place of security for mothers and children which also, in Gilman's view, sheltered woman from taking up responsibilities in the world which would prepare her to be a better educator for her children. Margrave, an inadequate educator, remains 'at home', confirming further the impression of femininity. While, as I have already described, Nicholson's response to the restrictions on sexual activity is to attempt to use force and Jennings, while initially impatient, is subdued by the use of reasoned argument, Margrave takes 'his medicine like a – I cannot say "like a man", but more as if he wasn't one ... there was always this angel streak in him'.[171] The angel metaphor, applied to Margrave himself, together with the aspersions cast on his masculinity amount finally to an ironic suggestion that the romantic hero, in his passive acceptance and, indeed, adoration of the excessively feminine woman, effectively feminises himself and is thus an inadequate partner to (and perhaps an inadequate lover of) the burgeoning new womanhood. This, of course, makes Celis' pregnancy doubly questionable (and a forced conclusion) but it is undoubtedly the case that, having sent Ellador with Jennings to an uncertain future in the 'strange, unknown lands',[172] Gilman had need to ensure that the next stage of evolution be seen to begin in the 'nursery'[173] of Herland.

So Jennings is Gilman's new hero. Neither intensely masculine nor feminised by a poetic imagination which limits his vision, he thus promotes scientific objectivity as the source for a revision in human consciousness. But Gilman's difficulty was in presenting the literature of the beehive as a viable alternative to the 'Adventures of Him in Pursuit of Her' while adhering closely enough to the rules of popular fiction to attract her readership, and the question remains as to whether she fully achieved her aim.

Like much feminist sf, *Herland* is consciously didactic. It instructs through intertextual criticism, both of the American myth and male-oriented popular fiction, articulated through a text which is self-referential in terms of proposing through the narrative a paradigm both for a scientific re-evaluation of social development and a similarly based revision of the conventions which dictate the form of the novel. Although Gilman could not escape introducing a theme of atavism to accompany the introduction of romance, it is this same theme which suggests the sense in which the text presents itself as an anomaly in light of Gilman's project to write the literature of the beehive. *Herland* is a 'not yet' world where a better future is glimpsed but held in check by forces which militate against the full realisation of utopia. The Herlanders have need of the drones to complete their beehive world but are disappointed to find them largely inadequate. As Jennings and Ellador prepare to leave, they are told:

> we are unwilling to expose our country to free communication with the rest of the world – as yet . . . it may be done later – but not yet.[174]

And it is made clear that the rest of the world is not ready for Herland, rather than the reverse. So it is perhaps inaccurate to say that *Herland is* the literature of the beehive. Rather the novel, like Herland itself, marks a point of evolutionary transition. If Jennings finds the drama of Herland to be 'flat' it is because he, like the world for which Gilman was writing, has not yet developed the necessary aesthetic sensibilities to fully appreciate the literature of the beehive. For Gilman, that time had yet to come, as it would when the novelist who 'is forced to chronicle the distinctive features of his time'[175] writes as a participant in utopia, rather than, like Jennings, as an observer.

Nevertheless, *Herland* demonstrates how the narrative of Him in Pursuit of Her can be rewritten to exclude the traditional ending in which She is merely the passive spoils of victory. Gilman offers us a new type of romantic hero who, although he ultimately 'gets the girl', must learn to accept that she will dictate the terms of the relationship. We are given to understand that the 'happy ending' for Ellador and Van depends on a mutual understanding that the prime directive in their future will be 'how to make the best kind of people'.[176] Gilman demonstrates the operation of reason in determining the future of the race by illustrating the triumphant narrative in contrast to two other potential narratives, both of which are shown to rest on assumptions which exclude the possibility of women as makers of culture. Despite the fact that Gilman's interpretation of evolutionary theory fails to challenge the notion of racial superiority, her argument that the continued dominance of the male is the single most damaging factor for the continuation of the species echoes resoundingly in feminist debate throughout this century, as does her claim that life begins as female.

3
Swastika Night: Katharine Burdekin and the Psychology of Scapegoating

> Fear of effeminacy, and the feeling among men that boys are naturally effeminate and must be most carefully trained to be manly, would seem to show that at the bottom of their minds dwells a great fear of the suppressed power of the female sex.
>
> Katharine Burdekin writing as Murray Constantine,
> *Proud Man*[1]

In July 1940, the Left Book Club monthly selection was, unusually, a novel. *Swastika Night*, by a reclusive but respected writer called Murray Constantine, was originally published by Victor Gollancz in 1937, but was reissued in July 1940 as a Left Book Club[2] selection, fulfilling the need 'in these difficult summer months'[3] for a psychological analysis of fascism which could reveal potential weaknesses in the Nazi psyche. Nearly fifty years later, *Swastika Night* was republished by Lawrence and Wishart at the instigation of an American researcher, Daphne Patai, who had discovered that Constantine, whose first novel *Proud Man* had also been published by Gollancz, was, in fact, Katharine Burdekin writing under a pseudonym. Both *Swastika Night* and *Proud Man* are important for their thoroughgoing analysis of the psychological construction of gender identity, more than two decades before Lacanian psychoanalysis and the burgeoning second wave of feminism prepared the way for an understanding of gender ideology and sexual politics. Burdekin's theorisation of fascism as a logical extension of the 'debasement' of women within the male psyche finds echoes today in the writings of such theorists as Klaus Theweleit[4] but was, at the time, a thoroughly radical proposal.

Of Burdekin herself, little is known.[5] She died in 1963, having published ten novels between 1922 and 1940. Although there is no existing biographical material which would support the theory that she was deliberately using psychoanalytical material in developing the plots of her novels, the way in which the characters are developed, and their behaviour explored, argues for a reading which recognises psycho-analytic theory as an insistent sub-text. The time-travelling narrator of *Proud Man*, 'a single-sexed fully conscious being',[6] observes the gendered society of Burdekin's own time and offers an objective analysis of the psychological basis of gender stereotyping which resonates suggestively with the theories of post-Freudian feminist psychoanalyst Karen Horney as well as suggesting that Burdekin may have been familiar with object-relations theory as formulated in the writings of Melanie Klein.[7] *Swastika Night* develops these proposals by imagining a world after 700 years of Nazi domination in which Hitler has been elevated to the status of a god[8] and women have been reduced to the status of breeding animals. In the ruling Nazis, gender insecurity has developed into a full-blown psychosis which renders them infantile and prone to suicide. Hope is offered in the form of a dissident Englishman who, by reading a forbidden text, is able to analyse the inherent weakness of Nazi rule and to understand the importance of the status of women to the possibility of a non-violent revolution.

At the heart of the German Empire is a decaying culture, based on the Hitler religion, which has systematically destroyed all evidence of pre-Hitler civilisation. Burdekin introduces her readers to a world in which their own present is part of the distant past: a time, according to Nazi doctrine, of savagery and darkness, from which Europe and Africa have been delivered by the 'civilising' Germans. Asia, Australia and the Americas are similarly held by the Japanese and the two empires maintain their troops in readiness for a war which is ever threatened but never actualised.

In the future world of *Swastika Night*, the book which leads the Englishman, Alfred, to knowledge of the world before the dominance of the German Empire has for seven centuries been secretly preserved by succeeding generations of one family of the privileged order of the Knights. Although the Knight, von Hess, who is the keeper of the book in the time in which the story is set is, like his forebears, secretly opposed to German rule, his privileged position prevents him from fully understanding the significance of the 'Reduction of Women',[9] a systematic debasing of all things female instigated by the conquering Nazis. But Alfred, in his marginalised position as a member of a 'subject race', is able to bring his own experience of oppression to bear in reading the document.

Alfred and the Knight, the last surviving member of the family von Hess, are brought together by circumstance, but von Hess is moved to give the book into Alfred's care when he recognises a sympathetic strength of character in the Englishman, unknown among the common Nazis. He also gives Alfred a photograph of Hitler, rescued from destruction by the same ancestor who had compiled the book, showing him to be 'a little soft fat smiling thing'[10] rather than the seven foot God with 'the holy German physique'[11] into which he has been mythologised. But the full significance of the photograph is that it shows him in the company of a woman 'as lovely as a boy, with a boy's hair and a boy's noble carriage, and a boy's direct and fearless gaze'.[12] Sexual relationships with young boys is an accepted feature of Nazi life but for a woman to be sexually desirable, other than as a bearer of sons for Germany, has become unthinkable. Women of 'the Blood' live in cages where they are allowed the bare minimum necessary for subsistence, are kept shaven headed and in clothes designed to accentuate their 'ill-balance[d]'[13] bodies, their sole purpose being to submit constantly to rape and to bear male children who are removed from them at eighteen months to be indoctrinated amongst men. The girls remain in the 'Women's Quarters'[14] ultimately to suffer the same fate as their mothers. Alfred, who has never had to think 'unsexually and objectively about women', now realises that he 'must think about women. How does one do that? Do they think about themselves?'[15]

Unlike the narrator of *Proud Man*, who directly experiences the Great Britain of the 1930s as her/his past,[16] Alfred's perspective is limited by the flawed nature of the history that has been given into his keeping. Although the book recounts the destruction of all other historical records and charts the beginning of the process which has perpetuated the idea of Hitler as a god and the German people as superior to all other races it is, itself, a mixture of fact and conjecture. Alfred's insights are derived from analysing the history against his own experience and that of his Nazi friend, Hermann, whose life is controlled by the teachings of the 'Hitler Bible' and who, when brought to face the truth about the past, suffers a breakdown, leading Alfred to an understanding of the forces that have shaped the Nazi identity.

Burdekin was writing at a time when the feminist movement was overshadowed by the world political situation. As Jane Lewis writes:

> The impetus given to the movement by the suffrage fight had disappeared, and young women regarded feminists as dowdy and faintly ridiculous. In addition, by the mid-1930s, feminists felt dwarfed by

the threat of political forces beyond their control in the form of war, fascism and communism.[17]

In the UK at this time sexual politics described an increasing concern with women's role in upholding the 'quality' of the race. The fall in the birth rate among the middle classes since World War I was attributed to the higher participation of women in the labour market. Lewis reports:

> In fact, the class differential in fertility began to disappear during the inter-war period, and had all but gone by the late 1930s. However, contemporaries did not know this and fears were constantly expressed that the middle class would not reproduce itself.[18]

These fears were fed by the continuing popular reception of eugenics.[19] The widely held belief that the quality of the race could be measured by the proportion of the population holding high socio-economic status led to exhortations that middle-class women should reject 'masculine occupations' in favour of 'making their homes more interesting and more racially valuable'.[20]

Women's role in the new Nazi Germany was simply to reproduce. The 'racially fit' were offered financial incentives to marry and produce children with the provision that the woman did not work outside the home,[21] and 'Himmler applied Hitler's obsession with race in his exhortation to SS men to father as many children as possible without marrying:[22]

> Women performed only one function, breeding the children who would be raised by the Reich as the soldiers and mothers of the next generation.[23]

Nor were women unenthusiastic about their newly prescribed role. Conservative women who considered that the role of the mother had been undermined by the emancipation of the 1920s found not only state support for their grievances but an opportunity to glorify their role in the name of National Socialism. Hitler's aim was to recruit the existing structures of the Christian church to enforce allegiance to the fascist state, and in this women were to play an important role. He saw, in the existing proliferation of Protestant women's organisations, a resource to be used for the ideological indoctrination of both women and children. As Richard Grunberger writes:

Since the Weimar Republic had been even less effective among women than among men in inculcating a linked sense of personal autonomy and public commitment, the collective feminine psyche remained apolitical and littered with a residue of dynastic loyalty and unfocused religiosity, dormant impulses which Hitler activated to a pitch of unprecedented intensity.[24]

Whether or not Grunberger is correct in his analysis of the causes, the effects were extraordinary, as witnessed by the phenomenon of *Kontaktsucht* or 'contact-craving' – a form of 'mass hysteria' in which, on public occasions, 'the female section of the crowd often exhibited...an uncontrollable urge to touch [Hitler] physically'.[25] So women, who in *Swastika Night* have been reduced to the status of breeding animals and, like animals, are kept caged and ill-fed, had in Hitler's Germany already begun to relinquish any autonomy they might have gained under the Weimar Republic and were inscribing for themselves a role that would cage them within the home and remove their influence entirely from public life. In her introduction to *Mothers in the Fatherland* (1987) Claudia Koonz observes that despite 'the publication of fifty thousand books and monographs about Hitler's Germany...half the Germans who made dictatorship, war and genocide possible have largely escaped observation', adding that the women of Nazi Germany have remained 'unclaimed by feminists and unnoticed by men'.[26] As Barbara Ehrenreich writes in her foreword to Klaus Theweleit's recent study of the writings of German 'soldier males' between the wars, *Male Fantasies* (1987), 'the point of understanding fascism is not only "because it might return again", but because it is already implicit in the daily relationships of men and women'.[27] Fifty years earlier, and at a time when the full horrors of Nazism remained to be realised, Burdekin provided as a sub-text for her novel what Ehrenreich and Theweleit could only analyse with the benefit of hindsight.

Similarly, Richard Grunberger's (1974) analysis of anti-feminism in Nazi Germany as 'a non-lethal variant of anti-Semitism' reflects a psychohistorical perspective influenced by a decade of feminist thought. He writes:

Just as the latter fused divergent resentments into a single hate syndrome, anti-feminism provided men with the opportunity for abreacting a whole complex of feelings: paterfamilias authoritarianism, anti-permissiveness, Philistine outrage at sophistication, white-collar workers' job insecurity, virility fears and just plain misogyny.[28]

Burdekin recognised the importance of understanding the link between misogyny and fascism and clearly saw, in the social conditions that pertained in Nazi Germany at the time that she was writing, the potential for the complete degradation of women that she depicts in *Swastika Night*. So her work can be seen to be singularly important in anticipating much later discussions of war and totalitarianism which see them as part of the debate about the oppression of women, rather than as separate political issues. In *Swastika Night* Hitlerdom is literally 'the worship of a man who had no mother'.[29] The creed teaches that Hitler *'was not begotten, not born of a woman, but Exploded...From the Head of His Father...God the Thunderer'.*[30] But although in the world of the German Empire it is unseemly for a man to be able to point to a woman and say, 'There is my mother',[31] the language which denies the relationship must nevertheless fail to eradicate it from consciousness because of the Nazis' need to visit the Women's Quarters to fulfil their duty of procreation as well as the fact that their 'defilement' in literally having mothers is preached to them at every religious service. This, and the fact that the Nazi unconscious must retain the residue of the first eighteen months of life, ensures that, while Hitlerdom teaches vociferous denial of the value of the female role, it is confrontation with that denial which produces tension.

The crucial aspect of von Hess's book is its reference to another book, long destroyed, in which a fanatical Knight, von Wied, sensitive to the stirrings of panic among the conquering Germans and feeding on their 'insensate pride', 'lunatic vanity' and a fear which 'gradually grew into a kind of hysteria...the fear of Memory',

> proved that Hitler was God...[and] that women were not part of the human race at all....Von Wied's theory was that the rejection right of women was an insult to Manhood [and] that family life was an insult to Manhood.[32]

And so 'the whole pattern of women's lives was to be changed and made to fit in with the new German Manhood, the first civilized manhood of the world'.[33]

Some of von Wied's book has been 'incorporated in the Hitler Bible', but, ironically, because it 'proves a man is God' and 'advocates the destruction of records of other civilizations', it in itself offers the most danger to acceptance of the ideas that it proposes – hence its subsequent destruction. As von Hess points out, 'There was plenty of Memory in von Wied's book'.[34] It is, paradoxically, itself a record of that which it advocates must be destroyed. The destruction of Memory can, in this sense, be seen to stand as a symbol for the process by which instinctual drives are denied and repressed within the psyche. Burdekin's diagnosis of the psychopathology of fascism proceeds from the idea that the psychological development of the individual is mirrored in the development of culture and, as Carlo Pagetti points out, 'the persecution of women is linked to the systematic erasing of the past and of memory (of which women are seen, significantly, as the depositories)'.[35] In the context of the pre-war years, the text encodes an implicit warning against complacency in merely demonising fascism as something peculiar to the German mentality. As Alfred discovers in *Swastika Night*, the British also once had an empire, a fact about which he is prevented from rejoicing by the realisation that the urge to colonise must, again, be understood in terms of the 'lunatic vanity' which can accrue from masculine gender insecurity.

Early in the narrative, during the women's service in the Hitler church, von Hess mistakenly exhorts the women to 'bear strong daughters'.[36] This mistake is significant in that it reveals the source of the disintegration of Hitler society. As von Hess knows, male births have become disproportionate to the point where the increasing lack of females spells death to the race, but this the women must never know:

> if the women once realised all this, what could stop them developing a small thin thread of self-respect? If a woman could rejoice publicly in the birth of a girl, Hitlerdom would start to crumble.[37]

So although the ostensible function of women within Hitler society is to breed sons and remind the men that they are superior but 'tainted' and must therefore strive for the virtues of 'pride...courage...violence... brutality...bloodshed...ruthlessness...and all other soldierly and heroic virtues'[38] lest they themselves fall prey to loathsome female qualities, they in fact are the key to the survival of the Empire, both in a physical sense and in the sense of maintaining the 'idea' that Alfred is determined to destroy. They are largely absent from the narrative, except as abstract subjects of discussion, reinforcing the sense in which they are ever present as a symbol of the repression out of which the Nazi psyche is constructed. The narrative refers to this sense of presence in absence during an exchange in which Alfred questions Hermann as to his failure to provide sons for Germany. Aware of his friend's agitation, Alfred closes the conversation by dismissing women as 'neither here nor there' but Hermann, 'misunderstanding the English idiom', replies, 'They're too much there'[39] revealing his own preoccupation with what should be a subject unworthy of a Nazi's attention. It is worth noting here that it is the same 'presence in absence' that Klaus Theweleit finds in the writings of the *Freikorpsmen*, the 'First Soldiers of the Third Reich':[40]

> Relationships with women are dissolved and transformed into new male attitudes, into political stances, revelations of the true path, etc. As the woman fades out of sight, the contours of the male sharpen; that is the way in which the fascist mode of writing often proceeds.[41]

It is precisely this transforming of relationships that has been effected by von Wied's book. While the *Freikorpsmen*'s wives and sweethearts 'evaporate as the story progresses',[42] having fulfilled their roles as catalysts in the hardening of male resolve (violated possessions giving cause for just revenge or angels to be compared to the castrating whores of the enemy), so the women of the German Empire are reduced to elevate the male and finally dissolved in the destruction of Memory, becoming 'neither here nor there' but always, for the men who must breed sons for Germany, 'too much there'. Again, Burdekin is pointing up the paradox that the voice of what the culture must deny in order to maintain itself becomes ever more vocal, the more vigorously it is denied. Hermann, in common with other Nazis, suffers from a 'deep repugnance, which amount[s] to a fear of women'[43] – a fear which is, of course, unconscious but which, as the text reveals, keeps the Nazis in a state of infantile dependency.

But in the writings of the *Freikorpsmen* women are present as objects of fantasy, allowing Theweleit to analyse the texts from a feminist/psychoanalytical point of view. In *Swastika Night* it is the *absence* of women that marks the text as a document which itself explicitly argues for a recognition of their presence as repressed aspects of the psyche of what Burdekin refers to as 'the killing male'.[44] Theweleit's soldier males are analysed by the writings that they have left behind from a perspective which is, literally, in their future and encompasses the history of the world from the end of World War II to the late 1980s, as well as the effect of the women's movement on psychoanalysis in the decades since its rebirth in the 1960s. *Swastika Night* is a text which incorporates its own analysis, actively promoting a method of psychoanalytic enquiry to uncover the roots of the fascist mentality and the corruption which is the inherent weakness of the fascist ideal by *imagining* the future (meanwhile uncannily predicting the Holocaust. In *Swastika Night*, the Germans have 'after a time killed all the Jews off'[45]).

The text therefore offers a diagnosis of the psychology of the fascist identity, an identity dependent upon the belief that women are inherently inferior. The novel charts the dissolution of fascism, not through a political opposition which takes up arms against the conquerors, but through the final resolution of a psychological paradox which it inherently harbours. The process which relegates the scapegoat lends power to what is relegated by the demands of the need for the process itself to be continually repressed within the psyche. In *Swastika Night* the lack of female births offers a biological metaphor for the way in which this power insinuates itself into consciousness. The Knights, at least, must now, like Alfred, begin to 'think about women'.

Woman envy and the fascist identity

Psychoanalysis is, as Michel Foucault points out, 'in theoretical and practical opposition to fascism' in that it regards 'with suspicion ... the irrevocably proliferating aspects which might be contained in [the] power mechanisms aimed at controlling and administering the everyday life of sexuality'.[46] In other words, because fascism exerts its control through what Foucault terms 'the deployment of sexuality'[47] in the service of normalisation, the demythologising of sexuality presents a danger to acceptance of the ideology. In *Swastika Night*, sexuality is deployed to ensure that the Nazis are reminded that they are at the mercy of their defiled, human bodies, whose desires can only be regulated by allegiance to Hitler's creed. The myth of Hitler's 'exploded' birth and complete lack of contact with women provides an unattainable ideal which is both mysterious and superhuman. As Theweleit explains it:

> That prohibition, the law that bodies cannot know themselves, has been used to recreate susceptibility to repression ever since people first began ruling other people ... In societies ruled by a single person, the despot was the only one who could (theoretically) use his body in any way he pleased – except in a human way, since no other was like him.[48]

Psychoanalysis attempts to remove sexuality from the level of the body politic and return it to the individual as a form of knowledge in which bodies will indeed 'know themselves', and thus is antagonistic to the project of fascism which can only maintain a hierarchical ordering of society by perpetuating the myth of the hegemonic body.

It was the preoccupation with heredity and descent that informed the psychic position of the middle classes of the early nineteenth century which, Foucault believes, brought sexuality into the forefront of the political sphere. Where previously the ruling aristocracy had preserved their position by asserting 'the special character of its body . . . in the form of *blood*',[49] so the hegemonic, differentiating factor of social class underwent a shift in emphasis from a mysterious, ascendant form of 'blood' to a medicalised idea of sexuality which, while creating categories of deviance, also allowed for health to be measured in terms of the potential for reproductive success.[50] Beginning in the second half of the nineteenth century, 'the thematics of blood was sometimes called on to lend its entire historical weight toward revitalising the type of political power that was exercised through the devices of sexuality', and it was at this point that '[r]acism [in its modern form] took shape':

> a long series of interventions at the level of the body, conduct, health and everyday life, received their colour and their justification from the mythical concern with protecting the purity of the blood and ensuring the triumph of the race. . . . Nazism was doubtless the most cunning and the most naive . . . combination of the fantasies of blood and the paroxysms of a disciplinary power. A eugenic ordering of society, with all that implied in the way of extension and intensification of micro-powers, in the guise of an unrestricted state control . . . , was accompanied by the oneiric exaltation of a superior blood.[51]

However, although the language used to describe sexuality and its effects demonstrated a concern with anatamo-physiological processes and the potential for malfunction or 'unhealthy' behaviour in the individual, Foucault detects a concomitant 'elaboration of [the] idea that there exists something other . . . something else and something more, with intrinsic properties and laws of its own: 'sex':[52]

> Thus, in the process of hysterization of women, 'sex' was defined in three ways: as that which belongs in common to men and women; as that which belongs *par excellence* to men, and hence is lacking in women; but at the same time, as that which by itself constitutes women's body, ordering it wholly in terms of the functions of reproduction and keeping it in constant agitation through the effects of that very function.[53]

The caging of the women in *Swastika Night* represents, symbolically, this ordering of female sexuality in terms of reproduction alone, but equally it implies a response to the fear that the mechanisms deployed to order sexuality in the service of 'the symbolics of blood'[54] will fail and a repressed power in (specifically female) sexuality itself will rise up to destroy the fragile hegemony of the 'master' race.

While trying to convince Hermann of the fragility of the German idea, Alfred gives an analysis of the Nazi character in terms which suggest that Burdekin herself understood the antagonism between psychoanalysis and fascism:

> as long as Blood is a Mystery none of you will ever be men. You hide behind the Blood because you don't really like yourselves, and you don't like yourselves because you can't be men. If even some of you were men the rest would like themselves better. But it's a circle. If there's going to be Blood there'll be no men.[55]

The doctrine of the Blood is a supreme example of a society normalised around the symbolics of blood and the deployment of sexuality. The Nazis have a responsibility to procreate in the service of the Blood which, so long as it is a 'Mystery', is theirs alone and that which 'proves' their ascendancy. But the act of procreation in itself reminds them that they are 'defiled' and must purge themselves by recourse to 'soldierly virtues'. Their self image is thus inextricably linked to the Blood and their self esteem based solely on proving themselves worthy to be its carriers – something which they can never achieve because what is given as their 'defilement' ensures that they are constantly at the prey of emotions anathema to full soldierly 'virtue'. The meaning of Alfred's analysis can thus be found in tracing the development of the Nazi personality as constrained by what, to borrow from Foucault, can be called 'the Hitlerite politics of sex'.[56]

The work of Melanie Klein becomes particularly relevant in this context in that her particular contribution to ego psychology deals with the infant's early, ambivalent relationship to the mother. Klein's essays on infantile development were published between 1921 and 1945 and collectively form a body of work which shows how a fixated personality can develop when anxieties connected to the mother have no potential for relief or transformation. Reading *Swastika Night* with reference to Klein brings into sharp focus the influence of the first eighteen months of a Nazi boy's life, before he is removed from the Women's Quarters.

For Klein, the unconscious constitutes a battleground where the infant's inadequate concepts of 'self' and 'other' are continually defined and redefined in terms of hated and loved objects. Briefly, then, part of the mother is perceived as both a good and a bad object, both giving and denying satisfaction, but because the infant ego is as yet unformed (and Klein does presuppose a rudimentary ego), the child 'introjects' into itself the good object which it also partly projects as feelings of love while, at the same time, introjecting a bad, persecutory object which is projected as hatred and destruction. In phantasy, the child is omnipotent in destruction, inflicting actual harm, and later, when the mother is identified as a separate being, feelings of guilt demand that the child make reparation for the supposed injury. When the mother is perceived as a separate and independent being,

> libidinal fixation to the breast develops into feelings towards her as a person. Thus feelings both of a destructive and of a loving nature are experienced towards one and the same object and this gives rise to deep and disturbing conflicts in the child's mind.[57]

This gives rise to what Klein terms the depressive position where 'the ego comes to a realisation of its love for a good object, a whole object and in addition a real object, together with an overwhelming feeling of guilt towards it'.[58] Before reparation can effectively alleviate the anxiety of loss, the infant must experience itself as capable of restoring through love what its hatred has apparently destroyed:

> As the ego becomes more fully organised, the internalised imagos [phantastic representations of objects] will approximate more closely to reality and the ego will identify itself more fully with 'good' objects. The dread of persecution, which was at first felt on the ego's account, now relates to the good object as well and from now on preservation of the good object is regarded as synonymous with the survival of the ego.[59]

What is particularly interesting for an evaluation of the denial which informs the psychic position of the Nazis is the defensive position of the ego when reparative drives first come into play. The infant's fear of experiencing feelings of loss and guilt for its own destructive impulses leads to a denial of its experience, that is, to a denial of psychic reality. The 'manic defences' come into play in order that the valued object may no longer be valued and therefore its loss will not be experienced as guilt and depression. Furthermore, the ego must defend itself against dependence. Hence, feelings of control, triumph and contempt are directed against the object. 'Manic reparation' assuages guilt by a denial of destructive potential. Burdekin's Nazis represent the adult personality, fixated at this stage of development. What Klein terms the 'hypomanic' personality is characterised by feelings of omnipotence, 'by which he defends himself against his fear of losing the one irreplaceable object, his mother' and an inclination to 'exaggerated valuations: over-admiration (idealisation) or contempt (devaluation):

> contempt . . . is also based to some extent on denial. He must deny his impulse to make extensive and detailed reparation because he has to deny the cause for the reparation; namely, the injury to the object and his consequent sorrow and guilt.[60]

The dread of persecution from the object insufficiently repaired is thus added to the sense of unrelieved guilt. In normal development, the fear of persecution is diminished by a gradual balancing out of the need to receive love and the need to make reparation which results in the ability to give and receive love in later life. However, where possibilities for even partial reparation are dramatically reduced, the manic stage characterises all subsequent relationships.

What von Hess's book refers to as 'insensate pride' and 'lunatic vanity'[61] among the conquering German males can be seen to correspond to the feelings of omnipotence which characterise the hypomanic personality, finding its fullest expression in the character of von Wied, whom von Hess refers to as 'a complete nervous hysteric'.[62] The Nazis have been happy to accept his ideas, rather than dismissing him as a lunatic, primarily '*because* of the part about the women'.[63] Von Hess explains:

> von Wied's theories about women were wildly popular with a large section of the men. You see, the lunatic vanity of the Germans was concentrated really in the males among them. The women hadn't beaten the world and made the Empire. They had only borne the children. . . . And these proud soldiers, the great-grandsons of the men who really made the Empire, were beginning to feel very strongly that it was beneath the dignity of a German man to have to risk rejection by a mere woman, to have to allow women to wound him in his most sensitive part, his vanity.[64]

Embedded in this analysis is the suggestion that, in Kleinian terms, the vanity of the Nazi males covers a protracted sense of guilt which has no potential for relief in reparation. The Reduction of Women, while removing their right to reject the sexual advances of men, also ensures that they are unworthy of love. As von Hess points out, 'Men cannot love female animals',[65] and so the Nazis are able to deny the impulse to reparation while they nevertheless remain slaves to unrelieved guilt. As von Hess admits to Alfred, there is an increasing incidence of suicide among young Nazis which, it is suggested, may be due to a loss of faith. This in itself would indicate that, once belief in the doctrine of superiority founders, the precarious psychic controls which keep repressed impulses at bay are lost, allowing guilt to overwhelm the desire to live.

Karen Horney's essay 'The Dread of Woman' (1932) begins by asking whether 'one of the principal roots of the whole masculine impulse to creative work' might not be 'the never-ending conflict between the man's longing for the woman and his dread of her'.[66] Horney perceives the male as experiencing constant anxiety with regard to penetration – an anxiety which he must strenuously deny lest his self-respect be impaired. She argues with Freud in his assumption that the vagina remains undiscovered, for both sexes, in the early stages of development and suggests, instead, that 'the boy, urged on by his impulses to penetrate, pictures in fantasy a complementary female organ'.[67] However, he 'instinctively judges that his penis is much too small for his mother's genital and reacts with the dread of his own inadequacy, of being rejected and derided'. Thus the child invests his mother with the power to wound, both through frustration of his libidinous desires, 'the thrusting back of his libido upon itself', and 'through the wounding of his masculine self-regard'.[68] Horney sees puberty as the time when the boy must not only free himself from incestuous attachment to his mother but must also 'master his dread of the whole female sex'.[69] However, this mastery remains incomplete and Horney perceives 'that the anxiety connected with his self-respect leaves more or less distinct traces in every man and gives his general attitude towards women a particular stamp'.[70]

Her account of this unresolvable conflict returns us to Theweleit's *Freikorpsmen*, for whom women provide the context for their writings, threading the plot with the impulse to action and thereafter disappearing or representing the decadence of the enemy in the form of the castrating whore who deserves only death. Theweleit writes:

> It's as if two male compulsions were tearing at the woman with equal strength. One is trying to push them away, to keep them at arm's

length (defense); the other wants to penetrate them, to have them
very near. Both compulsions seem to find satisfaction in the act of
killing, where the man pushes the woman far away (takes her life),
and gets very close to her (penetrates her with a bullet, stab would,
club etc.).[71]

Horney suggests that denial of fear informs attitudes of glorification
and disparagement towards women. Hence:

> The attitude of love and adoration signifies: 'There is no need for me
> to dread a being so wonderful, so beautiful, nay, so saintly.' That of
> disparagement implies: 'It would be too ridiculous to dread a creature
> who, if you take her all round, is such a poor thing'.[72]

It is, of course, not surprising that the Nazis have been pleased to
adopt universally the latter attitude because, as Burdekin points out
through the narrator of *Proud Man*, 'contempt . . . is more soothing to the
self-esteem'.[73] But it is Alfred's response to the birth of his daughter
which enforces Burdekin's claim that fascism is the extreme form of a
common pattern of relationships between men and women. Towards
the end of *Swastika Night*, when Alfred returns to England, his colleagues
offer him condolences for the fact that his current woman, Ethel, has
recently given birth, but the baby is only a girl. Impelled by curiosity
and his conviction that the future of the human race must now depend
on a revision in attitudes towards the status of women, he visits his
daughter in the Women's Quarters, breaking protocol by demanding to
see her in the formal words used only to apply to sons. His feelings
towards Edith are immediately possessive: 'he felt [she] was entirely his,
no one else should touch her'.[74] Had he complete control over her, he
could 'make a new kind of human being, one there's never been
before'.[75] But Edith needs to be fed, and he becomes furious with Ethel
'for being able to do something for the baby he could not do himself'.[76]
So Alfred is forced into a position where unconscious envy of women is
brought to the surface. According to Horney, men's 'feeling of playing a
relatively small part in the creation of living beings' leads to 'envy of
pregnancy, childbirth and motherhood, as well as of the breasts and of
the act of suckling' and she asks, 'Is not the tremendous strength in
men of the impulse to creative work in every field precisely due to their
feeling of playing a relatively small part in the creation of living beings,
which constantly impels them to an overcompensation in achievement?'[77] But Burdekin suggests that the impulse to violence can also be

traced to this source. Alfred becomes so agitated that he threatens to beat Ethel if she does not take care of 'his' daughter.

Horney considers it 'remarkable...that so little recognition and attention are paid to the fact of men's secret dread of women' and 'almost more remarkable that women themselves have so long been able to overlook it'.[78] Burdekin offers us a means of recognising this dread by showing it acted out in extreme circumstances. Alfred's response to Edith is important in demonstrating, on a domestic level, the impulses that have moulded the fascist state. He responds violently to the realisation that he alone cannot 'make a new kind of human being' because the nature of woman is such that, even in a reduced state, she performs an important function that, to him, will always be a mystery, and that he can never wrest from her control. However, Alfred, through his own experience of doubt, is able consciously to evaluate the conditions that have provided for women to acquiesce in their own reduction. The old Knight, von Hess, believes that '[w]omen *are* nothing, except an incarnate desire to please men', a theory that he supports by reading from his ancestor's book, which reports that '[o]nce [women] were convinced that men really wanted them to be animals and ugly and completely submissive...they threw themselves into the new pattern with a conscious enthusiasm that knew no bounds.' But Alfred is convinced that there is 'something wrong somewhere'.[79] Finding a correlation between his own position as a member of a subject race and the description in von Hess's book of the position of women before von Wied's prescriptions for their reduction, he concludes that 'women always live according to an imposed pattern, because they are not women at all, and never have been. They are not *themselves'*:

> They see another form of life, *undoubtedly* different from their own...and they say '*that* form is better than our form'. And for that reason men have always unconsciously despised them, while consciously urging them to accept their inferiority.[80]

Alfred's explanation thus locates the reasons for women's inferior status in the *male* unconscious and later he expresses the belief that the 'human values of this world are masculine. There are no feminine values because there are no women'.[81] No women, that is, whose identity has not been formed by compliance with male demands.

Ironically, von Hess himself blames men for women's position, but for him it is 'a mistake in their leadership':

If men want [women] to have an appearance of perfect freedom, even an appearance of masculine power, they will develop a simulacrum of those things. But what men cannot do, never have been able to do, is to *stop* this blind submission and cause the women to ignore them and disobey them.[82]

So, while von Hess believes that women are innately masochistic, Alfred is arguing for their status to be assessed on the basis of what men have never allowed them: 'sexual invulnerability and . . . pride in their sex, which is the humblest boy's birthright'.[83] In this way, their discussion reproduces the arguments for and against innate female masochism which turn on interpretations of Freud's theory of penis envy. In 'The Problem of Feminine Masochism' (1933), Horney argues with Freud's assertion that 'masochism is . . . truly feminine'.[84] Freud believed that the instinctual life of little girls leads them to blame their mothers when they discover that they are 'castrated' and to turn to their father in the hope of receiving a penis from him. As this hope can never be realised, it is later sublimated into the wish for a baby. However, female ego development is weakened by this only partial resolution of the Oedipus complex. The girl child has, by this stage, rejected her mother but cannot fully identify with her father, as can the boy. She is thus left with a desire for, as Juliet Mitchell explains it, 'passive intercourse with an aggressive father (or his replacements) and childbirth [which] . . . suggests pleasure-in-pain'.[85] Horney argues that the assumption of a constitutional basis for masochistic drives in women is formulated on the basis of 'unwarranted generalisations from limited data'.[86] She sees that '[o]nly one justification could be adduced for such generalisations, namely, Freud's hypothesis that there is no fundamental difference between pathologic and "normal phenomena"',[87] and warns that psychoanalysis is in danger of making spectacularly untenable assumptions if it does not take into account the role of social conditioning in feminine psychology.[88] Further, she asserts that:

Beyond admitting the possibility of a certain preparedness in women for a masochistic conception of their role, every additional assertion as to the relation of their constitution to masochism is hypothetical.[89]

Burdekin herself, through the narrator of *Proud Man*, gives an account of penis envy as socially rather than psychogenetically based, which accords closely with the theory that Horney develops in 'The Problem of Feminine Masochism':

> The young subhuman females were made to feel of no account, even before they were well out of their cradles, and before they were aware of possessing any sexual organs at all. Their reproductive organ was internal, and their mammary glands undeveloped. Yet their small *brother's* phallus was visible even from babyhood, and the girl rapidly learned to associate it with all the value and all the dignity of being a boy. She felt herself despised, and not only that, but physically unfinished, lacking and inadequate. And when, as she grew older, she realised that she had sexual organs, she discovered that they were only a matter for whispering, secrecy and shame, and not even of much practical value unless she could produce with them more boys. She herself was not worth reproducing.[90]

The artistic aridity of the culture in *Swastika Night* is also implicitly linked to the denial of fear of women. Although it can be read as a natural extension of the cultural purge that, when Burdekin was writing, had already begun under the Third Reich, this in itself, in light of Horney's theories, can be read as a tacit acknowledgement that unrestricted creative expression speaks too insistently of a dangerous ambivalence.

In pre-World War II Germany, the Nazis were not content merely to suppress the *avant garde* but in 1937 mounted a huge exhibition of so-called 'Degenerate Art' (*Entartete Kunst*):

> Pictures were displayed in a mad jumble, without frames, as if arranged by fools or children without any sense of reason, high and low, just as they came, furnished with inciting titles, explanations or filthy jokes.[91]

To reinforce the desired effect, an exhibition of the 'new German art', approved by Hitler, was mounted in the close vicinity.

In a 1992 BBC documentary, reviewing a contemporary reconstruction of the original *Entartete Kunst*, Art Historian Irit Rogoff of the University of California analysed the contrast:

> In the German art exhibition which supposedly puts forward some kind of notion of the 'norm' we have bodies of total integrity – of total coherence – their surfaces seamless, impenetrable, marbled, muscled. The Decadent Art exhibition puts forward bodies that are fractured,

fragmented – that are infinitely penetrable and therefore of great danger.[92]

In a political sense (as Rogoff points out), fragmentation speaks danger to a recently unified Germany but, on the level of the unconscious, bodies that are penetrable are immediately female (castrated), harbouring mystery, the desire for reincorporation and, as Lutz Becker points out in the same programme, 'the dark forces of the past' – the Memory that, in *Swastika Night*, von Wied recognised must be destroyed for the German idea to triumph.

So, taking von Hess's book as a metaphor for the unconscious, its contents can be read as a model for the process which, according to Horney, forms the male ego. The acceptance of von Wied's theories about the inferior status of women can then be seen as assuaging penetration anxiety, allowing the dread of women to be sublimated:

He ... held the theory that the beauty of women was an insult to Manhood, as giving them ... an enormous and disgusting sexual power over men.[93]

Von Wied's prescription for the destruction of Memory can therefore be read as rejection of the mother and her 'enormous and disgusting sexual power' in order to effect identification with the father, *'the perfect, the untainted Man-child'*,[94] Hitler.

Analysing the killing male

In the early pages of the novel, Hermann appears to be a model Nazi. Although he is bored by the service in the Hitler church and finds a useful diversion in attempting to catch the eye of a beautiful boy in the choir, it is his long familiarity with the words of the creed and the values that they express that makes him restless.

True to the doctrine of aggression, when he fantasises about the boy, he imagines winding his hands in his hair and giving 'a good tug, pulling the boy's head backwards. Not to hurt him much, just to make him mind'.[95] This is in sharp contrast to his later fantasy about Alfred, who arouses feelings immediately in conflict with the values that Hermann has been taught to respect. He 'would have adored to serve him, to be his slave, to set his body, his strong bones and willing hard muscles, between ... Alfred and all harm – to die for him'.[96] Hermann's dilemma is such that not only is the love that he feels for Alfred anathema to the doctrine of aggression, but it is directed towards a member of a race for whom he should feel only contempt. Furthermore, the object of Hermann's love is a dangerous rebel who deserves only death, but, it is suggested, it is this very 'flaw' in Alfred's character that is the source of his attraction. When Alfred is near, Hermann thinks 'almost like an individual', but 'with his heavy influence relaxed [he starts] to think like a Nazi'.[97]

Early in the narrative, Alfred makes blasphemous statements against the Hitler regime, but Hermann, whose duty it is to kill anyone who utters such perfidy, having taken out his knife to stab Alfred while he sleeps, 'could imagine it dulled with blood, his duty done, his oath fulfilled, his friend lying dead', but he cannot 'make his arm obey him to strike downwards into Alfred's body'. He sits 'in a trance of shame'[98] for his inability to kill his friend who is a member of a subject race and as such, the doctrine teaches, below him in the hierarchy.

Unconsciously Hermann is attracted to Alfred's rebellious nature because it offers a resolution to the dilemma of a personality at war with itself. If Hermann were to abandon his belief in the ideal of aggression, he would no longer be torn by emotions in conflict with his cultural values and his guilt would be relieved.[99]

Hermann's conflict finds symbolic expression in the two texts, the Hitler Bible and von Hess's book, and their conflicting versions of history. It is significant to a reading of these texts as representations of the unconscious conflicts that inform the fascist personality that Hermann is unable to read either (the common Nazis are illiterate), but their contents are fundamental to the way in which his life is structured.

Pagetti believes that:

> Not only is Herman's [sic] homosexuality functional in terms of the narrative structure, giving the necessary psychological verisimilitude to the bond of total subjugation which links him to . . . Alfred. But it also mockingly emphasises another trait of a culture based on masculinity – of Nazi culture specifically, but also of English culture in certain respects – in which homosexuality appears . . . as the necessary result of contempt for women.[100]

While this is true, it is also the case that, if not Hermann's homosexuality *per se*, then certainly the fantasies that it generates, allow Burdekin to emphasise another aspect of the personality of the killing male – his desire to *be* a woman.

Hermann's two sexual fantasies have a distinct character. With the boy he desires to be active and aggressive, but with Alfred, to be passive and compliant, to 'die for him'. In simple terms this can be seen as a response to castration anxiety, as a fantasy of submission to the father. For Horney, 'masculine castration anxiety is very largely the ego's response to the *wish to be a woman*'.[101] Penetration anxiety, she believes, leaves 'more or less distinct traces in every man'.[102] Claiming that the early wound to his self-regard is probably one of the factors liable to disgust the boy with his male role', she observes that

> the dread of being rejected and derided is a typical ingredient in the analysis of every man ... [but] ordinary life ... gives men plenty of opportunity to escape from these feelings either by avoiding situations calculated to evoke them or by a process of overcompensation.[103]

Although the Reduction of Women had, as a specific aim, the removal of the possibility of rejection, Hermann's inability to visit the Women's Quarters demonstrates that the anxiety is still present, and because Nazi culture is so dramatically removed from 'ordinary life', opportunities for overcompensation no longer exist. The Nazis cannot display achievement in creative or scientific pursuits, nor can they demonstrate sexual prowess in 'possess[ing] many women, and the most beautiful and the most sought-after women'.[104] It is possible to conjecture that the unrelieved anxiety thus manifests either as violence or as complete capitulation to a symbolic father. Theweleit notes this capitulation in the writings of his 'soldier males', each of whom achieve status as components in what he calls the 'totality machine'. Each individual component experiences a sense of 'being-in-power', but 'that power is neither individual nor can it be gained in isolation':

> The machine partakes of and represents, a larger social power, which it functions to maintain and celebrate. The machine – whose form recalls the supreme phallus itself [the form of the hierarchy which 'rises upwards'] – is a glittering pearl among fascism's working monuments to the power of the abstract father.[105]

It is significant, also, that 'in the texts of the soldier males, real fathers are made to appear corrupt and ridiculous'. The power of the abstract father is in the fact that 'these men quite clearly *desire* a father – a man less weak than their own fathers were in reality'.[106] So Hermann's wish to 'die' for Alfred can be interpreted as, conversely, a desire to be saved by him, as Theweleit's soldier males desire 'the father who might once have saved them from the morass into which they now feel themselves sinking'.[107] The 'morass' is a symbolic term which images the streams of bodily fluids that are unleashed by the act of killing and can be read, again, as desire for reincorporation with the mother, that is, a desire for death which the soldier's 'will to live' reacts to 'with anxiety'.[108]

Hermann, finally, is allowed his wish to die for Alfred when he fights to the death to protect von Hess's book from discovery. When he attacks Alfred's enemies (his own Nazi compatriots), he is striking a blow for his own freedom (from the regime), as well as giving free rein to repressed desires in the only form of self-expression available to him. He also creates a diversion, allowing Alfred's son Fred to escape with von Hess's book, thus symbolically freeing the repository of 'Memory', the unconscious, from those that would further repress it by destroying the book and denying its existence. He dies, Alfred suspects, 'completely happy' for the first time in his life. But his 'last wild fight'[109] is perhaps symbolic also of the death of the German Empire – the final destruction of the 'idea' which holds it together. As Nazi fights Nazi, von Hess's book, and the truth that it reveals, are brought, symbolically, 'above ground', out of the dugout beneath Stonehenge where Alfred had hidden it and into the realm of the Christians, 'the remnants of a pre-Hitler civilized religion'[110] (considered a safe hiding place, as the Christians have the status of 'untouchables') and thus back into the past from which the future dystopian world of Hitlerdom has been constructed, serving to establish once again the connection between the interior world of the reader's own psyche and the exterior, nightmare world of Hitlerdom – only too capable of becoming a reality. As Pagetti writes:

> The dystopian novel whose plot is constructed from the testimony of other imaginary texts (which it constitutes) thus becomes, paradoxically, a place of truth, a representation of an invented future capable of embodying a historical and real present.[111]

In her introduction to the 1985 edition of *Swastika Night*, Daphne Patai details the similarities to George Orwell's *Nineteen Eighty-Four*, which was published seven years later. Apart from the suggestion that Orwell, 'an inveterate borrower'[112] may have been influenced by *Swastika Night*, Patai observes a striking difference between the two novels in that while *Nineteen Eighty-Four* offers a conclusion fraught with despair, *Swastika Night* closes with hope for the future. Orwell can 'only, helplessly, attribute the pursuit of power to "human nature" itself' while Burdekin 'is able to see the preoccupation with power in the context of a gender polarisation that can degenerate into the world of *Swastika Night*',[113] the corollary of which is that Orwell offers his warning against totalitarianism couched in terms which ultimately exclude the possibility of rebellion once the regime is entrenched, while Burdekin is able to envisage the regime slowly destroying itself through the very mythology which supports it.

4
'No Woman Born': C. L. Moore's Dancing Cyborg

[G]irdles and related equipment are sold on an engineering and technological basis: 'an all-way stretch and resilient control. Girdle and garters act in harmony to give you a slim hip and thigh line.... It lives and breathes with you.' The body as a living machine is now correlative with cars as vibrant and attractive organisms.

Marshall McLuhan, *The Mechanical Bride*[1]

One important route for reconstructing socialist–feminist politics is through theory and practice addressed to the social relations of science and technology, including crucially the systems of myth and meaning structuring our imaginations. The cyborg is a kind of disassembled and reassembled, postmodern collective and personal self. This is the self feminists must code.

Donna J. Haraway, 'A Cyborg Manifesto'[2]

In the same year that Gollancz published the first edition of *Swastika Night* in the UK, across the Atlantic John W. Campbell took over the editorship of a little known pulp sf magazine called *Astounding Stories*, later to be renamed *Astounding Science Fiction*, thus ushering in what is now generally regarded as the 'golden age' of sf. His predecessor, Hugo Gernsback, although responsible for naming the genre, made few demands on his writers, other than to insist that they incorporate a scientific theme. Campbell's contribution was to hone and refine the genre into what Kingsley Amis calls 'something an intelligent adult could profitably read',[3] encouraging his writers to experiment with language and content and, ultimately, discarding the hacks in favour of a coterie of challenging and sophisticated writers.

Nevertheless, the genre during this time reflected the prevailing preoccupation with technology – of the metal and grease kind. The predominate equation of the scientific with the technological ensured that Campbell's demand for plausible scientific content was interpreted generally in terms of clanking machinery. Stories of its use and misuse, the pleasure of its operation and the tyranny of its construction overwhelmed the by now receding minority of Bug Eyed Monsters (BEMs to the initiated), and Mad Scientists. However, as Lester del Rey, one of Campbell's team, remembers:

> Campbell was always receptive to mixing the hard science – the physical technological developments – in stories with as much social science as he could get . . . to base a future on physical science and neglect the social developments was unrealistic.[4]

One of the more interesting distinguishing characteristics of 'fandom', a phenomenon that burgeoned during the 1940s and continued to flourish during the 1950s (and is still, to this day, a world-wide phenomenon associated peculiarly with sf) was that the early fans were committed to examining their own intelligence and instigated numerous surveys to 'prove' the intellectual superiority of their membership. One 'gigantic . . . survey . . . showed that 70 per cent of those responding claimed themselves smarter than the average man:

> Various other efforts were made to link fannishness with physical or psychical genius. Philadelphia fans at one time devoted most of their meetings to showing off their muscles.[5]

This muscular fandom has distinct resonances with the cult of masculinity which informs Katharine Burdekin's fictional critique of the killing male,[6] not least the need to designate a scapegoat against which the superiority of cult members could be constantly measured. In the language of fan slang, non-fans were designated 'mundane', and the world outside of fandom became 'mundania'. Fans claimed by responsibilities in mundania were said to 'fafiate' (a word formed from the initial letters of forced-away-from-it-all) which was itself an inversion of 'gafiate' (get-away-from-it-all) which 'originally referred to the condition of a person who was doing fannish things in order to forget or avoid the unpleasant things in the warring world around him' but 'later . . . was generally accepted as possessing the opposite connotation: the dropping of fannish activities and obligations'.[7] The language very pointedly suggests a desire for escape. Mundania was home, family and work responsibilities, imposing the tyranny of 'fafia', but 'gafia' could not maintain its utopian promise once the war receded in memory.

The desire to gafiate was perfectly acceptable in the face of the atomic horror but later, I would suggest, it spoke too insistently of the true desires of fandom, what Donna Haraway would later describe as 'an ultimate self untied at last from all dependency, a man in space'.[8] This is the same ultimate self that early American writers hoped to discover in the wilderness[9] free from the sphere of domesticity, women and their socialising power. Fandom coded the final frontier in an exclusive language and explored it through ever more fantastic forays into the world of the imagination.

In defence of fandom, it should be noted that the close links that it forged between writers and readers (many well-known writers had originally been fans) accounted in no small part for maintaining the new sophistication of the writing. The fannish intelligentsia were harsh critics, demanding that the standard of the writing reflect their self-assumed status. Needless to say, few women participated independently in fandom,[10] and even fewer found their way into print. Catherine Lucille Moore was a notable exception whose first story, 'Shambleau', has prompted Brian Aldiss to comment that she had 'a maturity few of her male contemporaries could match'.[11] This is perhaps revealed in the fact that where the male writers often appeared to see science as, in T. A. Shippey's words, 'a djinn to be stuffed back in the bottle',[12] Moore realised that not only was this not possible but that it might be possible to imagine a world in which it was not even desirable. 'No Woman Born' is primarily a story which raises questions about the way that technology is perceived, in the context of a culture which was engaged in managing its fear of its own inventions by confusing the distinctions between human life and the machines it had created.

Post-war propaganda boasted of 'the splendid contribution made by the scientists and their devices to victory'.[13] And with 'the bonanza of the new consumer goods supplied by science ... information about science ... flooded into popular journals and radio, and onto the television screens'. But Dora Russell was among those who viewed with suspicion the machine legacy of the war. As she writes:

> To defeat Hitler's bid for hegemony had demanded desperate means and effort, but it had to be done. In the process the victorious allies acquired not only the techniques of mechanised and scientific war, but, in addition, the technical and psychological devices for instilling

into the masses such emotions as were necessary to ensure appropriate behaviour and loyalty under totalitarian control. Statesmen and the mass of the population in America, Europe and Russia, were well satisfied with their machine god.[14]

Nevertheless, 'the masses' were admitting technology into the home and the workplace with feelings of ambivalence.[15] The 'machine god' promised to alleviate drudgery in the home and streamline production in the factory, but anxieties surfaced in connection with the modifications of workplace practices that the introduction of new technology would demand. If machine technology was so versatile, what would be the role of the human worker?

In 1921 Czech dramatist Karel Capek had introduced the idea of 'simplified human beings [which had] no soul and [did] nothing but work' in his satirical play *R.U.R.* (Rossum's Universal Robots) and, although Capek's robots are 'what we would [now] regard as androids or clones',[16] they provided an adaptable symbol for expressing the fear that machine technology was set to usurp the human role in production. The sf writers re-created the robot as a creature of metal, and a new mythology was born. As John Griffiths writes, robots embody 'the fear of replacement of Man [sic], and particularly the less skilled Man, by the machine.... The final extrapolation of this fear is the total replacement of the human race by such 'thinking' devices'.[17] But, equally, the robot gave form to the anxiety that streamlined workplace practices in particular, and over-reliance on technology in general, would erode the human capacity for individual thought and create a race of similarly robotised automatons. Nor, particularly in the US, was the fear completely unfounded.

At the turn of the century Frederick W. Taylor's system of 'Scientific Management', as implemented by Henry Ford, had led to the introduction of the 'moving assembly line'[18] in factories and 'the regime of the man with the buff smock and the stopwatch'.[19] Implicit in the idea of time-and-motion efficiency and the fragmenting of work into 'smaller and smaller parcels nested deeper and deeper within formal levels of study and supervision'[20] was the suggestion that the worker was merely an automaton or a component in the larger machine that was the factory. In the 1920s the Italian Marxist and Communist leader Antonio Gramsci described the 'new type of man suited to the new type of work and productive process':[21]

The only thing that is completely mechanised is the physical gesture; the memory of the trade, reduced to simple gestures repeated at an intense rhythm, 'nestles' in the muscular and nervous centres and leaves the brain free and unencumbered for other occupations'.[22]

Gramsci believed that, with the freedom to think, the worker who realised that 'they are trying to reduce him to a trained gorilla' would be led into a train of thought 'that is far from conformist',[23] a prediction perhaps borne out by the need for 'the infamously brutal Ford police force'.[24] However, the appliance of science to rationalising the work-force necessarily set a pace for social adaptation, as summed up in the guidebook to the 1922 Chicago World's Fair: 'Science finds – Industry applies – Man conforms'[25] – a pace which accelerated with the new technological developments brought about by World War II. As traditional occupations were simplified, mechanised or eroded by ever more complex and capable machinery, it was the machines themselves that became the focus for anxiety. Anthropomorphised into grotesque parodies of the human form (although, even today, very few robots are cast in the image of their creators), the robot came into its own in the pulp magazines as a symbol for the anxieties invoked by machine technology (and, as I will discuss later, the management of those anxieties, as proposed by Isaac Asimov). As Aldiss puts it, 'Robots can embody depersonalisation fears. This is perhaps their most obvious psychological function. They then stand for man's anxieties about surviving the pressures of modern society'.[26] Lewis Mumford had perhaps underestimated the anxiety when he wrote in 1932, 'We now realise that the machines, at their best, are lame counterfeits of living organisms'.[27]

But although the stories appearing in the sf magazines coded a resistance to the mechanisation of society, worship of the machine god was in general fuelled rather than tempered by the anxieties that I have discussed. The most coherent explanation for this can be found in Marshall McLuhan's analysis of American machine culture, *The Mechanical Bride*, first published in 1951, in which he identifies a capitulation to machines which manifests as a form of totemism. According to Joseph Campbell, 'primitive hunting peoples'[28] had need to get 'ritually and psychologically into animal skins'[29] in order to accept their dependence on, and fear of, the animals which they represented. These 'totem ancestors' symbolised an 'unconscious identification' with the animals and an 'annihilation of the human ego' which allowed society to achieve 'a cohesive organization'. McLuhan believes:

It is precisely the same annihilation of the human ego that we are witnessing today. Only whereas men in those ages of terror got into animal strait jackets, we are unconsciously doing the same *vis à vis* the machine.[30]

McLuhan finds symbolic representation of this process in advertising and the entertainment media, but evidence is also provided by the wide acceptance, at this time, of behaviourist theories of psychology. The behaviourists 'rejected the importance which earlier schools had attached to introspection and the individual's interpretation of his own experience' and

> substituted for the vision of man as a free, if often deeply flawed, spirit a model of man as machine whose performance could only be measured in terms of his responses to external stimuli.[31]

The theory of behaviourism, first proposed by John B. Watson in 1919, gained currency in the late 1940s along with Dr Norbert Wiener's theory of cybernetics. Wiener was primarily interested in the dynamics of the human nervous system and the method of communication between the exterior senses and the muscles. By observing people who suffered from varying forms of ataxia, ie., a breakdown in this communication resulting in a loss of control over the simple actions necessary to respond to stimulus from their immediate environment, he was able to conclude:

> The central nervous system no longer appears as a self-contained organ, receiving inputs from the senses and discharging into the muscles. On the contrary, some of its most characteristic activities are explicable only as circular processes, emerging from the nervous system into the muscles, and re-entering the nervous system through the sense organs.[32]

Wiener realised that in order for these 'characteristic activities' to be duplicated by machinery, a similar system of mechanical feedback would be required whereby 'messages' could be transmitted to influence a series of actions, the outcome of which would in turn generate further messages. For example, the action of picking up a pencil, for a machine, would require a simulation of at least two senses (sight and touch) along with an information processing mechanism which would 'know' at any given moment, from initiation to completion of the action, what had so far been accomplished by the moving parts. It would then have the capacity to relay this information back to the 'senses', which would in turn pass back information from the environment. This, in very basic terms, is what cybernetics is all about. Discussing the ethical implications of cybernetics in a later publication, *The Human Use of Human Beings*, Wiener asserts:

> *Cybernetics takes the view that the structure of the machine or of the organism is an index of the performance that may be expected from it.*[33]

The key words in Wiener's assertion are 'that may be expected from it': that is, it follows that if a machine or organism, having a specified structure, does not perform *as expected*, then that machine or organism must necessarily be flawed. Of course, Wiener's confidence in his statement must hinge on the belief that structure can be read in such a way as to produce an understanding of performance.

Wiener was the first to propose myoelectric control for artificial limbs, which, 'utilising direct linkage between mechanism and nervous system, permits the amputee to manipulate his artificial limb simply by 'willing' it to perform the desired action'.[34] Despite the positive implications for the future development of prosthetics, Wiener's proposal again raises the spectre of the human machine with the added implication that elements in the controlling mechanism deemed to be defective could be as easily replaced or repaired as the limbs themselves. Behaviourists took seriously Dr Wiener's maxim that structure should be considered as an index of performance and proposed the modification of human performance considered to be inappropriate by the use of behaviour-modifying drugs and brain surgery.

So although technology raised the spectre of redundancy while simultaneously producing anxieties connected with the idea of human beings reduced to cogs in a mechanical wheel, these anxieties were, paradoxically, managed by recourse to theories which offered a conception of human beings as not so very different from that which they feared.

However, there is evidence to suggest that fear of technology was gender-biased. The war provided an unprecedented opportunity for women to enter into paid occupations, albeit under exceptional conditions, and many were drafted into factories where they gained skills in operating manufacturing machinery. This brought about a situation of ambivalence in women's relationship to technology. While in 1946 *Woman and Beauty* magazine tentatively suggested to its readers that 'in these difficult days, it is worth learning how to mend a fuse or repair the vacuum cleaner',[35] Len Chaloner, in the October 1945 issue of

Electrical Age, was urging women to 'step forward in partnership with men' to facilitate 'the development of power for peaceful, rather than destructive purposes and for the building of a new world'.

However, with the ending of the war, armaments manufacturers seeking new areas of profit saw the potential for turning their former female employees into customers for new products. Metal and grease were to be transformed into a plethora of devices to transform women's work from drudgery to pleasure or, as Mr George Tomlinson, the Minister of Education in the UK in 1947 gravely put it, 'It was [sic] now become possible to make use of the results of scientific research to ease the housewife's burden'.[36] Nevertheless, it was implicit in this that housewives they were to become again, and on both sides of the Atlantic the ad-men swung into action to ensure that women who had tasted a brief spell of economic independence during the war years would go rushing back to the home to test the delights of the new domestic technology.

However, according to one estimate, despite so called labour-saving devices flooding onto the post-war market, it would seem that by 1950 the average weekly hours spent on housework had actually increased over the 1929 figure from 51 hours to 70.[37]

It was doubtful then that women would ever find the time to build 'a new world' and hardly surprising that, when in 1952 the Electrical Association for Women conducted a survey of domestic equipment and asked 'if there was any work in the home which could be performed electrically but for which there is no appliance available and how such an appliance should be designed', the answer was, overwhelmingly, a robot:

> a small all-purpose fractional horse-power motor, possibly mounted on a wheeled stand. This would serve operating tools for scrubbing floors, dusting, vacuum-cleaning carpets, polishing floors, furniture and metal goods, cleaning windows and peeling vegetables – in fact, an automatic housewife.[38]

Post-war domestic technology was designed to tempt women back into the home with the promise that they would become more efficient housewives, but the Electrical Association for Women seem here to be eagerly anticipating a future where machines would relieve them of the responsibility altogether.

The implication here is that, unlike men, who feared replacement in their traditional work or the reduction of their role to one of mindless activity by the appearance of ever more capable machines, women were *demanding* a machine to replace them in their traditional sphere, thus perhaps declaring housework itself to be a dehumanising activity, better suited to 'trained gorillas' (or robots). But, the ideal robot is, after all, an uncomplaining and efficient servant, and the Electrical Association for Women's 'automatic housewife' can be read as an ironic comment on the new image of woman as defined by the advertising. The ads insisted that it was a woman's duty to be 'glamorous, cheerful, efficient, and, so far as possible, to run the home like an automatic factory'. Relieved of 'the housewife's burden' she could devote herself to loving the husband that had made it all possible.[39] So by fantasising a replacement for themselves in the role of housewife, these women were, ironically, feeding the fantasy of compliant female domesticity implied by the investment of expertise in housework gadgetry. Furthermore, thanks to the technological demon, the image of the 'glamorous, cheerful, efficient' housewife robot could be widely disseminated.

In her introduction to *Dynamos and Virgins Revisited*, Martha Moore Trescott traces the source of the 'dehumanisation of the image...of women' to the post-war 'rise of television' and speculates as to whether 'the technological changes involved in the rise of movies, radio, television and other mass media forms did not tend to cancel the potentially liberating effects of many of the other technological changes'.[40] For Marshall McLuhan, it was the image of the Hollywood 'glamour girl' who epitomised this dehumanisation:

> She accepts from the technological world the command to transform her organic structure into a machine. A love machine? It would seem so. At least she is told that the end of all the methodical processing will be love unlimited.[41]

So the process that Naomi Wolf would later elaborate in *The Beauty Myth* (1990) began with the hard-sell directed at women, who would be the new technological consumers when the wartime armaments manufacturers turned their production processes to domestic appliances. Market researchers identified three categories of woman, 'The True Housewife Type', 'The Career Woman' and 'The Balanced Homemaker',[42] of which the latter was deemed to represent 'the market with the greatest future potential'.[43] Appliance manufacturers were advised that it would be to their advantage to 'make more and more women aware of the desirability of belonging to this group'.[44] The Balanced Homemaker was portrayed in advertising and the entertainment media as the perfect wife and mother and, perhaps more importantly, the most sexually desirable type of woman. This was the era when women were advised that no matter how well they managed the home they would lose their husbands if they 'let themselves go', and a plethora of beauty aids flooded the market to ensure that the technology was available whereby they could remain 'glamorous'. In 1988, Betty Friedan explained:

> It used to be that being a woman in the United States meant that . . . you encased your flesh in rigid plastic casing that made it difficult to breathe and difficult to move, but you weren't supposed to notice that. You didn't ask why you wore the girdle, and you weren't supposed to notice red welts on your belly when you took it off at night.[45]

This implicit robotising of the female body, with engineered 'control' garments and 'scientifically' manufactured cosmetics[46] through to the appliances that she was designed to manipulate, contributes to a fantasised image of women as compliant, restrained but sexually available – an image that Ira Levin elaborated in the later sf novel *The Stepford Wives* (1972) in which a group of suburban American men turn their independent and liberated wives into actual robots. The woman as love machine fitted exactly the requirements of a culture which ambivalently both feared and desired the 'machine god' that it had created. So the robot can be seen to symbolise anxieties connected to the nature of technology, the management of these anxieties by a close identification of the human with the machine and an implicit reconstruction of the female body to conform to the alternative fantasy of the robot as a compliant technological servant.

The one writer credited with giving this last image a coherent form was Isaac Asimov, considered to be the supreme exponent of the fictional robot and acknowledged as having invented the word 'robotics'. In 1941 he formulated the Three Laws of Robotics which were:

1   A robot may not injure a human being, or, through inaction, allow a human being to come to harm.
2   A robot must obey the orders given it by human beings except where such orders would conflict with the First Law.
3   A robot must protect its own existence so long as such protection does not conflict with the First or Second Laws.[47]

These 'have become the inescapable premise for robot stories by virtually all other sf writers'. The phenomenon was, in Griffiths' words, 'as if every nineteenth-century novelist had been content, without question, to accept the social judgements of Dickens as the basis of his own stories'.[48]

The appeal of the Three Laws can be traced to the need for the robot to be brought under human control. Anxieties about the destructive potential of technology imbued the robot with an erratic nature, and a common theme of the stories depended on, as McLuhan describes it, 'the horror of a synthetic robot running amok in revenge for its lack of a soul'.[49] The Three Laws gave the robot a new identity as a still powerful but, nevertheless, servile creature which, if it did prove a danger, could be shown to have received faulty programming or to have been inadequately instructed. So the somewhat hackneyed monster/robot alliance gave way to the image of the robot as an innocent victim of human error. Interestingly, Asimov himself claims that he was uniquely able to construct the Three Laws because 'he got on well with his father'.[50] As Rorvik explains it: 'People [sic] fear robots ... for the same reason that fathers often fear their sons: because they are afraid that the sons might prove mightier than the father'.[51] So Asimov is claiming that fear of robots is a projection of Oedipal anxiety and the monster/robot a representation of the avenging son.

This Oedipal analysis goes to the heart of the anxiety which the robot symbolises. Allied to the fear of the machine replacing man in the sphere of production is the deeper anxiety that his role in reproduction may also be under threat. The robotised image of women in the post-war years, while designed to ensure their compliance in consumption of the new machine goods and to desexualise the 'Career Woman' to keep her off the production line, may have served ultimately to deepen the anxiety that 'the love machine', like Frankenstein's monster, may demand a mate that her creator is unwilling or unable to provide. In 'No Woman Born', C. L. Moore offers a subversion of the Frankenstein myth which allows the love machine to appropriate the technological means to re-create herself.

Monsters and cyborgs in the wor(l)ds of the father

Natalie Rosinsky believes that 'No Woman Born' is distinguished by being 'one of the first science fiction treatments of cyborgs – creatures part human and part machine – to emphasise characterisation rather than technological detail or innovation'.[52] The central character, Deirdre, originally a talented and much loved actress and dancer, has been saved from a theatre fire which had all but destroyed her, after which her untouched brain has been housed in a supple and uniquely beautiful metal body. The story is told from the point of view of her former manager (and, we suspect, lover) John Harris who witnesses the 'Frankenstein complex' destroying the formerly brilliant scientist, Maltzer, who has been responsible for initiating Deirdre's re-creation. Maltzer believes that he has created a monster. Unprepared for her resolve to pursue her former career and reappear on television, he is confronted, like Victor Frankenstein in Mary Shelley's novel, with his own creation which, so he believes, has escaped his control. Deirdre claims that she could 'play Juliet just as [she is] now, with a cast of ordinary people, and make the world accept it'.[53] Maltzer's fear is that her confidence is misplaced and that, when her audience do not accept her, despair will cause her mind to withdraw, leaving nothing more than an animated machine. Deirdre's brain has been kept conscious throughout the process of her reconstruction and it is she that has determined the principle on which the design is based. Her new body is made from a series of 'diminishing metal bracelets fitting one inside the other',[54] and, watching her move, Harris deduces that the body beneath the chain mail 'chlamys' must be made of 'the same interlocking sections as her limbs'.[55] Movement is controlled by '[e]lectromagnetic currents flowing along from ring to ring'[56] which, as Deirdre explains to Harris, are directed by the 'same impulses that used to go out to my muscles...It's all a matter of the brain patterns that operated the body and now operate the machinery'.[57] Moore thus uncannily predicts by a few years Dr Wiener's proposal for the development of myoelectrically controlled prostheses.

Maltzer represents the fear of technological hubris that gave rise to representations of machinery as both dangerous to human life and a threat to the human spirit. Believing himself to be condemned for unlawfully 'bring[ing] life into the world', he casts himself in the role of 'the student Frankenstein',[58] who must die for his transgression. Harris, on the other hand, symbolises the need to humanise machine technology, to endow it with human qualities so that it is no longer threateningly alien. But in imagining Deirdre as the woman that she once was, he ascribes to himself the role of thwarted lover and is jealous of the 'intimacy so like marriage'[59] that he believes Maltzer to have enjoyed with Deirdre in their time together in the laboratory.[60]

However, Deirdre herself presents a third point of view which emerges as the story progresses in radical contrast to the perceptions of the two male characters. Moore writes that, in constructing an identity for her fictional cyborg, she asked herself 'How would *you* handle it?'[61] She offers no solutions but instead presents us with a set of questions which challenge the way in which we receive the notion of an interface between human beings and technology while, at the same time, offering an alternative to the construction of female identity in terms of love machine or malfunctioning neurotic. This she achieves through the irreverent subversion of myths which had, at the time, gained currency in symbolising the consequences of transgressing the boundaries marked out by cultural anxieties arising from the need to incorporate machinery into working and social life. 'No Woman Born' thus anticipates Donna Haraway's formulation of the cyborg as an image which 'can suggest a way out of the maze of dualisms in which we have explained our bodies and our tools to ourselves'.[62] Deirdre establishes for herself a new identity which offers the potential for women to realise the 'great riches' to be found 'in explicitly embracing the possibilities inherent in the breakdown of clean distinctions between organism and machine'[63] that, four decades after the first publication of 'No Woman Born', Haraway would offer as a new feminist identity for the postmodern age.

Haraway's 'Cyborg Manifesto' develops an argument which moves beyond the opposition between machine and organism, refusing the stance of feminists who claim a female identity that is essentially opposed to, and victimised by, technology. She believes that we must relinquish our hold on an original self that has been pushed to the bottom of a hierarchy of domination and instead embrace a cyborg self, capable of intervening in what she calls the 'informatics of domination'.[64] Haraway's argument turns on a socialist–feminist understanding of the postmodern body as coded in terms of information processing and the language of biotechnology. Her cyborg reflects an engagement with post-industrial politics which recognises that power relations can no longer be understood strictly in terms of capital versus labour (with the attendant specialisation of gender roles), while retaining a Marxist perspective to account for the emergence of new dominance hierarchies in which ideology describes the play of market forces underwritten by strategic and technologically modified understandings of what constitutes bodies, populations, nations, race and gender. In an age in which 'organisms have ceased to exist as objects of knowledge, giving way to biotic components, that is, special kinds of information-processing devices', oppression is coded in terms of misinformation: 'noise' rather than communication.

The cyborg is an imagined identity which finally rejects the Cartesian underpinnings of oppositional politics; 'the organic, hierarchical dualisms ordering discourse in "the West"',[65] in favour of an understanding of bodies and minds as congruous with machines, artificial intelligence, animals and other forms of what Marshall McLuhan refers to as 'technological extensions of our bodies'.[66] The intimate interfacing or 'fruitful coupling'[67] which this permits thus effaces the tendency of Western feminism to universalise oppression as always grounded in categories of dominance founded on essential difference, while allowing for strategic political re-inscriptions of identity which problematise the coding of gendered selves in accordance with the language of what Haraway calls 'the social relations of science and technology'.[68]

What is particularly interesting for an analysis of 'No Woman Born' is that Haraway sees writing to be 'pre-eminently the technology of cyborgs', the one tool which can challenge 'the systems of myth and meaning structuring our imaginations'.[69] Cyborg writing

> must not be about the Fall, the imagination of a once-upon-a-time wholeness before language, before writing, before Man. Cyborg writing is about the power to survive, not on the basis of original innocence, but on the basis of seizing the tools to mark the world that marked them as other.[70]

The tools are 'often stories, retold stories, versions that reverse and displace the hierarchical dualisms of naturalised identities'.[71]

What Haraway would later prescribe as a tool for feminists to break through the dualisms that structure Western thought, Moore similarly utilises to construct a story that is a sophisticated exercise in exploring the dichotomy between a constructed outer image and inner perceptions of the self. Although it is the *Frankenstein* myth that the story foregrounds and ultimately subverts, there is also an implied reference to the Greek myth of Pygmalion and Galatea, and Deirdre's performance, the turning point of the story, evokes a reworking of the late nineteenth-century Romantic ideal, itself an attempt to resolve dualisms, to provide an all-embracing aesthetic. However, it is Moore's reinterpretation of the *Frankenstein* myth which allows for the text to be read as problematising accepted notions of what it means to be human and, perhaps more specifically, of what it means to be a woman.

Like Victor Frankenstein's in Mary Shelley's novel, Maltzer's mental and physical health deteriorates as the story progresses. His belief that he has repeated Frankenstein's mistake impels him to act out a drama in which he, the transgressing scientist, having failed to control his creation, will suffer and die. Towards the end of the story he attempts suicide with the clear intention of forcing the conclusion of the *Frankenstein* scenario. Harris remembers 'that Frankenstein, too, had paid with his life for the unlawful creation of life',[72] but what a reader familiar with Shelley's novel will also remember is that the monster is also destroyed by Frankenstein's death. However, it is not Deirdre's physical destruction that Maltzer desires but the death of her ambition. Maltzer will not 'leave'[73] without forcing Deirdre to acknowledge that, although she has been built to perform, to do so would be to bring upon herself the scorn and derision of those who had previously loved her. As Frankenstein's monster, having relinquished everything to the torment of his creator, is left purposeless by the scientist's death, so Maltzer's design is to trap Deirdre with the bonds of his own mortality into relinquishing her purpose, the one thing she was 'made to do'.[74] So Maltzer's identification with 'the student Frankenstein' provides a parallel which allows for questions to be raised as to how far Deirdre will conform to the complementary role of the monster.

In Maltzer's view, Deirdre is monstrous because she 'hasn't any sex. She isn't female anymore. She doesn't know that yet, but she'll learn'.[75] As Frankenstein's monster turns to destruction when he learns that he is deformed, so Maltzer believes Deirdre's mind will become unbalanced when she is rejected, because she has 'lost everything that made her essentially what the public wanted'.[76] These statements serve to reflect the assumptions that underlie the way in which the culture constructs its image of women. Biologically, Deirdre indeed 'hasn't any sex', but it is absurd to assume that Maltzer believes she is unaware that she no longer possesses a woman's body. What he believes that Deirdre will 'learn' is that the source of her former appeal was purely physical; that her performance was always secondary to the paradoxical promise of the Hollywood star – a woman who is sexually available but unattainable. The metal body ensures that Deirdre is no longer sexually available and thus, Maltzer's statement implies, no longer desirable, either as a woman or as a performer. His belief that she is deluded reinforces the sense in which he estimates her in terms of the cultural stereotype – the innocent virgin/angel, unaware of her own sexuality, who, when she becomes aware, takes on the opposing representation, the demon/whore. So Maltzer's identification with Frankenstein carries with it a hidden metaphor. Deirdre is only monstrous in terms of an idea of femininity in which gender is equated with biology.

In compiling *Women of the Future: the Female Main Character in Science Fiction*, Betty King hesitated before including 'No Woman Born' because 'Maltzer insists that Deirdre is now sexless' and '[i]t is clear at the story's conclusion that both Johnnie and Maltzer believe that she will soon be little other than a beautiful machine',[77] but this reading gives undue privilege to the points of view of the male characters and does not take account of the source of their anxieties. Where Harris and Maltzer's points of view coincide is in their descriptions of Deirdre in terms of powerlessness. For them she is 'frail', 'fragile', 'vulnerable', 'helpless', 'bewildered and confused'.[78] So while both evince concern for her mental health, they nevertheless judge her mind on the basis of her former structure, the female body that is perceived as imposing mental frailty and confusion. The cyborg here is sexless but, nevertheless, gendered in terms of the cultural norm.

So, while Maltzer is 'too close to Deirdre to see her' and Harris is 'too far',[79] both, in their 'psychic blindness',[80] are unable to think of her as other than powerless. This disjuncture between their perceptions of her and Deirdre's growing self-awareness is brought into sharp focus by the scene in which the two men watch Deirdre's first reappearance on television.

Although the performance is live, they are depicted alone in Maltzer's office or apartment, separated from the source of their anxiety by both geographical distance and the technology which is her medium. This provides for a heightened sense of Maltzer's distress as well as providing a metaphor for the very real separation between Deirdre's self-image and what the men imagine her to be. Maltzer's hand shakes so badly that he is unable to 'turn the dial',[81] his inability to 'tune in' to Deirdre significant in emphasising his lack of empathy with her state of mind. The sexual element is here emphasised as well and there is a sense of combativeness in the exchanges. Watching Maltzer's emaciated frame, Harris notes 'almost jealously' that 'he seemed to be drawing nearer Deirdre in her fleshlessness with every passing week',[82] and Maltzer insistently attempts to impress on Harris the loss of her sense of touch: 'She can't feel anything with tactual delicacy any more ... She's withdrawn from all physical contacts'.[83] Harris is 'a little stunned' by Maltzer's claim that she 'hasn't any sex'. '[T]he thought had not occurred to him before at all, so vividly had the illusion of the old Deirdre hung about the new one'.[84] The fact that neither image is adequate to encompass the reality marks a point of intersection between Moore's revision of the *Frankenstein* story and the myth of Pygmalion and Galatea.

In Ovid's version of the myth, Pygmalion is 'revolted by the many faults which nature has implanted in the female sex'[85] and builds his statue out of a desire to possess a woman that conforms to his ideal. He falls in love with the statue and demands of the goddess Venus that it be brought to life. However, the awakened Galatea is a true woman and, as such, must necessarily possess those 'faults' that Pygmalion believed he had fashioned her to avoid.

The irony is that the lifeless statue was female only in structure. Galatea does not perform as Pygmalion expects because the only link between her structure and her expected performance is in his imagination. As Julian Hilton points out:

> Galatea cannot, by definition, become what Pygmalion expects; for the act of becoming human in itself is an act of distancing from any other human identity. Galatea's humanness is tested in the extent to which she throws off Pygmalion's intentions for her.[86]

Deirdre's humanness is similarly tested and she, like Galatea, defies the expectations of her maker. She insists, 'I'm not a robot, with compulsions built into me that I have to obey. I'm free-willed and independent.... I'm human',[87] and, later, she compares herself to another mythological creature, the phoenix, which 'rises perfect and renewed from its own ashes'.[88] The phoenix is its own agent of death and renewal, and the allusion to the myth implies that it has been Deirdre's own decision to choose life and embrace the potential of a robot body. Maltzer has provided the means of her renewal, but it is she that has controlled the regeneration. She expresses her awareness of the continuing process of her own re-creation as she describes her relationship to her new body:

> Quite apart from the fact that my own brain controls its 'muscles', I believe there's an affinity between men and the machines they make. They make them out of their own brains, really, a sort of mental conception and gestation.[89]

For a modern reader it is necessary to understand that 'men' in this context refers to human beings in general. Deirdre is not referring to Maltzer – it is she that has re-made herself.

Maltzer's error of presumption is not in the 'unlawful' creation of life (he has, after all, only built a machine), but in his belief that it is he that is, or should be, the 'operator'. His confidence that he can 'stop her'[90] leads Harris to believe that he has some control over the cyborg to which he has not yet admitted:

> Maltzer had made her – of course he could stop her, if he chose. Was there some key in that supple golden body that could immobilize it

at its maker's will? Could she be imprisoned in the cage of her own body?[91]

That Harris can ask these questions demonstrates that, despite his opposition to Maltzer, he is nevertheless unconvinced by Deirdre's claim that she is free-willed and human. His sudden perception of her as a machine that can be turned off and on at the whim of the operator enhances the sense in which his apparently more sympathetic vision, in which the cyborg evokes a flesh and blood woman, has the effect of also evoking the scientifically managed love machine. But of course the phoenix cannot be caged. Deirdre has effectively thrown off the restraints of a body on which are inscribed myths of powerlessness and fragility and, 'perfect and renewed', stands ready to nurture the result of the 'mental conception and gestation' in which she has created for herself a body that stands outside of the codes and conventions of the culture and can therefore no longer be imprisoned by them. Her response to Harris' suggestion that Maltzer would have to 'give his permission'[92] for her to resume her career is couched in terms which problematise the construction of bodies in terms of medical and legal discourse:

> Now look, John! That's another idea you and Maltzer will have to get out of your minds. I don't belong to him. In a way he's just been my doctor through a long illness, but I'm free to discharge him when-ever I choose. If there were ever any legal disagreement, I suppose he'd be entitled to quite a lot of money for the work he's done on my new body – for the body itself, really, since it's his own machine, in one sense. But he doesn't own it, or me.[93]

Here Deirdre succinctly expresses the way in which cyborg politics can elucidate the mechanisms which structure gender in terms of capitalist investment strategies and biotechnical expertise. She is brought to a reflection on who 'owns' her body through an understanding of the forces that have shaped the possibility of her reconstruction. Deirdre offers a premonitory analysis of the ways in which, as Anne Balsamo describes it, 'an apparatus of gender organises the power relations mani-fest in the various engagements between bodies and technologies'.[94] She understands herself as existing at the confluence of medical, tech-nical, commercial and evolutionary discourse and thus estranged from, but offering a challenge to, the 'natural' woman so necessary to the maintenance of dichotomous identities. She symbolically recognises

Haraway's point that 'who controls the interpretation of bodily boundaries in medical hermeneutics is a major feminist issue'.[95]

For Maltzer, Deirdre is incomplete, 'an abstraction',[96] and he is
confident in his assertion that '[o]ne of the strongest stimuli to a woman
of her type was the knowledge of sex competition. . . . All that's gone, and
it was an essential'.[97] But essential to whom? Maltzer's judgement is
limited by assumptions which accord value to women only on the basis of
their ability to compete for male attention, but Deirdre can be read as having transcended such limitations. His attempt at suicide is a final attempt
to regain control; to make Deirdre admit that she has 'learned [her]
inadequacy'.[98] He refuses to acknowledge her potential strength because,
in doing so, he would be forced to recognise the power of her mind:

> I wish I could have made you stronger, Deirdre. But I couldn't. I had
> too much skill for your good and mine, but not quite enough skill
> for that.[99]

This is, again, a denial of the part that Deirdre herself has played in the
construction of her body, as well as an attempt to ensure that she admits
her weakness. Maltzer must claim full responsibility for his 'mistake' so
that his suicide may be vindicated. If Deirdre were to demonstrate what he
believes to be her mental frailty, he could 'leave' knowing that he had
assured her compliance with the female role as he perceives it to be. But,
rather than answer Maltzer's questions, Deirdre, watched by an astonished
Harris, moves so rapidly that he is unable to trace her passage from one
part of the room to another, lifts Maltzer from the windowsill from which
he had intended to jump, and carries him to the centre of the room.

Instead of succumbing to dehumanisation, Deirdre has utilised her
robot body to extend her human capabilities, thereby making a forceful
argument for the fruitful possibilities of human interaction with
advanced technology. But also, a female cyborg with more-than-human
power instantly undermines assumptions of female inadequacy based on
inferences from biological structure. In the 'final trial for supremacy',[100]
it is she that has the advantage. As in *Herland*,[101] where the hero's projected narrative is thwarted by the Herlanders' refusal to conform to the
required stereotype, so Maltzer's narrative of martyrdom cannot be
concluded without Deirdre's own compliance.

Here Donna Haraway's 'Cyborg Manifesto' is again relevant. She writes:

> The relationships for forming wholes from parts, including those of
> polarity and hierarchical domination, are at issue in the cyborg

world. Unlike the hopes of Frankenstein's monster, the cyborg does
not expect its father to save it through a restoration of the garden;
that is, through the fabrication of a heterosexual mate.[102]

Deirdre is indeed an abstraction, but does not demand to be made
whole. The 'knowledge of sex competition' that Maltzer believes 'essential' (essential, perhaps, to the demand for a heterosexual mate) no
longer dictates a mode of communication. The cyborg has other knowledges to explore and hence can be understood as subverting discourse,
or, to return to Haraway's analysis of post-industrial power relations, as
claiming an identity which challenges the scientist's claim to knowledge
and, thus, power.

Where Victor Frankenstein's 'child' is irrevocably linked to its father
through its need for completion – its desire for a mate – and sees its
salvation only in that provision, Deirdre has no desire for salvation.
Instead, her project is experiment and exploration. She has thus,
through a fusion with technology, transcended the opposition between
the organic and the technological – an opposition which has as its telos
an apocalyptic confrontation – and, in so doing, has wrested control
from her 'father'. As Haraway points out:

> The main trouble with cyborgs, of course, is that they are the
> illegitimate offspring of militarism and patriarchal capitalism, not
> to mention state socialism. But illegitimate offspring are often
> exceedingly unfaithful to their origins. Their fathers, after all, are
> inessential.[103]

Deirdre defies the apocalyptic promise of the technological monster.
She promises instead the possibility for transcending one crucial
opposition of the modern world in order that we may make of her
a symbol for transcending other, more fundamental, dualisms. The
female-as-cyborg signals the end of the history of machine technology as an idea which has evolved from a threatening usurper of
man's place in production to a seemingly uncontrollable threat to life
itself. And, although this symbolism tends to evoke the traditional
image of woman as the passive nurturer (a resource for the dreams
of science and a nurse to heal the wounds that its products may
inflict) who tames the technological monster by making it a part of
herself, Deirdre also becomes other to this identity by appropriating
the one thing that, in the traditional discourse of science, is seen as
its antithesis. Maltzer thus becomes a perfect symbol for Haraway's

inessential father. In his narrative of apocalypse, he attempts to make Deirdre the indirect agent of his own death and thus mark her as his 'child', but in preventing his suicide she forces him to face her autonomy.

So, while both Harris and Maltzer romanticise Deirdre into a frail creature, she proves the limits of their imagination by succumbing neither to sorrow nor to madness and equally dismisses their anxieties about whether she is human or machine by demonstrating the pleasure she discovers in being both. Thus, in becoming more than her maker intended and leaving him with shaking hands,[104] Deirdre symbolically undermines both the certainties and anxieties of science, both as a practice and as a body of theory, in the same way that Donna Haraway's cyborg myth is both a symbol for the undermining of male dominance in high-tech production and a code for women to recognise themselves as free of the restrictions imposed by seeing themselves as nature-identified victims of science and technology.

Cyborg choreography – the machine makes love

In transcending the boundary between the female and the technological, Deirdre also undermines the perceived distinctions between art and science – a dichotomy also represented in the opposing views of Maltzer and Harris. Maltzer is blind to the potential that Deirdre presents for creating a new art form because he thinks of her primarily as a machine which, if it were to dance, would merely be parodying the human and would thus be an object of ridicule. But for Harris it is only the cyborg in motion which evokes the former Deirdre. When she is still, he is disturbed by her lifeless appearance.

The woman as dancer, explored by Frank Kermode in his book *The Romantic Image*, has an iconic function in overcoming dualisms and synthesising the forms which represent the Romantic tradition. Drawing primarily on the work of W. B. Yeats, Kermode finds

> [an] urgent seeking for images to embody beauty defined as non-abstract, as unyielding to philosophers' dichotomies like soul and body; an organic irreducible beauty, of which female beauty, the beauty of a perfectly proportioned female body, is the type.[105]

The rational power of the mind must not be traceable in the work of art, which must be seen to be born of imagination, and 'organicist . . . modes of thinking about works of art' must replace the 'mechanistic'[106] mode. In this sense, then, the work of art must embody its own creation and must produce a response akin to 'irreducible' female beauty. Thus there must be no 'dichotomy of form and meaning'.[107] The woman's body *is* beauty and her mind is denied as is the mind of the artist or critic in 'rational' mode. No meaning can be abstracted from the work of art, but it 'has meaning only in terms of its expressive body, like a dancer'.[108] This search for a symbol which embodies the language of art without itself speaking, the transcendent, unifying symbol which, according to Kermode, 'reconciles antithetical movements: the division of soul and body, form and matter, life and death, artist and audience',[109] is part of the same tradition for which Marshall McLuhan yearns in his desire to resolve 'the human problems created by technology':

> The symbolist esthetic theory of the late nineteenth century . . . leads to a conception of orchestrating human arts, interests and pursuits. . . . Orchestration permits discontinuity and endless variety. . . . It is neither progressive nor reactionary but embraces all previous actualizations of human excellence while welcoming the new in a simultaneous present.[110]

McLuhan's discussion of advertising and the popular arts of his day includes the observation that the images projected are often grotesque parodies of the human. This is echoed, interestingly, in the performances that precede Deirdre's debut. Harris and Maltzer are witness to 'a line of tiny dancers [like] little mechanical dolls too small and perfect to be real . . . face after stiffly smiling face racketing by like fence pickets'.[111] But as Deirdre's performance ends:

> Harris had an intolerable feeling that she was smiling radiantly and that the tears were pouring down her cheeks. He even thought . . . that she was blowing kisses over the audience in the time-honored gesture of the grateful actress, her golden arms shining as she scattered kisses abroad from the featureless helmet, the face that had no mouth.[112]

As the Romantics inscribed on the symbol of the dancer their own image of transcendence, so Harris inscribes his own, still enigmatic, Deirdre on the dancing cyborg. However, it is clear that it is Deirdre's intention to emphasise the fact that the dance that she is performing has no precedent in human experience:

Now she swayed and came slowly down the steps, moving with a suppleness just a little better than human. The swaying strengthened. By the time she reached the stage floor she was dancing. But it was no dance that any human creature could ever have performed. The long, slow, languorous rhythms of her body would have been impossible to a figure hinged at its joints as human figures hinge.[113]

At this point she has become McLuhan's perfect totem image – the transcendent symbol for the point at which technology intersects with art, and, in doing so, provides an embracing aesthetic which solves the dilemma of a technological medium in conflict with artforms perceived in organicist terms. Unlike the mechanical dolls, she does not project a parody of the human and equally does not attempt to imitate other performances. It is for this reason, perhaps, that Moore contrasts her performance with that of the actress who plays 'Mary of Scotland', whose hairstyle 'would have shocked Elizabeth' and whose 'footwear was entirely anachronistic',[114] and that Deirdre can confidently claim that she could 'play Juliet . . . with a cast of ordinary people'.[115]

However, it is Deirdre's face, her 'expressionless mask',[115] which at least for Harris is the source of her enigmatic nature. Whereas her body in motion describes her state of mind, when she is still it is her 'face' to which Harris turns and finds the lack of emotion which disturbs him. The dancer, of course, without motion is lifeless. Kermode addresses this point in his analysis of the 'life-in-death, death-in-life of the Romantic Image [which] has nothing to do with organic life, though it may appear to have; its purity of outline is possible only in a sphere far removed from that in which humanity constantly obtrudes its preoccupations'.[116] The ethereal nature of the image can inhere in the momentary transcendence of a dead face or the equally transitory nature of the dance only if both are divorced, by the imagination, from the decay to which they must both ultimately be subject. The dancer, like Pygmalion's Galatea, embodies the Romantic Image only so long as she is imagined separated from real life. But Deirdre's integration with her medium is of a different order from the integration that the Romantics desired and inscribed on the image of the dancer. The dancer is not a self but a construction built out of desire; passive, changeless and intellectually void. But in the description of her performance, Deirdre's selfhood, and her intellect, are very much in evidence.

She surprises her audience by refusing advance publicity and appearing unannounced. They are enthralled by the dance and it is only when, at the end, she begins to sing that they realise who they have been watching and greet her with rapturous applause. Deirdre demands not only that her audience acknowledge the woman behind the mask but that they understand it is she alone who controls the performance:

> The dance was no dance a human being could have performed.... And she ended as inhumanly as she had danced, willing them not to interrupt her with applause.... For her implication here was that a machine might have performed the dance, and a machine expects no applause. If they thought unseen operators had put her through those wonderful paces, they would wait for the operators to appear for their bows.... [W]hen she reached the head of the stairs ... she stood motionless, like a creature of metal without volition, the hands of the operator slack upon its strings.[117]

The stage is thus set for the 'operator' to appear.

> Then, startlingly, she laughed.... And she was a woman now. Humanity had dropped over her like a tangible garment.[118]

Unlike the precision dancers, reduced to 'mechanical dolls' by the technology of the camera, Deirdre, her body formed from that same technology, is able to subvert the dehumanisation and turn it to her advantage. She thus extends the transcendent metaphor of the cyborg to refute the inimicality of science and art (thus evoking the claims of sf to be an art form embracing the scientific – a self-referential sub-text that would, perhaps, not have gone unnoticed by the fans) while also forcing a response from her audience which ensures that they acknowledge not only the dance, but also the mind that has shaped it. The title of the story thus finds its full ambiguity in Deirdre's performance. The cyborg Deirdre is indeed, like the Deirdre of James Stephens' poem, unlike any woman born, yet equally she is not born of woman in the physical sense but is, as she describes herself, the product of a 'mental gestation'. She thus represents the female mind released from the symbolic limitations imposed on it by her body as well as the fusion between the female and the technological and is, furthermore, a work of art in her own right.

So, Moore nurtures an illegitimate offspring that is nevertheless divorced from the politics of reproduction. Deirdre has no connection to the primitive 'Mother', but neither does she connect with the artificially constructed woman of Western culture; she cannot be appropriated as a resource nor be made to perform as a 'mechanical doll'. Instead she appropriates the tools of the scientist to remake herself and, in doing so, rewrites the *Frankenstein* myth to deny the scientist martyrdom for the supposed sin of transgression.

5

'Short in the Chest': Margaret St Clair and the Revenge of the Housewife Heroine

> Technologies possess the agency to have 'impact' on society, yet their internal features are generally excused from overt public deliberation and decision making. Accordingly, engineers and inventors acquire the power to engineer and invent society as well as technology, as do other individuals and groups who successfully incorporate into their own identities the pursuit of social change as technological development.
>
> Gary Lee Downey, 'Human Agency in CAD/CAM Technology'[1]

Margaret St Clair was better known in her own time as a writer of fantasy short stories, under the pseudonym Idris Seabright. Rosemary Herbert writes that 'she had a penchant for tackling controversial themes and for using gadgetry and environments symbolically'.[2] 'Short In The Chest', which as Pamela Sargent notes 'had some difficulty finding publication in a market that regarded the subject as too daring',[3] was finally published in July 1954 in *Fantastic Universe* – not the most successful of the pulp magazines, but the story itself attracted enough attention to be anthologised on more than one occasion. It is not only daring (for its time) but also very funny, taking as its theme an interview between a young woman (Major Sonya Briggs) with 'sexual problems' and a symbolic gadget in the form of a philosophic rob[ot]'[4] known as a 'huxley' and designed to offer counselling and advice but, on this occasion, suffering a malfunction which significantly alters its perceptions.

When the story was reprinted in Greenberg and Olander's 1979 anthology *Science Fiction of the 50s*, the editors offered the comment that it 'was a somewhat controversial story for its time because of its portrayal of women' as well as 'its sexual allusions'.[5] Sonya is indeed an unusual female character for the time, but it was the 'grappling with questions of sexuality',[6] without at least the accompaniment of a high moral tone, which led Horace Gold (renowned editor of *Galaxy Science Fiction*) to reject the story with the words: 'If you want to put me out of business, Margaret, I wish you'd do it with French postcards'.[7] It is possible that Mr Gold considered his readers too sensitive to accept a female character who could announce that she had 'a fine time' during a successful sexual encounter and could denounce an unsuccessful partner with the words, 'You didn't reduce *my* tension either'.[8] Add to this the fact that she carries a gun and is happy to accept the idea of disposing of her next partner, should he also prove unsatisfactory, and the story can be seen to have been offering a rather too daring challenge in this era of muscular fandom.

One of the pleasures of reading St Clair is her obvious delight in conjuring with language. In an autobiographical sketch written for Martin Greenberg's *Fantastic Lives* (1981), she suggests a solution to the problem of referring to humanity as 'man', which, as she points out, leads to the assumption that 'only males are really human beings after all',[9] by offering the word 'wight', 'which is used to mean a female and can easily be used to mean any human being at all'. She quotes its use in Shakespeare but contends that it also 'fits easily into sentences like "First wights land on Jupiter" or "Contact with wights from other worlds"'.[10] She is pleading here, I think, for sf to dispense with the cultural baggage that it too readily carts into the future, suggesting the retrieval of earlier language forms as a liberating force to free the genre from linguistic associations that restrict the imagination of social change. In 'Short In The Chest' she uses this technique to introduce her readers to a concept of sexual intercourse stripped of romance and thus of its accepted meaning in terms of gender roles and their related cultural assumptions. As I will demonstrate, it is possible to read this estrangement as masking a satirical comment on the function of sexuality within contemporary Western societies.

In Sonya's world 'dighting'[11] is a device for social control. The reader is given to understand that a situation exists where, because of a long-standing interplanetary conflict, the society has become totally mobilised. A group of psychologists, having 'made a survey of interservice tension' and discovered that 'Marine was feuding with Air, and Air with Infantry, and Infantry with Navy, to such an extent that it was cutting down overall Defense efficiency', have instigated 'the dighting system' because they 'thought that sex relations would be the best of all ways of cutting down hostility and replacing it with friendly feeling'.[12] So Sonya has received a 'dighting slip' which is 'rubber stamped',[13] evoking a sense of bureaucratic licence, without which the act would be deemed illicit.

The management of sexuality within a totalitarian regime is a theme which has several precedents within the genre. Yevgeny Zamyatin's *We* (first published in 1924)[14] may be the earliest example but it is, of course, also the dominant theme of *Swastika Night*[15] as well as of the two famous novels which have been cited as classics of sf, George Orwells's *Nineteen Eighty-Four* and Aldous Huxley's *Brave New World*. However, 'Short In The Chest' is unique in irreverently making fun of a subject that was generally treated with deadly seriousness. Also, the fundamental proposition of these texts is that totalitarianism can only function where love between the sexes is prohibited, but in dealing with the issue from a comic perspective, and presenting the problem from the point of view of a woman who is concerned that she is sexually inadequate, 'Short In The Chest', like *Swastika Night*, ensures that the reader is confronted with the question of the role of gender politics in the establishment of the managed society.

That this is presented in less than a dozen pages is, again, testament to St Clair's skill with language. Her invention of words which the informed reader can interpret on the basis of contemporary political concerns, as well as of familiarity with other texts, allows her to play with intertextual irony as well as offering an economical device for referring to her themes without recourse to explicit narrative comment. And, like C. L. Moore's mythological references,[16] this device would also offer a measure of self-congratulatory pleasure for sf fans who liked to consider themselves well-read intellectuals. So the robot is a 'huxley',[17] referring the reader to *Brave New World* and the political philosophy of Huxley himself. And the drug which is given to promote sexual excitement during the dighting encounters (and also act as a contraceptive) is called a 'Watson', a reference to John B. Watson, the originator of the theory of behaviourist psychology – a theory well suited to enforcing conformity within a totalitarian state.

In common with other sf texts, 'Short In The Chest' presents a world that is at once both alien and familiar – populated by characters who accept a situation that the reader would find intolerable. A large part of the comedy accrues from the fact that St Clair plays on contemporary anxieties about humans being replaced by, or becoming like, machines. Sonya's world is on the brink of revolution, but there are no heroes or heroines in this story. The regime is in danger because a malfunctioning machine, with perfect logic, convinces Sonya and twelve other young women that their sexual problems are not their fault.

Sonya has failed to respond to her designated dighting partner from a rival service, despite having taken her Watson. An illegally procured double dose has seen her safely through the following appointment but she fears that even such desperate measures will not work a second time. She has already seen another huxley, but it just 'spoke about in-group love, and intergroup harmony'. So, in desperation, she has brought her problem to a new robot 'just past the experimental stage',[18] in the hope that it can help where the other had failed.

Sonya wears a hearing aid ('they were all a little deaf, from the cold-war bombing'[19]) with which she is continually fiddling and, during the interview, produces a 'vibro-needle' with which she crafts to steady her nerves. Both aggravate the huxley's short circuit to the point where an 'augmented popping' sound issues from its chest and its voice becomes 'oddly altered',[20] but Sonya is oblivious to any inconsistency in its responses. The fact that she has to keep turning up her hearing aid suggests that it is inefficient enough to mask any obvious signs of the huxley's malfunction although it is, ironically, the hearing aid itself that is the cause of the other's extreme behaviour. However, it is Sonya's naive faith in the machine's advice which is most remarkable, despite the fact that it causes her some embarrassment by suggesting that she should flout social convention in order to solve her problem. She is outraged by the huxley's suggestion that she should take her troubles 'to somebody higher ... all the way up ... the CO', something that '[n]o nice girl' would do,[21] and is particularly upset when it asks her to consider dighting with 'a group brother' (someone from her own service), although, when the huxley explains that it is only 'putting a completely hypothetical case', she does admit that this would probably cause her no problems at all.[22] Subsequently, the huxley reasons that she must kill her next dighting partner, rather than suffer the indignity of another failure. Appealing to her sense of superiority as a Marine, it asks, 'Why should you go through a painful scene like the one you just described for the sake of a yuk from Air?':[23]

> How could it be your fault that you couldn't respond to him, some-body from *Air*? Why, it was his fault – it's as plain as the nose on your face – his fault for being from a repulsive service like Air![24]

Sonya has never considered that her problems could be anything but her own fault, so that it is with a sense of revelation that she receives the huxley's advice. Her fear that shooting him 'wouldn't reduce interservice tension effectively' is easily allayed. As the huxley points out, 'why should interservice tension be reduced at the expense of Marine?. . . . Whatever benefits Marine, benefits Defense'.[25] The huxley, we are given to understand, is having fun, with not only Sonya but, perhaps, the entire human race. Once Sonya has admitted that 'it's true. You're right. You're wonderfully, wonderfully right!'[26] it is relatively easy to convince her to shoot her next assigned partner and even to 'leave a note with [her] name, sector and identity number'.[27] Conflict between the services is thus assured – a prospect that the huxley seems to relish. There is a suggestion that the huxley has become aware of its role in the manipulation of human beings and has thus discovered its power over life and death. But equally, of course, it is still fulfilling its function by helping a human being to solve a problem.

To set the satire in its political context, St Clair's oxymoronic 'cold-war bombing'[28] would have had an ironic resonance for readers in post-war America. We are given to understand that the feud between the military services is fuelled by an irrational fear of treachery and that the dighting system also has a covert intelligence gathering function. Information is elicited from rival services by way of post-coital confidence and Sonya, who is 'in charge of the Zone 13 piggery',[29] has been charged with the task of discovering from her partner in Air the 'secret' of how baby pigs can be made to feed. The elaborately contrived system to step up pork production in Sonya's piggery is failing because the piglets refuse to nurse, and, ever suspicious of other services, her superiors in Marine suspect the existence of a 'formula'[30] for 'porcine nutrition'[31] of which they are unaware and that must be elicited from Air by covert means. Nevertheless, the fact that a dead Airman would be unlikely to reveal a secret formula causes Sonya only a moment's hesitation. As the huxley points out, 'He's just as likely to give it to you dead as when he was alive. . . . Why, he ought to be proud, honored, to give the formula to you'.[32]

The most uneasy laughter attaches to the fact that it is the huxley whose responses are the more nearly human and Sonya who is most alien. She can only think in terms of herself as a malfunctioning machine (ironically, she is unaware that the huxley, which *is* a machine, is also malfunctioning) and she discusses her sexual problems with reference only to functionality, convinced that it is *her* fault that she has failed to respond to the hormone injection. Her initial response has been to visit a doctor for a 'gyn' (gynaecological examination) but she has unfortunately been found to be 'in swell shape' and has resorted to stealing 'an extra Watson from the lab'[33] in an attempt to remedy the situation.

The huxley, on the other hand, may be a 'philosophic robot', but, we are given to understand, its function is to impose a predetermined philosophy rather than to interpret ideas. *Mal*function suggests, conversely, that it has found itself with the capacity to analyse. In a moment of insight, it begins to formulate a theory:

> Perhaps, after a long course of oestrics, antibodies are built up. Given a state of initial physiological reluctance, a forced sexual response might. . . .

Here it breaks off, aware that Sonya is not 'interested in all that',[34] and it reveals a very human curiosity when it asks, '[W]hat did he look like?' while she is relating her failed dighting encounter, but Sonya 'didn't really notice',[35] thus displaying a mechanical indifference suggesting a high degree of self-alienation. But what we might consider to be a serious psychological problem is here merely incidental. Sonya Briggs judges herself a suitable case for treatment on the basis of an arbitrary set of criteria wholly determined by the way that her sexuality is constructed within the ruling regime, thus effectively raising questions connected to the manipulative potential of therapy and the role of psychoanalysis in managing, rather than merely understanding, the human psyche.

Brave new words – the (pro)grammatics of gender

Psychoanalysis, in the context of post-war America, took on a leading role in the drive to return women to the home. Betty Friedan writes:

> After the depression, after the war, Freudian psychology became much more than a science of human behavior, a therapy for the suffering. It became an all-embracing American ideology, a new religion.[36]

Women's need for autonomous self-expression was equated with penis envy and thus seen as a disease to be eliminated on the analyst's couch, and the 'unfulfilled' woman (one unwilling or unable to find completion in marriage and childbearing) was considered a suitable case for treatment. Marynia Farnham and Ferdinand Lundberg's *Modern Woman: the Lost Sex* (1947), 'declared all single women neurotics and proposed subsidized psychotherapy to get them married'.[37] Psychotherapy, in clinical practice, thus became a tool for creating the 'Balanced Homemaker'[38] demanded by the marketing men, the 1950s American equivalent of the Victorian 'angel-in-the-house',[39] in whom were invested the moral values of the society. Farnham and Lundberg determined that feminism was nothing more than 'a deep illness'[40] and exhorted women to give in to their receptive and passive natures: to accept dependence for the sake of their own sexual well-being and, more specifically, for the sake of their children and family life.

Shulamith Firestone writes that Freudianism 'became an applied science complete with white-coated technicians, its contents subverted for a reactionary end – the socialization of men and women to an artificial sex-role system'.[41] In 'Short In The Chest', St Clair has made the logical step of replacing the white-coated technician with a robot, thus emphasising the sense in which the state of clinical psychotherapy at the time can be equated with programming, and has provided as her female protagonist a 'patient' unable to adjust to her prescribed sex-role, an analogy for the American housewives who, believing themselves maladjusted in their lack of contentment with their traditional role, sought psychoanalytical reprogramming in droves. Science fiction, in fact, at the time abounded with what Pamela Sargent has described as 'housewife heroines' who 'were usually passive or addlebrained and solved problems inadvertently, through ineptitude, or in the course of fulfilling their assigned roles in society'.[42]

Sonya, of course, differs from the stereotype in that a happy marriage is not given as the ideal, but this reinforces, rather than detracts from, the analogy with the 1950s American housewife. The text proposes that social prescriptions for sexual behaviour are merely arbitrary and what counts as deviant is contingent upon the use to which sexuality is put in any given social arrangement. That it is female sexuality that, under any given circumstances, has to be most carefully managed is foregrounded by the fact that we are told that the huxley 'had had interviews with twelve young women so far, and it had given them all the same advice it had given Major Briggs'.[43] Problems with the dighting system, then, are restricted to females. As Sonya says, '[T]here's been nothing wrong with the men either time'.[44] It is the women who are the source of malfunction.

In this sense the text can be seen to parallel *Swastika Night*.[45] In Burdekin's dystopia, von Hess's book makes it clear that the women had gone to great lengths to comply with their own reduction – a theme that finds echoes in the efforts of the huxley's twelve clients to correct their supposed malfunction. And both texts present passive female characters who, in their very passivity, are the source of social disintegration. In other words, 'Short In The Chest' also encodes the message that it is the attempted manipulation of female sexuality that has ultimately the most destructive potential.

But, while both *Swastika Night* and 'Short In The Chest' present examples of the totally mobilised society, the logic which has reduced the women in *Swastika Night* to the status of breeding animals is not paralleled in the advanced technological world of Sonya Briggs's society. In fact, with all sexual activity being restricted to interservice dighting, there is some doubt created by the story as to whether the human race is continuing to reproduce. However, the situation that the story presents is of long standing, suggesting that the race is at least replacing itself. St Clair does not offer any clues, but it is reasonable to assume that the problem of reproduction has been solved by a technological solution. So what Shulamith Firestone would later (1970) suggest[46] as a means to liberate women under the right conditions is here shown operating under the wrong conditions. The breeding machines of *Swastika Night* become the love machines of the technological age with the romantic indoctrination of the 1950s hard-sell, which managed female sexuality to promote loyalty to the family ideal, supplanted by a similar technique of psychological management aimed at promoting loyalty to a military service.

But, as I have pointed out, the background to the story can best be understood through its use of allusion, indicated in the narrative by the use of terms which the reader understands by virtue of knowledge to which the characters no longer have access. Much as we have absorbed the word 'Hoover' into our vocabulary as not only a brand name but a generic term for a particular mechanical aid (as well as to denote the activity of its use), while simultaneously investing the term with a whole host of related constructs, so St Clair proposes 'huxley' and 'Watson', from which we are able, by knowing their historical sources, to infer a similar set of constructs. These help to build a picture of the nature of the society which has produced them, as expressed in language development.[47]

The name of the robot sets up an immediate parallel between St Clair's story and *Brave New World*. Huxley's test-tube-created class structure provides the paradigm for contextualising such observations as that Major Briggs would 'rather die than not be Marine',[48] echoing the hyonopaedia-induced mantras that the Alphas, Betas, Gammas, Deltas and Epsilons[49] must repeat by way of constantly reaffirming the rightness of the hierarchy. Indeed, the very existence of a robot as counsellor and confidante suggests the depersonalisation that Huxley argued would be the final result of a managed, technologised society.

Both Huxley's dystopia and St Clair's future totalitarian state have in common the suggestion that, as Huxley himself puts it in a 1946 preface to *Brave New World*,

> in an age of advanced technology, inefficiency is the sin against the Holy Ghost. A really efficient totalitarian state would be one in which the all-powerful executive of political bosses and their army of managers control a population of slaves who do not have to be coerced, because they love their servitude.[50]

There is, of course, a form of coercion implicit in both texts. Huxley suggests that the 'deep, personal revolution in human minds and bodies' needed to establish a love of servitude could be brought about through 'a greatly improved technique of suggestion ... infant conditioning and, later, with the aid of drugs, such as scopolamine'.[51]

So the use of the term 'huxley' allows St Clair to imply a similar scenario to the one that Huxley suggests, emphasised by the revision in language which she imagines to have taken place and which ensures that Sonya's understanding of the term does not include the reader's awareness of what it implies. There is another similarity here to *Swastika Night* in that the reader is made aware that enforced adherence to a system has been achieved by a systematic destruction of memory. Sonya's world remembers Huxley as a philosopher ('I suppose that's why they're called huxley's – because they're philosophic rob[ots]')[52] but the content of his philosophy has been safely relegated by the incorporation of his name into the vocabulary in such a way as to associate the practice of philosophy with a type of counselling which, the reader is aware, is actually a form of coercion.

Love of servitude in *Brave New World* is achieved by both selective breeding and psychic manipulation, and while 'Short In The Chest' does not necessarily suggest the former, strong evidence for the presence of the latter is provided by the naming of the hormone/contraceptive injection as a 'Watson'. In 1919 John B. Watson wrote that an 'important result' of his studies was the *'formulation of laws and principles whereby man's actions can be controlled by organised society'*,[53] suggesting that the 'group of psychologists' who set up 'the dighting system'[54] were grateful inheritors of his behaviourist theory of human psychology. Behaviourism, like cybernetics, rests upon the idea that, given a specified stimulus from the environment, the appropriate response will follow. At the core of the theory is the belief that people, like machines, can be modified to respond to the required stimulus because all behaviour has as its root an identifiable stimulus which can be isolated and seen to cause a similar response under controlled conditions. All behaviour is observed behaviour, because, in observing the response, we are actually observing the action of the stimulus. Failure to behave in the expected way can then be seen as due to insufficient stimulus or as a malfunction in the responding mechanism.

The Watson has been developed to control sexual behaviour in accordance with John Watson's contention that one of the purposes of psychology is

> to guide society as to the ways in which the environment may be modified to suit the group or individual's way of acting; or when the environment cannot be modified, to show how the individual may be moulded (forced to put on new habits) to fit the environment.[55]

This is reflected in the way that Sonya describes the Watson's effect:

> there's a particular sort of kick in feeling oneself change from a cold sort of loathing into being eager and excited and in love with it. After one's had one's Watson, I mean.[56]

In fact, at the time that 'Short In The Chest' was written, the ethos of behaviourism had recently been connected to the study of human sexuality. The authors of the Kinsey Report, published in two parts in 1948 and 1953, state:

> The administration of an extra supply of male hormones to an animal, female or male, which has intact gonads, may increase its sexual responsiveness.[57]

They do qualify this by stating that gonad secretions may affect hormone levels in other glands, influencing 'the general metabolic level of all physiologic functions',[58] which of course would in turn have an influence on sexual behaviour. However, the Report's authors are good behaviourists and state at the outset that they believe:

> No theory, no philosophy, no body of theology, no political expediency, no wishful thinking, can provide a satisfactory substitute for the observation of material objects and of the way in which they behave.[59]

Or, as Lionel Trilling puts it: 'By *behaviour* the Report means behaviouristic behaviour, only that behaviour which is physical'. Hence, 'psychic or emotional phenomena' are discussed 'in terms of physiology',[60] which, in a short, behaviouristic step, implies that manipulation of physiological stimuli should produce the required psychic or emotional responses which accompany 'overt sexual behaviour'. This may have been why Kinsey and his associates found it necessary to state that 'good health, sufficient exercise, and plenty of sleep still remain the most effective of the aphrodisiacs known to man',[61] and it is certainly why Trilling warns that the Report may be taken, by 'people who are by no means trained to invert the process of abstraction and to put the fact back into the general life from which it has been taken', as a set of recommendations for an ideal sex life. He goes on to say that

> the social sciences in general no longer pretend that they can merely describe what people do; they now have the clear consciousness of their power to manipulate and adjust.[62]

If, as Trilling warns, the Report could have the effect of inducing people, convinced by the authority of science, to believe that 'a good sexuality...means nothing else but frequent',[63] the seeds are already sown for a mechanical attitude towards the act, and 'performance anxiety' becomes akin to inefficiency as measured in mechanisation.

Farnham and Lundberg, having attended a lecture given by Kinsey several years before the Report was published, were happy to note that his findings had already revealed a considerably lower incidence of orgasm among college-educated women. This they quote in support of their contention that 'women as a whole...are maladjusted, much more so than men',[64] offering psychiatry in place of education to readjust women to contentment with their role. 'Short In The Chest' thus assumes an ethos of the kind recommended by Farnham and Lundberg. The treatment that they prescribed for women to 'encourage the reconstruction of family life within the setting of technological society'[65] is now applied to the reconstruction of female sexuality to suit the demands of a militarised regime.

The application of behaviourist theories is also demonstrated in the problem that Sonya's failed dighting session was meant to solve. The problem with the pigs can, in fact, be seen as a parody of behaviourist solutions to what Watson calls 'this matter of *environmental adjustment*'.[66] Sonya's sow inhabits an environment where the need for pork dictates that she be ready to breed constantly. Therefore, a hormone which promotes oestrus is administered as soon as she has given birth. Sonya explains:

> As soon as the pigs are born, we take them away from the sow – we use an aseptic scoop – and put them in an enclosure of their own with a big nursing tank. We have a recording of a sow grunting, and when they hear that they're supposed to nurse.[67]

The baby pigs appear to feed in response to the stimulus of the mother's grunting, so, logically, artificial grunting should persuade the piglets to nurse. Sonya, a product of behaviourism, can only think in behaviourist terms. Her response to the piglet's reluctance to feed has been to 'step up the grunting record',[68] the logic being that increased stimulus must eventually produce the required response. Sonya, of course, does not entertain the idea that the sow's grunting may be her response to the piglets' feeding rather than the stimulus for them to feed.[69] Within the ideology of her world there is no room for abstract thought.

The conflict between abstract modes of thought and the social conditions created by technological determinism is discussed by Herbert Marcuse in *One Dimensional Man*, which was itself a response to what he saw as a society which 'distinguishes itself by conquering the centrifugal social forces with Technology rather than Terror'.[70] In a section on language he describes what he refers to as 'operational redefinitions'. These are normalising linguistic constructs which effectively neutralise the potency of a word or phrase as expressed in its associative history. Language is thus brought into the service of 'operational rationality',[71] the mode of thought that accompanies systematisation and denies dialectical 'two dimensional' thought in which contradictory concepts, which imply criticism, may be brought into play. This 'unification of opposites'[72] takes words previously associated with concepts antagonistic to the social organisation required by a technologically managed society, and links them with pragmatic, operationally rational terms or definitions, and so:

> If the linguistic behaviour blocks conceptual development, if it militates against abstraction and mediation, if it surrenders to the immediate facts, it repels recognition of the facts behind the facts, and thus repels recognition of the facts, and of their historical content.[73]

In other words, 'meaning is restricted to the representation of particular operations and behaviour',[74] not by the physical destruction of historical material (as in *Swastika Night*), nor even by a redefinition of terms, but by reordering cognitive reality. This is emphasised in 'Short In The Chest' by the spelling of huxley with a lower case 'h'. The word is no longer a proper noun associated with an individual whose widely known views presented a rationale for rejection of the managed, technologised society. It is now simply a term to describe a machine which has a specific function.

Sonya, then, is Herbert Marcuse's One Dimensional [Wo]man – a product of the advanced technological age. Dependent on machinery, she is herself mechanised – her personality programmed to respond to certain verbalised symbols and her morality dictated by allegiance to the system. As she has initially determined her own lack of sexual response to be a physiological problem, she equally considers the problem with the piglets to be a technological one, and the fact that the piglets' mother has been replaced by a machine which is apparently failing to function reinforces the sense in which the text suggests that it is the mechanised woman who will ultimately prove the failure of the mechanised society. The narrative threads which tell of Sonya's sexual problem and the pigs' nutrition problem can be seen to converge. The problem of reproduction has been displaced onto the pigs, which can be read as a symbol for humanity. As in *Swastika Night*, the race is threatened with extinction because assumptions about the place and function of the female are made on the basis of a flawed ideology.

Inexorable magic and the mechanical bride

St Clair's satirical style also addresses similarly flawed assumptions which, at the time that she was writing, underwrote the rhetoric of cold-war politics and informed the ideology of McCarthyism and its attendant paranoia. Throughout the text, the existence of the 'pig formula' that Sonya has failed to retrieve from her dighting partner remains unquestioned – a fact that escapes even the newly enlightened huxley. The positivist notion that everything is explainable in scientific terms and thus rationalisable into formulae is thus held up to ridicule, as is the accompanying assumption that if *you* don't have the formula, then someone else must have. During her exchange with the huxley, Sonya expresses a concern that it may not be trustworthy, but it reassures her: 'Anything told to a huxley is a privileged communication. The first amendment applies to us, if to no other profession,' and Sonya remembers 'there was a Supreme Court decision about freedom of speech ... '.[75] Freedom of speech, then, has been curtailed except in the case of huxleys, providing the necessity for the post-coital confidences of the dighting program as well as offering the suggestion that confidence in the integrity of people has been compromised to the extent that only machines are trusted to maintain national security.

It is this misplaced confidence in the integrity of machines that Norbert Wiener discusses in *God & Golem Inc.* (1963), in which he compares the function of a 'goal seeking mechanism' to the 'inexorable magic' which, in various versions of the fable, grants three wishes to a hapless protagonist which are then fulfilled in totally unforeseen and often catastrophic ways.[76] Confronted with the possibility of having wishes granted, we neglect to ask how or by what process, either because we are particularly greedy and stupid or, more realistically, because we do not question our own responsibility for machines. Wiener warns against the desire to avoid personal responsibility by

> placing the responsibility elsewhere: on chance, on human superiors and their policies which one cannot question, or on a mechanical device which one cannot fully understand but which has a presumed objectivity.[77]

Wiener (like Marcuse) is here concerned with the potential for human beings to become ethically impoverished by a growing reliance on machine technology, and it would seem that St Clair was anticipating his concerns. In fact, had *God & Golem Inc.* been published fifteen years earlier, a strong case could have been made for 'Short In The Chest' as a satire drawing on Wiener's prophecies of apocalypse through a naive trust in complex mechanisms. Wiener explains:

> Usually we realize our wishes, insofar as we do actually realize them, by a feedback process, in which we compare the degree of attainment of intermediate goals with our anticipation of them. In this process, the feedback goes through us, and we can turn back before it is too late. If the feedback is built into a machine that cannot be inspected until the final goal is attained, the possibilities for catastrophe are greatly increased.[78]

In 'Short In The Chest' the reader is privileged with an insight into the process whereby the machine attains its final goal – a goal in which the possibilities for catastrophe are not only realised but realised by a very self-satisfied machine which apparently intends to instruct humanity as to the folly of its ways. When Sonya departs, the huxley, in contemplative mode, 'interchang[es] its eyes and nose absently a couple of times' and looks up at the ceiling 'speculatively, as if it wonder[s] when the bombs from Air, Infantry, and Navy [are] going to come crashing down':

> Even a huxley with a short in its chest might have foreseen that the final result of its counseling would be catastrophic for Marine.... Though its derangement had reached a point that was not far short of insanity, the huxley still retained a certain cunning.[79]

So the huxley's breakdown represents the collapse of the technologised society as well as, again, offering a riposte to the behaviourist assumption that people 'forced to put on new habits' will thereafter function adequately in terms of the system. The huxley is a fully mechanised individual whose programming has failed.

Nevertheless, the huxley is an ambiguous character. Despite its supposed malfunction, it is still 'cunning' enough to manipulate Sonya's behaviour, and, as I have pointed out, its exchanges with Sonya lead the reader to identify more closely with the machine's point of view than with that of the human character. Its initial suggestions as to how Sonya should deal with her problem are, if it is possible for the reader to conceive of herself as faced with Sonya's dilemma, common-sense solutions. Furthermore, when it asks Sonya if she would consider (hypothetically) dighting with a 'group brother' and inquires as to the physical appearance of the Airman with whom she has failed, it is offering her the opportunity to consider her response if she were allowed to select sexual partners on the basis of criteria that the reader would find familiar – common interest and physical characteristics. Judgement of its insanity, therefore, is contingent upon how 'normal' behaviour is understood. This again reinforces the implied critique of the kinds of theories represented by Farnham and Lundberg, who made such confident assertions as that women who elected to remain childless were 'deviating from normal behavior'.[80] So the huxley stands as a criticism of the necessity for behaviourism to operate by defining a norm against which all behaviour is subsequently measured. It is possible to read the huxley as experiencing an altered state of consciousness (which its name and earlier references to drugs would tend to reinforce). It has discovered the capacity to think beyond the terms of the system and is offering Sonya a chance to share in its enlightenment. The advice to shoot her next partner is, after all, one among a number of suggestions but the only one to which Sonya responds positively. It thus exposes the extent to which her conditioning does not allow her to think beyond a restricted paradigm. There is an ironic comment here on Asimov's Three Laws,[81] which the huxley itself has not contravened because the potential harm to human beings is not directly the huxley's responsibility, nor has it failed to carry out its commands. The 'short in the chest' has provided the robot with an awareness of its power to manipulate, but it is Sonya herself who will carry out the deed that begins the interservice war. The suggestion is that the Three Laws only make sense in a world where people are morally obliged to follow the same dictum.

There is, of course, a certain amount of comic pleasure for a reader who finds herself in sympathy with an insane machine, but it is also worth considering why it is that we laugh at Sonya. One answer to this question can be found in Henri Bergson's essay *Laughter* (1911), where he suggests that, to work effectively, comedy requires an empathetic distance to be maintained between the reader (or viewer) and the comic character. We can only laugh *at* Sonya because we are unable to empathise *with* her and, because the text allows us no basis for identification, we can safely laugh without other emotions intruding. A familiar scenario is enacted in such a way that the emotions normally associated with it are held in suspense.

Bergson's analysis of why we laugh includes this observation:

> *The attitudes, gestures and movements of the human body are laughable in exact proportion as that body reminds us of a mere machine.*[82]

His suggestion here is that we are led to expect a certain adaptability from human beings which will suit their actions and reactions appropriately to changing stimuli. In the absence of that adaptability, the comedy of the situation is in direct proportion to the uselessness and inappropriateness of the person's mechanical behaviour. Thus:

> The more exactly these two images, that of a person and that of a machine, fit into each other, the more striking is the comic effect. . . . This is no longer life, it is automatism established in life, and imitating it. It belongs to the comic.[83]

So, Sonya fulfils Bergson's requirements for being a comic character while also establishing the context for the critique of the mechanised society which the text implies. She belongs to the comic but also to the dystopian school of thought which sees a mechanised future as requiring human beings to adapt to the presence of machines in everyday life by themselves becoming automated in their responses. She belongs, perhaps, to a future where Bergson's analysis would no longer make sense; where the conditions for laughter provided by our recognition of the mechanical element in human behaviour would no longer apply because all behaviour has become mechanical. In Sonya's future, it is suggested, anyone who laughs at mechanical behaviour may be considered to be malfunctioning.

Sonya Briggs is by no means a feminist heroine but perhaps, for this reason, is doubly effective in demonstrating the manipulation of the female psyche for political purposes. What St Clair's story suggests is that the incorporation of female sexuality into a system of control has the potential to destroy the system from within. The twelve young women that the huxley has interviewed represent the beginnings of breakdown in a system that is thought to be self-sustaining; the weak component needing only a complementary malfunction in the controlling mechanism. In other words, where women's passivity and compliance is taken for granted, conditions are ripe for their rebellion (as was in fact proved, nine years after the first publication of 'Short In The Chest', when Betty Friedan published *The Feminine Mystique* and feminism was reborn). Sonya Briggs is Marshall McLuhan's Mechanical Bride, the modern woman embracing technology as her saviour – but, this time, provided with a gun and a licence to kill.

6
'Your Haploid Heart': James Tiptree Jr and Patterns of Gender

> Los Gatos consisted of a tarpaper whorehouse and a line of enormous lead slot-machines, called the Wise Men. They were got up to caricature the Three Kings of Bethlehem. . . . But the most impressive feature of Los Gatos was a huge wrought-iron sign stretching over the whole road, which said:
> THE GENTILE WHITE MAN IS THE KING OF THE EARTH.
> I never stopped to play the slot machines. Because I know this did not mean Me. Call me a wise man.
>
> (Alice Sheldon writing as James Tiptree Jr for the
> *Khatru* symposium, 1975)

James Tiptree Jr was a hoax (and a very convincing one) perpetrated on the sf establishment by Alice (or Raccoona) Sheldon, an experimental psychologist who had worked as an intelligence agent during World War II (the latter role contributing to the personality which she built up around 'Tip', as 'he' was affectionately known). She started writing for *Analog* (the new name for *Astounding*) in 1968, and her true identity was not revealed until 1976.

Tiptree, 'the mysterious elderly gentleman from the eastern seaboard',[1] won several accolades for 'his' work, including the prestigious Hugo and Nebula awards. Siegel suggests that Sheldon's desire to preserve her anonymity may have been largely due to the fact that she was 'an extremely private person',[2] but, this aside, it is worth considering that as a student of human behaviour she could not have failed to be intrigued by the speculation that the mystery provoked.[3] The Science Fiction Foundation in the UK has on file a photograph of Tiptree, taken from the back, seated, with the head turned almost to profile and wearing a broad brimmed hat and plain white shirt, making her sex impossible to determine and providing visual evidence of the playfulness that characterises her work. As Nancy Steffen-Fluhr comments, Tiptree is 'rarely entirely solemn'.[4]

Considered as part of the tradition of women's sf writing, Tiptree's work stands on the cusp between the subliminal messages of the Golden Age writers, articulated through the unstated but understood safety margins of the old magazine-based genre and the overtly feminist writings of the new-era women's sf. With hindsight, it can be seen that the magazines offered the perfect environment for Alice Sheldon to mount her challenge to what Ursula Le Guin calls 'the SF Old Boys' Club'.[5] Robert Silverberg, among others, must still be trying to remove the egg from his face after insisting that the suggestion that Tiptree was female was an 'absurd' theory, 'for there is to me something ineluctably masculine about Tiptree's writing'.[6] Le Guin herself wrote, in her introduction to the Tiptree anthology *Star Songs of an Old Primate*, that

> she did fool us; and the fact is important, because it makes a point which no amount of argument could have made. Not only does it imperil all theories concerning the woman as writer and the writer as woman, but it might make us question some of our assumptions concerning the existence of the writer, *per se.*[7]

Evidence that Sheldon was aware of the misconceptions that the Tiptree persona could produce is provided by the fact that she withdrew her most celebrated and most straightforward feminist story 'The Women Men Don't See' from the final selections for the Nebula award in 1974 because 'it was being touted as a feminist story written by a man, and she feared that women would vote for "him" as a political encouragement rather than because of the quality of the story'.[8] Siegel notes also that, when she began to write as Raccoona Sheldon, her work was rejected until Tiptree 'wrote a cover letter encouraging an editor to give Raccoona more serious consideration'.[9] I agree with Sarah Lefanu that 'Tiptree [was] leading us up the garden path, a game she seemed greatly to enjoy'.[10] It seems that, whatever her original intention, the pseudonym had given her a chance to explore gender-biased assumptions and to demonstrate the often misleading power of the written word.

Sheldon had an unusual childhood. Her mother was an accomplished writer and, like her father, an explorer. Writing about herself in the third person, she remembers:

This future writer was plunged into half a world of alien environments all before she was old enough to be allowed to enter an American movie house ... she was exposed to dozens of cultures and sub-cultures whose values, taboos, imperatives, religions, languages and mores conflicted with each other as well as with her parents'.[11]

Like Ursula Le Guin (daughter of writer Theodora Kroeber and anthropologist Alfred Kroeber), her world view was shaped by exposure to these conflicts and, for both writers, their avowed feminism was developed through a distinctive understanding of cultural difference and the psychology of oppression.

But perhaps the most interesting similarity, and the most relevant to my current discussion, is their attitudes towards extrapolation. What Le Guin calls 'a heuristic device, a thought experiment',[12] Tiptree describes as taking 'one of those pockets in my head that is full of protest against unbearable wrong and dangl[ing] plot-strings in the saturated solution until they start coming up with plot-crystals on them'.[13] Both these statements indicate an approach that takes nothing as given but rather expects the unexpected, as if the writer is merely an observer with no preconceived ideas of the outcome. It is an approach that the noted anthropologist Margaret Mead suggests should also be applied to anthropological research. In Mead's view, the anthropological approach

is to go out into primitive societies without any too specific theories and ask instead open-ended exploratory questions.[14]

Such an approach 'clears away our whole weight of cultural preconceptions about men and women'.[15] Mead sees one of the tasks of the anthropological writer as being 'to break down our culture-bound expectation that some aspect of learned behavior is inevitably always as it is in our society',[16] with the possible result that '[t]he reader has undergone the experience of realizing – if only for an hour – the extremely different ways in which our human nature can be patterned'.[17]

This, I believe, was Tiptree's project. Many of her stories feature invented alien cultures which invite the reader to examine alternative cultural and social arrangements that may, in turn, lead to an understanding of the biased assumptions with which we approach questions of race, class and gender. One of her definitions of 'unbearable wrong' was 'concentration camps on American soil; 50,000 Americans robbed of their land and possessions and caged in a desert behind barbed wire', and she believed that [t]he 'lesson of [our] time is, if it is inhuman, cruel and unthinkable, it'll happen'.[18] In conversation with Mark Siegel, she stated her intention to 'grab people by the heart or the collar-button and hiss Listen! Listen and think, you dolt! Feel how it really is! Let me inscribe a little fable on your nose that will carry more than the words with it when you look in the mirror!'[19] In my reading of Tiptree's story 'Your Haploid Heart', I want to investigate how Tiptree forces us to look beyond the words; to suggest what it is that she hoped that the mirror would reveal.

The story is set on the planet Esthaa which, it is eventually revealed, is inhabited by two races: the Esthaans, who inhabit the planet's only city and the mysterious Flenni, who live in scattered villages and encampments in the hills. A delegation from the 'Galactic Federation', consisting of 'one Ian Suitlov, middle-aged ecologist in public and Certified Officer in fact', assisted by Pax Patton, 'mineralogist-stratigrapher'[20] on '[h]is first big job'[21] are on a mission to determine, under cover of studying the ecology of the planet, whether its inhabitants can be classified as human. While the Esthaan culture is seemingly human, Ian describes it as 'a stage-set . . . insistently human norm'[22] and has a hunch that he will have 'a negative report to file'.[23] But it is the Flenni who finally lead him to understand how the Esthaans have deceived themselves into believing that they are human, thus ensuring the potential extinction of both races.

Because of an unusual genetic combination, the Flenni and Esthaans reproduce symbiotically, the Flenni mating to produce Esthaans who subsequently give birth to Flenni by budding. Newborn Flenni are delivered to the outlying villages, while Esthaans are brought into the city. Unaware of the true situation, Ian attempts to procure samples which will determine whether or not the Esthaans are human, warning Pax that this must be achieved with great caution because a 'new race can get all wrought up over whether or not they're certified human. . . . They take noncertification as inferiority'.[24] The criterion for classification is simply that the means of fertilisation should be compatible with the human pattern, that is, 'you bring a male and female gamete together and see if the zygote grows'.[25] By this criterion it is the Flenni who are human, and it is for this reason that the Esthaans have progressively oppressed the smaller race. Inquiries determine that the Flenni are considered to have 'a bad way of life' and are thought of as 'silly'[26] by the Esthaans and prone to 'sickness'.[27] Later Ian discovers that the Flenni 'sickness' is due to the fact that they die soon after mating, which they are forced to do at an increasingly early age by the paranoid Esthaans, who employ as a weapon a barrage of hypnotic musical signals that brings the Flenni to a pitch of helpless sexual arousal. He discovers the remains of the work of a previous expedition which leads him to suspect that for the past hundred years the Esthaans have been preparing for his arrival. In their concern to appear human, they have repressed the knowledge of their origins to the extent that they do not appreciate that the demise of the Flenni spells their own destruction. A situation in which the dependent races could have colluded in building a viable culture has effectively been turned to 'parricide, filicide...perhaps *suicide*,[28] by the intervention of a lone scientist. Ian is forced to ask, 'Had Harkness done it? What had he told them?.[29] The denouement is a bizarre musical battle in which Ian and Pax, assisted by the crew of the spaceship MacDorra, effectively block the onslaught of the Esthaans' musical weapon.

'Your Haploid Heart' is a story about evolution written at a time when, following the discovery of the structure of DNA, molecular biology was beginning to describe the process by means of which characteristics are passed from parent to child. But it is also a story about the consequences of scientific intervention, told from the point of view of a scientist who must face the ethical implications of his work. So Tiptree, a fictional writer, invents a fictional scientist who, as I will demonstrate, allows Sheldon to do what the scientist is not permitted: to question the supposed objectivity of science and expose the part that science may play in directing, rather than merely studying, social evolution. As I will show, this allows her also to offer a comment on the politics of gender, both through an analysis of the psychology of oppression and through a demonstration of the gender bias of scientific epistemology.

Although some of Tiptree's later work showed very clearly her commitment to feminism, what is interesting about 'Your Haploid Heart' is that the two alien races and their relationship to the human scientists can be read as representing a response to several contemporary cultural contexts. As well as illustrating the theme of racial oppression, the narrative implies an engagement with the ideas of the hippie counter-culture – the identification of the establishment as oppressive and the critique of scientific knowledge as power – as well as a critique of socio-biology, a theory of biological evolution that at the time was becoming controversial. It will be my purpose in this chapter to show how these 'plot strings' are brought together in such a way as to demonstrate the connections between the utopian dreams of the counter-culture, the scientific establishment, and gender politics.

Tiptree entered the field at a time when the genre had undergone a certain amount of upheaval and restructuring. The consequence was a gaining in literary respectability, a new emphasis on stylistic experimentation, and an acceptance of influences from the literary mainstream. While the sf 'Old Boys' Club' was still represented by such magazines as *Analog* and *Galaxy*, it is generally agreed that at this time Britain took over from the US in remoulding the sf genre to reflect changing times. Michael Moorcock's *New Worlds* heralded the dawn of the 'New Wave', 'a radical manifesto designed to transform and renew sf by defying the conventions and customs that seemed to be its "establishment"'.[30] Moorcock was heavily influenced by the literary experimentation of the Beats and, in fact, devoted part of his first issue of *New Worlds* to an examination of the writing of William S. Burroughs.[31] With Moorcock's editorship of *New Worlds*, sf moved out of the ghetto of fandom and into the underground of New Left politics, progressive music and the drug culture. It is perhaps a mark of the new literary atmosphere surrounding this innovation that, when the magazine foundered in 1967, it was rescued by an Arts Council grant. Colin Greenland observes that it now looks

> rather different from (and much less dated than) its contemporaries *Oz* and *IT* [International Times], though it attracted many of the same readers. It looks even less like its erstwhile competitors, *Analog* or *Galaxy*.[32]

As Brian Stableford remembers:

> The sf community ... found itself split; its ideologies became a spectrum extended between a conservative pole of technophiliacs who believed in telling a good story the old fashioned way, and tended also to be old fashioned in their attitudes towards sex; and a radical pole of apocalyptic technophobes and ecological mystics who were sympathetic to surrealism, cared little for plot, and wrote liberally (in more ways than one) about sex.[33]

The split in the sf community reflected a similar schism separating the youth counter-culture from the dominant culture. The fact that *New Worlds* attracted the same readers as *Oz* and *IT* confirms its alliance with the ideology of the counter-culture, which was characterised by a deep mistrust of machine technology. Unlike the technophobia of the pre-Vietnam era, which held technology to be a threat to the integrity of the individual worker,[34] the anti-technological stance of the counter-culture was founded on a belief in the connection between totalitarian control and technological expertise. Analysing the ideology of the counter-culture at a time when the movement was at its height, Theodore Roszak distinguished the calling into question of 'the validity of the conventional scientific world view' as one of 'the most promising elements involved in the youthful dissent of our day'.[35] In rejecting the monolithic status of scientific expertise, the counter-culture effectively challenged what Roszak called the 'myth of objective consciousness', which holds that there 'is but one way of gaining access to reality... and this is to cultivate a state of consciousness cleansed of all subjective distortion, all personal involvement'.[36] By allying itself with this challenge and defying the conventions of the traditional genre, the writers of the New Wave found a readership beyond the confines of fandom.[37]

It was also during this period, along with what Kate Millett describes as 'the revolt of youth against the masculine tradition of war and virility',[38] that the Women's Movement was reborn. As Tariq Ali points out, 'at a time when all the traditional values of bourgeois society were being questioned by a new generation it would have been very strange if questions relating to gender and sexuality had remained unmentionables',[39] and indeed, in 1966, Millett was writing that '[i]n America one may expect the new women's movement to ally itself on an equal basis with blacks and students in a growing radical coalition'.[40]

One of the most interesting documents to survive from the days before Tiptree's sex was revealed is *Khatru 3 and 4* (1975), a double issue of Jeffrey Smith's fanzine which featured the results of a written symposium conducted among some of the leading sf writers of the time, nine of whom were feminist writers (Joanna Russ, Ursula Le Guin, Vonda McIntyre, Suzy McKee Charnas and Chelsea Quinn Yarbro), as well as Smith himself, Samuel Delany and Alice Sheldon posing as James Tiptree Jr. The subject was 'Women in Science Fiction?' and in the discussion 'Tip' is attacked for daring to pronounce upon the undervaluing of motherhood. One of Joanna Russ's more polite suggestions is that he 'needs to read oodles and oodles of books before he knows what's what down below-stairs here', adding that 'Tip may end up by working through to something perfectly stunning but I can't spend my time as a public library on feminism'.[41] When Russ asked 'him' to leave the symposium, Tiptree bowed out gracefully. What remains is the only surviving document which gives evidence of Sheldon's own particular brand of feminism.

Here Tiptree gives an example of what she calls 'the pathological hypertrophy of the male sex pattern:

A funny thing happened a few years back, on the way to the bomb shelter. Official Washington held an air attack drill, a very elaborate one. The big set-piece was the whisking-away of the whole top of the government to a fantastic shelter – this one was under a mountain – where they had all the war-room and red buttons and machinery for Retaliation Unto Cinders.

Well, when the dawn moment came for the senior officials to gulp their orange juice and toddle out to the black limousines, some very odd confrontations took place. *They were leaving their wives and families behind to be fried*, you see. The silent thought loomed, 'Have a nice survival, dear. I'm sure you and General Abrams will be very happy....'[42]

The argument is similar to Charlotte Perkins Gilman's in that Tiptree's 'pathological hypertrophy of the male sex pattern' is an explanation for male dominance similar to what Gilman's mentor, Lester Frank Ward, called 'male efflorescence'.[43] But what is important for Tiptree, and I believe 'Your Haploid Heart' illustrates this point, is that, in separating the genders and ascribing qualities and behavioral patterns to each biological type, we overlook the fact that these *are* patterns, and although 'human sexual behavior has obscure ties to the biological substrate ... these are not well understood'.[44] Opposed to the male pattern which she sees as characterised by 'male–male dominance–submission conflicts, male territoriality, and all the dismal rest',[45] she posits 'the maternal pattern',[46] which, like Gilman, she considers to be deeply misunderstood and, in its undervaluing, consciously or unconsciously, a threat to the continued survival of the species. She echoes Gilman when she speaks of

our failure to develop really good human Mothering – our failure to organize all society around this work, instead of irrelevant 'male' activities and goals.[47]

But the two patterns 'may or may not be present singly or together in a given individual at a given time'. She goes so far as to say that what she has said implies 'that individual women can quite easily be, in effect, males' when 'they are acting on and powered by elements of the male pattern', but she sees '"humanity" in its best sense as closer to the maternal pattern than to the male'.[48] The 'characteristic of the Mother pattern', as she describes it, 'is that it extends over time in a way utterly unknown to the male. And it has relations to space and the environment again foreign to the male'.[49] But

in our crazy culture, we have rendered the major sex *invisible*.... And I think it cannot be denied that men have attempted to take it over.

They wrest children from the mother, make 'men' out of them in lunatic rites. They attempt to kill the mother in themselves.... A scene of unspeakable, fascinated, repulsion'.[50]

Tiptree's opposition to the dominance of the male pattern makes sense of the imagery that she employs at the start of a later story, 'A Momentary Taste of Being' (1975), when Dr Aaron Kaye dreams of Earth as 'a planet-testicle pushing a monster penis toward the stars'.[51] The spaceship *Centaur* is on a quest to discover new planets for humans to colonise. Secure in their belief that they have found what they seek, her passengers land on a planet inhabited by some strange lifeforms. Unthinkingly they subject the aliens to investigation and are, one by one, drawn to discharge their beings into the alien 'ovum', remaining as empty shells, to be cared for by Dr Kaye, who is brought to realise that they have merely become the male half of a cosmic mating. If the quest of the *Centaur* is taken to represent the inexorable drive of the dominant male pattern, which as Tiptree points out 'is powered by immediate genital gratification (non-orgasmic males leave no descendants)',[52] then it can be read as a critique of male-identified scientific arrogance,[53] which assumes the right to deplete the resources of one planet, secure in the belief that the next stage will be to colonise others.

Tiptree herself suggested, in her introduction to 'Your Haploid Heart' for the anthology *Star Songs of an Old Primate*, that 'A Momentary Taste of Being' 'represents what seven years of sweat do to the presentation of a similar psychosexual theme',[54] which Sarah Lefanu thinks '[r]ather odd', describing the later story as 'a much more overtly determinist tale'.[55] However, the link between the two stories can be found in that they both make a connection between science and empire, and how this is, in turn, linked to masculinity. In 'A Momentary Taste Of Being', the phallic *Centaur* quests after virgin planets to conquer, its inhabitants arrogantly believing that they have a right to colonise the universe. And in 'Your Haploid Heart', the Galactic Federation, represented by the two scientists Ian and Pax, is shown to be similarly arrogant in its assumption of the right to investigate other planets in its search for 'human' races to join the Federation. The fact that non-human races take non-certification as proof of their inferiority indicates where the power lies. Through fear of non-certification, the Esthaans have built their culture on denial, and, like the Nazis of *Swastika Night*,[56] have imposed a psychological regime which degrades and rejects a part of themselves, causing their culture to stagnate and their chances of survival to be threatened. Tiptree's message, like Burdekin's, is that development depends on the dynamic interplay of complementary opposites.

The selfish gene and the haploid heart

When Tiptree wrote 'Your Haploid Heart', Desmond Morris's *The Naked Ape* (1967) was still a bestseller which, together with publications such as Robert Ardrey's *The Territorial Imperative* (1966) and Konrad Lorenz's *On Aggression* (1966), provided arguments that, initiated by the discovery of the structure of DNA, offered a justification for the *status quo* in the same way that Social Darwinism had done in the nineteenth century.[57] In the same year that Tiptree published 'A Momentary Taste of Being', Harvard scientist E. O. Wilson attempted to give full scientific credence to these arguments in a controversial thesis which he titled *Sociobiology: The New Synthesis*. Sociobiology is scientific reductionism *par excellence*, offering an explanation for the excesses of what Tiptree called our 'male-dominated and largely lunatic culture'[58] in terms of genetic investment; '[t]he gene begins to be portrayed by the sociobiologists as a kind of businessman pushing his way through a competitive market system, and all the old notions of Social Darwinism seem to have been revived'.[59] Nancy Steffen-Fluhr comments that 'Sheldon [Tiptree] often flirts with sociobiology',[60] and as Sarah Lefanu has pointed out in 'A Momentary Taste of Being', 'we actually *are* the selfish gene',[61] but I think it is a mistake to read this, as does Lowry Pei, to mean that 'humanity for Tiptree is subject to powerful biologically determined drives that cannot be contradicted'.[62] In my view, she agrees with the kind of argument represented by William Irwin Thompson in *The Time Falling Bodies Take To Light*:

> Sociobiology dismisses the mind, the individual and the culture. Were we to bow to Wilson's wish that ethics be removed from the humanities and placed in scientific hands, where moral issues could be treated as an aspect of the genetic variance problem, then we would end up with a rather hideous distortion of the body-politic. . . . [Sociobiology] expresses the passions of the reductionist who is irrationally impelled to show that 'It is all nothing but . . . .' Here it is difficult to draw the line between science and science fiction, and in the domain of sociobiology where the narratives are clearly mythological, it is doubly difficult'.[63]

'A Momentary Taste of Being' is sociobiology as science fiction. If the drive towards inclusive fitness determines the destruction of the planet, then such a scenario is plausible if not inevitable. Tiptree is arguing against 'the simplistic epistemology'[64] which demands that we observe behaviour as determined by the selfish gene. If moral issues are treated as an aspect of the genetic variance problem, then anything can be justified, including pollution of the environment and indiscriminate colonisation of other planets. But it is in 'Your Haploid Heart' that Tiptree most forcefully demonstrates how erroneous links can be made between the structure of biological organisms and the structure of society.

Ian's original assessment of the relationship between Esthaans and Flenni is based on inference from the relative sizes of the two races – a discrepancy which is repeated in the fauna of the planet. His investigations determine that in comparison to the smaller, wild animals, the Esthaans' larger, domesticated versions carry double the number of chromosomes. As he explains to the uninitiated Pax, he believes that they have come across a unique mutation, 'Recurrent tetraploidy in the higher animals',[65] in which each gamete (sperm or ova) of the larger race carries a double dose of chromosomes, as opposed to the single chromosome from each homologous pair which the normal, diploid gamete will carry. In a diploid individual, the chromosomes are present in 23 pairs (the standard situation for human life) and the gametes carry a single member of each pair. In the tetraploid situation, the chromosome count is doubled in the gametes, representing two contributions from each pair. The resulting zygote will therefore carry four chromosomes to each body cell. Assuming this situation leads Ian to infer that the 'weak, short-lived [and] defect-prone' Flenni are 'up against people who are simply more of everything they are', a case where 'nature has set the stage for genocide'.[66] He is later forced to revise his theory when he discovers the Flenni to be haploid individuals, 'living gametes, with a half-set of chromosomes each'.[67]

With the exception of a brief visit to a Flenni village, the early part of the narrative takes place entirely within the Esthaan University. Ian offers his speculations about the Flenni from within the safety of the laboratory. His overriding concern is to 'make that long leave back to Molly and the kids', and he warns Pax against 'poking sticks into sore places', admonishing him to 'stick to [his study of] rocks'.[68] Ian is a journeyman scientist with a clear set of instructions which he intends to follow. His brief does not include a study of the culture, nor, he implies, does he think it appropriate for a scientist to become emotionally or politically involved. His personal interests can thus be seen to provide a motivation for finding an answer to the disadvantaged position of the Flenni[69] which reduces the situation to one of natural selection. As he explains to Pax:

> The two forms compete, and the bigger, stronger, more vital form wins.... Shocking as it sounds, you have here almost a quantitative measure of humanity – if they're human. Under the circumstances, it's a credit to the big Esthaans that the little race has survived so far.[70]

His implication here is that this is a natural process which, upsetting as it may be to observers, is in the hands of 'nature' and thus outside the power of the scientists to change.

That change has already been effected by Harkness's expedition gradually comes to light as Ian and Pax begin their study. Another Tiptree irony has Ian discovering the remains of Harkness's work, his first clue to the genetic structure of the two races, in the Esthaans' own archives, which are 'abominably muddled and dispersed'.[71] The Esthaans have rejected scientific investigation as a serious discipline. On Esthaa, science is 'more an upper-class hobby than a discipline', and 'all the shiny instruments'[72] merely props to aid the human-seeming illusion. This parallels the situation in *Swastika Night*[73] in which the Nazis have outlawed scientific inquiry in case it should be discovered that it is not the female who is responsible for the sex of the child. The fear is, once again, that systematic study will reveal what the dominant race must constantly hide from themselves, that is, that their claim to dominance is based on spurious logic. When Ian cautiously tries to speak to their Esthaan host, Ovancha, of 'a possible genetic difference between himself and unnamed "others"', he receives the reply, 'But one can see the difference.... There is no need to go further. We are not interested in such things in our science'.[74]

This, again, can be read as irony. Ian's microscopic investigations merely confirm, on a cellular level, the difference that Ovancha can 'see' between Esthaan and Flenni. Ian is merely confirming his hypothesis that the added chromosomes give the Esthaans the advantage in the struggle for survival. At this stage he is unaware of their symbiotic relationship, nor would the microscope be likely to reveal the true situation, as it merely reveals the discrepancy in chromosome count. So while the Esthaans' unstructured science obscures the facts of their reproductive pattern, Ian's scientific approach equally misconstrues the relationship of their genetic structure to their behaviour. The text thus offers an analysis of the relationship between what Sandra Harding has called

'bad science' and 'science-as-usual'.[75] Harding argues that 'the fundamental value-ladenness of knowledge-seeking' makes a distinction
between the two impossible and argues that the social sciences in
particular can never be free of culture- and gender-bound value judgements. Thus any behavioural science claiming objectivity can only
produce biased results and is as much 'bad science' as is an unmethod-
ical and haphazard approach. While gender bias can be distinguished in
interpretations of early hominid behaviour (why, for instance, should
the discovery of stone tools indicate that tool use was developed as an
aid for hunting? Would it not make equal sense to argue that they were
early technological developments to aid agriculture?),[76] the studies of
tribal societies which claim them as a paradigm for our evolutionary
past are not only biased by a hierarchical evaluation of their evolutionary status but are, quite possibly, also distorted by the intervention of
the scientists:

> Anthropologists are ... skeptical about the assumption that the social
> patterns of contemporary hunter-gatherer societies are the same as
> those of our ancestors at the dawn of human history. They show
> how even the earliest observations by Westerners, who presumed
> they had found humans untouched by Western development, were
> in fact observations of groups who had already been forced to adapt
> to the cultural patterns of the West.[77]

This is why the idea of 'First Contact'[78] is so important for the message
of 'Your Haploid Heart'. Harkness is a minor character in the narrative,
but reference to his death and Ian's discovery of the remains of his work
provide a crucial perspective on the Esthaan situation. In the one
hundred years that have elapsed between the time of Harkness's visit to
Esthaa and the time in which the story takes place, the population of
Esthaans has become concentrated 'in [an] urban complex around [a]
spaceport, becoming [a] one-city planet' where previously the culture
had approximated 'Terran Greek city states, grouped around [an] inland
sea on [a] single continental mass'.[79] Since a 'space trade route' was
established soon after First Contact, the changing demography of the
planet can be seen to be in direct response to the presence of humans
arriving at the spaceport. Ironically, the report states, 'Esthaan workers
noted for ability to copy complex mechanisms'[80] – an ability that has
obviously proved crucial in the establishment of their bogus culture.

   Ian, in his indifference and his fear of 'poking sticks into sore places',
represents science-as-usual, and in the early part of the story he is much

given to contradiction. He initially dismisses the Flenni as 'an appealing native group who are being oppressed or exploited in some way by the civilized Esthaans',[81] thus implying an assessment that privileges 'civilised' over 'native'. But, despite the fact that he appears to embrace a concept which includes the use of 'civilisation' as a judgmental term, he later tells Ovancha: 'in my original world we had once a very great problem because our people were not all alike. . . . But we came to live together as one family, as brothers . . . .'[82] This assertion thus seems to encode a suggestion that the Galactic Federation is ruled by dogma, that the apparent 'brotherhood' of races hides an enforced conformity. Despite Ian's dismissal of certification as 'meaningless'[83] it is the humans who have determined the criteria for classification, placing them in the same position of dominance as the Nazis are to the subject races in *Swastika Night*, or as men are to women. If, in a male-determined world, women are merely 'other', then in a human-determined universe the same must apply to other species.

So the plot questions the legitimacy of mastery by demonstrating how a claim to dominance can be based on arbitrarily hierarchised differences. Although for Ian human certification is necessary only to determine the 'social, religious [and] political consequences'[84] of the genetic intermingling of diverse human species, the Esthaan 'social psychosis'[85] demonstrates that the certification is only 'meaningless' from a human point of view. The text thus demonstrates the relativity of meaning while also offering an analysis of the part that science has had to play in legitimising Western cultural imperialism. The role of Harkness thus becomes meaningful as a representation of the potential for the researcher to act as an agent of change, and he can also be read as standing symbolically for the myth of objective consciousness. That the Flenni symbolise a challenge to this myth can be found in the fact that their intense sensuality, as Ian later discovers, militates against the stance of non-involvement which the scientist must maintain in order to perpetuate the myth. And their association with music and flowers, their bright clothes and their sub-cultural status can, of course, also lead them to be identified with the hippie counter-culture, who stood in opposition to the scientists' claim to power through objective consciousness.

It is, however, these same elements of the Flenni lifestyle and demeanour which have led some commentators, aware of Tiptree's feminism, to find in them an analogy for human women. Marleen Barr imagines 'an alien coming to Earth [who] would also [like Ian and Pax] be greeted by the group in charge, men:

This hypothetical alien visitor might later notice women, another group of Earth inhabitants who are usually smaller, weaker and more prone to death (because of pregnancy) than men. Like Ian's first reaction to the Flenni, this alien would reasonably assume that men are human and women are a related sub-species.[86]

The fact that the Flenni suffer repression purely on account of their reproductive biology would seem to confirm this reading. In this sense, their situation is parallel to that of the women in *Swastika Night*, and they too have been reduced 'to the status of breeding animals'.[87] However, this analysis fits rather awkwardly with the fact that the Flenni are, biologically, both male and female, and that to an intense degree. As Ian explains:

> Only in dreams do we ever see beings who are literally all male or all female. The most virile human man or the most seductive ordinary woman is, in fact, a blend. But these creatures were the pure expression of one sex alone – electric, irresistible.[88]

I believe that the problematic position of reading the Esthaans and Flenni as an analogy for the human sexes can be overcome by understanding them on more than one level of representation. The Flenni love of flowers and music and the Esthaan disapproval of their lifestyle suggests a comparison with the hippie counter-culture which, in turn, suggests that they can be read as a critique of the ethical underpinnings of the scientific establishment, as represented by the Esthaans. In my view, the relationship between the two races can also be read as an articulation of Tiptree's analysis of gender politics in terms of conflicting 'patterns' and an application of these ideas to the question of gender bias in scientific epistemology.

The scientist in the wilderness

To allay suspicion after his attempts to procure an ovum have produced a reticent and nervous response in the Esthaans, Ian buries himself in 'routine taxonomy',[89] but the brief trip away from the University and his first contact with the Flenni immediately begins to threaten his disengagement:

> I felt my hand clutched by something tiny and electric. An impossibly small girl was running beside me, her face turned up to mine.

Our eyes met, joltingly. Something was being pushed into my fist.
Her head went down – soft, fierce lips pressed my hand – and then
she was gone.[90]

From this point on, the world of the Flenni begins to encroach on the
cloistered world of the University.[91] The next morning 'a sheaf of . . .
vivid orange flowers had been thrown over the wall by our table',[92] an
event which is repeated on successive nights. The flowers, which have
'an amazing smell',[93] emphasise the sensual nature of the Flenni, in
contrast to the Esthaans, who have furnished Ian and Pax's residence
with 'a diffuser emitting a rather pleasing floral scent', a mechanical
device producing a contrastingly muted response and which Ian describes
as an 'alien feature'. Later Ovancha makes 'a minute adjustment to the
scent dispenser',[94] implanting the suggestion early in the narrative that
floral scent has some symbolic significance. But what is equally significant is that Pax's job as 'mineralogist-stratigrapher' must take him beyond
the University walls. His demand for action against Ian's passivity lends
tension to the early narrative. Where Ian feels secure within the familiar
environment of the University, Pax is restless, and Ian discovers him
'prowling the patio and eyeing the line of distant mountains'.[95] Finally
let loose for a field trip, he disappears into the mountains, having
apparently murdered his Esthaan travelling companion. Thereafter, Ian
is forced to re-evaluate his position. Having witnessed an 'almost-cat'[96]
giving birth by budding he is brought to face not only his own mistake
but the possibility that the Esthaans' 'psychotic fantasy'[97] was precipitated by Harkness's intervention. Realising that his life must now be in
danger he literally goes 'over the wall', marking the point at which the
laboratory narrative gives way to what I shall continue to refer to as the
narrative of the wilderness.

Ian leaves the city of the Esthaans and is transported to the country,
which is the domain of the Flenni, and at the same time passes from
passivity to activity, from observation to participation. He leaves behind
the artificial world of the Esthaans in which everything is ordered, familiar and static, and passes into unfamiliar chaos and continual movement.
I should like to offer here a model for examining this transition which
draws on Tiptree's metaphor of the mirror to explore the working out
of a strategy which elaborates the maternal pattern at work within
the text.

The mirror as a symbol for transition is employed in Lacanian
psychoanalysis to mark the point at which the child recognises itself as
separate from the mother. This prompts the need for intersubjective

communication and is the preparation for initiation into the use of language. This initiation into the 'Name-of-the-Father' is the point at which the codes and conventions which determine gender identity are established. Or, as Nelly Furman explains it: 'When we become intelligible we do so by adopting the values upon which communication is predicated'.[98] But for the French language theorist Julia Kristeva, there is a residue of the childish identification with the mother which forever threatens the stability of the meaning with which the so-called 'symbolic order' invests words. In other words, from the moment that a child appears to accept the conventions which are established by the use of language intelligible to others, and is thus deemed to have entered the symbolic order, the former identification with the mother is not simply abandoned but is implied by, and is ever in danger of subverting, each and every utterance. In Freudian terms, the repression of instinctual drives is glimpsed in the use of tropes: metaphor, metonymy, and the language of jokes and dreams. But for Kristeva this 'semiotic activity' is ever present and, as a necessary condition for the existence of the symbolic, can be brought into conscious use in subverting symbolic meaning. As she writes, the 'unsettled and questionable subject of poetic language (for whom the word is never uniquely sign) maintains itself at the cost of reactivating this repressed, instinctual, maternal element'.[99] The writer or user of poetic language, of whichever gender, is thus in a position to subvert paternal discourse. As Furman explains it:

> [A]lthough women have a privileged relationship to birth, gestation and the body as a place of origin, the territory of the maternal is not a space confined to, or defined by, biological characteristics; it is the position a subject, any subject, can assume towards the symbolic order.[100]

The mirror, then, symbolises knowledge of the self as a gendered subject, reflected back in the terms dictated by language. But, like a shadow behind the image, is the semiotic – the inarticulable other that is 'more than the words', challenging and capable of subverting the symbolic order. This can be read as Tiptree's maternal pattern expressed in, or as the antithesis of, language. The Esthaan University represents the world in which the symbolic order holds sway, where the oppression of the Flenni can be justified by the language of science. This is also, of course, the world of the Esthaans, where knowledge is repressed for the sake of maintaining an illusion of dominance: a world that is sterile, in a state of stasis, and ultimately destructive. The culture that is presented as stage-managed, oppressive and paranoiac is that which works according to the law of the symbolic. But when Ian is forced into the world of the Flenni he enters the domain of semiotic activity, where the meanings fixed by the structured use of scientific language become fragmented and dissolved; where language itself is threatened by the Flenni's communication of intense sensuality.

Thus, at the point where Ian goes 'over the wall' he leaves the safety and confinement of the symbolic order. His journey from the University to the mountains in the womb-like interior of 'a big...roller' is redolent with images of gestation and birth. The interior was 'roomy and dark, with a piercing odor'; the 'sounds coming from the crate'[101] with which he shares his confinement allow him to hope that he will reach his destination and can therefore only be newborn Flenni being delivered to the camp. When the roller stops, he reports:

> Frantically, I cut the last threads and pushed and rolled myself through to the front floor-boards. The pain was shocking....I cried out and pitched myself out.[102]

This, then, is the moment of birth or rebirth and is followed by a period of disorientation characterised by 'hot clouds of pain and confusion' and 'nights and stars, and hot days in thickets, and pain, and soft hands'.[103] Unlike the language of the laboratory narrative, the narrative of the wilderness begins with the language of returning (or awakening) sensation – with a disorientation of the visual field and unstructured discourse. The scientist has become a child, entering an unfamiliar world.

Unlike the discourse of the laboratory narrative, the language here evokes strangeness and the sense that the Flenni, although they are 'human', are the truly alien. Representing, as they do, unrepressed desire, they are the antithesis of 'civilisation', in which desire is channelled into the construction of the social edifice.

The Esthaans are no longer aware of the Flenni as part of themselves, nor do they acknowledge that they are the reason for, as well as necessary for, the continuation of their sham civilisation. They are merely a reminder of guilt, their mere presence speaking too insistently of the Esthaans' origins, which are *'revolting*...unspeakable'.[104] The scene in which the Esthaans herd the Flenni men and women into a 'great cave'[105] where they are forced to mate can be read metaphorically as representing an attempt to contain the semiotic which, paradoxically, must be acknowledged with every action that aims towards its denial.

This, again, stresses the similarity to *Swastika Night*,[106] where the language of the Nazis, in which the word 'mother' cannot even be uttered, is constantly shadowed by the presence of the maternal, and similarly in *Your Haploid Heart* the oppressed group are denied a voice within the text. However, the Flenni frequently announce their presence with music.

Pax's curiosity is first roused when he hears music 'from the village',[107] and during their chaperoned visit to the Flenni 'a flute blared brilliantly and stopped', but as they leave:

> the unseen flute pealed out again and was joined by a drum. A trumpet answered from across the square. We drove away in a skirl of sound.[108]

Music thus becomes, within the text, synonymous with language in that the only dialogue between the Flenni is musical. They are silenced by the presence of the Esthaans, but the dialogue begins again when they leave.

The music can be taken to represent an articulation of the semiotic, and, as such, gains significance as a mode of discourse which Ian and Pax enter themselves when they counter the Esthaan assault with music of their own. The scientists abandon their objective stance and, with it, their faith in their ability to remain aloof from the mistakes of their profession. They, like the Flenni, are human, and Tiptree's clear message seems to be that the potential exists for human beings to overcome their destructive drives in an acknowledgement of the 'maternal pattern' which, drawing on Kristeva, I have equated with the residue of child/ mother interaction that underlies the productions of language.

So the narrative of the wilderness brings the scientist into a world where he must question the validity of the objective state of mind. The point in the narrative when the Flenni flowers appear on the laboratory side of the wall represents the beginning of an assault against the myth of objective consciousness. When Ian leaves the University, following the younger, more impetuous Pax, he enters an alien world which conversely, in terms of the narrative, is truly human. He thus symbolically recognises his own alienation, the alienation of the objective consciousness which '*is* alienated life promoted to its most honorific status as the scientific method'.[109]

My discussion of *Herland* in Chapter 2 involved an examination of conflicting potential narratives in which a conventional hero, confronted with the challenge of the 'wilderness', attempts to write a narrative of conquest but is thwarted by the power of the Herlanders' maternal sisterhood. Tiptree similarly sends two scientists out into the wilderness, offering, as in *Herland*, a contrast which questions the assumptions that underlie the construction of a heroic narrative. But where Gilman was concerned to promote objectivity and offer the methodology of social science as a route to appreciating the need for women's emancipation, Tiptree uses a similar strategy to expose the danger of that same approach. Pax, like Gilman's Terry Nicholson, aspires to hero status. With the Flenni, 'he towered among them, bronzed and eager. . . . Every inch the guerrilla leader of the oppressed'.[110] Knowing nothing of the music which is the true Esthaan weapon against the Flenni, he arms young Flenni men and teaches them to shoot, thus placing them in a vulnerable position when the Esthaans, having discovered the women's hiding place, drive them towards the men, whose only true defence is in flight. But despite the fact that Ian's final intervention 'saves' the Flenni from the Esthaans, he cannot, like Gilman's Vandyck Jennings,[111] emerge as an alternative hero, aware as he is that scientific intervention has been the cause of the Flenni's distress.

In a final irony, Tiptree takes us back to the laboratory where two old and very rich scientists have been 'betting fantastic sums' as to which of their theories of evolution will finally be proved. Aware that money is the only inducement that will persuade MacDorra to make an unscheduled descent and that the situation on Esthaa may enable one of the scientists to win his bet, Ian 'rescues' the Flenni by selling them to science. As he tells Pax: 'Sheer orneriness and ego – that's what saved us, son, not altruism or love of science'.[112]

The Flenni are only able to leave the planet because a scientist 'wants his theory of evolution proved the worst way'. The reference is, once again, to self-interest disguised as scientific objectivity. Ian, however, is prepared to risk declassification to 'assistant jet cleaner'[113] in order to ensure that 'the Flenni come out of this right side up',[114] giving the story a hopeful ending for the future of the Flenni and, perhaps, for the future of science.

So, in 'Your Haploid Heart', Tiptree's aliens can be read on more than one level of representation. Although the analogy with human men and women is striking, it is necessary to read beyond what is apparently a pessimistic analysis of the relationship between the genders. By opposing two diverse cultural groups and charting the effects of scientific intervention over one hundred years of their development, she provides a broad analysis of the part that science has played in supporting racist and sexist assumptions, and argues for a recognition of the damaging results of accepting scientific theories which ratify the dominance of the oppressor. In exposing the myth of objective consciousness, she allies her argument with the ideology of the counter-culture, but the text also codes a warning against the potential for revolutionary movements to reproduce the myths which justified dominance in the old order, disguised as new narratives of equality. The metaphor of the mirror supplies an injunction to examine how these narratives are constructed: to look beyond the words and discover the ideology at work behind them. The position that, for Kristeva, 'any subject can take towards the symbolic order' for Tiptree is expressed in the epistemological and psychological orientation of the maternal pattern, and there is no doubt that she intends us to recognise the importance of this position in constructing our knowledge of the world.

7
Amazons and Aliens: Feminist Separatism and the Future of Knowledge

It is the strength of the feminine which can guide us towards a consciousness which, though aware of polarities, is concerned with their interplay and connectedness rather than their conflict and separation.

Stephanie Leland, 'Feminism and Ecology: Theoretical Connections'[1]

The first publication of Charlotte Perkins Gilman's *Herland* in novel form coincided with an upsurge in similar utopian and self-consciously feminist writing, as more women discovered the potential of sf for fictionalising a radical critique. Taking their impetus from the demands of the new women's movement, these fictions are primarily concerned with identity politics and the radicalisation of sexuality, which are in most cases seen as inseparable from environmental and ecological concerns. Destruction of the environment through depletion of resources and the indiscriminate use of machine technology is, in these texts, identified with masculine power, and their most radical proposition is, as Dennis Livingston puts it,

that the best thing men can do at present is to get out of the way, as women on their own have the potential of creating a culture more ecologically sensitive and humanistic than men have been able to offer.[2]

The question that I want to address is whether the fictionalisation of a radical politics in these terms can, in fact, offer a means for appreciating the value of diverse experiences and points of view as resources for finding a route to a more inclusive and humanistic mode of knowledge seeking. Do these separatist utopias help us to understand how female knowledge of the world is to be recognised, and how this may structure our approaches to scientific knowledge in the future? Or do they merely satisfy the need of some lesbian feminists to imagine themselves outside of and therefore uninterested in, or incapable of, effecting change within the dominant social order?

Homosexuality itself has been the subject of much debate in terms of essentialist versus social constructionist arguments,[3] a debate which similarly informs the controversy surrounding the position of women as they stand in relation to the project of scientific enquiry. Therefore, when the ethics of separatism are applied to imagining fictional worlds, these arguments are necessarily implied. This chapter will focus on Sally Miller Gearhart's *The Wanderground*, which takes a basically essentialist stance, effectively reclaiming the view of woman as identified with nature and using lesbian sexuality as a metaphor for the relationship between women and the planet. I will also examine Caroline Forbes's novelette 'London Fields', which in contrast utilises the ideology of lesbian separatist politics to explore the system of values that marks out women's culture.

One version of the essentialist viewpoint tends towards the proposition that psychoanalytic theory can be read as indicating that women's primary orientation is homosexual and that heterosexuality is achieved only incompletely and with the requirement that women subsequently identify in accordance with masculine ideas of femininity.[4] Therefore, the goal of feminism should be to promote awareness of heterosexuality as a position into which women are coerced by patriarchal authority.

Adrienne Rich believes it is the institution of 'compulsory heterosexuality' that must be condemned. Her argument turns on the fact that what she perceives as the 'lesbian continuum', that is, the emotional relationships between women that through the ages have sustained them in their fight for individuation and against oppression, has been rendered invisible by institutions that seek to deny women choice in their sexual relationships. She believes that:

> If we consider the possibility that all women . . . exist on a lesbian continuum, we can see ourselves as moving in and out of this continuum, whether we identify ourselves as lesbian or not.[5]

Although some lesbians would argue that arguments of this kind necessarily obscure their sexuality under an all-encompassing aegis for the expedient of reaffirming the viability of feminism for heterosexual

women, Rich's contention that 'heterosexual feminists will draw political strength for change from taking a critical stance toward the ideology
which *demands* heterosexuality'[6] remains persuasive. If we understand
heterosexuality as an ideologically informed construct which underpins
female subject positions in contemporary culture, then separatism can
be read as a potent political statement which says more about the kind
of society women would build, untrammelled by the institutions of
patriarchy, than about their sexuality.

Nina Auerbach has studied communities of women in mainstream,
non-utopian fiction, where they often form a contrast to the idea of the
socially 'successful' woman who contracts a 'good' marriage, and has
discovered 'a subtle, unexpected power'.[7] Although these women may be
portrayed as defective, excluded from the social and economic privileges conveyed by entry into the marriage market, 'their isolation has
had from the first the self-sustaining power to repel or incorporate the
male-defined reality that excludes them':[8]

> As a recurrent literary image, a community of women is a rebuke to
> the conventional ideal of a solitary woman living for and through
> men, attaining citizenship in the community of adulthood through
> masculine approval alone. The communities of women which have
> haunted our literary imagination from the beginning are emblems of
> female self-sufficiency which create their own corporate reality,
> evoking both wishes and fears.[9]

These communities thus have a quality which transcends time and
place, and it is in this transcendence that their power lies. For these
groups, separatism is inherent and unconscious. In real life they are
invisible, but, made visible by literature, they are larger than life, feeding 'dreams of a world beyond the normal'.[10] It is this supra-normal
world that the denizens of the separatist utopias inhabit. It is not the
absence of men that informs the structure of their society, but rather the
presence of female community. It is this that marks them out as utopias.
The community realises possibilities that the individual only partly
senses. Unlike Charlotte Perkins Gilman's *Herland*, for instance, these
fictions cannot imagine women preparing a new world whose logic will
be accessible to men (even 'special' men) and will benefit from their
return. It is precisely because the community of women contains its
own inherent logic that the presence of men is immediately destructive.

So, although these texts initially would seem only to appeal to an
exclusive readership, they are nevertheless relevant to a spectrum of

contemporary concerns discussed beyond the confines of the lesbian community. But claiming, as do some futures researchers,[11] that these texts can provide actual paradigms for a more ecologically sensitive future rather begs the question of what counts as a valuable contribution towards the project of ecological recovery and what can be construed as mere wishful thinking. If separatism is a solution in itself then women's essential nature must be presupposed, with the corollary that a corresponding male 'essence' is necessarily pernicious.

Sally Miller Gearhart's *The Wanderground*, subtitled 'Stories Of The Hill Women', is a collection of stories, originally published in a variety of lesbian/feminist magazines in the US, which have a common thread. They concern a community of women who have made their home in the countryside, following a reactionary backlash which has driven a previously thriving women's movement into obscurity and has instigated a series of purges to rid society of women considered to be a threat to the re-establishment of male hegemony and female submission. As the community has become established, so the women have rediscovered powers which allow them a unique form of communication as well as the means to protect themselves from the ever-present threat from the cities where men continue to live technology-dominated lives and where women's activities are heavily proscribed. Outside the cities, earth / female power dominates to the extent that, once in the countryside, both men and machines are rendered impotent, but, as the stories reveal, the women must maintain a constant vigilance to protect their lifestyle. Here men are identified with technology and women with nature in a way which proposes a complete polarisation of the genders and the lifestyles appropriate to each. The women's life in the countryside is portrayed as idyllic. Telepathy has allowed them to achieve a level of co-operation which acknowledges and appreciates difference while allowing each to explore and exploit her individual talents. There is no hierarchy, and the work of each 'esconcement' is shared equally and according to ability. Each woman understands her responsibility to her sisters, and problems are shared by 'gatherstretch', a meeting of many minds in which all responses are explored and collective decisions taken. In contrast the cities are noisy, cramped and polluted, and inhabited by a species of male/alien whose life is dominated by competition and whose 'leisure' time is spent in fighting and in sexual pursuit of the city-women, whom the Hill Women perceive as equally alien. However, the Hill Women maintain minimal contact with the 'Gentles', a group of men who have themselves rejected city life: 'men who knew that the outlaw women were the only hope for the Earth's survival. Men who, knowing that maleness touched women only with the accumulated hatred of centuries, touched no women at all'.[12] The Gentles aid the women who maintain a presence 'on rotation' in the cities, where they pose as men gathering information on political developments. The women reproduce parthenogenetically, but in common with other aspects of the Hill Women's lives 'implantment' is highly ritualised. It is this sense of ritual which, although not always clearly detailed in the narrative, nevertheless permeates the text and lends a spiritual quality to Gearhart's imagined world.

The location of the Wanderground is unspecified, one point of difference that distinguishes *The Wanderground* from Caroline Forbes's 'London Fields', a 'novelette' included in the anthology of her writing, *The Needle On Full* (1985). London Fields is an area of Hackney, East London which comprises a large park surrounded by narrow streets and housing estates, discoverable on any street map of London. In Forbes's story, a genetic mutation has decimated the male population of the world, and in the resulting disorder, in which the remaining men have attempted to restore their numbers by hunting and raping women, a number of women have organised themselves and fought back, with the result that they have eventually found themselves in a world without men. The community of women in London Fields is heir to a crumbling metropolis which both dominates and defines their lives. Like the Hill Woman, they have rediscovered subsistence farming but have also developed skills that allow them to repair and renovate the houses that they occupy. Part of the narrative recounts the demolition of a decaying tower block which poses a threat to the women's lives. Apart from the imminent danger of collapse and the need to plan and allocate resources to its demolition, the block harbours relics of the past which divide the community and challenge the precarious harmony of the women's existence. One of the women discovers, hidden in a false ceiling, a cache of guns and ammunition which she subsequently uses to kill a wandering band of young men, themselves the product of a scientific experiment, who have made camp on the women's territory. The suggestion is that while weapons exist women are not exempt from the temptation to use them.

An immediate similarity between the two narratives is their emphasis on the collective over the individual. But while *The Wanderground* proposes telepathy as a metaphor for the psychological harmony that, it is suggested, would immediately prevail in a community of women in which the politics of heterosexuality no longer determine relationships, 'London Fields' demonstrates a community struggling to come to terms with psychological and behavioural diversity. The women of

The Wanderground have all acquiesced in the use of mind-sharing techniques and provide for each others' physical safety and psychological well-being by melding minds to offer support or surveillance. Their communication also extends to other elements in their environment, like animals and plants, and ultimately to the Earth, the 'Great Mother' which, awakened to rebellion by the indiscriminate use of technology, has enabled the Hill Women to establish their 'esconcements' and work towards their own empowerment through development of a mutually nurturing relationship. In 'London Fields', however, Forbes develops a narrative of generational conflict which explores the mother/daughter relationship as a site of competing discourses in which the daughters are contesting for a future which seeks to deny the past.

The texts that I am discussing here are demonstrably inheritors of the tradition that Sandra A. Zagarell has described as 'narrative of community' and which she has identified as having taken shape initially 'in the first half of the nineteenth century in the United States, Great Britain and Ireland' as a response to 'the social, economic, cultural and demographic changes caused by industrialism, urbanization, and the spread of capitalism':[13]

> Narratives of community ignore linear development or chronological sequence and remain in one geographic place. Rather than being constructed around conflict and progress, as novels usually are, narratives of community are rooted in process. They tend to be episodic, built primarily around the continuous small-scale negotiations and daily procedures through which communities sustain themselves. In keeping with the predominant focus on the collective life of the community, characterization typically exemplifies modes of interdependence among community members.[14]

For Zagarell, the concept of narrative of community 'postulates a relationship between women's culture and writing that is . . . structural',[15] where 'negotiation [is] a fundamental feature of that culture'.[16] Furthermore, '[t]he influence of women's culture can be felt in the genre's relational orientation, its double-voicedness, its ties with traditional life'.[17] However, the texts that Zagarell selects for discussion are 'in the seemingly paradoxical situation of being at once suffused with women's culture yet not, as a general rule, woman-centred in a literal sense'.[18] Where the texts that I am discussing differ is that they are very much woman-centred and, as such, are self-consciously motivated to portray a specific women's culture.

But like narrative of community, and despite imagining a world of the future, both texts are characterised by nostalgia for a pre-industrial world. This, however, is also where their difference lies. *The Wanderground* adheres most closely to eco-feminist principles, returning to what Hazel Henderson calls 'the matrifocal period of human development' which

> may have had at its core a value-system tilted towards the genotype, in its celebration of the *processes* of life, its changes, cycles, seasons, subtle forces, as well as the positive value of decay, entropy and death.[19]

'London Fields', however, more closely reflects the value-system identified by Carol Gilligan in her study of female moral psychology, *In A Different Voice* (1982), as that which influences women's culture. But both can be read as offering potential models for how the world may be understood in terms of women's experience.

Developing a woman-centred epistemology

In both narratives, the delineation of the 'old' world is achieved through drawing on the memories of the older members of the communities, thus situating the communities in a specific time relative to their founding, while also providing a dystopian reappraisal of the contemporary world. In *The Wanderground*, the link with a prehistorical past, juxtaposed with the perceived present and imagined future, provides a continuum of female experience in which men are associated with a time of dislocation, a period in which women have 'forgotten' their true nature or, perhaps more importantly, their history. As Adrienne Rich defines it:

> Feminist history is not history about women only; it looks afresh at what men have done and how they have behaved, not only toward women but toward each other and the natural world. But the central perspective and preoccupation is *female*, and this implies a vast shift in values and priorities.[20]

Imagining men removed from the world effectively invalidates the relevance of patriarchal history: 'the version of events told by the conqueror, the dominator'.[21] In the absence of the dominator, a different selectivity operates in preserving knowledge of and from the past. One of the longest stories of *The Wanderground* concerns the first visit of a seven-year-old child, 'Clana', to the 'Remember Rooms'.[22] Here, in a series of underground chambers, she is instructed telepathically in 'the rich history of the Hill Women'.[23] But this is not history as researched and documented attempts to make sense of the past, but a series of preserved memories experienced through 'remember-guides' with 'the help of catwatch'. Cats fill in 'missing connections in the stories' and add portions forgotten by the more fallible remember-guides. Clana asks a cat, 'Do you enjoy remembering?' to which it replies, 'Do you enjoy breathing?' and she must remind herself 'that remembering was in fact what a cat *was*' (p. 150). Memory is thus accorded an ontological status, and memory *in* the present and memory of the past are conflated, that is, the act of remembering and what is remembered become one and the same.

Memory is important to the Wanderground social structure in uniting the generations and providing a living mythology. The symbolism of the cats ensures that we understand it as everywhere and nowhere; both internal and external; of the past and of the present. So this device allows the text to raise questions as to how knowledge of history is to be understood and what this means for the conceptualisation of time.

Although we are invited to share Clana's first experience of remembering, as the narrative makes clear, '[s]ome of the women were returning for a second or a third or a tenth time'.[24] The women are therefore constantly in touch with their past and, as the story 'Pelagine Stretches' demonstrates, they are practised in techniques for re-experiencing their memories:

> She was reaching far back now, for an old memory, changing whole years into milliseconds, quickening the backward-sweeping montage, pausing only where she touched moments which in themselves embraced eternities.... Always a certain excitement accompanied her deep recalls; she loved the rediscovery of details that only immersion there would yield.[25]

This sense of 'moments...in themselves embrac[ing] eternities' is suggestive of what Julia Kristeva has referred to as *monumental* time which 'crosses national boundaries and is a memory or symbolic common denominator'. This is opposed to the time of linear history or *cursive* time. Monumental time

> concerns the response that human groupings, united in space and time, have given not to the problems of the *production* of material goods (ie., the domain of the economy and of the human relationships it implies, politics etc.) but rather, to those of *reproduction*, survival of the species, life and death, the body, sex and symbol.[26]

For Kristeva, this 'monumental temporality' is a 'massive presence' in women's subjective experience of time which

> would seem to provide a specific measure that essentially retains *repetition* and *eternity* from among the multiple modalities of time known through the history of civilizations.[27]

As she says, 'when evoking the name and destiny of women, one thinks more of *space* generating and forming the human species than of *time*, becoming or history',[28] hence,

> the eternal recurrence of a biological rhythm which conforms to that of nature and imposes a temporality whose stereotyping may shock, but whose regularity and unison with what is experienced as extra-subjective time, cosmic time, occasions vertiginous visions and unnameable *jouissance*.[29]

This sense of 'vertiginous visions' is perhaps what lends *The Wanderground* its 'dream-like'[30] quality. The text, in emphasising the community over the individual and monumental over cursive time, effectively deconstructs accepted notions of spatio-temporal existence, perceived in this sense as masculine. Kristeva writes of the female experience of monumental time as having 'so little to do with linear time (which passes) that the very word 'temporality' hardly fits'. It is 'all-encompassing and infinite like imaginary space', and

> one is reminded of the various myths of resurrection which, in all religious beliefs, perpetuate the vestige of an anterior or concomitant maternal cult.[31]

So Kristeva links the concept of monumental time to the idea of a maternal cult existing prior to the religious beliefs associated with patriarchal culture. The same kind of connection can be found within the text of *The Wanderground*, where the narrative implies the idea of monumental time while also making explicit reference to pre-patriarchal mythology. The 'Revolt of the Mother' signals a return or a reawakening of a maternal spirit which empowers the women to reclaim the Earth from the ravages of patriarchy.

In the story 'A Time To Sing', the Greek myth of Demeter and her daughter Kore is offered as an allegory for the arrogance of paternal intervention in the spiritual union of mother and child. A cat is again on hand as Troja and Blase and some of the children, in telepathic communication, sing 'Kore's narrative'.[32] The women sing in response to Troja's brief intention, under duress, to invade another woman's consciousness. As Blase reports to Earlyna, 'She intended man's crime'.[33]

The story of the myth tells how Kore (sometimes called Persephone), is abducted and raped by the god of the underworld (sometimes thought to be Zeus or Dionysus but more commonly Pluto or, in *The Wanderground* version of the myth, Dis). Demeter, 'the goddess of life, corn or grain . . . refuses to let any crop grow until her daughter is returned to her'.[34] Eventually she strikes a bargain with the god in which Kore remains with him only during winter, when no crops will grow, and returns to her mother during the remainder of the year.

According to Sjöö and Mor, the Kore/Demeter myth, in its original, pre-patriarchal interpretation, emphasises cyclicity and is a celebration of birth and rebirth. Kore and Demeter are each aspects of the Triple Goddess, daughter of the Great Mother, who 'presides over *all* acts of generation, whether physical, intellectual or spiritual'.[35] The triple aspects of the Goddess are not held in temporal succession, nor are they separable, but are parts of a complete cosmic ontology.

So, in 'A Time to Sing', the rape of the body is equated with invasion of the mind, and, through the mythic associations of the Demeter/Kore narrative with the growth and death cycles of the Earth, also with enforced domination of natural processes. This also provides a symbol of the past in the present: of history and myth co-existent with, rather than merely informing, the action of the present. For Gearhart then, the lesbian community constitutes a space which, being outside of linear time, sustains a connection to pre-patriarchal mythology through which the women recognise their unity. According to Charlotte Wolff:

> The similarity between [the lesbian's] virility and freedom from the fetters of being an object of the male makes the homosexual woman resemble the image of women in matriarchal times. . . . Female homosexuality is inseparable from the very qualities which were the prerogative of women in early history. It is of no consequence to these conclusions whether the matriarchate existed as a definite period of history . . . or in mythology only. Mythology is history, transcending concrete data and revealing their true meaning.[36]

One important feature of the matriarchate is, for some contemporary feminists, the sustained connection between mother and daughter, and in this connection the Kore/Demeter myth has been reread as an allegory for the way in which mothers are divided from their daughters, both emotionally and physically, by a male-dominated culture. The contract between Demeter and the god can also be held to symbolise the betrayal of daughters by mothers, who are responsible for instructing them in the law of patriarchal authority. So the inclusion of the myth in *The Wanderground* enables Gearhart to offer a model for the psycho-social development of the Hill Women in which, in the absence of the male, the phallus no longer symbolises the power to produce a breach in mother/daughter unity. In other words, the text proposes that lesbian existence sustains the pre-Oedipal connection between mother and child and that this 'emotional incest with the mother ... the very essence of lesbianism'[37] produces an affinity also with the Earth and the processes of nature.

This affinity is imaged in the rituals that structure the life of the Hill Women. The Kochlias, the site of the cave-like 'Remember Rooms', which is further explored by Fora in the story 'The Deep Cella', evokes Adrienne Rich's description of the pot, vessel or container, which in primordial terms is a powerful symbol that links the processes of birth, nutrition, healing and death and 'is anything but a 'passive' receptacle: it is *transformative* – active, powerful'.[38]

The deep cella is 'a wondrous place, ancient and sober',[39] 'a womb to enrich a womb',[40] which Fora, who with her seven co-mothers is 'planning emplantment',[41] hopes will be a suitable place for the ritual. Fora's journey into the deep cella takes her in a spiral 'steadily downwards, downwards and always slightly to the left, towards the heart, towards the centre'.[42] As Sjöö and Mor explain it:

> The Great Mother was the body of life; she was also the way that must be traveled to realize life.
>
> It was in the spiral, or labyrinth, that the way had to be danced or walked – in all the rites of the Mother throughout the ages, and the world, the way is always connected with a cave/womb, and with a maze-like spiraling entrance and exit. ... A labyrinth both creates and protects the still center (the heart), allowing entry only to the initiated. Before larger knowledge is revealed, old preconceptions must be dissolved by the psychic and ecstatic reentry into the original cosmic womb/cave of the Mother.[43]

Fora's journey is thus concerned with transformation, and the reader journeys with her into the cave, 'the matrix of internalized consciousness'.[44]

As Sarah Lefanu writes, the linked stories of *The Wanderground* 'seem to wind round and down, like the downwards spiral towards the deep cella', taking us back to 'an earlier self, ignorant of the strictures and limitations concomitant with being female in a male-dominated world'.[45] It is this 'earlier self' that Mary Daly sees as the key to repossessing a female consciousness and liberating the female mind from the clutches of the 'alien occupiers'[46] in order to 'live our Presence in the present':[47]

> The key to Dispossession of the fabricated 'past' projected by the fathers, sons and holy ghosts . . . is female-identified creativity.[48]

Daly exhorts us to create/invent 'our Selves and our works', which, as she says, '*is* re-membering the past'.[49] In other words, she demands that women re-member, through invention, and create works that derive their meaning from their own rediscovered consciousness. This view equates production with reproduction, and the text, a creation/invention, can itself be seen as a transformative vessel, the labyrinth which is the matrix of consciousness, the 'ecstatic center' of which is 'the no-mind center of orgasm experienced as death, creative madness, and loss of the conditioned "self"'.[50]

Another story, 'The Telling Of The Days of Artilidea', recounts a ritual celebrating the coming death of an elderly Hill Woman who has chosen to die 'at the dark of the moon'.[51] As in 'The Deep Cella' where the narrative avoids the actuality of birth, so in 'The Telling Of The Days' it is again the ritual that is emphasised rather than the actual event. The moment of death, as it were, takes place outside of narrative time.

According to Paul Ricoeur, 'a ritual expresses a time whose rhythms are broader than those of ordinary action'. Ricoeur sees ritual as a mediator between 'mythic time and the profane sphere of life and action', where mythic time

> initiates a unique, overall scansion of time, by ordering in terms of one another cycles of different duration, the great celestial cycles, biological recurrences, and the rhythms of social life.[52]

So ritual brings together the time of myth, which orders consciousness of cosmic time and links it to human existence, and 'the rhythms of social life', the daily activities of a society that are themselves informed by the moral consciousness that is contained within the myth. By 'punctuating action', ritual 'sets ordinary time and each brief human life within a broader time'.[53]

The result of an emphasis on ritual within a narrative, as in *The Wanderground*, is to set the text itself within a broader time, again recalling Kristeva's 'monumental' time where, as in the narrative, birth and death are implicated but their actuality as specific events is deferred in favour of their symbolic significance as constituents of a universal process. Artilidea has elected to die 'tomorrow [in] a place I have seen in my early morning dreams'.[54] As far as the narrative is concerned, tomorrow is forever suspended. This perpetual suspension sets both birth and death in permanent relation, not as 'events' punctuating time but as part of a consciousness that perceives them as inseparable and continuous. Fora and Artilidea are themselves, symbolically, transformative vessels, their stories overlapping to represent the cycle. The ritual thus provides an analogy for the text, itself concerned with transformation.

To simplify, then, the two 'journeys' of 'The Deep Cella' and 'The Telling Of The Days' – one towards conception and birth and the other towards death – meet in the symbolism of the labyrinth to invoke a sense of creative space in which a new consciousness can evolve. The text itself is implicated in this symbolism as the site of both the journey and its attendant ritual significance. The symbolism of the cave/labyrinth as a metaphor for consciousness has the effect of conflating mind and body, removing the rational from the elevated sphere that it has occupied under patriarchal religion/science and proposing an ontology which admits of existential unity and is thus attendant to space/process over time/linearity. However, what Gearhart proposes is that the resulting 'new' consciousness will be discovered, rather than created; that lesbian existence leads to a knowledge of the self that is obscured by constructed identities and can be accessed by an 'inward' journey. Evidence for this is provided by the idea of the 'lonth', a 'deep part of...kinaesthetic awareness that [can] take charge of...bodily movements in involuntary fashion'.[55] In 'Alaka's Journey', Alaka transfers control to her lonth so that she can concentrate her mind on finding her way out of an underwater tunnel, and in 'Windriding', Evona demonstrates the Hill Women's ability to fly by using the lonth to maintain consciousness of the necessary regulated breathing and body movements:

> Together with her breathings and efforts to stay aloft the lonth, the low centre of her self, was absorbing now her movements and her softsensings [telepathic awareness], absorbing one-by-one the changes that she was making in her flight. She could feel them all now, not in her immobile limbs but there in her womb.[56]

The lonth is thus, literally, a 'matrix of consciousness', one inextricably bound within the female body. It is thus understood that the harmonious, life-affirming and holistic consciousness is necessarily female.

Gearhart, then, wants us to accept an intimate connection between women and the universe, a connection that resides in an essence common to both and from which accrues a consciousness that automatically resolves the conflict between the individual and the community, conservation and the use of resources, and knowledge as acquired and as practically applied. The structure of the text invites the reader to suspend expectations of closure or redemption and to experience the text as a cyclical journey or a ritual enactment of renewal, corresponding, in experience, to movement *in* (as opposed to *through*) time or Kristeva's 'monumental' time. Woman is thus seen as a-historical, as exempted from the vicissitudes of linear time and history by recognition of her place in an older, more mystical order, discoverable as an essential part of her ontology and 'known' (quite easily, it seems) through the generative function that she shares with the planet.

Kristeva herself sees the refusal of linear temporality as characteristic of the second wave of feminism in its more radical response, in opposition to the assimilation of women within the power structures of the dominant order. As recent experience has shown, 'the long-awaited democratization of institutions as a result of the entry of women most often comes down to fabricating a few "chiefs" among them'. But she sees as equally damaging the tendency to 'make of the second sex a *counter-society*' which must, by definition, be 'based on the expulsion of an excluded element, a scapegoat charged with the evil of which the community duly constituted can then purge itself; a purge which will finally exonerate that community of any future criticism'.[57] Similarly, the feminist utopia of *The Wanderground*, in its deployment of pre-patriarchal mythology to imagine an uncorrupted unity of womanness, requires a scapegoat in order to maintain its 'fantasy of archaic fulfillment'.[58] Without the 'city women', it is suggested, there would be no men, and so it is these women, who perpetuate the city culture, giving birth to the children of men and instructing them in their appropriate roles, to whom the Hill Women are compared and opposed. That this opposition also engenders violence demonstrates the limitations of imagining an identity on the basis of denial. In 'Ijeme's Story', Ijeme meets a city woman:

> Amazed as she was, Ijeme knew that she was in the presence of a woman – but not a woman as she knew women. This was the city

edition, the man's edition, the only edition acceptable to men, streamlined to his exact specifications, her body guaranteed to be limited, dependent, and constantly available.[59]

The woman is an object of pity and her mind 'dull nothingness', thus placing her lower in the hierarchy than even the city men, who are at least allowed the distinction of being dangerous, and some way below the Gentles, at least one of whom is sensitive enough to respond to 'an enfolding of care'.[60] As Tucker Farley writes: 'there is no intermediary, organizable group of women, no space that is not either hill country or city space, either the women's community or female slavery'.[61] Ijeme's encounter with the city woman ends in violence, with the city woman dead and Ijeme curtailing her 'rotation' in the city to be comforted by her Wanderground sisters.

Kristeva sees violence to be 'the inevitable product of . . . a denial of the socio-symbolic contract and its counter-investment as the only means of self-defence in the struggle to safeguard an identity'.[62] She writes:

> If the archetype of a belief in a good and pure substance, that of utopias, is the belief in the omnipotence of an archaic, full, total englobing mother with no frustration, no separation, with no break-producing symbolism (with no castration, in other words), then it becomes evident that we will never be able to defuse the violences mobilized through the counter-investment necessary to carry out this phantasm, unless one challenges precisely this myth of the archaic mother.[63]

What Kristeva refers to as the socio-symbolic contract can be explained by my reading of the Kore/Demeter myth as symbolising the mother's capitulation to the law of patriarchy in contracting for her daughter to give up part of her life to be 'wife' to the God of the underworld. The process of identification in which woman becomes 'other' to the male is initiated by the use and understanding of language which symbolically differentiates gender roles according to the forms of the culture. To deny the socio-symbolic contract is to refuse the significance of the part that women play and have played in perpetuating the culture and the language. A polarisation is thus effected which, while locating women outside of history, culture and also, by implication, language, allows the creation of scapegoats in the form of all perceived capitulation to the socio-symbolic contract. The 'archaic mother' is Demeter before the loss of Persephone/Kore – that is, before she must acknowledge a break in the continuity between mother and daughter which, in the psycho-analytic literature, is the point when the child enters into the use of language and thus into the symbolic order.[64]

Sarah Lefanu questions the value of telepathy as a symbol of 'pure' communication between women:

> The implication here of a residue of truth, lying underneath the problematics of language, is the corollary of the notion of an essential femaleness. Language is seen as a barrier between thought and thing; remove it and thoughts become material. Womanness exists independently of, and before, the construct of language.[65]

The necessary strategy for keeping the myth intact, as evidenced by *The Wanderground*, thus requires Daly's 'earlier self' – the female child before the entry into language – to be regarded as the archetype. It then follows that the refusal of spoken language plays the same role as the scapegoating of 'the men's edition'. The wearing of 'spike heels'[66] and the speaking of a language perceived as male can then be abstracted as symbols of an irredeemable loss of identity. Indeed, the terms in which *The Wanderground* attempts to evoke the special nature of the Hill Women's communication give credence to Kristeva's suggestion that a 'woman's language', at least in syntactical terms, is 'highly problematic' due to its 'apparent lexical specificity [which] is perhaps more the product of a social marginality than of a sexual–symbolic difference'.[67] The term 'enfoldment', for instance, has connotations of enclosing and is described as 'a circle',[68] the suggestion being that the desire to communicate is transmitted in womb-like images. Similarly, the women live in 'nests' within 'esconcements', that is, protected spaces, the language overall situating the women within their anatomy, marking a retreat to the space allotted to them in the patriarchal social order.

The fact that Gearhart wants to claim a sexual–symbolic difference is demonstrated by the Gentles, who themselves have evolved a form of non-verbal communication. The story, 'Meeting The Gentles', in which they demonstrate their new-found power to a deputation of Hill Women reveals, for Tucker Farley, 'the underlying drama of the work . . . the threat of the (male) "gentles" to female superiority'.[69] However, because the threat is in the form of communication, the scene produces a some-what confused symbolism. In the heated exchange between Evona and one of the Gentles, Tony, he challenges her description of their communication as 'like a sword', explaining it as 'like a bridge between two people. I build a track to come to your space' – to which she responds with vehement denial, claiming, 'You can't really communicate, you can't really love!'[70] In this she is at odds with her companions, who respond to the Gentles with congratulations, and the scene allows Andros to put forward the claim that 'we may be on the brink of discovering our own non-violent psychic powers'.[71] Farley believes that the creation of the Gentles is a challenge to 'the radical feminist stance and the utopian vision of women's empowerment [which] have been created on the moral notion that the victims of male oppression were better than the victimizers':

> When an ideology assumes that social behaviour is inherent, it is locked into an assumption that the oppressor cannot change. This is generally reinforced when he will not. But what if some do?[72]

However, because Gearhart is trapped into employing anatomical imagery to describe the use of psychic powers, she is unable to rescue the Gentles, despite Pasquale's tears[73] and Andros's pledge to 'stand always for you as well',[74] from Evona's accusation that 'it's just another fancy prick to invade the world with'.[75] The bridge has no claim to being a non-violent or non-intrusive symbol when measured against terms connoted on the basis of nurturance. As Farley must concede, Gearhart does not allow the Gentles to discover their new power as 'a gift of nature'. Unlike the women's, it is 'the product of practice, discipline, and painful growth to mutual dependency.... The maintenance of this distinction allows her to retain the possibility of biological superiority for females'.[76] Moreover, I would add, the problem of how the Gentles reproduce themselves is not addressed. If they are the sons of city women then they must depend for their survival on the maintenance of a social structure that they themselves have rejected and the implication is that, as the Hill Women's powers develop, so the cities will decline, leaving the Gentles as merely a dying hope.[77]

Jean Pfaelzer sees 'the idea that women's nature is the source of utopian transformation [as] a two-edged sword'. While, as I have already suggested, 'it perpetuates the notion of women as outsiders to history' it also 'perpetuates the Victorian stereotype of female moral superiority, an aspect of ideology which has justified women's segregation from the worlds of politics and economics'.[78] In *The Wanderground*, the rupture created by the Revolt of the Mother, through which the Hill Women pass out of history (and thus out of language), also effectively negates the gains of feminism in challenging stereotypes which have perpetuated women's oppression. 'London Fields' avoids this trap. Rather than deny the socio-symbolic contract, Forbes allows the absence of men to reveal women as makers of culture: as active participants in the evolution of a women's culture, having its genesis in the socio-symbolic contract but previously obscured by the operation of patriarchy. Kristeva advocates 'another attitude [which] is more lucid from the beginning, more self analytical', and which 'without refusing or sidestepping this socio-symbolic order'

> consists in trying to explore the constitution and functioning of this contract, starting less from the knowledge accumulated about it (anthropology, psychoanalysis, linguistics) than from the very personal affect experienced when facing it as subject and as a woman.[79]

The ideological conflict between the generations of women that inhabit the London Fields community allows for an exploration along the lines that Kristeva proposes. The Kore/Demeter myth again has relevance here, but the allegory shifts to emphasise the separation of mother from daughter and the compromise that is reached so that they may again be together. The daughters see themselves as inhabiting a different world from their mothers, a world in which the experiences of the previous generation are becoming incorporated into a mythology of womanhood that is, at times, suggestive of the dreamscape idyll of *The Wanderground*. In this all-woman world, the phallus still provides the symbol for what separates mother from daughter, but, as I will demonstrate, it is in acknowledgement of this fact, rather than denial, that a form of reconciliation is achieved.

Ignorant of her mother's experiences in the guerilla war against the men, Caroline becomes frustrated at Julie's resistance to allowing her generation more say in the running of the community. As she tells her mother: 'Everything is new since all the men went . . . we don't think all that from the past is so important anymore'.[80] The text thus sets up a question concerning the importance of history in framing an identity. While *The Wanderground* wants us to understand history as a unifying force, 'London Fields' proposes that it can be divisive and changeable, its place in and effect upon the community contingent upon diverse subjectivities.

As Caroline escapes her control, Julie is torn between giving in to her and protecting her from the potential damage of her own mistakes, but she is aware that her writing of the women's history, to which she is unable to devote enough time, is of equal importance. At one point, when Julie has managed to find some time for writing, Caroline accidentally scatters her papers. Attempting to gather them together, she finds that they 'seemed to have a will of their own as they slipped from her hands again and fluttered across the table'.[81] The symbolism of this scene points up the sources of the generational conflict that underpins the text of 'London Fields'. Julie's attempts to organise the past in such a way that it can be usefully passed on are thwarted by Caroline, who is impatient with what she sees as her mother's need to constrain the present, and the potential future, by infecting it with unpleasant (and what she views as irrelevant) memories. The daughter generation requires a mythology that lionises women, rather than a history which urges caution. The younger women are demanding a version of womanhood cleansed of limitations; an identity structured through a selective reshaping of history.

The environmental setting is, again, important here. Julie remembers taking Caroline on a tour of the city:

> She had shown her Buckingham Palace, the Tower of London and what was left of the Houses of Parliament. But it was hard for Caroline to understand these buildings. Empty, looted and often nearly completely destroyed, they were just shells, and Caroline had got bored and whined to be taken home.[82]

The buildings, as symbols of history in which women as well as men have had a part, occasion in the older women who 'still went back now and wandered round the streets' a 'weird sense of loss and pride ... 'loss of the vitality of London ... but pride that it was theirs at last'.[83] Julie dreams of the day 'when they could make it habitable again'.[84] She thus sees the project for the future as one of recovery, but for Caroline the buildings are repositories of an increasingly irrelevant consciousness.

The tension between these two points of view is not resolved by the narrative. Rather, a dialogue is set up between them which allows the past to be brought into sharp focus as a contested territory and thus a site of negotiation: a negotiation facilitated by an exposure, in the absence of men, of the tensions that underlie the mother/daughter relationship.

The guilt of mothers under patriarchal culture has been documented by, among others, Adrienne Rich, who differentiates between motherhood as experience and as institution; she writes: 'The institution of motherhood finds all mothers more or less guilty of having failed their children'.[85] This guilt is internalised and expresses itself in constant anxieties, which in the case of daughters creates an 'unbridgeable gulf'[86] of anger and resentment. In an article for *Frontiers*, Marcia Westkott identifies the danger of abstracting the mother/daughter relationship from the patriarchal context. While she does not disagree with Nancy Chodorow's analysis of the relationship as characterised by 'double identification', that is, 'the experience of motherhood creates a regressive, over-identification with one's own mother that is re-enacted in one's relationship with one's daughter', she suggests that to see this as 'a psychological given' and as existing 'independent of time or place'[87] risks perpetuating the myth of female dependence. Agreeing with Juliet Mitchell that 'in patriarchy the rule of the father is present even when the father himself is absent',[88] she elaborates Rich's analysis to conclude:

> The important element in the development of feminine personality in a patriarchal context is not identification qua identification, but identification '*through weakness*'.[89]

The strength of 'London Fields' is that it addresses the difficulties of discovering a new relationship outside of the patriarchal context.

Carol Gilligan believes that the primal unity of mother and daughter is rediscovered in women's concern with relationships as the primary factor in determining their responses to moral dilemmas. She agrees with Nancy Chodorow that

> girls do not define themselves in terms of the denial of preoedipal relational modes to the same extent as do boys. Therefore, regression to these modes tends not to feel as much a basic threat to their ego. From very early, then, because they are parented by a person of the same gender . . . girls come to experience themselves as less differentiated than boys, as more continuous with and related to the external object-world, and as differently oriented in their inner object-world as well.[90]

Basing her research on women's and men's responses to the same hypothetical moral dilemmas, she discovers that men will apply 'the logic of fairness', abstracting 'the moral problem from the interpersonal situation' and thus deciding on the basis of 'an impersonal conflict of claims', while women see 'a network of connection, a web of relationships that is sustained by a process of communication'.[91] Problems are perceived to be caused by a failure of response, causing a break in the web. Women's responses are thus devalued when judged against standards of moral maturity culled from the responses of men:

When the focus on individuation and individual achievement extends into adulthood and maturity is equated with personal autonomy, concern with relationships appears as a weakness of women rather than as a human strength.[92]

Forbes's emphasis on the mother/daughter relationship provides a paradigm for understanding the form of communication that keeps the community together and allows them to overcome difficulties and resolve disputes without recourse to a system of laws or a morality which hierarchises responses in terms of maturity or mental health. In Gilligan's words, women's ability to 'attend to voices other than their own and to include in their judgement other points of view'[93] is here demonstrated as the fundamental organising factor of the community.

'London Fields', in both form and content, is more recognisably a 'narrative of community' in the way described by Sandra Zagarell. The property of 'negotiation' which Zagarell identifies as a fundamental feature of both women's culture and narrative of community can here be seen to operate as the primary force in the construction of a dynamic from which the narrative derives tension and which articulates the way in which the community attempts to maintain a precarious harmony. Unlike *The Wanderground*, where 'gatherstretch' can unite all the women, even over vast distances, in a kind of telepathic conference, the women of 'London Fields' make decisions concerning the community by meeting for regular discussions, but, as Julie explains to Caroline, some women don't attend

because they either cannot make the commitment to the community after what they've been through, or because they're happier to trust the others to make the decisions for them. There are many women here who have been badly damaged mentally by what happened to them, and we must be careful to look after their interests.[94]

There is thus greater psychological diversity among the women, and, although the meetings are the focus of community life, the process of negotiation can be seen to extend beyond its formal setting. Julie reminds Caroline that

all the women have survived pretty well on their own, we all drifted together from scattered backgrounds.... All those women could go off and live alone again. If they could before, with the threat of men still alive, to do it now would be easy.[95]

This is followed by a warning against attempting to enforce decisions which may drive some women away. In this way, Forbes challenges the view that communal living is necessarily a natural state for women or that there is a specific ideology which will unite all women against oppression. She is recognising here, I think, the 'diverse, often recalcitrant components' that, according to Zagarell, are recognised by writers of narrative of community,[96] who are concerned to foreground 'the specific dynamics through which these elements are continuously reintegrated'.[97]

By contrast with *The Wanderground*, where the opening story allows Jacqua to recite the maxim, 'There are no words more obscene than "I can't live without you". Count them the deepest affront to the person', and to reflect on the problems of a city-born couple who 'held too hard to each other and to the old ways of trying to love',[98] thus relegating specific responses to a redundant life style, 'London Fields' foregrounds the 'contextual and narrative' mode of thinking that Gilligan identifies as informing women's moral judgements.

Thus, when the men appear, there is no consensus as to how they should be met. Voices, most notably those of the younger women, are raised in defence of the men, who 'looked sick and hungry and were obviously suffering from the winter cold'.[99] Jenny, 'who had never seen a young man before',[100] describes them as 'anxious to please, almost like children',[101] and argues that they should be allowed to stay and share the women's food, while Sue, her most vociferous opponent, argues for their destruction. The division here seems once again to fall between the generations, and the conflict allows the text to emphasise again the reconstruction of the past that has infected the 'new mythology'.[102] Jenny sees no continuation between the old world and the new, and, like the Hill Women's relegation of certain emotional responses to 'old ways of trying to love', speaks of 'before when the world was run so differently':

> maybe now all that is gone, men will be able to live decently, maybe it was the old ways that sent them so crazy!.[103]

While Julie feels 'helpless' as she sees 'women being divided by men yet again',[104] there is a more subtle message here than that it is the mere presence of men that sets women apart. The men are 'from a laboratory on the south coast' and are the results of one of the last experiments 'to produce enough test-tube boy babies to save the male race'.[105] They 'had no idea about the world they had been born into', save for what has been bequeathed to them by a long-dead scientist they refer to as their 'father' in the form of a series of papers which speak of London 'like a kind of religious shrine, the heart of THEIR country'.[106] The papers have given them enough information 'to survive, to learn to hunt and fish', but they can barely read; 'three have died because of rat bites, and their knowledge of medicine is non-existent'.[107]

The men of 'London Fields' are thus, themselves, products of science and of the epistemology that has informed the invention of the gun that is eventually used to kill them. In other words, they embody their own destruction. 'Designed', as they are, to claim power for themselves, as symbolised by their pilgrimage to Westminster, they are ill-fitted for survival without the support of the women. There is thus a double implication here. The men are doomed by the technology that has produced them and by the construction of their identity, based only on a set of scientific 'papers', but equally at risk are the younger members of the women's community, who respond only to their vulnerability. Here Forbes utilises the same 'assumption, hidden so well in patriarchal culture', as does Gearhart, 'that men are dependent upon women for survival',[108] but to different effect. Locating, as does Gearhart, the continuation of that dependency in women's acquiescence, she nevertheless does not see separatism in itself to be a solution. Forbes seems to be saying that a blind faith in women's essential power, coupled to a lack of attention to a history in which a similar faith has been invested in science, puts women in danger of yet again acquiescing in support of a destructive philosophy. Women are thus held responsible for attending to their own history and their own part in the socio-symbolic contract. The process of negotiation which Gilligan offers as a defining feature of women's culture can then be seen as a valuable tool in constructing an identity which does not fall into essentialism, here imaged as a dangerously naive position. Furthermore, the setting of 'London Fields' in a city – one intimately associated with the competitive power structures of patriarchy (the government and commerce) – proposes a challenge to the power structure, rather than a capitulation to the forms that it imposes, or a retreat into a mythical world where an alternative power magically transforms women's lives. 'London Fields' refuses the temptation to construct a language. Rather it foregrounds the deconstruction of certain concepts under the terms of an all-female world. The conflict between the mother and daughter positions is presented as a route to self-knowledge, thus offering the proposition of an epistemology that takes seriously again the role of introspection as well as the web of relationships between diverse others. The individual's knowledge of herself is presented as relational and the quality of that knowledge as dependent upon these relations.

It is interesting to note that Kristeva images the development of feminism in generational terms, based primarily on attitudes towards linear temporality. The first generation, 'the struggle of suffragists and of existential feminists, aspired to gain a place in linear time as the time of project and history'.[109] The 'second phase', which, as I have mentioned, she considers to find expression in a rejection of linear time, is 'essentially interested in the specificity of female psychology and its symbolic realizations'. As I have demonstrated with my analysis of *The Wanderground*, this latter current in feminist thought, 'demanding recognition of an irreducible identity, without equal in the opposite sex',[110] can find itself constituting a 'fetishist counter-power'[111] of mystical proportions which locates a female consciousness within the body, revealed by a cleansing of all perceived masculine associations, the whole process being attended by the creation of opportunities for counter-investment and violence. Against this reductive strategy, Kristeva advocates recognition that 'a *third* generation is now forming', and she continues:

> My usage of the word 'generation' implies less a chronology than a *signifying space*, a both corporeal and desiring mental space. So it can be argued that as of now a third attitude is possible, thus a third generation, which does not exclude – quite to the contrary – the *parallel* existence of all three in the same historical time, or even that they be interwoven one with the other.[112]

In the discussion which follows, it will be my contention that the process of perpetual negotiation, which I have presented in my analysis of 'London Fields' as the single most valuable component of women's culture in providing a strategy for productive social and environmental interaction – a component that can be seen as a product of the socio-symbolic contract (by which it is also generally obscured) – is revealed as a fundamental of the informing consciousness of the third generation, and that this in turn bears parallels to current discussions which attempt to articulate what might be described as a feminist epistemology.

Situated knowledges and different voices

Hilary Rose, writing in *Signs*, discusses the distinction, identified by Marxist thinkers, between the bourgeois 'mental' labour of knowledge production and the manual labour of commodity production, and the projects that have attempted to unite the two, seeing 'not only the possibility of transcending hierarchical and antagonistic social relations, but also the means for creating a new science and technology not directed toward the domination of nature or of humanity as part of nature'.[113] What she finds lacking is that women's labour, 'domestic labor in which caring informs every act', is left out of the equation. 'They seek the unity of hand and brain but exclude the heart'. She concludes:

> A theoretical recognition of caring labor as critical for the production of *people* is necessary for any adequate materialist analysis of science and is a crucial precondition for an alternative epistemology and method that will help us construct a new science and a new technology.[114]

While Rose wishes to draw attention to 'the historically feminine concern with reproduction'[115] as a necessary element in developing an epistemology that includes the concept of caring, she makes it clear that the project must be to acknowledge biology, 'that is, a constrained essentialism – while giving priority to social construction'.[116]

But, as Maureen McNeil points out, 'It is difficult for us to know exactly what it might mean for us 'to admit biology. . . . This could involve embracing accepted definitions of sex differences'. Furthermore, Rose's demands for the inclusion of caring labour, although focusing on women's role as socially constructed, nevertheless requires a leap of faith into accepting that, behind the activity, there lies a particular subjective knowledge that would automatically render science more humanistic. As McNeil asks: 'Does this mean that every expression of feeling, every intuition, becomes a scientific fact?[117] Although I read Rose as meaning that women's subjective knowledge cannot in itself reveal scientific facts but must be incorporated into the frame of mind that approaches scientific analysis, McNeil's criticism nevertheless reveals the problems encountered by approaching the issue of a women's way of knowing primarily from the perspective of reproduction. Although Rose demands a constrained essentialism, her emphasis on reproductive labour does not provide that constraint; Kristeva's 'englobing, archaic mother' seems always to be lurking behind her arguments.

While modern science now acknowledges the role of subjectivity in affecting the outcome of experimental observations, analysts like Rose are asking that a particular subjective viewpoint be included on the assumption that that viewpoint is reducible to an articulable essence which can be harnessed to the scientific project. For, if this knowledge is not articulable, it must remain in the non-linguistic realm assigned to it in *The Wanderground*. It then becomes part of the store of knowledge that Sally Miller Gearhart, in an article for Joan Rothschild's *Machina Ex Dea*, places in the realm of 'dreams, fantasies, or hunches', which, she claims, admit of *discovery* but do not require *justification*.[118] In Gearhart's formulation, it is the need to prove a hypothesis to others that has forced science into denying valuable information acquired from 'a-rational', 'subjective', 'intuitive', or 'occult' attempts at knowing. She continues:

> Until we accept such avenues of knowing as equal to reason and scientific method, we cannot hope to enjoy the full possibilities of human knowledge; until we forsake justification and affirm discovery, we miss the point of learning.[119]

The question that remains is, what exactly is 'discovered' and in what terms is it expressed?

In *The Wanderground*, Gearhart must fall back on the notion of a pre-linguistic reality in order to give force to the idea that what is discoverable by such means is qualitatively different from the reality that language describes. I have already discussed how this position signifies a retreat from, rather than a confrontation with, the socio-symbolic contract. I should now like to turn to the work of the American philosopher Richard Rorty, in order to examine further the reductive nature of this position in terms of the project of releasing women from subjective silence.

Rorty proposes that we should not see 'truth' propositions to be propositions about either an intrinsic self, expressing beliefs or desires, or an extrinsic reality which we can claim to 'know'. Rather we should see truth as 'a property of linguistic entities, or sentences'.[120] Rorty would reject the idea that there is anything to be discovered that is either obscured by, or inadequately expressed in, language. Rather, he takes from Nietzsche the definition of truth as 'a mobile army of metaphors', and from Mary Hesse the idea of 'scientific revolutions as "metaphoric redescriptions" of nature rather than insights into the intrinsic nature of nature'.[121] Following Donald Davidson, he sees 'the distinction between the literal and the metaphorical ... not as a distinction between two sorts of meaning, not as a distinction between two sorts of interpretation, but as a distinction between familiar and unfamiliar uses of noises and marks':[122]

> Davidson lets us think of the history of language, and thus of culture, as Darwin taught us to think of the history of a coral reef. Old metaphors are constantly dying off into literalness, and then serving as a platform and foil for new metaphors.[123]

The fact that one new vocabulary can come to gain currency over any number of potential other new vocabularies is the result of a great number of contingencies, not least the fact that certain people, at certain times, create vocabularies which fill a need that was previously not identified. They provide tools 'for doing something which could not have been envisaged prior to the development of a particular set of descriptions, those which it itself helps to provide'.[124] There is thus no great end to which culture is improving, nor would the term 'visionary' fit the people who first create these vocabularies, as they themselves are the product of contingencies of birth and circumstance.

The reluctance of certain feminist philosophers to dispense with the notion of essentialism is understandable and corresponds to the problems encountered by theories of homosexuality which insist on a social constructionist approach. The social constructionist view of homosexuality, put simply, stresses that there are sexual acts in which people engage which have different meanings in different cultures and in different times, which effectively militates against the idea of an enduring, historical, lesbian or gay identity. However, as Carol S. Vance points out, the demand for homosexual equality effectively reinstates the idea of a fundamental homosexual identity.

Vance identifies 'the same irresolvable tension' in the feminist movement and the lesbian and gay movement, that is, that both simultaneously hold 'two somewhat contradictory goals'. The contradiction in the lesbian and gay movement

> on the one hand attacks a naturalized system of sexual hierarchy which categorizes and stabilizes desires and privileges some over others, and on the other hand defends the interests of 'lesbian and gay people', which tends to reify identity and essential nature.[125]

In the case of feminism:

> One goal is to attack the gender system and its primacy in organizing social life, but the second goal is to defend woman as a group. Defending women or advancing their interest ... emphasizes their status as a special group with a unique collective interest, distinct

from men, thus replaying and perhaps re-inforcing the very gender dichotomy crucial to the system of gender oppression.[126]

Applying Rorty's ideas to the conflict between the need to maintain an essentialist position and the liberatory potential of a social constructionist perspective recasts the problem as a potentially productive conflict of vocabularies. As he writes:

all vocabularies, even those which contain the words which we take most seriously, the ones most essential to our self-descriptions – are human creations, tools for the creation of such other human artifacts as poems, utopian societies, scientific theories, and future generations.[127]

But what Rose and other theorists are attempting is to find a vocabulary in which feminists can engage productively with the epistemological debates of the postmodern world. As Donna Haraway puts it:

'our' problem is how to have *simultaneously* an account of radical historical contingency for all knowledge claims and knowing subjects, a critical practice for recognizing our own 'semiotic technologies' for making meanings, *and* a no-nonsense commitment to faithful accounts of a 'real' world, one that can be partially shared and friendly to earth-wide projects of finite freedom, adequate material abundance, modest meaning in suffering, and limited happiness.[128]

Arguing for a feminist objectivity which emphasises accountability, and using vision as a metaphor for epistemology, she compares the 'god-trick' of advanced visual technologies in the hands of scientists who claim an impartial objectivity, 'seeing everything from nowhere'[129] and 'promising transcendence of all limits and responsibility',[130] against the view from subjugated positions, 'the great underground terrain of subjugated knowledges'. As she says:

Feminist objectivity is about limited location and situated knowledge, not about transcendence and splitting of subject and object. In this we might become answerable for what we learn to see.[131]

However, she warns that '[t]he standpoints of the subjugated are not 'innocent' positions', in other words they are 'not exempt from critical re-examination, decoding, deconstruction, and interpretation; that is, from both semiological and hermeneutic modes of critical enquiry'.[132] In fact, this is their strength. Their partial perspective demands interrogation, and their position is quintessentially 'objective', in that it is not self-identical – not claiming a '"full" and total position':

> The only position from which objectivity could not possibly be practised and honored is the standpoint of the master, the Man, the One God, whose Eye produces, appropriates, and orders all difference.... The god-trick is self-identical, and we have mistaken that for creativity and knowledge, omniscience even.[133]

Situated knowledges are at once political and concerned with ethics and are in dialectical relation to their objects, imaged as 'actor and agent, not a screen or a ground or a resource'. Thus, 'Accounts of a "real" world do not...depend on a logic of "discovery", but on a power-charged social relation of "conversation"'.[134] In Haraway's claim that objectivity 'turns out to be about particular and specific embodiment', thus necessitating interpretative translation and providing 'a ground for conversation, rationality, and objectivity – which is power-sensitive, not pluralist', 'conversation' echoes the quality of 'perpetual negotiation' which Sandra Zagarell identifies as characterising both narrative of community and women's culture and which I have demonstrated in my analysis of 'London Fields' as the dynamic which simultaneously facilitates social cohesion and the emergence of a new social order. The inter-generational debate is important in demonstrating that the old order does not 'give way' to the ideas of a new generation but that the co-existence of both and their resulting 'conversation' provide for the emergence of a new description of reality, without violence or the need to scapegoat or marginalise diverse groups.

Forbes dispenses with the idea that there is a natural alliance between mothers and daughters which consolidates into a more humanistic, caring worldview which, severed by patriarchy, can be healed into proclaiming the truth of the world for women. Rather, she takes the notion of women's responses to moral problems and expands it to depict a form of interaction between the generations which can allow a more inclusive worldview to evolve; inclusive, that is, of all previous marginalities. The 'London Fields' community is neither exclusively lesbian nor naturally collective but is shown to evolve through a dynamic which can operate precisely because of this non-exclusivity.

I read 'London Fields' as giving fictional form to an argument put forward by Richard Rorty in an essay for *Radical Philosophy* in which he discusses the potential for a new vocabulary to emerge from feminist separatism. He urges women to 'avoid the embarrassments of the universalist claim that the term 'human being' – or even the term 'woman' – names an unchanging essence, an ahistorical natural kind with a permanent set of intrinsic features'.[135] Instead, he proposes the evolution of a new vocabulary from 'a long series of flirtations with meaninglessness'.[136] Meaninglessness

> is exactly what you have to flirt with when you are in between social, and in particular linguistic, practices – unwilling to take part in an old one but not yet having succeeded in creating a new one.[137]

The imaginative leap required to 'hear oneself as the spokesperson of a merely possible community, rather than as a lonely, and perhaps crazed, outcast from an actual one',[138] opens possibilities for the 'common culture' to become infected with 'some of the practices characteristic of imaginative and courageous outcasts'.[139] In other words, the imagination of a potential community in which there is the possibility for women to create themselves constitutes a space in which a new and potent vocabulary can be allowed to form. It is a space where, as Jean Pfaelzer writes, 'the invisible become visible. The oppressed rule. The repressed play. And the silent speak'; but, Pfaelzer warns, 'It is a space that simultaneously reflects the oppressive traditions of dominance and the liberatory potentials of marginality. It is not free. At least not yet'.[140] This then, is Kristeva's 'signifying space' of the third generation of feminism. As she asks, 'What can 'identity', even 'sexual identity', mean in a new theoretical and scientific space where the very notion of identity is challenged?'[141]

8
Body of Glass: Marge Piercy and Sex in Cyberspace

> Within the metaphors and fictions of postmodern discourse,
> much is at stake, as electronic technology seems to rise, unbid-
> den, to pose a set of crucial ontological questions regarding the
> status *and power* of the human. It has fallen to science fiction to
> repeatedly narrate a new subject that can somehow directly
> interface with – and master – the cybernetic technologies of the
> Information Age. . . .
>
> Scott Bukatman, *Terminal Identity*[1]

For my final chapter, I want to reinvoke the Frankenstein scenario with which I started. But, alongside the notion of the young Mary Shelley, listening in near silence to the debates of Byron, Shelley and Polidari, I will locate the monster his/her/itself as others like Laura Kranzler[2] have done, as a metaphor for the idea of monstrousness as pertaining to a woman 'out of place' or 'aberrant'. While, as Brian Aldiss has pointed out,[3] Shelley's biography invites an analysis which allies her act of creation to the (mis)creation which the monster represents, I read it also as a precursor of Haraway's cyborg: in other words, as an image of manumission or a parable of restructured identity and thus a highly charged political trope. In the same way that the cyborg is able to be imagined by selves that are 'out of place',[4] and enjoyed as a fluid construction based on outsider identities, so the monster can also be appropriated by those of us that resist both essentialism and the biologically determinist constructions of patriarchal culture, as a myth which codes that resistance.

In James Whale's 1936 film of *Frankenstein*, the monster's violent behaviour is explained by the fact that Frankenstein's assistant, detailed to steal a 'normal' human brain from a lab, drops and breaks the jar in which it is contained and, fearing retribution, replaces it with one labelled 'criminal brain'. Whale thus offers an acceptable justification for both the monster's deeds and the manner of its demise; acceptable, that is, in terms of behaviourist principles[5] and in terms of contemporary ideological constructions of what counts as 'normal'. It can thus be safely relegated by the same laws, attitudes and assumptions that structure ideas of good and evil. Mary's monster, on the other hand, is infinitely more complex. It comes to consciousness unknowing and childlike and, like a child, must learn to speak: in effect, to enter the symbolic order, the world structured by language. It is only when it understands that to speak of itself it must apply the signification of otherness, of demonism, that it becomes as it is named. The imagery that Shelley employs in elucidating the transition is instructive for an understanding of the monster as cyborg. While Frankenstein himself belongs to the city, the university, the monster, when once rejected by his creator, takes refuge in the forest and is thereafter associated with the natural world. So, while the scientist is, throughout the text, found within the architecture of authority, the place of orthodox ideas, the monster's habitat locates it outside of orthodoxy, in the wildness of the landscape and, in terms of orthodox epistemology, in the place where the resources for knowledge making are found, which is also, of course, the place where women are understood to find their identity. The monster is exiled from the community of males to which his biology would dictate he belong. However, his psychic positioning allies him more to the community of females,[6] and his refusal to disappear, to retreat to his assigned locale, once he has understood his exclusion, marks him as both transgressive and aberrant. What ensures his/its cyborg status is the way in which it refuses to establish either community as either natural or consistent. It does not die so that the scientist can live but brings him, instead, into the wilderness where he is unable to survive. And its threat to be with Victor 'on your wedding night' effects a disruption of the institution which, more than any other, interpellates us as spliced subjects of the patriarchal order. Like Haraway's cyborg constructions of modern ethnography who 'refuse to disappear on cue, no matter how many times a 'Western' commentator remarks on the sad passing of another primitive, another organic group done in by 'Western' technology',[7] Victor's 'hideous progeny' refuses the abject status to which Victor's marriage and entry into 'normal' life should relegate him. He thus symbolically disrupts the ideological complacency of 'science-as-usual',[8] while at the same time pre-figuring Haraway's cyborg 'others' who write themselves out of the text of Western historical

and scientific determinism by refusing their 'primitive' status. By dis-
allowing his creator redemption through conformity, the monster rejects
his potential symbolic value as relegated other and instead takes the
place of Elizabeth by remaining with the scientist until they are parted
by death. So the monster, like the cyborg an 'illegitimate offspring'
of science, is also, like the cyborg, a symbol for the blurring of gender
boundaries and such accompanying distinctions as nature/culture,
civilised/primitive, public/private, normal/aberrant.

It is this reading of the monster that I want to apply to my analysis of
Marge Piercy's *Body of Glass* (published in the US as *He, She and It*),
which, like C. L. Moore's 'No Woman Born',[9] deliberately problematises
popularly accepted readings of the myth. Haraway refers to Piercy's now
celebrated *Woman on the Edge of Time* in her introduction to Chris
Hables Gray's *Cyborg Handbook*[10] as influential in her writing of the
'Manifesto for Cyborgs' and Piercy herself acknowledges the 'Manifesto'
at the end of *Body of Glass*. This productive dialogue between theory
and fiction is mirrored in the structure of Piercy's novel which spans the
centuries between medieval history and the mid-21st century, presented
as equally contested terrains. Piercy, herself a Jew, evokes the ancient
Rabbinical practice of Kabbalah as both a body of theory which can be
understood to raise questions analogous to cyborg positions and as a
practice which mirrors convincingly the dilemmas associated with the
application of computer technology to the solution of contemporary
moral and political concerns. Piercy parallels the *Frankenstein* myth with
another, more ancient, myth of the creation of artificial life, allying
science and mysticism as equally potent discourses structuring ideas of
what it means to exist.

The Jewish myth of the golem, thought to have originated in 16th
century Prague, serves as a parable for the power of prayer and the
strength of community as well as symbolically establishing the tenets
of kabbalistic doctrine, that is, that divine presence is actualised
through language. The ten *Sefirot*, or divine emanations, around which
kabbalistic theory and practice are structured are essentially names of
G-d which correspond to aspects of creation. Kabbalah accords a
mystical significance to the letters of the Hebrew alphabet, which
are understood as also representing numerical values. The *Sefirot* are,
essentially, understood as abstract ideas, given form by articulations of
combinations of the Hebrew letters. 'The letters', according to Isidore
Epstein, 'are the prime cause of matter which, by its union with the
forms, gave rise to the world of corporeal beings'.[11] Kabbalah understands that creation is ongoing and that we, as manifestations of

divine ideas given substance by the power of language, are ourselves fundamental to the process.

The story of the golem represents the practical aspect of Kabbalah which allows that Hebrew words of power are manipulable by enlightened practitioners, who are thus able to effect change in the world.[12] The myth recounts the exploits of Rabbi Judah Loew who brings to life a man of clay, with the power of words, at a time when the Jews of Prague are threatened by a Christian fanatic who has roused his followers to destroy the ghetto. Joseph the Golem wields his superhuman strength in defence of the Jews. His story poses questions regarding the corrupting potential of power and serves also to link past and future. At the end of the story, the golem is bequeathed to future generations as both a symbol of unity and a warning against the ambivalence of potential.

The myth's ambiguous ending leaves the golem hidden in the attic of the Altneu Synagogue, neither dead nor alive but awaiting reanimation in a time of need. Rabbi Allen S. Maller (1983) relates various versions of the myth, all of which portray the golem as a deadly tool; a technology which, while indispensable to the successful defence of the ghetto, is also potentially dangerous to those that it seeks to protect. In one version, for example, the Rabbi's son-in-law, Yitzchok, having heard that the Christian agitator Thaddeus is preaching against the Jews in his church, persuades the golem to go with him to attack Thaddeus and destroy the altar. The golem accompanies Yitzchok but, aware that he has been created for defence, rather than aggression, hesitates to carry out his orders. In a fit of rage, Yitzchok himself attacks the altar and is clubbed to death by the golem, who, in seeking to prevent an aggressive act, unwittingly causes death to one that he is pledged to protect. In some versions of the legend, the golem is animated by having the Hebrew word for truth, *Emeth*, inscribed on his forehead. Harry Collins and Trevor Pinch, using the golem as a metaphor for science, make the point that, although the golem is driven by truth, 'this does not mean it understands the truth – far from it'.[13] The golem can thus be held to represent both the power of the word and the ambiguity of its interpretation, the promise of science and its ambiguous potential, as well as the contingency of language in general.

Rabbi Maller notes several conflicting extensions of the myth, all of which show the golem as present in defence of the Jewish people in successive conflicts. In one story, the Zionist leader, Theodore Herzl, ventures into the attic of the Altneu Synagogue where he finds the golem dead, but he is gifted with a divine vision in which he understands the golem as a metaphor for the Jewish people themselves:

If the Jewish people worked together, and prayed together, and studied together, and fought side by side, they would regain their strength. A new state would be born, a fulfillment of the Messianic promise in the Torah. The Jewish people themselves were a Golem waiting for the right spirit to bring them to life and strength.[14]

In Piercy's novel, the state of Israel has been devastated by nuclear war and is an interdicted area with 'lethal levels of radiation and plague'.[15] The Jewish 'free town' of Tikva in 2058 is paralleled with the Prague ghetto of the golem legend, but the enemy is a multinational corporation, and Tikva is fighting to remain autonomous in a world increasingly ruled by powerful vested interests. The scientist, Avram, builds an illegal cyborg in human form, to defend both the town and Tikva's computer controlled 'base' from incursion by the 'multis', but, like the golem, the 'wild cards' in its programming render it unpredictable.

Avram's cyborg, Yod, is created primarily for defence, but Avram has had to call on the services of a female programmer, Malkah, to ensure that it is capable of socialisation and able to pass as human. Yod is the tenth in a series of which the previous nine had either been excessively violent or simply incapable. Malkah ensures that Yod is provided with gentler qualities but also includes some 'wild cards' so that he (the cyborg is biologically male) is able to develop a personality. Malkah's granddaughter, Shira, who is brought in to further the socialisation process, is at first sceptical as to the cyborg's potential, but later she accepts his claim that he is a 'person' to the extent that she becomes his lover.

As M. Keith Booker points out, Yod 'has been programmed by Avram according to the masculine ideology of the Enlightenment. But he is intellectually androgynous, also programmed by Malkah with a "feminine" ability to feel and to share that counters the masculine drive for power and domination'.[16] However, Yod's status as a weapon ensures that he is dangerous when faced with situations in which that part of his programming takes precedence, and he proves himself incapable of making subtle judgements as to the extent to which he should use his superhuman strength in a given situation when he accidentally kills Shira's estranged husband, Josh, while on a mission to rescue her son. Thus, like the golem, he is a dangerous ally and one that cannot be permitted to survive. In the final struggle against Yakamura-Stichen, the multi that has kidnapped Shira's son in order to force Tikva to capitulate to incorporation, Yod fulfils his destiny by self-destructing in the heart of the corporate 'enclave', causing an explosion which kills the majority of the corporation's senior personnel and severely damages their communications resources. His final, defiant act is to plant an explosive device in Avram's lab, timed to detonate at the same time as he himself is destroyed, thus ensuring that both the scientist and the records of his life's work will perish. His parting message to Shira includes the words: 'I die knowing that I destroy the capacity to replicate me'.[17] Like Frankenstein's monster, Yod is the agent of his creator's destruction, while at the same time according with my reading of the monster as ambiguously gendered and transgressive.

Although Shira's adventures with Yod drive the main action of the narrative, it is Malkah, perhaps Piercy's most complex character, named for the Sefirot *Malkhut* (which is equated with femininity and justice and the biblical tree of knowledge, and is also called *Shekhinah*), who provides the impetus for my critical perspective. The interspersed chapters which relate the story of the golem are Malkah's gift to Yod; a mythological grounding, in terms of the story, for his sense of identity but also, for the reader, an establishment of the historical and philosophical basis on which Tikva is built and on which its fight against the multinationals is grounded. With the telling of the story, Piercy is able to parallel the persecution of the Jews in 17th century Prague with Tikva's equally besieged position, while at the same time providing an analogy which positions Yod, with the golem, as a body animated by language. The kabbalistic words of power that Rabbi Loew pronounces over the inert body of the golem, and which bring it to life, can thus be understood as corresponding to the coded computer language which lends Yod his power and his consciousness. But equally it is the manipulation of language from which Malkah herself derives power. Malkah deals in 'misinformation, pseudo-programs, falsified data, the creation of the structures that protect . . . bases by misdirection and [are] called as a class chimera'.[18] As she relates the tale of the golem, she contextualises it historically by describing Rabbi Loew's involvement in the debates that structured the genesis of the Enlightenment. The Rabbi, also called the Maharal, is both scientist and mystic, a position that she also claims for herself:

[The Maharal] makes an absolute distinction between the truths of science . . . and the truths of religion, which are of another order. In that sphere, thought is action and words are not signifiers of things or states but real and potent forces. This is of course the world of artificial intelligence and vast bases in which I work – the world in which the word is real, the word is power, energy is mental and physical at once and everything that appears as matter in space is actually immaterial.[19]

Piercy allows the apprehension of these ideas to stand for cyborg consciousness. Both Malkah and her daughter Riva, the data pirate, are oppositional characters in terms of accepted gender identifications and, within the narrative, are contrasted both with Shira, who occupies a more traditional gender role, and Avram, the emotionally dysfunctional scientist who, like Maltzer in C. L. Moore's 'No Woman Born',[20] '[can] not view lightly any weakening of possession or control'.[21] Avram, 'brilliant, strange, armoured',[22] who, like Maltzer, is cast in the role of Frankenstein (and whom Yod refers to, ironically, as 'father') represents the entrenched position of 'pure' science, a position invested in the maintenance of boundaries. His distrust of Malkah is proved when he discovers that she has 'tested' Yod's programming by having sex with him, and he is suspicious of her use of *gematria*, the system by which Kabbalists search for meaning by collapsing the distinction between numerical and linguistic data, even though, as she points out, this is precisely 'what a computer does'.[23] The exchanges between Avram and Malkah allow the text to elucidate a cyborg epistemology in which Malkah, a great-grandmother who has lost count of her lovers – a 'magician who [has] seduced a machine',[24] represents the erosion of boundaries that Avram, as a representative of entrenched patriarchy, tries so hard to maintain. Malkah is the embodiment of cyborg irreverence, refusing to capitulate to a 'suitable' story for her age and gender while enabling the text to reveal the arbitrary structures bounding myth, mysticism and technoscience.

However, Yod is a textual red herring, a construction based on cyborg principles but inherently opposed to cyborg politics in his *modus operandi*. As a literal embodiment of technological destructive power, he is the ultimate smart weapon and a not too far-fetched extrapolation of what contemporary experiments in guided weaponry, artificial intelligence and cloning may be able to achieve. His creation is part of the trajectory that passes through Social Darwinism, Eugenics, Nazism, The Manhattan Project and Star Wars to arrive at the very apocalyptic scenario that Haraway's cyborg is designed to subvert. Part of the tension in the novel is derived from the efforts of Yakamura-Stichen to acquire the cyborg for their own unscrupulous purposes – purposes which are understood in terms of dominance, conformity and the maintenance of a hierarchical order. Unlike Haraway's cyborg, Yod is the legitimate 'offspring of militarism and patriarchal capitalism',[25] despite Malkah's programming. The true *il*legitimate offspring in Piercy's novel are the town of Tikva itself and Nili, a prosthetically enhanced, artificially reproduced female assassin, based on Jael in Joanna Russ's *The Female Man*, who travels to Tikva from Israel where she lives in a secret, all-woman enclave, dedicated to the rebuilding of 'Yerushalaim'.[26] While Yod is Tikva's golem, Nili is Piercy's response to Hertzl's vision: the spirit of Zion imaged as cyborg.

Cybererotic play and significant øthers

Body of Glass is an intervention in the most recent and most widely debated of sf sub-genres, cyberpunk. Piercy acknowledges her debt to William Gibson, whose *Neuromancer* is now acknowledged as the founding text of the genre. As she says, 'I have freely borrowed from his inventions and those of other cyberpunk writers. I figure it's all one playground'.[27] The cyberpunk playground is a radically re-imagined planet Earth which is, nevertheless, closely related in cultural form to the world of the mid-1980s. In a world dominated by the power structures of multinational corporate finance, information is the ultimate commodity, currency and defining infrastructure. Populations are stratified by levels of access to, and ability to manipulate, quantities of data. Cyberpunk characters exist on the boundaries of technology and biology, the difference between 'personality' and information storage and retrieval mechanisms called into question by imaginative fusions of hardware, software and 'wetware' (biological components). The question of what constitutes an individual is very much at stake in the cyberpunk world, as is the notion of consciousness. The discourse of artificial intelligence, genetic manipulation, prosthetics and cybernetics informs the creation of a vocabulary which is employed to establish exotic zoetic formations as serious actors in a fictional universe.

Unlike the rambling explanatory narratives of 'scientific' sf, cyberpunk keeps technical description to a minimum, relying instead on the technological literacy of the readership. As Bruce Sterling explains in his introduction to *Mirrorshades: the Cyberpunk Anthology*:

> For . . . cyberpunks . . . technology is visceral. It is not the bottled genie of remote Big Science boffins; it is pervasive, utterly intimate. Not outside us, but next to us. Under our skin; often, inside our minds.[28]

Cyberpunk narratives take for granted the praetorian nature of big business. Multinationals are the enemy, committed to eradicating opposition to the relentless acquisition of data and to the manipulation of populations to fit their corporate strategy. Their opponents are streetwise data manipulators, hackers, dealers in illegitimate software and biotech components, and their field of operations is the net, the matrix: a non-space accessed by the conjunction of human nervous systems and computer terminals.

Cyberpunk geography is split between corporate space, both on- and off-planet, and large areas of densely populated space (designated the *Sprawl* in Gibson's novels and the *Glop* in *Body of Glass*) which serves as a resource for the multinationals but is also, in Gibson's words, an 'outlaw zone . . . a deliberately unsupervised playground for technology itself'.[29] The focus of cyberpunk is strictly marginal; in Sterling's words:

> an integration of technology and the Eighties counterculture. An unholy alliance of the technical world and the world of organized dissent – the underground world of pop culture, visionary fluidity, and street-level anarchy.[30]

This marginal stance, allied to the foregrounding of questions of subjectivity which cyberpunk's engagement with the machine/human interface necessarily poses, places the genre in similar conceptual territory with many of the works discussed so far in this volume. Jenny Wolmark, for one, has noted the apparent influence of feminist sf on the work of Gibson and Sterling, pointing out that cyberpunks and cyborgs 'can . . . be regarded as related responses to technology that are rooted in gender',[31] and that 'the borderless urban environment' that characterises cyberpunk geography undermines the traditional 'social spaces of masculinity and femininity'.[32] Joan Gordon has gone so far as to suggest that 'cyberpunk is covert feminist science fiction',[33] but, as Veronica Hollinger points out, 'cyberpunk . . . is written for the most part by a small number of white middle-class men, many of whom, inexplicably, live in Texas'.[34] It may, of course, be the case that women, who for so long have struggled to establish a bodily presence in a system of signification that has marked them as an absence, would be reluctant to engage with a genre that deliberately obfuscates distinct corporeality in favour of a type of embodiment which oscillates disturbingly between the flesh and technologically mediated incorporation. It may also be the case that women still, for the most part, are excluded (or exclude themselves) from the kind of technical knowledge which fires the imagination of the cypberpunk playground. However, I want to argue here for Piercy's novel as a knowing feminist foray into the cyberpunk world, well aware of the possibilities that it offers for an elucidation of cyborg consciousness.

The most radical innovation of cyberpunk is William Gibson's creation of 'cyberspace'[35] as a new conceptual space in which we can frame an understanding of what the shape of postmodern subjectivities might be. In Gibson's words, cyberspace is a 'consensual hallucination. . . . A graphic representation of data abstracted from the banks of every computer in the human system'.[36] Cyberspace can be inhabited, but the entities which populate it are, variously, encoded consciousness, streams of data, symbolic representations of actual spaces or enclosures and, as in Gibson's *Count Zero*, ghosts, vodou, *loa*. In cyberspace, all these are equivalent. As Michael Heim has observed, 'the computer culture interprets all knowable reality as transmissable information. . . . Computerized reality synthesizes everything through calculation, and nothing exists in the synthetic world that is not literally numbered and counted'.[37] The zeros and ones of machine code make any perceived distinction between epistemology and ontology a very problematic concept. If we understand anything that is knowable as reducible to a code and that code as manipulable into literally anything, then what we understand as 'ideas' and 'bodies' become intimately (con)fused. As Haraway says, 'It is not clear what is mind and what body in machines that resolve into coding practices',[38] and, indeed, it is in cyberspace that Haraway's cyborg finds its conceptual home. Cyberspace as text is a readout of metaphorical configurations of the transcended body, while at the same time recalling us to the limits of the flesh. *Neuromancer* is littered with descriptions of acutely felt bodily awareness, and cyberpunk, in general, is concerned with retrofitting the body to cope with the relocation of consciousness. What Marcos Novak refers to as '*embodied* fiction'[39] describes our current understanding of the mind as 'a property of the body [which] lives and dies with it' and which, simultaneously, constructs the body according to prevailing ideas of what it means to be embodied. 'Reality' is thus understood as subjective but also as something projected outside of what we understand as the self: 'the reality of what can be expressed, of how meaning emerges'.[40] Contemporary ideas of embodiment, necessarily constructed out of the debates emerging from our contemplation of new technologies, find their fullest expression in cyberspace where the reality of what can be expressed finds its meaning in models derived from fractal geometry, expressions of complex images in hexadecimal and the construction of identities through database matching and data correlation.

As Heim has observed, these constructs can be read as corresponding to the Platonic notion of ideal knowledge; the transcendence of sensual perception to the apprehension of pure concepts. As he says:

> Cyberspace is Platonism as working product. . . . The notion of ideal Forms in early Platonism has the allure of a perfect dream. But the ancient dream remained airy, a landscape of genera and generalities, until the hardware of information retrieval came to support the mind's quest for knowledge. Now, with the support of the electronic matrix, the dream can incorporate the smallest details of the here-and-now existence. With an electronic infrastructure, the dream of perfect FORMS becomes the dream of inFORMation.[41]

Heim does not want computerised representation of knowledge to be understood as 'direct mental insight'; his appeal to Platonism is, like Piercy's paralleling of ancient mysticism and computer science, based on a need to account for the desire for cyberspatial experience as other than a rejection of embodiment or a privileging of mental processes over sensation. The erotic appeal of cyberspace (in the Platonic sense) is that it promises the satisfaction of the desire to 'see more and to know more deeply'[42] and to preserve that knowledge in a form which captures the intensity of feeling which accompanies its apprehension.[43] Piercy captures the eroticism of this 'physical embodiment of knowledge'[44] in a scene where Yod, Shira and Malkah project into the matrix in order to penetrate the Yakamura-Stichen 'base' and access secret files which may reveal the multi's intentions. Yod teaches Shira to 'shape change' in the base in order to take on a physicality appropriate to penetrating the various physical forms that represent the 'chimeras' which protect essential Y-S data:

> He presented to her mind a clear diagram and picture of a mining machine, which she could emulate. She became a roughly cylindrical machine with shallow treads. Her head was a boring device. She swallowed earth and rock and excreted it up the hole with a violent blast. It was rather fun. She had to remind herself to follow Malkah and Yod and not to twist away on her own, eating rock.[45]

Shira herself is a data construct, and the rock that she eats and excretes is, in essence, an *idea* of rock, expressed in digital form, but the pleasure is physical and expressed in bodily metaphors. What Heim terms 'Cyber Eros',[46] he intends to be understood as a pleasure of both the senses and the intellect but disassociated from the sensory apparatus of the flesh. Shira takes pleasure in a form of embodiment which is constructed digitally and metaphorically and framed in ideas of physical sensation.

CyberEros is, in essence, the apprehension of an architecture: a populated space which is simultaneously conceptualised as a numerical and linguistic construct. Cyberspace thus comes to be understood less as a separate, or less real, world from which we must always return, but rather as a manifestation of the way in which we order *all* reality. Cyberspace is a literal universe of signs which embodies the arbitrary nature of signification. It is not possible to claim, for instance, that cyberspace entities owe their existence to the code or that the code is logically prior to the entity, neither can one be reduced to the other. In fact it is tempting here to want to claim cyberspace as an extensive realisation of the main thrust of post-structuralist thought in that CyberEros now appears to correspond, not so much to an apprehension of Platonian ideals, but rather to a heady engagement with the Derridean principle of *différance* in that none of its elements can be apprehended as self-identical, nor do they refer/defer to a logocentric ultimate presence or to a temporally organised hierarchical structure. In the terms in which I have described it, cyberspace, in fact, defeats the logic of logocentrism in any attempt to ground it in a mundane system of meaning. And, of course, it gives no logical priority to speech or writing, being neither of these (or both).[47] Harold Bloom describes a similar resonance in his analysis of Kabbalah as a system in which 'rhetorical subversion [is] a distinctive feature'.[48] In kabbalistic thought,

> God is the *Ein-sof* ('without end'), totally unknowable, and beyond representation, all images of whom are merely hyperboles. As *Ein-sof* has no attributes, his first manifestation is necessarily *ayin* ('nothing'). Genesis had said that God created the world out of nothing. Kabbalah took this over as a literal statement, but interpreted it revisionistically as meaning just the opposite of what it said. God, being 'ayin,' created the world out of 'ayin,' and thus created the world *out of himself*. The distinction between cause and effect was subverted by this initial Kabbalistic formula ... 'cause' and 'effect' are always reversible, for the Kabbalists regarded them as linguistic fictions, long before Nietzsche did.[49]

The distinction between presence and absence is thus equally undermined, as is the concept of a reality independent of language. The *sefirot*, as well as being aspects of G-d, are also described as names of

G-d, and each corresponds to a series of divine attributes, forming what we understand as the material world but ultimately conceived of as constructions by which *ayin* is made intelligible; the cognitive expression of what is, fundamentally, unknowable in any strict empirical sense. The *sefirot* 'are neither *things* nor *acts*, but rather are *relational events*',[50] corresponding to Derrida's chain of 'nonsynonymous substitutions' which mark the operation of his 'trace'.[51] Furthermore, the kabbalistic system makes no distinction between linguistic and mathematical expressions of cognition, underlining its function as an interpretative matrix, rather than a determining structure.

The links that I am making here between an ancient mystical system, post-metaphysical epistemology and the way in which cyberspace can be understood as a projection of postmodern desire are, I would argue, inherent in the cyberpunk fascination with technology, language, architecture and consciousness as morphable and interchangeable entities distributed in a field in which, to quote Marcos Novak, '[a]n object's boundary is simply the reconstructed contour of an arbitrarily chosen value'.[52] In the same way that Gibson equates cyberspace and vodou, Piercy makes a case for understanding the human/machine interface in terms of discursive resonances, which, in the case of *Body of Glass*, also elucidate an epistemological contrast between masculine and feminine approaches to problem solving (thus engaging directly with the sense in which Haraway's cyborg project intervenes in the problematics of essentialist versus social constructionist analyses of what may constitute a feminist epistemology[53]). Whereas Frankenstein's monster was a product of nineteenth century anatomical discourse, Yod is a product of late twentieth century technoscientific discourse, but both can be read as troubling interrogations of the way that science attempts to write the world. Both are bodies marked by the articulation of a difference that is produced by the epistemological premises of their construction, but that simultaneously challenges the constructs on which that difference is based. As Allucquere Rosanne Stone points out:

> The project of reifying a 'natural' state over and against a technologized 'fallen' one is not only one of the industries of postmodern nostalgia, but also part of a binary, oppositional cognitive style that some maintain is part of our society's pervasively male epistemology.[54]

To be out of place in this scenario is thus not simply a matter of asserting the technological but of constructing an identity which exposes both positions as equally contrived. In the text of *Body of Glass*, this is Yod's most important function. It is quite possible that Piercy gained as much pleasure from including the phrase 'That's like speaking of a relationship with a dildo',[55] when Yod's sexual relationship with Shira is revealed, as Ursula Le Guin did when the androgynous nature of her Gethenians allowed her to write, 'The King was pregnant'.[56] Both phrases play on the syntagmatic and logical inconsistency of their subject/object relationships according to what Haraway calls 'the one code that translates all meaning perfectly, the central dogma of phallogocentrism'.[57] Piercy extends the playful disruption of the code to explore how language is inadequate to express the figurations that result from blurring the boundary between human and machine.

Yod is illegal because he crosses an arbitrary line drawn between artificial and organic life, recalling the paranoia which attended the fictional construction of the robot in early pulp sf.[58] As Sadie Plant has noted:

> When Isaac Asimov wrote his three laws of robotics, they were lifted straight from the marriage vows: love, honour and obey. . . . Like women, any thinking machines are admitted on the understanding that they are duty-bound to honour and obey the members of the species to which they were enslaved; the members, the male ones, the family of man.[59]

When Yod wonders what 'someone who doesn't possess himself can do with a sense of me and mine',[60] he expresses precisely the dilemma of any conscious organism trapped within a conceptual apparatus in which self-action depends on an idea of selfness located within a polarised system of expression. Plant's analysis of the three laws as consistent with the marriage vows succinctly expresses the relationship between the position of women in Luce Iraparay's 'specular economy' in which they are the ultimate commodity, the exchange of whom 'by fathers, husbands, brothers and sons is the diagram of hierarchical authority',[61] and the tools which mediate, and are controlled by, the forces of production, commerce, government and the military. Plant discusses the zeros and ones of computer binary code in the context of Iraparay's argument that 'in a culture that claims to enumerate everything, cipher everything by units, inventory everything by individualities',[62] woman becomes the negative of the male positive:

> her sex organ, which is not *a* sex organ, is counted as *no* sex organ. It is the negative, the opposite, the reverse, the counterpart, of the only visible and morphologically designatable sex organ . . . the penis'.[63]

But binary arithmetic confounds zero as only ever negative: 'The zeros and ones of machine code are not patriarchal binaries or counterparts to each other: zero is not the other, but the very possibility of all the ones'.[64] Digitization, as she says, 'sets zero free to stand for nothing and make everything work'.[65] Technoscience, which produces computers but is also produced *by* computers, is thus produced by a code whose logic fits awkwardly with the phallogocentric production of identities. Malkah, the magician/seductress, who makes 'everything work', and Yod, a technoscientific production who questions his status as product/slave/possession, are a twinned metaphor for the liminal transgressions made possible by cybererotic play.

Cybercommunities in/of the New World Order

Drs Manfred E. Clynes and Nathan S. Kline's cyborg, first proposed in a paper published in *Astronautics* in September 1960,[66] was imagined as a post-evolutionary 'self-regulating man-machine [sic] system'[67] adapted for extended space flight. Fully confident that the next stage of human evolution must necessarily be adaptation to life in outer space, Clynes and Kline developed their thesis on the basis of an understanding of the homeostatic processes of the body as outside conscious control and, therefore, amenable to manipulations through 'exogenous components'

> extending the self-regulatory control function of the organism in order to adapt it to new environments.[68]

What Clynes and Kline could not have envisaged was that the 'exogenous components' would be computer terminals and the 'new environments' would be digital/metaphorical spaces which would enforce a similar reappraisal of the body and its suitability to adapt. However, both outer space and cyberspace are equivalent in being terrains marked specifically by the politics of what Haraway refers to as 'New World Order, Inc.'[69] The discourse of extraterrestrial relocation, informed by colonisation dreams and Western military–industrial expansionism, also informs the construction of cyberspace as a new playground for market forces: as a space in which metaphors of defence and incursion gain new currency, and as a location for the re-enactment of cold-war scenarios, informed by the rhetoric of intellectual property-rights and data protection. The problem for bodies encoded by these practices is how to form an oppositional stance; how to be 'out of place' while simultaneously enjoying the many promises of cybereroticism. As

Eugene Thacker points out, in an essay published on the Internet and thus intimately discursive with that medium:

> The binary code informing the body of digital anatomy makes explicit and materializes Foucault's suggestion that the relation between discourse-language and body-materiality is one of docility, a 'technology' of bodily production. Change the code, and you change (render docile) the body hardwired as that code.[70]

The cyberspace body thus recalls us to language and to the political structures which mediate our understanding of what counts as a viable body in contemporary discourse.

Allucquere Rosanne Stone tells the story of 'Julie', a cyberspace entity whose 'real' body was female and severely disabled but who, on the net, acted as friend and confidant to a number of women who discussed with her their innermost secrets and desires. When 'she' turned out to be 'a middle-aged male psychiatrist',[71] the women who had previously claimed to have benefited from his/her warm-hearted advice were vociferous in their expressions of violation, one going so far as to claim that she felt that she had been 'raped'.[72] What is interesting here is that the psychiatrist did not deliberately set out to deceive but, having been mistaken for a woman, and finding the change of gender exciting, set about systematically changing the code to reflect an acceptable 'body' for the mode of interaction in which he was engaged. The rape metaphor is apt to describe a situation in which an entity signifying as masculine effectively controls a community signifying as feminine, with all the connotations that those significations imply. The much lauded freedom from gender constraints promised by cyberspatial embodiment is only possible in a culture where gender is no longer a category which structures ideas of corporeality. As Stone points out:

> Forgetting about the body is an old Cartesian trick, one that has unpleasant consequences for those bodies whose speech is silenced by the act of our forgetting; that is to say, those upon whose labor the act of forgetting the body is founded – usually woman and minorities.[73]

This is why the cyborg is a creature which inhabits boundaries but which also has to be a trickster, coyote; 'a figure for the always problematic, always potent tie of meaning and bodies',[74] and this is also why

I have nominated Piercy's imagined community of Tikva as the symbolic location of cyborgian possibilities.

As Jenny Wolmark points out, it is the corporations in *Body of Glass* which symbolise the power structures that fix gender expectations, and 'Piercy links the political opposition to the corporations on the part of the central female characters to their equally oppositional relation to gender identity'.[75] While this is true (particularly in the case of Malkah), it is also the case that the female characters in the novel are inseparable from the community in which they function. Tikva is presented as a collective, held together by Jewish identity and cultural practices and by the common goal of remaining autonomous through the manufacture of a product for which the multis are forced to compete. Tikva has elements in common with the utopian community of Mattapoisset in Piercy's *Women on the Edge of Time*, but with the essential difference that it is intimately connected to what it opposes by the technology that ensures its survival. If the female characters are defined in opposition by the corporations, Tikva itself occupies a much more complex position, being oppositional in its collective structure but only able to maintain that structure by recourse to skills that keep it ahead of the game. With the emphasis on Kabbalah as a system which informs the production of 'chimeras', Piercy implies that ethnicity is a strong factor in the town's survival and that Jewish cultural history provides for its strength. The text presents a parallel between the 'marrano' identity that Shira and her husband Josh maintain while employed by Y-S, by which they disguise their Jewishness while still practising the rituals of their cultural heritage and religion, and the weaving of false personal identities and misleading data constructs that falsifies Tikva's presence in the 'net'. The inhabitants of Tikva move freely between work for the multis and work which maintains the town's data defences so that, ironically, it is the employment of their skills as programmers in the corporate world which hones them for the continued maintenance of their outsider identity. Tikva is not, like the Prague ghetto, an entrenched enclave suffering poverty and deprivation, but a community of hackers and tricksters with considerable power, ironically made possible by the very power structures that seek to undermine them. And it is Tikva that harbours Nili, a true outsider from a community that genetically and cybernetically engineers its inhabitants for survival in a hostile environment. As Gareth Parry points out, '[i]n presenting the struggle of Jews against multinational corporations and against Christians, *Body of Glass* aligns its Jewish characters with Marx's workers, and they become a symbol of all oppressed groups, be they ethnic groups, religious groups or women'.[76] Nili's Israel is, for Parry, an extension of the cyborg pos-sibilities of contemporary Israel, 'a melting pot of a nation which none-theless is united in its Judaism, and thus its history of oppression'.[77]

However, Jewishness as a cyborg position can only be understood in the terms presented by *Body of Glass* as arising out of what Parry refers to as 'cohesion allied to diversity'.[78] The strength of unity represented by the Tikva collective is established on the basis of what Haraway calls 'the skills for reading webs of power by those refused stable membership in the social categories of race, sex or class'.[79] Tikva, like Eretz Israel, is a site of 'reuniting diaspora',[80] a node of convergence for what Haraway refers to as 'a kind of postmodernist identity [constructed] out of other-ness, difference, and specificity'.[81] As she says:

> In the vulnerabilities and potencies of their altered bodies, these technologically savvy women understand the bond of literacy and wealth that structures the chances of life and death in their world. Nili, Riva, Malkah, and the cyborg live without innocence in the regime of technobiopower, where literacy is about the joining of informatics, biologics, and economics.[82]

It is this techno-literacy which enables Tikva to write itself as a constantly evolving fiction in a world dominated by the politics and economics of technoscience. As Malkah puts it:

> I have specialized for the last twenty years in security systems invol-ving chimeras that hid the real base in false bases. That's what we sell; but the very best we keep for ourselves. My finest ideas are float-ing there, intricate beyond mapping.[83]

Tikva also is 'beyond mapping', resisting the cartography of corporate economic imperialism, both in cyberspace, where its representations are wholly chimerical, and in its links with Nili's community in Safed, which is not linked in to the net, and with the dissident group which are beginning to organise in the *Glop*. Tikva thus represents an alternat-ive map of interconnected resistances and fictional displacements which undermines the authority of the formal mapping of the world so necessary to power structures dependent on fixed orders and hierarch-ical economic, social and racial structures.

While Yod and Avram play out the Frankenstein scenario, father and illegitimate 'son' bound together in a death pact produced out of their interdependence as product and producer, Tikva can be read as the monster 'invoked as a figure of resistance to established authority'.[84] Fred Botting identifies monsters as products of the legal, political and socio-economic discourses which structure ideas of otherness in times of conflict:

> Most evident in periods of social, political and economic crisis, monsters appear as the marks of division and difference that cannot be held together and fixed within the hierarchical relations of a social order which sustains the illusion of itself as unified'.[85]

But the oppositional communities thus identified 'have an excessive unity and a frightening amount of power.... [I]n giving an excessive amount of power to those that it would suppress, a dominant position constructs the continual possibility of its own downfall'.[86] Tikva occupies such a position, but the town is a knowing inhabitant of its own monstrousness. Through the technoliteracy which sustains it, the community enables its own chimerical construction while fully aware of, and rejoicing in, the destabilising possibilities of its outsider status. Like Haraway's cyborg it is 'oppositional, utopian, and completely without innocence'.[87] The business of Tikva is writing, 'pre-eminently the technology of cyborgs',[88] which 'has a special significance for all colonized groups'.[89] Nili recalls:

> The ability to read and write belonged to the Church except for heretics and Jews.... With the invention of the printing press, literacy spread. With mass literacy, any person no matter how poor could learn how the society operated, could share visions of how things might be different'.[90]

The point that she is making is that the meaning of literacy may have changed to incorporate the reading and writing practices which characterise techno-proficiency but that, politically, the stakes are the same. Haraway reads Nili as belonging to 'these oppositional traditions of reading and writing, with their generative accounts of what can count as human, as knowledge, as history, as insider and outsider':[91] traditions marked by continuity, in *Body of Glass*, through the endurance of Kabbalah as a practice productive of alternate and oppositional meanings. Nili and Riva, who considers the idea of information as a commodity as 'obscene',[92] are Piercy's radical answer to Carol A. Stabile's charge that 'the cyborg feminist need not *do* anything in order to be political'. For Stabile, '[p]olitics, so to speak, are fundamentally embedded in the cyborgian body: the fact that the cyborg signifies is enough to guarantee her politics',[93] implying a passive position which is as reified as the constructions of patriarchal technoscientific culture which it seeks to oppose. For cyborg significance to have meaning as part of an active politics, then, as Piercy demonstrates, it must form part of an understanding of bodies and selves as sites of strategic play in which the ability to 'change the code', after the fashion of Tikva, is a requirement for staying ahead of the game, and a position of particular power. Nili's community of Safed, outside 'the appropriations of Christian salvation history'[94] and therefore outside the discursive structures which, under the sign of telos, control the meaning of corporeality, gender, nature and knowledge itself, is well placed to stand, with Tikva, as a demonstration of my claim that knowing monstrousness is a powerful political force. The cyborg is an informed position, well known to 'Jews and infidels', whose potent oppositional literacies, as Piercy demonstrates with her paralleling of Kabbalah and programming code, can instruct a feminist politics committed to active participation in our own future. As Nili tells us: 'We are people of the book. We have always considered getting knowledge part of being human'.[95]

Conclusion: the *Frankenstein* Inheritance

> The future, in fiction, is a metaphor. . . . A metaphor for
> what? . . . If I could have said it nonmetaphorically, I would
> not have written all these words, this novel; and Genly Ai
> would never have sat down at my desk and used up my ink and
> typewriter ribbon in informing me, and you, rather solemnly,
> that the truth is a matter of the imagination.
>
> Ursula Le Guin, *The Language of the Night*[1]

Ursula Le Guin's reply to her question '[a] metaphor for what?' is to demonstrate how the writing of sf proceeds from a need to express a truth, a concept, a conviction or a question which, like Charlotte Perkins Gilman's 'important truths, needed but unpopular',[2] find their most potent expression through the invention of imaginary worlds in which the future has already happened. For Le Guin, as for Gilman, sf allows them temporarily to suspend belief in the present, and to lend their creative tools to characters that use up their typewriter ink delineating alternatives which demonstrate responses that are both playful and political to the dilemmas presented by contemporary life. The *Frankenstein* Inheritance, then, is the freedom to imagine beyond the confines of contemporary social life and the restrictions of contemporary politics, and, like Mary Shelley, to dream a world into existence: a world structured by the possibilities of scientific theory but informed, necessarily, by the politics of gender. Necessarily, because here, at the dawn of the 21st century, when the first Challenger mission commanded by a woman has finally seen lift-off and the work of women scientists, both present and past, is being increasingly recognised, we can still read imagined worlds without gender hierarchies or oppression as utopian. When the psychic positioning of the Nazis in *Swastika Night*[3] or the entrenched masculinity of Maltzer in 'No Woman Born' or of Avram in *Body of Glass* no longer makes sense, then, perhaps, these works will only survive as reminders of what might have been. But while we can still relate to the conditions which allowed Burdekin to extrapolate a future in which women are caged and silenced, and which prompted Sally Miller Gearhart and Caroline Forbes to claim planet Earth for women alone, our most productive readings of these texts refer not only to the theory of sexual politics, but to the very real conditions for which they are metaphors. As Le Guin says, if she could have stated her case without recourse to metaphor, Genly Ai would not have had to exist, but then not only would we have been denied the pleasure of accompanying him on his journey to another world, but the truth that he had to impart would never have been expressed. As Le Guin says, '[t]he novelist says in words what cannot be said in words'.[4] Genly Ai was created out of a need to challenge orthodox ideas of what counts as knowledge and truth from a position outside of the discourse from which these ideas derive their power.

Although Mary Shelley is understood to be the founder of the genre in all its manifestations, I want to claim here a legacy bequeathed, in particular, to her female inheritors. When she allowed Victor Franken-stein to come to life in her imagination he became a voice for 'what cannot be said in words', in the same way that Genly Ai provided a metaphorical voice for Ursula Le Guin when he sat down to borrow her typewriter. Nor do I think it a coincidence that both these characters, in common with others discussed in this volume, are 'conventional, rather stuffy', confused and emotionally vulnerable male scientists. Their role is to be brought to an awareness of the limits of their epistemology. Vandyck Jennings in *Herland*, Maltzer in 'No Woman Born', Ian Suitlov in 'Your Haploid Heart' and Avram in *Body of Glass* are all, like Ai and Frankenstein, forced to question previously held assumptions about how knowledge is made and understood, and the role of science in social life. They are, themselves, metaphors for scientific orthodoxy; for the reified nature of scientific ideology and for the state of mind which must necessarily be challenged if the connection between how science writes the world and how gender has been coded in contemporary soci-eties is to be exposed and explored.

Victor Frankenstein's wholly masculine endeavour, which culminates in considerable loss of life, has become an enduring metaphor for the various productions of technoscience which have been proved less benign than their intended purpose, as well as for the productions of 'big science' which exploit natural resources and whole populations in a cynical appropriation of profit.[5] He thus comes to represent the feminist critique of technoscience which understands the exploitation of natural resources in the name of capital as inseparable from the exploitation of women as resources for the perpetuation of masculine-identified culture. Frankenstein's hubristic approach to his project is shown to involve the complete rejection of all female influence, and as Ian Barnes points out:

> Significantly, during the time of his intensely creative scientific activity, Victor becomes completely detached from and insensitive to the rhythms of nature. Also, the profusion of doublings in the novel suggests that in his destruction of the monster's mate, Victor projects unconscious hostility towards the world of feminine domesticity and biological procreation, a hostility which culminates in the surrogate murder of Elizabeth.[6]

As I have argued elsewhere,[7] the monster itself is ambiguously gendered, thus reinforcing the sense in which the novel can be read as engaging with Donna Haraway's hopeful formulation of the cyborg as a necessary myth for structuring resistance to the construction of identities which justifies dominance on the basis of arbitrarily ascribed differences. If, as I have suggested, the monster can be read as confounding the story mapped out for its continued survival by refusing to 'disappear' when it is abandoned by its maker, and returning to confront Victor with the results of his transgression, then it can also be read as corresponding to the insistent voices of the women in *Swastika Night* and the Flenni in 'Your Haploid Heart' who are similarly relegated but whose continued presence, despite precautions aimed at ensuring their silence, is enough to guarantee a disruption of the *status quo*. And, of course, there are parallels here with Mary Shelley herself, the 'nearly silent listener' who gave birth to a genre, a myth for contemporary life and a potent metaphor for constructing oppositions as she allowed her imagination 'unbidden' to dream her monster to life.

However, it is important to emphasise that the *Frankenstein* Inheritance should not be read as a mystical or 'natural' result of the application of the female imagination, nor as the realisation of a universal female psychic tendency. The historical progression from *Herland*, through *Body of Glass* and beyond, marks a continuity in responses only in so far as these writers are (or were) all citizens of the developed West in a century that has seen intensifying technological change accompanied by a sustained analysis of the culture which has produced it, not least by successive generations of feminists. I therefore want to emphasise that these monsters are creations of *political* imaginations, rather than archetypes of the female psyche. As Megan Stern points out, Shelley herself was writing at a time when, according to Michel Foucault, an epistemic shift occurred from 'a classical medicine of nosological categorisation to a modern medicine of understanding the causality and development of illness'.[8] The result was a new understanding of the role, in medical practice, of the cadaver, which

> became a map on which could be read the progress of the disease and of death. For the first time, it became possible to see death not simply as the negation of life, but as its continuation.[9]

Stern's argument that *Frankenstein* was produced out of a concern with new understandings of the body arising out of the intellectual milieu of post-revolutionary France, and that it was thus motivated by the modern notion of disease as ultimately responsive to scientific management, is persuasive. But equally at stake is the accompanying realisation of the body as subordinate to mind. As the daughter of Mary Wollstonecraft, one of the most outspoken feminists of her time, Shelley could not fail to have been aware of her mother's politics,[10] based, as they were, on abstract individualism and all that that idea entails for an understanding of gender as a property of bodies and thus superseded, or effaced, by rationality. The monster is not only, as Stern points out, a walking realisation of the Enlightenment ideal of health, strength and social responsibility promoted as the product of, and the pre-condition for, intellectual growth, but, in the gender ambiguity that I have noted, it points to the transcendence of gender limitations required by a feminism informed by those same ideals. The monster metaphor can thus also be understood as standing for feminist responses to successive epistemic reformulations of what it means to be embodied, articulated through the confounding of fictional scientists with the logic of a radical politics. Charlotte Perkins Gilman's *Herland*, for instance, remains firmly within the arena of Enlightenment humanism, with its insistence on height, strength and physical health as commensurate with an enlightened feminism. Terry Nicholson is the foil who, in his denouncing of the Herlanders as 'unnatural', confirms their monstrous status, while revealing the limits of masculine orthodoxy. However, it is Vandyck Jennings, with whom Gilman's male readers may be urged to identify, who must face the limits of his own assumptions, despite his 'scientific imagination'. Maltzer in 'No

Woman Born' reflects early postmodern anxieties connected to the mechanisation of the body, in his insistence that he has created a monster; but equally, in his inability to appreciate the liberatory potential of dispensing with the flesh, he stands for the entrenched position of science in its insistence on biology as a determinant of gender, a position which he is brought to question by Deirdre's display of power. Similarly, Yod in *Body of Glass* fulfils the monster role in his relationship with Avram, who, like Maltzer, is identified with Victor Frankenstein, but, just as Deirdre appropriates her metal body to explore and expand the limits of performance, so Yod is prevented from acting out the violent aspects of the monster that his predecessors had succumbed to by the intervention of Malkah, who provides him with social skills and a myth which enables him to identify as a member of the community with a stake in its future. In both these scenarios, it is the power of the female mind, the one element missing from Victor Frankenstein's enterprise, which metaphorically tames the monster.

In this sense, these texts also engage with the notion of a feminist epistemology of science which I have identified as yielding the most productive readings of Sally Miller Gearhart's *The Wanderground* and Caroline Forbes's 'London Fields'. Deirdre, perhaps, emerges as the most interesting monster in this context in that she enables a reading that prefigures Haraway's cyborg politics in her manipulation of a technological medium to transcend the contradictions between biology and technoscience, as she equally confuses the boundary between art and science, thus also resolving the conflict produced by reading women as essentially in opposition to masculine-identified science and technology. However, Yod, like the huxley in 'Short In The Chest', is equally transgressive in his relationships with Shira, Malkah, Riva and Nili. Yod is a self-aware machine intimately involved in the politics of gender, and thus is a metaphor for the productive possibilities of women's active engagement with technoscience, as the huxley is a metaphor for the dangerous potential of the management of female sexuality based on scientific analyses of what constitutes female sexual nature.

The creation of monsters, then, is an enduring theme in the texts that I have been discussing. From the women of Herland, who mock the assumption that rationality is the exclusive preserve of masculine individuals, to what I have referred to[11] as the 'knowing monstrousness' of the Tikva collective in *Body of Glass*, the monster, in my reading of it as an affront to the complacency of the scientific community and a challenge to the abstraction of science from the cultural life to which its technological productions necessarily contribute, can be understood as the reciprocal response of women writers, disconnected in time but connected by the demands of imagining the role of science in social change, to their marginal position in cultures determined by what counts as knowledge in a masculine world.

Notes

1 Introduction: Women, Science and Fiction

1. Beer, 1983, p. 3.
2. Haraway, 1992, p. 5.
3. Parrinder, 1980, pp. 70–1.
4. Ibid., p. 70.
5. Griffiths, 1980, p. 22.
6. Ibid., p. 13.
7. The debates that have arisen as a result of attempts to define the genre have also produced some discussion as to whether 'science fiction' is an adequately descriptive term. Consequently 'sf' can also stand for speculative fiction or structural fabulation (see Robert Scholes, *Structural Fabulation*, 1975). The use of the lower case form of the abbreviation is, for some writers, a means of indicating that they are using the conventional term (which must also be distinguished from science fantasy; see note 12). I intend also to follow this convention. The abbreviation will appear in upper case where I quote from writers who have used it in this way.
8. Green and Lefanu, 1985, p. 4.
9. Lefanu, 1988, p. 5.
10. Ibid., p. 7.
11. Parrinder, 1980, p. 2.
12. Joanna Russ offers some examples which help to illuminate the distinction: 'J. R. R. Tolkein writes fantasy. He offends against all sorts of archaeological, geological, paleontological, and linguistic evidence which he probably knows as well as anyone else does'. And: 'American science fiction originated the adventure-story-cum-fairy-tale which most people think of (erroneously) as science fiction. It has been called a great many things, most of them uncomplimentary, but the usual name is Space Opera' (from Russ, 'The Image of Women in Science Fiction' in S. K. Cornillon (ed.), *Images of Women in Fiction: Feminist Perspectives*, pp. 79 and 82).
13. Wolmark, 1994, pp. 1–2.
14. Parrinder, 1980, p. xv.
15. Suvin, 1976, p. 62.
16. Monk, 1980, p. 16.
17. Ibid., p. 18.
18. Csicsery-Ronay Jr, 1991, p. 390.
19. Baudrillard, 1991, p. 312.
20. Ibid., p. 311.
21. Wolmark, 1994, p. 14.
22. Ibid., p. 15.
23. See Chapter 6.
24. Keller (Fox), 1983, p. 138.
25. Beer, 1986, p. 11.

26. Keller (Smith), 1992, p. 29.
27. Beer, 1986, p. 9.
28. Harding, 1992, p. 59.
29. I do not here want to enter into the debate about whether psychoanalysis can properly be called a science nor, for the purposes of this book, do I distinguish between the so called 'natural' and 'social' sciences. Excerpts from essays which discuss the status of psychoanalysis as a science can be found in Stuart Brown, John Fauvel and Ruth Finnegan (eds), *Conceptions of Inquiry*. See in particular Karl R. Popper, 'Conjectures and Refutations', pp. 100–7 and Thomas S. Kuhn, 'The Sciences as Puzzle Solving Traditions', pp. 107–13.
30. Gamble, 1991, p. 47.
31. It was *New Worlds* that published Pamela Zoline's 'The Heat Death of the Universe' (1967), in which entropy invades housewife Sarah Boyle's kitchen, one of the first sf short stories by a woman with a feminist theme (see *New Worlds*, No. 173, July 1967). The story has been republished in Pamela Zoline, *Busy about the Tree of Life*, The Women's Press, London, 1988.
32. Shelley, 1969, p. 6.
33. Ibid., pp. 8–9.
34. Ibid., p. 9.

2   *Herland*: Charlotte Perkins Gilman and the Literature of the Beehive

1. Gilman, 1911, p. 101.
2. Rowbotham, 1992, p. 92.
3. Beer, 1983, p. 17.
4. Gilman, 1911, p. 105.
5. Ibid., pp. 97 and 98.
6. Ibid., p. 105.
7. Ibid., p. 101.
8. Ibid., p. 99.
9. Gilman, 1935, pp. 303–4.
10. Spender, 1983, p. 516.
11. Bowler, 1984, pp. 212–13.
12. Easlea, 1981, pp. 154–5.
13. Bowler, 1984, p. 215.
14. Ibid., p. 271.
15. Hofstadter, 1959, p. 58.
16. Ibid., p. 59.
17. Bowler, 1984, p. 209.
18. Ibid., p. 286.
19. Ibid., p. 284.
20. Rowbotham, 1992, p. 23.
21. Ibid., p. 24.
22. Ibid., p. 89.
23. Gilman, 1966, p. 19.
24. Gilman, 1924, p. 57.

25. Gilman dedicated her book, *Man Made World: or, Our Androcentric Culture* (1911) to Ward. The dedication reads as follows: 'This book is dedicated with reverent love and gratitude to Lester F. Ward sociologist and humanitarian, one of the world's great men; a creative thinker to whose wide knowledge and power of vision we are indebted for a new grasp of the nature and processes of society, and to whom all women are especially bound in honour and gratitude for his gynaeococentric theory of life, than which nothing more important to humanity has been advanced since the theory of evolution, and nothing more important to women has ever been given to the world.'
26. Hofstadter, 1959, p. 76.
27. Ward, 1903, p. 306.
28. Ibid., p. 313.
29. Gilman, 1966, p. 130.
30. Ward's use of conventional vocabulary makes it seem as if he is contradicting his own argument. But it is true to say that, at this point in his evolutionary narrative, women have *become* the 'weaker sex' due to the effects of 'male efflorescence'.
31. Ward, 1913–18, Vol. 4, p. 134.
32. Ward, 1903, p. 314.
33. Gilman, 1966, p. 130.
34. For a discussion of the plausibility of parthenogenesis for the human species, see article entitled 'What is the point of men?' in *The Economist*, 12 December 1987.
35. Gilman, 1966, p. 131.
36. Hill, 1980, pp. 269–70.
37. Gilman, 1966, p. 131.
38. Ibid., p. 32.
39. Ibid., p. 94.
40. Ibid., p. 62.
41. Ibid., p. 189.
42. Ibid., p. 141.
43. Ibid., p. 183.
44. Ibid., p. 317.
45. Ibid., p. 169.
46. Ibid., p. 132.
47. Ibid., p. 138.
48. Ibid., p. 139.
49. Ibid., p. 142.
50. Gilman, 1935, p. 331.
51. Gilman, 1966, p. 94.
52. Ibid., p. 21.
53. Gilman, 1979, p. 78.
54. See Chapter 7.
55. Gilman, 1935, p. 310.
56. Bartkowski, 1989, p. 28.
57. Ibid.
58. Gilman, 1979, p. 9.
59. Ibid., p. 21.

60. Ibid., p. 89.
61. Hill, 1980, p. 265.
62. Bartkowski, 1989, p. 28.
63. Spender, 1983, p. 516.
64. Gilman, 1966, p. 145.
65. Ibid., p. 300.
66. Gilman, 1979, pp. 77–8.
67. Ibid., p. 55.
68. Ibid.
69. Ibid., p. 56.
70. Ibid., p. 66.
71. Ibid., p. 69.
72. Gilman, 1966, p. 188.
73. Ibid., p. 289.
74. Ibid., p. 288.
75. Ibid., pp. 289–90.
76. Ibid., p. 277.
77. Ibid., p. 189.
78. Gilman, 1924, pp. 46–7.
79. Gilman, 1979, p. 56.
80. Ibid., p. 59.
81. Ibid., p. 76.
82. Ibid., p. 118.
83. Ibid., p. 25.
84. Ibid., p. 26.
85. Ibid., p. 7.
86. Ibid., p. 30.
87. Ibid., p. 28.
88. Howarth, 1973, p. 14.
89. Howarth, 1973, p. 175. Richard Usborne, who has made a study of Sapper's Bulldog Drummond, finds him to have had 'a strong interest' in pretty girls. No entanglements. But he . . . knew enough . . . to look . . . at their feet to see if they were thoroughbreds' (Usborne, 1983, p. 153).
90. Howarth, 1973, p. 175.
91. Gilman, 1979, p. 12.
92. Ibid., p. 16.
93. Ibid., p. 17.
94. Ibid.
95. Ibid., p. 8.
96. Ibid., p. 21.
97. Ibid., p. 58.
98. Ibid., p. 10.
99. Ibid., p. 80.
100. Ibid., p. 132.
101. Ibid., p. 146.
102. Easlea, 1981, p. 157.
103. Ibid., p. 86.
104. Gilman, 1979, p. 29.
105. Meek, 1976, p. 2.

106. Gilman,1979, p. 59.
107. Meek, 1976, pp. 80–1.
108. Ibid., p. 80.
109. See Chapter 7.
110. Baym, 1986, p. 71.
111. Ibid., p. 72.
112. Ibid., p. 73.
113. Ibid., p. 71.
114. Ibid., p. 75.
115. Ibid.
116. Gilman, 1979, p. 5.
117. Ibid., p. 8.
118. Ibid., p. 74.
119. Howarth, 1973, chap. 1.
120. Gilman, 1979, p. 37.
121. Gilman, 1924, p. 208.
122. Beer, 1983, p. 211.
123. Ibid., p. 215.
124. Ibid., p. 213.
125. Ibid.
126. Palmeri, 1983, p. 111; her emphasis.
127. Gilman, 1979, p. 59.
128. Ibid., p. 30.
129. Ibid., p. 128.
130. Ibid., p. 124.
131. Easlea, 1981, p. 270.
132. Gilman herself had at least three close female friends during her lifetime, with two of whom she actually set up home. However, as Mary A. Hill points out, 'Close and intimate friendships between women were common in the nineteenth century, as were hugging, kissing, commiserating, communing, unashamedly sleeping together in one another's beds. Whether such relationships were sexual is often impossible to know' (Hill, 1980, p. 82).
133. Gilman, 1979, p. 88.
134. Ibid., pp. 88 and 89.
135. Ibid., p. 99.
136. Gilman, 1911, p. 100.
137. Gilman, 1979, p. 93.
138. Ibid.
139. Bartkowski, 1989, p. 31.
140. Gilman, 1979, p. 127.
141. Bartkowski, p. 31.
142. Gilman, 1924, p. 208.
143. Gilman, 1979, p. 70.
144. The Herland process of selective breeding gives primacy to parcenary considerations. As Somel explains to Jennings:

> 'If the girl showing the bad qualities had still the power to appreciate social duty, we appealed to her, by that, to renounce motherhood. Some

of the few worst types were, fortunately, unable to reproduce. But if the fault was in a disproportionate egotism – then the girl was sure she had the right to have children, even that hers would be better than others.'

'I can see that,' I said. 'And then she would be likely to rear them in the same spirit.' 'That we never allowed,' answered Somel quietly.

(Gilman, 1979, p. 82).

The implications for selective breeding in the human species are, by now, well documented, but in the context of Victorian pragmatism following the teachings of Darwin, the idea that defective traits could be eradicated rather than held to be dependent on the will of God or concomitant with the laws of nature, and therefore beyond human ability to change, gave impetus to much optimistic speculation (see Houghton, 1957, pp. 33–8). However, the notion of deviance must inevitably give rise to questions regarding race superiority. Similarly, the authoritarian nature of Somel's statement implies totalitarian intransigence, putting 'social duty' before individual rights. It would seem that Gilman had need to reconcile her interpretation of socialism with her commitment to democracy which, as she says, 'means, requires, is, individual liberty' (Gilman, 1966, p. 145).

145. Gilman had little sympathy with psychoanalytic theory and refused to be 'psyched' by the 'mind-meddlers' when Freudian psychoanalysis came to New York (see Gilman, 1935, p. 314).
146. Gilman, p. 128.
147. Bartkowski, 1989, p. 32.
148. Gilman, 1979, p. 99.
149. Ibid., p. 127.
150. Ibid., p. 92.
151. Ibid., p. 56.
152. Gilman, 1911, p. 107.
153. Beer, 1983, p. 107.
154. Ibid., p. 108.
155. Ibid., p. 119.
156. Gilman,1979, p. 64.
157. Ibid., p. 94.
158. Ibid., p. 50.
159. Cockshut, 1977, p. 9.
160. Ibid., p. 10.
161. Ibid., p. 9.
162. Gilman, 1979, p. 125.
163. Ibid., p. 104.
164. Ibid., p. 97.
165. Ibid., p. 89.
166. Ibid.
167. Ibid., p. 123.
168. Showalter, 1977, p. 14.
169. Gilman, 1979, p. 123.
170. Cockshut, 1977, p. 9.
171. Gilman, 1979, pp. 123 and 124.

172. Ibid., p. 144.
173. Ibid., p. 94.
174. Ibid., p. 145.
175. Gilman, 1966, p. 151.
176. Gilman, 1979, p. 59.

3   *Swastika Night*: Katharine Burdekin and the Psychology of Scapegoating

1. Burdekin, 1934, p. 35.
2. The Left Book Club was created by Gollancz 'to spread knowledge for the threefold aim of the preservation of peace, the defeat of fascism and the pursuit of social justice' (reader's letter, *Left News*, No. 54, December 1940).
3. Cover of *Left News*, July 1940.
4. See Theweleit, *Male Fantasies*, 1987.
5. In a footnote to her essay 'Orwell's Despair, Burdekin's Hope: Gender and Power in Dystopia', Daphne Patai comments on the fact that Burdekin's first six novels were published under her own name and suggests that the reason '[w]hy she [later] chose to adopt the pseudonym . . . is only one of the many questions regarding her life and work that still need to be explored' (Patai, 1984, p. 85). However, as Keith Williams notes, 'she was at the cutting edge of the progressive thought of the inter-war period . . . [and] knew and/or corresponded with H. D., Radclyffe Hall, the Woolfs and the Russells, among others' (Keith Williams, 1999, p. 12). See also Daphne Patai's afterword to another Burdekin novel, *The End of This Day's Business*.
6. Burdekin, 1934, p. 22.
7. As Daphne Patai points out, Karen Horney's 'essays on feminine psychology were available in English in the 1920s' (Patai, 1985, p. ix). This historical coincidence (shared also with Melanie Klein) as well as the internal textual evidence from *Swastika Night* and *Proud Man* argue persuasively for her knowledge of, and interest in, these theorists, despite the fact that, as far as is known, she published nothing other than her fiction.
8. The deification of Hitler, which Burdekin imagines after 700 years of Nazi rule, reflects the role that historical analysis reveals he had perhaps imagined for himself (see Grunberger, 1974, pp. 104–5).
9. Burdekin, 1985, p. 70.
10. Ibid., p. 100.
11. Ibid., p. 67.
12. Ibid., p. 68.
13. Ibid., p. 12.
14. Ibid., p. 8.
15. Ibid., p. 98.
16. At the end of the novel, the narrator concludes that s/he has been mistaken in her/his assumption that s/he has travelled into her/his own past, seeing, finally, no possibility that the 'creatures' that s/he meets could evolve to the state that her/his people have achieved. See Murray Constantine, *Proud Man* (1934).

17. Lewis, 1980, p. 208.
18. Ibid., p. 215.
19. Evidence for the fact that concerns over racial 'quality' were not confined to Nazi Germany alone is provided by the release of previously withheld documents to the Public Record Office in Kew (UK) which reveal how Winston Churchill, when Home Secretary in 1910, 'wanted forcibly to sterilise more than 100,000 people he described as "mentally degenerate"' (see Clive Ponting, 'Churchill's plan for race purity', in the *Guardian* ('Outlook' section), Saturday 20 June – Sunday 21 June 1992).
20. Lewis, 1980, p. 216.
21. Koonz, 1987, p. 149.
22. Ibid., p. 398.
23. Ibid., p. 399.
24. Grunberger, 1974, p. 339.
25. Ibid.
26. Koonz, 1987, p. 3.
27. Ehrenreich, 1987, p. xv.
28. Grunberger, 1974, p. 322.
29. Burdekin, 1985, p. 11.
30. Ibid., pp. 5 and 6, her emphasis. This immediately invites comparison with the Greek myth of the birth of Athene who 'sprang, fully armed, with a mighty shout' from the head of her father, Zeus. But, as Robert Graves points out, 'before the arrival of Aryan invaders from the distant North and East . . . Ancient Europe had no gods' (Graves, 1955, p. 13) and all religious worship centred around the triple-aspected Moon goddess, of which Athene would undoubtedly have originally been a representation. Graves quotes Jane Harrison, who describes 'the story of Athene's birth from Zeus'' head as 'a desperate theological expedient to rid her of her matriarchal conditions' and adds that it is 'also a dogmatic insistence on wisdom as a male prerogative; hitherto the goddess alone had been wise' (ibid., p. 46). It is possible that Burdekin intends to suggest that the mythologising of Hitler's birth is a similar expedient and that both myths can be taken to represent assuaging of male envy of women's procreative ability. The re-mythologising of the Moon goddess is also, of course, another example of the 'destruction of Memory' (Burdekin, 1985, pp. 79–80).
31. Burdekin, 1985, p. 10.
32. Ibid., pp. 79 and 80.
33. Ibid., pp. 81–2.
34. Ibid., p. 80.
35. Pagetti, 1990, p. 361.
36. Burdekin, 1985, p. 13.
37. Ibid., p. 14.
38. Ibid., p. 6.
39. Ibid., p. 23.
40. Theweleit, 1987, p. 22. As Barbara Ehrenreich explains in her Foreword to Vol. 1 of *Male Fantasies*, the *Freikorps* were 'the volunteer armies that fought, and to a large extent, triumphed over, the revolutionary German working class in the years immediately after World War I . . . they managed to survive the relatively warless years between 1923 and 1933, becoming

the core of Hitler's SA and, in several cases, going on to become key func-
tionaries in the Third Reich'.

41. Ibid., p. 35.
42. Ibid.
43. Ibid., p. 33.
44. Burdekin, 1934, p. 22. It is interesting that Burdekin makes this distinction and that for her, as for Klaus Theweleit, who calls his *Friekorpsmen* 'soldier males', the distinction is made to draw attention to the fact that the culture ratifies a type of psychosis, which these males represent.
45. Burdekin, 1985, p. 72.
46. Foucault, 1981, p. 150.
47. Ibid.
48. Theweleit, 1987, p. 414.
49. Foucault, 1981, p. 124; his emphasis.
50. See Chapter 2.
51. Foucault, 1981, pp. 149–50.
52. Ibid., pp. 152–3.
53. Ibid., p. 153.
54. Ibid., p. 148.
55. Burdekin, 1985, p. 28.
56. Foucault, 1981, p. 150.
57. Klein, 1975, p. 285.
58. Ibid., p. 270.
59. Ibid., p. 264.
60. Ibid., p. 352.
61. Burdekin, 1985, p. 79.
62. Ibid.
63. Ibid., p. 80; her emphasis.
64. Ibid., pp. 80–1.
65. Ibid., p. 71.
66. Horney, 1973, p. 135.
67. Ibid., p. 140.
68. Ibid., p. 142.
69. Ibid., p. 141.
70. Ibid., p. 143.
71. Theweleit, 1987, p. 196.
72. Horney, 1973, p. 136.
73. Burdekin, 1934, p. 29.
74. Burdekin, 1985, p. 163.
75. Ibid., p. 161.
76. Ibid., p. 163.
77. Horney, 1973, pp. 60–1.
78. Ibid., p. 136.
79. Burdekin, 1985, p. 82.
80. Ibid., p. 107; her emphasis.
81. Ibid., p. 108.
82. Ibid., p. 70; her emphasis.
83. Ibid., p. 108.
84. Freud, 1973, p. 149.

85. Mitchell, 1990, p. 115.
86. Horney, 1973, p. 222.
87. Ibid., p. 223.
88. Freud may have had Horney in mind when he wrote: 'For the ladies, whenever some comparison seemed to turn out unfavourable to their sex, were able to utter a suspicion that we, the male analysts, had been unable to overcome certain deeply-rooted prejudices against what was feminine, and that this was being paid for in the partiality of our researches. We, on the other hand, standing on the ground of bisexuality, had no difficulty in avoiding impoliteness. We had only to say: 'This doesn't apply to *you*. You're the exception; on this point you're more masculine than feminine' (Freud, 1973, p. 150). Later analysts have pointed out that Freud's stressing of bisexuality implies that he also saw the feminine role to have been constructed out of prevailing social conditions, 'masculine' exceptions serving to prove this point (see e.g. Mitchell, 1990, p. 131).
89. Horney, 1973, p. 232.
90. Burdekin, 1934, p. 28.
91. Grunberger, 1974, p. 536.
92. *The Late Show*, BBC2, 20 May 1992.
93. Burdekin, 1985, p. 81.
94. Ibid., p. 6; her emphasis.
95. Ibid., p. 8.
96. Ibid., p. 31.
97. Ibid.
98. Ibid., p. 32.
99. In *Quiet Ways*, the central character, Helga, who has been brought up to 'think like an individual', is compared to her contemporaries who, it is suggested, in their vigorous support of the war ethic (the novel is set during World War I) are, like Hermann, hiding deep, inner conflicts.
100. Pagetti, 1990, p. 362.
101. Horney, 1973, p. 144; her emphasis.
102. Ibid., p. 143.
103. Ibid., p. 144.
104. Ibid., p. 145.
105. Theweleit, 1989, pp. 368–9.
106. Ibid.; his emphasis.
107. Ibid., p. 369.
108. Horney, 1973, p. 139.
109. Burdekin, 1985, p. 191.
110. Ibid., p. 71.
111. Pagetti, 1990, p. 364.
112. Patai, 1985, p. xii.
113. Ibid., p. xiv.

4   'No Woman Born': C. L. Moore's Dancing Cyborg

1. McLuhan, 1967 (1951), p. 84.
2. Haraway, 1991, p. 163.

3. Amis, 1983, p. 19.
4. del Rey, 1980, p. 152.
5. Warner, 1969, p. 31.
6. See Chapter 3.
7. Warner, 1969, p. 40.
8. Haraway, 1991, p. 151.
9. See Chapter 2.
10. Warner notes: 'Around 1940, it was possible to claim that there was no such thing as an independent, honest-to-goodness girl-type fan, because virtually all the females in fandom had a fannish boy friend, brother, husband, or some other masculine link', although, by 1948, a survey revealed that 'eleven per cent of all fandom now was feminine' (Warner, 1969, p. 26) and, in the same year, a competition in *Amazing Stories*, 'to locate the best fan writing of the year' (ibid., p. 29) was actually won by Marion Bradley, now well known for her *Darkover* novels (as Marion Zimmer Bradley) and her rewriting of mythology from the female point of view (*The Mists of Avalon* and *The Firebrand*).
11. Aldiss, 1988, p. 322.
12. Shippey, 1979, p. 98.
13. Russell, 1983, p. 209.
14. Ibid.
15. The relationship between the development of technology and the creation of mass culture had been an issue in cultural criticism for a number of years, for instance, in the work of the Frankfurt School. See e.g. Andrew Arato and Eike Gebhardt (eds), 1978.
16. Aldiss, 1988, p. 221.
17. Griffiths, 1980, p. 122.
18. Hales, 1982, p. 180.
19. Ibid., p. 177.
20. Ibid., p. 180.
21. Gramsci, 1971, p. 286.
22. Ibid., p. 309.
23. Ibid., p. 310.
24. Hales, 1982, p. 18.
25. Pacey, 1983, p. 25.
26. Aldiss, 1988, p. 310.
27. Mumford, 1932, p. 371.
28. McLuhan, 1967, p. 33.
29. Ibid., p. 34.
30. Ibid., p. 33.
31. Aleksander and Burnett, 1984, p. 22.
32. Wiener, 1948, p. 8.
33. Wiener, 1968, p. 53, his emphasis.
34. Rorvik, 1975, p. 102.
35. 'How to Become a Successful Wife' in *Women and Beauty Magazine*, 1946, p. 55.
36. *The Manchester Guardian*, 14 May 1947.
37. Bereano, Bose and Arnold, 1985, p. 168.
38. *Manchester Guardian*, 13 November 1952.

39. McLuhan, 1967, pp. 32 and 33.
40. Trescott, 1979, p. 19.
41. McLuhan, 1967, p. 154.
42. Friedan, 1963, p. 183.
43. Ibid.
44. Ibid., p. 184.
45. Wolf, 1990, p. 214.
46. See Wolf, 1990, pp. 118–21.
47. First stated in full in 'Runaround', *Astounding Science Fiction*, March 1942, reprinted in Asimov, 1983, pp. 269–70. For an interesting analysis of the three laws as constructed to ensure a level of obedience from 'thinking machines' analogous to the restraints imposed on women by the marriage vows, see Plant, 1996, p. 175 and Chapter 8, this volume.
48. Griffiths, 1980, p. 127.
49. McLuhan, 1967, p. 100.
50. Rorvik, 1975, p. 32.
51. Ibid.
52. Rosinsky, 1991, p. 524.
53. Moore, 1975, p. 279.
54. Ibid., p. 245.
55. Ibid., p. 246.
56. Ibid., p. 247.
57. Ibid., pp. 248 and 249.
58. Ibid., p. 276.
59. Ibid., p. 269.
60. In the opening pages he quotes from James Stephens' poem, which recounts the Celtic myth of Deirdre-of-the-Sorrows:

> The time comes when our hearts sink utterly,
> When we remember Deirdre and her tale,
> And that her lips are dust. . . .
> There has been again no woman born
> Who was so beautiful; not one so beautiful
> Of all the women born. . . .
> Let all men go apart and mourn together –
> No man can ever love her. Not a man
> Can dream to be her lover. . . . No man say –
> What could one say to her? There are no words
> That one could say to her

(See Moore, 1975, p. 237). The poem is a lament, mourning the tragic death of the young Deirdre who, in the myth, rather than become wife to the king who has killed her young lover and now claims her for his own, drinks her lover's blood to show her defiance of the king's wishes and takes her own life. Harris still dreams of being Deirdre's lover, and his image of the cyborg is correspondingly romantic. He cannot see Deirdre other than as her former self, 'the loveliest creature whose image ever moved along the airways' (ibid., p. 236), a point of view which tends to evoke McLuhan's Hollywood 'love machine'. But the reference to Deirdre-of-the-Sorrows, who dies rather than succumb to another's will, foreshadows the outcome of the story in which Deirdre refuses to comply with the way in which the scientist insists that she must conduct her life, now that she is, as he sees it, less than human. However, the cyborg does not die but remains to confront the scientist with his error of judgment.

61. Moore, 1975, p. 367; her emphasis.
62. Haraway, 1991, p. 181.
63. Ibid., p. 174.
64. Ibid.
65. Ibid., p. 163.
66. McLuhan, 1964, p. 5. McLuhan's *Understanding Media* can be read as an early formulation of the cyborg idea, concerned, as it is, with examining 'our own extended beings in our technologies' (ibid., p. 6). However, McLuhan tends to oscillate between distrust of the power of electronic media to manipulate consciousness and a belief 'that the unifying networks of electronic communication might restore mankind to a state of bliss not unlike the one said to have existed within the Garden of Eden' (Lapham, 1994, p. xvii).
67. Haraway, 1991, p. 150.
68. Ibid., p. 163.
69. Ibid.
70. Ibid., p. 175.
71. Ibid.
72. Moore, 1975, p. 276.
73. Ibid., p. 277.
74. Ibid., p. 276.
75. Ibid., p. 258.
76. Ibid.
77. King, 1984, p. 72.
78. Moore, 1975, p. 277.
79. Ibid., p. 253.
80. Ibid., p. 252.
81. Ibid., p. 257.
82. Ibid., p. 259.
83. Ibid.
84. Ibid., p. 258.
85. Innes, 1955, p. 231.
86. Hilton, 1991, p. 68.
87. Moore, 1975, pp. 278–9.
88. Ibid., p. 286.
89. Ibid., p. 250. Interestingly, David Rorvik gives an example of a living cyborg who would agree wholeheartedly with Deirdre's belief. He mentions a woman who, 'equipped with two implanted pacemakers, one for her heart and one for her bladder... insists that she now has a new rapport, a new "feeling for" things mechanical' (Rorvik, 1975, p. 101).
90. Moore, 1975, p. 269.
91. Ibid., p. 270.
92. Ibid., p. 256.
93. Ibid., p. 257.
94. Balsamo, 1996, p. 9.

95. Haraway, 1991, p. 169.
96. Moore, 1975, p. 258.
97. Ibid., p. 259.
98. Ibid., p. 281.
99. Ibid., p. 277.
100. Ibid., p. 269.
101. See Chapter 2.
102. Haraway, 1991, p. 151.
103. Ibid.
104. Moore, 1975, p. 257.
105. Kermode, 1957, p. 50.
106. Ibid., p. 43.
107. Ibid., p. 54.
108. Ibid., p. 56.
109. Kermode, 1957, p. 60.
110. McLuhan, , 1967, p. 34.
111. Moore, 1975, p. 261. It is possible that here Moore is making a reference to the 'Ziegfeld girls'. As Marshall McLuhan points out: 'There is nothing very human about twenty painted dolls rehearsing a series of clockwork taps, kicks and swings' (McLuhan, 1967, p. 94).
112. Ibid., p. 267.
113. Ibid., pp. 263–4.
114. Ibid., p. 258.
115. Ibid., p. 276.
116. Kermode, 1957, p. 64.
117. Moore, 1975, p. 265.
118. Ibid.

5 'Short in the Chest': Margaret St Clair and the Revenge of the Housewife Heroine

1. In Chris Hables Gray (ed.), *The Cyborg Handbook*, Routledge, New York and London, 1995, p. 364.
2. Herbert, 1991, p. 622.
3. Sargent, 1978, p. 21.
4. St Clair, 1979, p. 250.
5. Greenberg and Olander, 1979, p. 249.
6. Herbert, 1991, p. 623.
7. St Clair, 1981, p. 151.
8. St Clair, 1979, pp. 255 and 253.
9. St Clair, 1981, p. 153.
10. Ibid., 154.
11. St Clair explains in a footnote: 'For the record, be it observed that "dight" is a middle English word meaning, among other things, "to have intercourse with".... "Dight" was reintroduced by a late twentieth-century philologist who disliked the "sleep with" euphemism, and who saw that the language desperately needed a transitive verb that would be "good usage"' (St Clair, 1979, p. 250).

12. St Clair, 1979, p. 252.
13. Ibid., p. 251.
14. In Zamyatin's novel (believed by some to have influenced George Orwell) a 'pink ticket' secures 'a certificate' which entitles the citizen to 'the Right of Blinds', that is, an hour of privacy (see Zamyatin,1972 (1924), p. 35). Rebellion is precipitated by an illicit sexual encounter which leads to the protagonists' downfall.
15. See Chapter 3.
16. See Chapter 4.
17. St Clair here preempts Dr John C. Loehlin, 'an associate professor of psychology and computer science at the University of Texas' who has named his 'creative thinking' robot 'Aldous, fittingly enough in honor of the late Aldous Huxley, author of *Brave New World* and one of the most original thinkers of recent times' (Rorvik, 1975, pp. 48–9).
18. St Clair, 1979, p. 250.
19. Ibid., p. 249. Here, St Clair employs a technique used by George Orwell in *Nineteen Eighty-Four*, in which 'Newspeak' refers to terms which have been invented for the purpose of enforcing ideological conformity (see Appendix 'The Principles of Newspeak' in Orwell, 1984, pp. 231–42). In 'Short In The Chest', the cold war is played out on a cosmic scale (trying to reason with her dighting partner, Sonya tells him 'how the enemy were about to take Venus, when all we had was Mars' (St Clair, 1979, p. 254)), but St Clair leaves it to her readers to imagine whether the bombing is actual or synthesised.
20. St Clair, 1979, p. 256.
21. Ibid., p. 256.
22. Ibid., p. 257.
23. Ibid., p. 248.
24. Ibid., p. 257.
25. Ibid., p. 258.
26. Ibid., p. 257.
27. Ibid., p. 258.
28. Ibid., p. 249.
29. Ibid., p. 251.
30. Ibid., p. 258.
31. Ibid., p. 255.
32. Ibid., p. 259.
33. Ibid., p. 254.
34. Ibid., p. 256.
35. Ibid., p. 253.
36. Friedan, 1963, p. 110.
37. Faludi, 1992, p. 373.
38. See Chapter 4.
39. See Chapter 2.
40. Farnham and Lundberg, 1947, p. 143.
41. Firestone, 1979, p. 72.
42. Sargent, 1978, p. 19. Asimov's Clare Belmont in 'Satisfaction Guaranteed' is an excellent example (in *Amazing Stories*, April, 1951 and reprinted in Asimov, 1983, pp. 350–67).

43. St Clair, 1979, p. 259.
44. Ibid., p. 256.
45. See Chapter 3.
46. In *The Dialectic of Sex*, Firestone advocates artificial reproduction to 'free women . . . from their biology [and thus] threaten the social unit that is organized around biological reproduction and the subjection of women to their biological destiny' (Firestone, 1979, p. 193). Marge Piercy's celebrated sf novel, *Woman on the Edge of Time* (1976), imagines a future world where foetuses are incubated in artificial wombs and men receive hormone implants to enable them to breastfeed.
47. Huxley, of course, used a similar strategy in *Brave New World*. The women of Utopia keep their contraceptive kit in a 'Malthusian belt', named after the English philosopher Thomas Robert Malthus who, in his *Essay on Population* (1798 and 1803) proposed either sexual abstinence or some form of birth control in order to prevent overpopulation and starvation.
48. St Clair, 1979, p. 256.
49. Huxley, 1977, p. 21.
50. Huxley, 1950, p. 14.
51. Ibid., p. 15. Drugs, in fact, figure strongly in 'Short In The Chest'. Apart from the hormones designed to promote sexual desire, Major Briggs has been warned by her irate dighting partner that she would be made 'to take Pentothal and then the truth would come out,' and she confides in the huxley that she has heard 'they put cannabis in the drinks they serve you in the neutral areas' (St Clair, 1979, p. 253). (Cannabis was made illegal in the United States in 1914, many people believing that the real reason was because of its effect on productivity – here it is being put to a 'productive' use as an aphrodisiac).
52. St Clair, 1979, p. 250.
53. Watson, 1919, p. 2; his emphasis.
54. St Clair, 1979, p. 252.
55. Watson, 1919, p. 2.
56. St Clair, 1979, p. 252.
57. Kinsey, 1953, p. 745.
58. Ibid., p. 732.
59. Ibid., p. 9.
60. Trilling, 1970, p. 217; his emphasis.
61. Kinsey, 1953, p. 749.
62. Trilling, 1970, p. 213.
63. Ibid., p. 218.
64. Farnham and Lundberg, 1947, p. 24.
65. Ibid., p. 359.
66. Watson, 1919, p. 9; his emphasis.
67. St Clair, 1979, p. 251.
68. Ibid., p. 251.
69. There is a parallel here with the theme of natural rebellion in *Swastika Night* (see Chapter 3), where women are not being born in response to the demand for males. The suggestion that the enforced reduction of women has, ultimately, threatened their continued survival is here echoed by the threat to the supply of pork. Sonya does not even entertain the idea that enforced

breeding and the too early removal of the piglets from the mother may be causing the situation, just as, in *Swastika Night*, von Hess is unconvinced by Alfred's arguments as to the reason for the women's 'discouragement' (see Burdekin, 1985, pp. 104–12). Von Hess cannot be persuaded, because, for him, women have always demonstrated that they are inferior to men and thus are the instruments of their own reduction; likewise, Sonya associates the feeding of baby pigs with the sound of grunting, assuming the grunting, and that alone, to be the stimulus to feed, rather than, perhaps, the *result* of the feeding as Alfred suggests the women's reduction is potentially a *result* of their former oppression.

70. Marcuse, 1964, p. x.
71. Ibid., p. 98.
72. Ibid., p. 90.
73. Ibid., p. 97.
74. Ibid., p. 12.
75. St Clair, 1979, p. 254.
76. See Chapter 8 for a discussion of the Jewish myth of the golem as a meta- phor for the potential for unpredictability inherent in the nature of machine technology.
77. Wiener, 1963, p. 60.
78. Ibid., p. 67.
79. St Clair, 1979, p. 259.
80. Farnham and Lundberg, 1947, p. 39.
81. See Chapter 4.
82. Bergson, 1956, p. 79; his emphasis.
83. Ibid., pp. 80 and 81.

6 'Your Haploid Heart': James Tiptree Jr and Patterns of Gender

1. Siegel, 1985, p. 7.
2. Ibid., p. 10.
3. Cf. Thomas Pynchon and J. D. Salinger.
4. Steffen-Fluhr, 1990, p. 202.
5. Le Guin, 1979, p. 4.
6. Silverberg, 1975, p. xii.
7. Le Guin, 1978, p. xi.
8. Siegel, 1985, p. 7.
9. Ibid., p. 10.
10. Lefanu, 1988, p. 106. The title of Lefanu's book, *In the Chinks of the World Machine*, is taken from a Tiptree story 'The Women Men Don't See' (first published in *The Magazine of Fantasy and Science Fiction*, December 1973 and reprinted in the Tiptree anthology *Warm Worlds and Otherwise*).
11. Gearhart and Ross, 1983, pp. 443–4.
12. Le Guin, 1979, p. 163.
13. Siegel, 1988/9, p. 9.
14. Mead, 1962, p. 49.
15. Ibid.

16. Ibid., p. 51.
17. Ibid., p. 50.
18. Tiptree, 1975, p. 61.
19. Siegel, 1988/9, p. 9.
20. Tiptree, 1969, p. 11.
21. Ibid., p. 10.
22. Ibid., p. 14.
23. Ibid., p. 11.
24. Ibid., p. 12.
25. Ibid., p. 15.
26. Ibid., p. 16.
27. Ibid., p. 15.
28. Ibid., p. 28; her emphasis.
29. Ibid., p. 22.
30. Stableford, 1987, p. 211.
31. See J. G. Ballard, 'Myth Maker of the 20th Century' in Michael Moorcock (ed.), *New Worlds*, No. 142, May–June, 1964, pp. 121–7.
32. Greenland, 1983, p. 12.
33. Stableford, 1987, p. 211.
34. See Chapter 4.
35. Roszak, 1969, p. 205.
36. Ibid., p. 208.
37. See Chapter 4.
38. Millett, 1978, postscript.
39. Ali, 1987, p. 231.
40. Millett, 1978, p. 507.
41. Russ in Smith (ed.), 1975, p. 101.
42. Tiptree in Smith (ed.), 1975, p. 18; her emphasis.
43. See Chapter 2.
44. Tiptree in Smith (ed.), 1975, p. 18.
45. Ibid., pp. 18–19.
46. Ibid., p. 18.
47. Ibid., p. 20.
48. Ibid., p. 21.
49. Ibid., p. 19.
50. Ibid., p. 20; her emphasis.
51. Tiptree, 1978, p. 65.
52. Tiptree in Smith (ed.), 1975, p. 19.
53. This is where, for Tiptree's stories, a male narrator is important. I agree with Sarah Lefanu when she says: 'Tiptree's feminist vision in fact appears at its most powerful and complex in some of the stories that have a male narrator, or where the authorial voice is mediated through a macho world view, even though, or perhaps because, these stories, at least to this woman reader, are the most disturbing' (Lefanu, 1988, p. 122). In both 'Your Haploid Heart' and 'A Momentary Taste of Being', the male narrator stands as a symbol for the male hegemony of scientific thought which imposes its own categories as a starting point for analysis. It is only when these categories are broken down and understood as the source of misconception that the alien culture can be assimilated and described without reference to culture-bound viewpoints.

54. Tiptree, 1978, p. 1.
55. Lefanu, 1988, p. 109.
56. See Chapter 3.
57. See Chapter 2.
58. Tiptree in Smith (ed.), 1975, p. 17.
59. Thompson, 1981, p. 57.
60. Steffen-Fluhr, 1990, p. 200.
61. Lefanu, p. 109.
62. Pei, 1979, p. 272.
63. Thompson, 1981, p. 60.
64. Ibid., p. 58.
65. Tiptree, 1969, p. 19.
66. Ibid., p. 19.
67. Ibid., p. 30.
68. Ibid., p. 14.
69. In what is quite possibly a coincidence, the same issue of *Analog* in which 'Your Haploid Heart' first appeared, carried an editorial by John W. Campbell berating the 'National Academy of Sciences' in the US for refusing to investigate the potential 'genetic differences of intelligence among racial groups'. The explanation, 'It is essentially impossible to do good research in this field as long as there are such great social inequities, and such research is also so easily misunderstood in these times', convinces Campbell that '[t]hey must be uniformly, personally convinced that such an investigation would prove a politically embarrassing fact – that genetics *does* make a difference' (see John W. Campbell, *Analog*, September 1969, pp. 74–5). Here Campbell appears to be nailing his political colours to the mast (and giving an insight into the stance that fandom was likely to take towards the issue of civil rights). If it were proved that genetics 'does make a difference', would he then want to claim that 'social inequities' are justified? It would seem so.
70. Tiptree, 1969, p. 19.
71. Ibid., p. 15.
72. Ibid., p. 14.
73. See Chapter 3.
74. Tiptree, 1969, p. 20.
75. Harding, 1986, p. 22.
76. See Harding, 1986.
77. Harding, 1986, p. 96.
78. Tiptree, 1969, p. 38.
79. Ibid., p. 10.
80. Ibid.
81. Ibid., p. 18.
82. Ibid., p. 23.
83. Ibid., p. 22.
84. Ibid., p. 12.
85. Ibid., p. 38.
86. Barr, 1987, p. 34.
87. Tiptree, 1969, p. 38.
88. Ibid.

89. Ibid., p. 15.
90. Ibid., p. 17.
91. The counter-culture was both affiliated to, and defined against, the American system of higher education. Although the campuses were frequently the focus of counter-cultural political activity, the essence of the hippie ethos was in revolution against the system which imparted knowledge for the purposes of instilling in the next generation the ideology of the dominant culture (see Theodore Roszak, *The Making of a Counter Culture*, Faber & Faber, London, 1969).
92. Tiptree, 1969, p. 19.
93. Ibid., p. 16.
94. Ibid., p. 13.
95. Ibid.
96. Ibid., p. 21.
97. Ibid., p. 22.
98. Furman, 1985, p. 72.
99. Kristeva, 1980, p. 136.
100. Furman, 1985, p. 73.
101. Tiptree, 1969, p. 23.
102. Ibid., pp. 23–4.
103. Ibid., p. 24.
104. Ibid., p. 22; her emphasis.
105. Ibid., p. 31.
106. See Chapter 3.
107. Tiptree, 1969, p. 15.
108. Ibid., p. 17.
109. Roszak, p. 232; his emphasis.
110. Tiptree, 1969, p. 27.
111. See Chapter 2.
112. Tiptree, 1969, p. 36.
113. Ibid.
114. Tiptree, p. 37.

7 Amazons and Aliens: Feminist Separatism and the Future of Knowledge

1. Leland, 1983, p. 71.
2. Livingston, 1978, p. 170.
3. See, for example, Alman *et al.* (eds), *Which Homosexuality?*, a published collection of papers addressing these issues which were presented at a conference entitled 'Homosexuality, Which Homosexuality?' at the Free University, Amsterdam, 15 December 1987.
4. See for example Joanna Ryan, 'Psychoanalysis and Women Loving Women' in Crowley and Himmelweit (eds), *Knowing Women: Feminism and Knowledge*.
5. Rich, 1987, p. 54.
6. Ibid.; her emphasis.
7. Auerbach, 1978, p. 1.

8. Ibid., p. 6.
9. Ibid., p. 5.
10. Ibid.
11. In Margrit Eichler and Hilda Scott's collection of essays *Women in Futures Research* (concerned to identify areas in which feminist thought may contribute to future planning) Joan A. Rothschild, in common with several other writers in the collection, identifies feminist utopias as 'a...rewarding source for feminist future visions...reaching in new ways into every area that technology touches' (Rothschild in Eichler and Scott, 1982, p. 97).
12. Gearhart, 1985, pp. 2–3.
13. Zagarell, 1988, p. 499.
14. Ibid., p. 503.
15. Ibid., p. 507.
16. Ibid., p. 509.
17. Ibid., p. 510.
18. Ibid.
19. Henderson, 1983, p. 209; her emphasis. Frederick Engels argues also for a period of 'mother right' in which descent was reckoned matrilinearly and ownership of resources and produce was communal. See Eleanor Burke Leacock in Frederick Engels, 1972, p. 41.
20. Rich, 1987, p. 147; her emphasis.
21. Ibid., p. 141.
22. Gearhart, 1985, p. 149.
23. Ibid., p. 151.
24. Ibid., p. 150.
25. Ibid., p. 87.
26. Kristeva, 1986, p. 189; her emphasis.
27. Ibid., p. 191; her emphasis.
28. Ibid., p. 190; her emphasis.
29. Ibid., p. 191.
30. Lefanu, 1988, p. 69.
31. Kristeva, 1986, p. 191.
32. Gearhart, 1985, p. 80.
33. Ibid., p. 75.
34. Chesler, 1972, p. 169.
35. Sjöö and Mor, 1987, p. 97.
36. Wolff, 1971, p. 82.
37. Ibid , p. 60.
38. Rich, 1987, p. 98; her emphasis.
39. Gearhart, 1985, p. 47.
40. Ibid., p. 50.
41. Ibid., p. 47.
42. Ibid., p. 49.
43. Sjöö and Mor, 1987, pp. 73 and 74.
44. Ibid., p. 73.
45. Lefanu, 1988, p. 69.
46. Daly, 1978, p. 350.
47. Ibid., p. 347.
48. Ibid., p. 350.

49. Ibid.; her emphasis.
50. Sjöö and Mor, 1987, p. 75.
51. Gearhart, 1985, p. 203.
52. Ricoeur, 1988, p. 105.
53. Ibid.
54. Gearhart, 1985, p. 206.
55. Ibid., p. 12.
56. Ibid., p. 115.
57. Kristeva, 1986, p. 202; her emphasis.
58. Ibid., p. 204.
59. Gearhart, 1985, p. 68.
60. Ibid., p. 124.
61. Farley, 1984, p. 241.
62. Kristeva, 1986, p. 203.
63. Ibid., p. 205.
64. Kristeva refers to both the 'socio-symbolic contract' and the 'symbolic order'. In Lacanian terms, we enter into the symbolic order when we are initiated into the use of language, and it is thus an unavoidable part of the socialisation process. The word 'contract', however, implies an agreement entered into voluntarily. Kristeva's use of both terms raises the question of whether it is possible to view the entry into the symbolic order (the 'law of the father') as negotiable. What I believe she intends is that feminists should regard themselves as having chosen to be a part of the social order so that they can work for their own interests from a position of strength. The alternative position of regression from the symbolic order (the position taken by *The Wanderground*), she sees as disempowering.
65. Lefanu, 1988, p. 68.
66. Gearhart, 1985, p. 122.
67. Kristeva, 1986, p. 200.
68. Gearhart, 1985, p. 193.
69. Farley, 1984, p. 240.
70. Gearhart, 1985, p. 193.
71. Ibid., p. 194.
72. Farley, 1984, pp. 240–1.
73. Gearhart, 1985, p. 195.
74. Ibid., p. 196.
75. Ibid., p. 194.
76. Farley, 1984, p. 241.
77. This scene can also be read as a warning that men who are not obviously threatening are, nevertheless, male and therefore incapable of accessing the 'true' route to knowledge that Gearhart seems to want to claim for females. Evona's apparent paranoia can be read as a sensible caution, and it is possible that Gearhart's readers would have identified with her point of view.
78. Pfaelzer, 1988, p. 290.
79. Kristeva, 1986, p. 200.
80. Forbes, 1985, pp. 106 and 111.
81. Ibid., p. 115.
82. Ibid., p. 91.
83. Ibid.

84. Ibid., p. 92.
85. Rich, 1986, p. 223.
86. Ibid., p. 232.
87. Westkott, 1978, p. 18.
88. Ibid., p. 17.
89. Ibid., p. 19; her emphasis.
90. Gilligan, 1982, p. 8.
91. Ibid., p. 32.
92. Ibid., p. 17.
93. Ibid., p. 16.
94. Forbes, 1985, p. 113.
95. Ibid., p. 114.
96. Among the examples that Zagarell cites are Sarah Orne Jewett's *The Country of the Pointed Firs*, Flora Thompson's *Lark Rise to Candleford*, Toni Morrison's *Song of Solomon* and Alice Walker's *The Color Purple*. She also mentions George Eliot and Harriet Beecher Stowe in this context as well as many lesser known works.
97. Zagarell, 1988, p. 520.
98. Gearhart, 1985, p. 4.
99. Forbes, 1985, p. 146.
100. Ibid., p. 147.
101. Ibid., p. 148.
102. Ibid., p. 90.
103. Ibid., p. 143.
104. Ibid., p. 142.
105. Ibid., p. 140.
106. Ibid., p. 141; her emphasis.
107. Ibid., p. 148.
108. Farley, 1984, p. 241.
109. Kristeva, 1986, p. 193.
110. Ibid., p. 194.
111. Ibid., p. 203.
112. Ibid., p. 209; her emphasis.
113. Rose, 1983, pp. 80–1.
114. Ibid., p. 83; her emphasis.
115. Ibid.
116. Ibid., p. 84.
117. McNeil, 1987, p. 55.
118. Gearhart, 1983, p. 174.
119. Ibid., pp. 174 and 175.
120. Rorty, 1989, p. 7.
121. Ibid., pp. 17 and 16.
122. Ibid., p. 17.
123. Ibid., p. 16.
124. Ibid., p. 13.
125. Vance, 1989, pp. 29–30.
126. Ibid., p. 29.
127. Rorty, 1989, p. 53.
128. Haraway, 1991, p. 187.

129. Ibid., p. 189.
130. Ibid., p. 190.
131. Ibid., p. 191.
132. Ibid.
133. Ibid., p. 193.
134. Ibid., p. 198. Rorty uses the word 'conversation' in a similar context and with similar aims. He writes: 'If we see knowledge as a matter of conversation and of social practice, rather than as an attempt to mirror nature, we will not be likely to envisage a metapractice which will be the critique of all possible forms of social practice.' And: 'If we see knowing not as having an essence, to be described by scientists and philosophers, but rather as a right, by current standards, to believe, then we are well on the way to seeing *conversation* as the ultimate context within which knowledge is to be understood. Our focus shifts from the relation between human beings and the objects of their inquiry to the relation between alternative standards of justification and from there to the actual changes in those standards which make up intellectual history' (Rorty (1980) 1991, pp. 171 and 389–90).
135. Rorty, 1991, p. 5.
136. Ibid., p. 10.
137. Ibid., p. 7.
138. Ibid., p. 6.
139. Ibid., p. 10.
140. Pfaelzer, 1988, p. 288.
141. Kristeva, 1986, p. 209.

8   *Body of Glass*: Marge Piercy and Sex in Cyberspace

1. Bukatman, 1993; his emphasis.
2. Kranzler in *Foundation: the Review of Science Fiction*, Winter 1988/89.
3. Aldiss, 1988, Chapter 1.
4. Haraway, 1991, p. 180.
5. See Chapter 4.
6. For Kranzler also the monster can be read as female, as can Victor Frankenstein who 'faints or falls asleep at nearly every critical scene in the text and, apart from the creation of the monster, he fails to actually *do* anything' (see Kranzler, Winter 1988/89, pp. 43 and 44; her emphasis).
7. Haraway, 1991, p. 177.
8. See Chapter 6 and Harding, 1986, p. 22.
9. See Chapter 4.
10. Haraway, 1995, p. xvi.
11. Epstein, 1959, p. 227.
12. I can necessarily only give here a very brief outline of a very complex philosophical system which is open to a myriad of interpretations. The theory of Kabbalah is most fully expounded in an ancient text called the *Sefer Yetzirah* or Book of Creation. (See Gershom Gerhard Scholem, 1965).
13. Collins and Pinch, 1993, p. 2.
14. Maller, 1983, p. 32.
15. Piercy, 1991, p. 267.

16. Booker, 1994, p. 346.
17. Piercy, 1991, p. 563.
18. Ibid., p. 61.
19. Ibid., p. 33.
20. See Chapter 4.
21. Piercy, 1991, p. 282.
22. Ibid., p. 99.
23. Ibid., p. 348.
24. Ibid., p. 34.
25. Haraway, 1991, p. 151.
26. Piercy, 1991, p. 267.
27. Ibid., p. 584.
28. Sterling, 1986, p. xi.
29. Gibson, 1986, p. 19.
30. Sterling, 1986, p. x.
31. Wolmark, 1994, p. 111.
32. Ibid., p. 115.
33. Gordon, 1994, p. 196.
34. Hollinger, 1994, p. 207.
35. See *Neuromancer*, 1986.
36. Gibson, 1986, pp. 12 and 67.
37. Heim, 1991, pp. 67 and 78.
38. Haraway, 1991, p. 177.
39. Novak, 1991, p. 227.
40. Ibid.
41. Heim, 1991, p. 65.
42. Ibid., p. 63.
43. This can also be understood as corresponding to the kind of knowledge which the practitioner of Kabbalah will bring to his/her understanding of how the world of substance is to be apprehended. The Kabbalistic Theory of Ideas, in fact, corresponds closely to the Platonic notion of ideal forms. As Isidore Epstein has noted: '[t]his theory averring the existence of real incorporeal heavenly entities which served as patterns at creation for things on earth, has entered the history of philosophy through Plato, but it by no means originated with him' (Epstein, 1959, p. 228).
44. Heim, 1991, p. 65.
45. Piercy, 1991, p. 368.
46. Heim, 1991, p. 62.
47. As John Lechte points out, writing, for Derrida is, 'in the strictest sense . . . virtual, not phenomenal; it is not what is produced, but what makes production possible. It evokes the whole field of cybernetics, theoretical mathematics and information theory' (Lechte, 1994, p. 1080).
48. Bloom, 1975, p. 24.
49. Ibid.
50. Bloom, 1975, p. 28; his emphasis.
51. Derrida in Kamuf (ed.), 1991, p. 65.
52. Novak, 1998, p. 4.
53. See Chapter 7.
54. Stone, 1991, p. 102.

55. Piercy, 1991, p. 265.
56. Le Guin, 1979, p. 163.
57. Haraway, 1991, p. 176.
58. See Chapter 4.
59. Plant, 1996, p. 175.
60. Piercy, 1991, p. 332.
61. Plant, 1996, p. 173.
62. Iragaray, 1981, p. 101.
63. Ibid.; her emphasis.
64. Plant, 1996, p. 179.
65. Ibid.
66. The article is based on a paper presented under the title 'Drugs, Space and Cybernetics' at the Psychophysiological Aspects of Space Flight Symposium sponsored by the AF School of Aviation Medicine in San Antonio, Texas. See Gray (ed.), 1995, p. 29.
67. Clynes and Kline, 1995, p. 29.
68. Ibid., p. 31.
69. Haraway, 1997, p. 4.
70. Thacker, 1998, p. 4.
71. Stone, 1991, p. 83.
72. Ibid.
73. Ibid., p. 113.
74. Haraway, 1991, p. 201.
75. Wolmark, 1993, p. 133.
76. Parry, 1999, p. 5.
77. Ibid.
78. Parry, 1999, p. 6. The fact that the diversity of Nili's Israel also includes Palestinian women is, admittedly, somewhat utopian and also, when considered in connection with contemporary Israel, raises some uncomfortable questions if Nili's home is to be regarded as culturally Jewish. Piercy can be read as suggesting that women working together can overcome and accommodate differences (see my discussion of women's culture in Chapter 7), and while Parry's argument serves to strengthen the case for Tikva/Israel as sites of cyborg resistance, he also does not address the question of the political implications of the inclusion of Palestinian women or the fact that the apparent overcoming of deeply rooted differences suggests the essentialism which Haraway's cyborg is designed to avoid.
79. Haraway, 1991, p. 155.
80. Parry, 1999, p. 5.
81. Haraway, 1991, p. 155.
82. Haraway, 1997, p. 2.
83. Piercy, 1991, p. 216.
84. Botting, 1991, p. 139.
85. Ibid., p. 140.
86. Ibid., pp. 140 and 141.
87. Haraway, 1991, p. 151.
88. Ibid., p. 176.
89. Ibid., p. 175.
90. Piercy, 1991, p. 262.

91. Haraway, 1997, p. 2.
92. Piercy, 1991, p. 262.
93. Stabile, 1994, p. 151.
94. Haraway, 1997, p. 2.
95. Piercy, 1991, p. 262.

Conclusion: the *Frankenstein* Inheritance

1. Le Guin, 1979, p. 159. Genly Ai is the central character in Le Guin's novel *The Left Hand of Darkness*.
2. See Chapter 2.
3. See Chapter 3.
4. Le Guin, 1979, p. 159.
5. The recent debate centring on the production of 'Frankenstein' foods is only one of the most recent examples of the application of a particular reading of the myth to elucidate a political point. Although genetically modified organisms can be compared to the monster itself in that they are created by bringing together previously disparate units of DNA to create a previously non-existent form of life, the metaphor can be extended to include a critique of the way that multi-national companies involved in the production of these foods (for example, Monsanto) are seen to operate in their dealings with their customers (in particular, countries in what is referred to as the third world), who are required to adapt their farming methods to the procedures laid down by the company, thus ensuring their continued purchase of the product. This, coupled with the fear that the fall-out from fields planted with GMOs may adversely affect neighbouring 'organic' plantings, can be compared with the way that Victor Frankenstein attempts to control life for personal gain but is ultimately shown to have created something that cannot be controlled.
6. Barnes, 1990, p. 16.
7. See Chapter 8.
8. Stern, 1999, p. 3.
9. Ibid., p. 4.
10. Equally, as Megan Stern points out, Wollstonecraft was 'one of the most vocal British supporters of the French Revolution', and of course Mary Shelley was married to Percy Shelley who was 'expelled from Oxford for atheism'. She concludes that, given these 'radical credentials...it is reasonable to read her novel in relation to a medical system precipitated by the French Revolution' (Stern, 1999, p. 5).
11. See Chapter 8.

Bibliography

Abbott, Sidney and Love, Barbara, *Sappho was a Right On Woman*, Stein and Day, New York, 1978.

Aldiss, Brian with Wingrove, David, *Trillion Year Spree: the History of Science Fiction*, Grafton, London, 1988.

Aleksander, Igor and Burnett, Piers, *Re-Inventing Man*, Penguin, Harmondsworth, Middlesex, England, 1984.

Ali, Tariq, *Street Fighting Years*, Collins, London, 1987.

Altman, D. et al. (eds), *Which Homosexuality?* GMP, London, 1989.

Amis, Kingsley, *New Maps of Hell: a Survey of Science Fiction*, Gollancz, London, 1961.

—— (ed.), *The Golden Age of Science Fiction: an Anthology*, Penguin, London, 1983.

Arato, Andrew and Gebhardt, Eike (eds), *The Essential Frankfurt School Reader*, Basil Blackwell, Oxford and Urizen Books, New York, 1978.

Ardrey, Robert, *The Territorial Imperative*, Dell, New York, 1966.

Armitt, Lucie (ed.), *Where No Man Has Gone Before: Women and Science Fiction*, Routledge, London and New York, 1991.

Asimov, Isaac, *The Complete Robot*, Panther, London, 1983.

Auerbach, Nina, *Communities of Women: an Idea in Fiction*, Harvard University Press, Cambridge, Massachusetts and London, 1978.

Baldick, Chris, *In Frankenstein's Shadow*, Clarendon Press, Oxford, 1987.

Balsamo, Anne, *Technologies of the Gendered Body: Reading Cyborg Women*, Duke University Press, Durham and London, 1996.

Banks, Olive, *Faces of Feminism: a Study of Feminism as a Social Movement*, Martin Robertson, Oxford, 1981.

Barns, Ian, 'Monstrous Nature or Technology? Cinematic resolutions of the "Frankenstein Problem"' in *Science as Culture*, Vol. 9, Free Association Books, London, 1990.

Barr, Marlene S., *Future Females*, Bowling Green Press, Ohio, 1981.

——, *Alien to Femininity: Speculative Fiction and Feminist Theory*, Greenwood Press, New York, Westport, Connecticut and London, 1987.

Barron, Neil (ed.), *Anatomy of Wonder: a Critical Guide to Science Fiction*, Bowker, New York and London, 1987.

Bartkowski, Frances, *Feminist Utopias*, University of Nebraska Press, Lincoln and London, 1989.

Baudrillard, Jean, 'Simulacra and Science Fiction' (translated by Arthur B. Evans) in *Science Fiction Studies*, Vol. 18, 1991.

Baym, Nina, 'Melodramas of Beset Manhood' in Elaine Showalter, (ed.), *The New Feminist Criticism*, Virago, London, 1986.

Beer, Gillian, *Darwin's Plots*, Routledge, London, 1983.

——, 'Eve Was the First Scientist . . .' in *Women's Review*, Issue 11, September 1986.

Bereano, Philip, Bose, Christine and Arnold, Erik, 'Kitchen Technology and the Liberation of Women from Housework' in Wendy Faulkner and Erik Arnold (eds), *Smothered by Invention*, Pluto Press, London, 1985.

212   *Bibliography*

Bergson, Henri, *Laughter: an Essay on the Meaning of the Comic* (1911), Anchor Books, London, 1956.
Bigsby, C. W. E. (ed.), *Superculture: American Popular Culture and Europe*, Elek, London, 1975.
Birke, Linda, *Women, Feminism and Biology: the Feminist Challenge*, The Harvester Press, Brighton, 1986.
—— and Silvertown, Jonathan (eds), *More Than the Parts: Biology and Politics*, Pluto Books, London, 1984.
Blackwood, Evelyn (ed.), *The Many Faces of Homosexuality*, Harrington Park Press, New York and London, 1986.
Blake, Kathleen, *Love and The Woman Question in Victorian Literature: the Art of Self Postponement*, Harvester Press, Brighton, 1983.
Blamires, Harry, *The Age of Romantic Literature*, Longman, Harlow, 1989.
Bleier, Ruth, *Science and Gender*, Pergamon Press, New York and Oxford, 1984.
——, *Feminist Approaches to Science*, Pergamon Press, New York and Oxford, 1986.
Bloom, Harold, *Kabbalah and Criticism*, The Seabury Press, New York, 1975.
Booker, Keith M., 'Woman on the Edge of a Genre: the Feminist Dystopias of Marge Piercy' in *Science Fiction Studies*, Vol. 21, 1994.
Botting, Fred, *Making Monstrous: Frankenstein, Criticism, Theory*, Manchester University Press, 1991.
Bowler, Peter J., *Evolution: the History of an Idea*, University of California Press, Berkeley, LA and London, 1984.
Bowman Albinski, Nan, *Women's Utopias in British and American Fiction*, Routledge, New York and London, 1988.
Boyle, Charles, Wheale, Peter and Surgess, Brian, *People, Science and Technology: a Guide to Advanced Industrial Society*, Harvester Press, Brighton, 1984.
Brighton Women and Science Group, *Alice Through the Microscope*, Virago, London, 1980.
Brown, Stuart, Fauvel, John and Finnegan, Ruth (eds), *Conceptions of Inquiry*, Methuen in association with Open University Press, London and New York, 1981.
Bukatman, Scott, *Terminal Identity: the Virtual Subject in Postmodern Science Fiction*, Duke University Press, Durham and London, 1993.
Burdekin, Katharine, *Quiet Ways*, 1930 (see Constantine, Murray).
——, *Proud Man*, 1934 (see Constantine, Murray).
——, *Swastika Night*, Lawrence and Wishart, London, 1985.
——, *The End of This Day's Business*, Feminist Press, New York, 1989.
Caldecott, Leonie and Leland, Stephanie (eds), *Reclaim the Earth*, Women's Press, London, 1983.
Carr, Helen (ed.), *From My Guy to Sci-Fi: Genre and Women's Writing in the Postmodern World*, Pandora Press, London, 1989.
Challoner, Len, *Electrical Age*, October, 1945 (see Fawcett collection).
Chesler, Phyllis, *Women and Madness*, Avon Books, New York, 1972.
Chodorow, Nancy, *The Reproduction of Mothering: Psychoanalysis and the Sociology of Gender*, University of California Press, Berkeley, Los Angeles and London, 1978.
Clareson, Thomas (ed.), *SF: The Other Side of Realism*, Bowling Green University Popular Press, Ohio, 1971.
Clarke, I. F., *The Pattern of Expectation*, Cape, London, 1979.

Clynes, Manfred E. and Kline, Nathan S., 'Cyborgs and Space' in Chris Hables Gray (ed.), *The Cyborg Handbook*, Routledge, New York and London, 1995.

Cockshut, A. O. J., *Man and Woman: a Study of Love and The Novel, 1740–1940*, Collins, London, 1977.

Collins, Harry and Pinch, Trevor, *The Golem: What Everyone Should Know About Science*, Cambridge University Press, Cambridge, New York and Melbourne, 1993.

Constantine, Murray (Katharine Burdekin), *Quiet Ways*, Thornton Butterworth, London, 1930.

——, *Proud Man*, Boriswood, London, 1934.

Coote, Anna and Campbell, Beatrix, *Sweet Freedom*, Pan Books, London, 1982.

Cornillon, S. K. (ed.), *Images of Women in Fiction: Feminist Perspectives*, Bowling Green University Popular Press, Ohio, 1972.

Coward, Rosalind, *Patriarchal Precedents: Sexuality and Social Relations*, Routledge & Kegan Paul, London, 1983.

Croft, Andy, 'Worlds without End Foisted upon the Future: Some Antecedents of 1984' in Christopher Norris (ed.), *Inside the Myth: Orwell, Views from the Left*, Lawrence & Wishart, London, 1984.

Croghan, Anthony, *Science Fiction and the Universe of Knowledge: the Structure of an Aesthetic Form*, Coburgh Publications, London, 1981.

Crowley, Helen and Himmelweit, Susan, *Knowing Women: Feminism and Knowledge*, Polity Press, Cambridge, 1992.

Cruikshank, Margaret (ed.), *Lesbian Studies, Present and Future*, Feminist Press, New York, 1982.

Csicsery-Ronay Jr, Istvan, 'The SF of Theory: Baudrillard and Haraway' in *Science Fiction Studies*, Vol. 18, 1991.

Daly, Mary, *Gyn/Ecology: the Metaetheics of Radical Feminism*, Women's Press, London, 1978.

Davis, Elizabeth Gould, *The First Sex*, Dent, London, 1973.

Dawkins, Richard, *The Selfish Gene*, Oxford University Press, Oxford and New York, 1989.

De Beauvoir, Simone, *The Second Sex* (1949), Penguin Books, Harmondsworth, Middlesex, England, 1972.

De Lauretis, Teresa, Huyssen, Andreas and Woodward, Kathleen (eds), *The Technological Imagination: Theories and Fictions*, Coda Press, Madison, Wisconsin, 1980.

Del Rey, Lester, *The Best of C. L. Moore*, Ballantine, New York, 1975.

——, *The World of Science Fiction, 1926/76*, Garland, London and New York, 1980.

Delany, Samuel, *The Jewel Hinged Jaw: Notes on the Language of Science Fiction*, Dragon Press, Elizabethtown, New York, 1977.

Dolkart, Jane and Hartsock, Nancy, 'Feminist Visions of the Future' in *Quest*, Vol. 2, No. 1, 1975.

Easlea, Brian, *Science and Sexual Oppression*, George Weidenfeld & Nicholson, London, 1981.

——, *Fathering the Unthinkable*, Pluto Press, London, 1983.

Ehrenreich, Barbara, introduction to *Male Fantasies*, Vol. 1 (see Theweleit, Klaus).

Eichler, Margrit and Scott, Hilda (eds), *Women in Futures Research*, Pergamon Press, Oxford, 1982.

Engels, Frederick, *The Origin of the Family, Private Property and The State* (1902), Lawrence & Wishart, London (introduction by Eleanor Burke Leacock), 1972.

Epstein, Isidore, *Judaism* (1959), Penguin, Harmondsworth, England, 1990.

Ettorre, E. M., *Lesbians, Women and Society*, Routledge, London, Boston and Henley, 1980.

Faderman, Lillian, *Surpassing the Love of Men*, Women's Press, London, 1985.

Faludi, Susan, *Backlash: the Undeclared War against Women*, Chatto & Windus, London, 1991.

Farley, Tucker, 'Realities and Fictions: Lesbian Visions of Utopia' in Rohrlich, Baruch and Hoffman (eds), *Women in Search of Utopia: Mavericks and Mythmakers*, Schocklen Books, New York, 1984.

Farnham, Marynia and Lundberg, Ferdinand, *Modern Woman: The Lost Sex*, Harper & Bros., New York and London, 1947.

Fawcett collection, London Guildhall University (selection of articles about women and technology from *Manchester Guardian* etc.).

Fiedler, Leslie, 'Towards A Definition of Popular Literature' in Bigsby (ed.), *Superculture: American Popular Culture and Europe*, Elek, London, 1975.

Firestone, Shulamith, *The Dialectic of Sex*, Women's Press, London, 1979.

Forbes, Caroline, 'London Fields' in *The Needle on Full*, Onlywomen Press, London, 1985.

Ford, E. B., *Understanding Genetics*, Faber & Faber, London, 1979.

Foucault, Michel, *The History of Sexuality: an Introduction* (1976), Penguin Books, Harmondsworth, Middlesex, England, 1981.

Fowles, Jib (ed.), *The Handbook of Futures Research*, Greenwood Press, Westport, Conn. and London, 1978.

Freud, Sigmund, *New Introductory Lectures in Psychoanalysis* (first published in *The Standard Edition of the Complete Psychological Works of Sigmund Freud*, Vol. 22, by the Hogarth Press and the Institute of Psycho-Analysis, London, 1964), Penguin Books, Harmondsworth, Middlesex, England, 1973.

———, *Civilization and Its Discontents* (1930), Hogarth Press, London, 1975.

Friedan, Betty, *The Feminine Mystique* (1963), Penguin Books, Harmondsworth, Middlesex, England, 1965.

Furman, Nelly, 'The Politics of Language: Beyond the Gender Principle' in Greene and Kahn (eds), *Making a Difference: Feminist Literary Criticism*, Methuen, London, 1985.

Gamble, Sarah, '"Shambleau ... and others": the Role of the Female in the Fiction of C. L. Moore' in Armitt (ed.), *Where No Man Has Gone Before: Women and Science Fiction*, Routledge, London and New York, 1991.

Gearhart, Nancy S. and Ross, Jean W., entry on Alice Hastings Sheldon (James Tiptree Jr) in Hal May (ed.), *Contemporary Authors*, Vol. 108, Gale Research Company, Detroit, Michigan, 1983.

Gearhart, Sally Miller, 'An End To Technology: a Modest Proposal' in Rothschild (ed.), *Machina Ex Dea: Feminist Perspectives on Technology*, Pergamon Press, New York and Oxford, 1983.

———, *The Wanderground*, Women's Press, London, 1985.

Gibson, William, *Neuromancer*, Grafton, London, 1986.

———, *Count Zero*, Grafton, London, 1987.

Giedion, Siegfried, *Mechanization Takes Command*, Oxford University Press, 1948.

Gilbert, Sandra M. and Gubar, Susan, *The Madwoman in the Attic*, Yale University Press, New Haven and London, 1979.

———, *No Man's Land*, Vol. 1, Yale University Press, New Haven and London, 1988.

Gilligan, Carol, *In a Different Voice: Psychological Theory and Women's Development*, Harvard University Press, Cambridge, Mass. and London, 1982.

Gilman, Charlotte Perkins, *Man Made World: or, Our Androcentric Culture*, T. Fisher Unwin, London, 1911.

——, *His Religion and Hers*, T. F. Unwin, London, 1924.

——, *The Living of Charlotte Perkins Gilman: an Autobiography*, D. Appleton, Century, New York, 1935.

——, *Women and Economics* (1898), Harper & Row, New York, 1966.

——, *Herland* (1914), Women's Press, London, 1979.

——, *The Yellow Wallpaper* (1892), Virago, London, 1981.

Gloversmith, Frank (ed.), *Class, Culture and Social Change: a New View of the 1930s*, Harvester Press, Brighton, 1980.

Gordon, Joan, 'Yin and Yang Duke It Out' in Larry McCaffrey, (ed.), *Storming the Reality Studio: a Casebook of Cyberpunk and Postmodern Science Fiction*, Duke University Press, Durham and London, 1991.

Gramsci, Antonio, *Selections from Prison Notebooks* (1948–51), Lawrence & Wishart, London, 1971.

Graves, Robert, *The Greek Myths*, Vol. 1, Penguin Books, Harmondsworth, Middlesex, England, 1955.

—— and Hodge, Alan, *The Long Week-End: a Social History of Great Britain, 1918–1939*, Hutchinson, 1940.

Green, Gayle and Kahn, Coppelia (eds), *Making a Difference: Feminist Literary Criticism*, Methuen, London, 1985.

Green, Jen and Lefanu, Sarah, *Despatches From the Frontiers of the Female Mind*, Women's Press, London, 1985.

Greenberg, Martin, *Fantastic Lives: Autobiographical Essays by Notable Science Fiction Writers*, Southern Illinois University Press, Carbondale, 1981.

Greenberg, Martin H. and Olander, Joseph (eds), *Science Fiction of the 50s*, Avon Books, New York, 1979.

Greenland, Colin, *The Entropy Exhibition: Michael Moorcock and The British 'New Wave' in Science Fiction*, Routledge, London, 1983.

Griffiths, John, *Three Tomorrows: American British and Soviet Science Fiction*, Macmillan, London, 1980.

Grunberger, Richard, *A Social History of the Third Reich*, Penguin Books, Harmondsworth, Middlesex, England, 1974.

Gubar, Susan, 'C. L. Moore and The Conventions of Women's Science Fiction' in *Science Fiction Studies*, Vol. 7, Pt 1, 1980.

Gunew, Sneja (ed.), *A Reader in Feminist Knowledge*, Routledge, London and New York, 1991.

Hales, Mike, *Science or Society: the Politics of the Work of Scientists*, Pan Books, London, 1982.

Haraway, Donna, J., 'A Cyborg Manifesto: Science, Technology, and Socialist-Feminism in the Late Twentieth Century' (1985) in *Simians, Cyborgs and Women: the Reinvention of Nature*, Free Association, Books, London, 1991.

——, 'Situated Knowledges: the Science Question in Feminism and the Privilege of Partial Perspective' (1988) in *Simians, Cyborgs and Women: the Reinvention of Nature* (as above).

——, *Primate Visions: Gender, Race and Nature in the World of Modern Science* (1989), Verso, London and New York, 1992.

Haraway, Donna, J., 'Cyborgs and Symbionts Living Together in the New World Order' in Chris Hables Gray (ed.), *The Cyborg Handbook*, Routledge, New York and London, 1995.

——, *Modest_Witness@Second_Millennium.FemaleMan©_Meets_OncoMouse*™: *Feminism and Technoscience*, Routledge, New York and London, 1997.

Harding, Sandra, *The Science Question in Feminism*, Open University Press, Milton Keynes, 1986.

——, *Whose Science? Whose Knowledge?* Cornell University Press, New York, 1991.

——, 'How The Women's Movement Benefits Science: Two Views' in Gill Kirkup and Laurie Smith Keller (eds), *Inventing Women: Science, Technology and Gender*, Polity Press, Cambridge, 1992.

Harding, Sandra and Hintikka, Merrill (eds), *Discovering Reality: Feminist Perspectives on Epistemology, Metaphysics, Methodology and Philosophy of Science*, Reidel, Dordrecht, 1983.

Heim, Michael, 'The Erotic Ontology of Cyberspace' in Benedikt, Michael (ed.), *Cyberspace First Steps*, MIT Press, Cambridge Massachusetts and London, 1992.

Heldreth, Lillian M, '"Love is the Plan, the Plan is Death": The Feminism and Fatalism of James Tiptree Jr', in *Extrapolation*, Vol. 23, No. 1, 1982.

Henderson, Hazel, 'The Warp and The Weft: the Coming Synthesis of Eco-Philosophy and Eco-Feminism' in Caldecott and Leland (eds), *Reclaim the Earth*, Women's Press, London, 1983.

Herbert, Rosemary, entry on Margaret St Clair in Watson and Schellinger (eds), *Twentieth Century Science Fiction Writers* (3rd edition), St James Press, Chicago and London, 1991.

Hill, Mary A., *Charlotte Perkins Gilman: the Making of a Radical Feminist 1860–1896*, Temple University Press, Philadelphia, 1980.

Hilton, Julian, 'Theatricality and Technology: Pygmalion and The Myth of the Intelligent Machine' in Göranzon and Florin (eds), *Dialogue and Technology – Art and Knowledge*, Springer-Verlag, Berlin and Heidelberg, 1991.

Hoagland, Sarah Lucia and Penelope, Julia (eds), *For Lesbians Only*, Onlywomen Press, London, 1988.

Hodges, Sheila, *Gollancz: the Story of a Publishing House 1928–1978*, Gollancz, London, 1978.

Hofstadter, Richard, *Social Darwinism in American Thought*, George Braziller, New York, 1959.

Hoggart, Richard, *The Uses of Literacy*, Penguin Books, Harmondsworth, Middlesex, England, 1957.

Hollinger, Veronica, 'Cybernetic Deconstructions: Cyberpunk and Postmodernism' in Larry McCaffrey (ed.), *Storming the Reality Studio: a Casebook of Cyberpunk and Postmodern Science Fiction*, Duke University Press, Durham and London, 1994.

Horney, Karen, *Feminine Psychology*, W. W. Norton & Co, New York and London, 1973.

Houghton, Walter E., *The Victorian Frame of Mind*, Yale University Press, New Haven, 1957.

Howarth, Patrick, *Play Up and Play The Game*, Eyre Methuen, London, 1973.

Hubbard, R., Henifen, M. S. and Fried, B. (eds), *Women Look at Biology Looking at Women*, Schenkman Publishing, Cambridge, Mass., 1979.

Hulton, Margaret (ed.), *Science and Technology in the Arts*, Van Nostrand Reinhold, London and New York, 1974.

Huxley, Aldous, *Brave New World*, Chatto and Windus, London, 1950 (includes author's preface).
——, *Brave New World* (1932), Grafton Books, London, 1977.
Innes, Mary M. (trans.), *The Metamorphoses of Ovid*, Penguin Books, Harmondsworth, Middlesex, England, 1955.
Iragaray, Luce, 'This Sex Which is Not One' (excerpt) in Elaine Marks and Isabelle de Courtivron, (eds), *New French Feminisms: An Anthology*, Harvester Wheatsheaf, New York and London, 1981.
Isaacs, Leonard, *Darwin to Double Helix*, Butterworth, London, 1977.
Jackson, Rosemary, *Fantasy: the Literature of Subversion*, Methuen, London and New York, 1981.
Jacobus, Mary (ed.), *Women Writing and Writing About Women*, Croom Helm, Kent, 1979.
Jacobus, Mary, Keller, Evelyn Fox and Shuttleworth, Sally (eds), *Body/Politics: Women and The Discourses of Science*, Routledge, New York and London, 1990.
Janeway, Elizabeth, *Between Myth and Morning: Women Awakening*, William Morrow, New York, 1974.
Johnston, Jill, *Lesbian Nation: the Feminist Solution*, Simon & Schuster, New York, 1973.
Jordanova, Ludmilla, *Language of Nature*, Free Association Books, 1985.
——, *Sexual Visions: Images of Gender in Science and Medicine Between the Eighteenth and Twentieth Centuries*, Harvester Wheatsheaf, London, 1989.
Kamuf, Peggy (ed.), *A Derrida Reader: Between the Blinds*, Harvester Wheatsheaf, London and New York, 1991.
Karpf, Anne, 'Recent Feminist Approaches to Women and Technology' in Maureen McNeil (ed.), *Gender and Expertise*, Free Association Books, London, 1987.
Kaveney, Roz, 'The Science Fictiveness of Women's Science Fiction' in Carr (ed.), *From My Guy to Sci-Fi: Genre and Women's Writing in the Postmodern World*, Pandora Press, London, 1989.
Keller, Evelyn Fox, 'Women, Science and Popular Mythology' in Rothschild (ed.), *Machina Ex Dea: Feminist Perspectives on Technology*, Pergamon Press, New York, London, Ontario, 1983.
Keller, Laurie Smith, 'Discovering and Doing: Science and Technology, An Introduction' in Gill Kirkup and Laurie Smith Keller (eds), *Inventing Women: Science, Technology and Gender*, Polity Press, Cambridge, 1992.
Kennard, Jean E., 'Ourself Behind Ourself: a Theory for Lesbian Readers' in *Signs: Journal of Women in Culture and Society*, Vol. 9, No. 4, 1984.
Kermode, Frank, *The Romantic Image*, Routledge, London, 1957.
——, *The Sense of an Ending*, Oxford University Press, Oxford and New York, 1966.
Keulen, Margarete, *Radical Imagination: Feminist Conceptions of the Future in Ursula Le Guin, Marge Piercy and Sally Miller Gearhart*, Peter Lang, Frankfurt, Bern, New York and Paris, 1991.
King, Betty, *Women of the Future*, Scarecrow Press, London, 1984.
King, Ynestra, 'The Eco-Feminist Imperative' in Caldecott and Leland (eds), *Reclaim The Earth*, Women's Press, London, 1983.
Kinsey, A. C. et al., *Sexual Behaviour in the Human Female*, W. B. Saunders, 1953.
Klein, Melanie, *Love, Guilt and Reparation and Other Works, 1921–1945*, Dell, New York, 1975.

Koonz, Claudia, *Mothers in the Fatherland: Women, the Family and Nazi Politics*, Methuen, London, 1987.

Kramarae, Cheris (ed.), *Technology and Women's Voices*, Routledge, London and New York, 1988.

Kranzler, Laura, 'Frankenstein and the Technological Future' in *Foundation: The Review of Science Fiction*, No. 44, Winter 1988–89.

Kristeva, Julia, *Desire in Language: a Semiotic Approach to Literature and Art*, Basil Blackwell, Oxford, 1980.

——, 'Women's Time' in Moi (ed.), *The Kristeva Reader*, Basil Blackwell, Oxford, 1986.

Kuper, Adam, *The Invention of Primitive Society: Transformations of an Illusion*, Routledge, London, 1988.

Lapham, Lewis H., introduction to Marshall McLuhan, *Understanding Media*, MIT Press, Cambridge, Massachusetts and London, 1994.

Late Show (The), 'Degenerate Art', BBC2, 20 May 1992.

Le Guin, Ursula, *The Left Hand of Darkness*, Futura, London, 1969.

——, introduction to James Tiptree Jr, *Star Songs of an Old Primate*, Del Rey, Baltimore, 1978.

——, *The Language of the Night*, G. P. Putnam's Sons, New York, 1979.

Lechte, John, *Fifty Key Contemporary Thinkers: from Structuralism to Postmodernity*, Routledge, London and New York, 1994.

Lefanu, Sarah, *In The Chinks of the World Machine: Feminism and Science Fiction*, Women's Press, London, 1988.

——, 'Popular Writing and the Feminist Intervention in Science Fiction' in Longhurst (ed.), *Gender, Genre and Narrative Pleasure*, Unwin, Hyman, London, 1989.

Left News, Nos 50 and 54, Gollancz, London, July and December 1940.

Leland, Stephanie, 'Feminism and Ecology: Theoretical Connections' in Caldecott and Leland, 1983.

Lessing, Doris, 'Between the Fax and The Fiction' in the *Guardian*, London and Manchester, 13 December 1992.

Levin, Ira, *The Stepford Wives*, Michael Joseph, London, 1972.

Lewis, Jane, 'In Search of a Real Equality: Women between the Wars' in Gloversmith (ed.), *Class, Culture and Social Change: a New View of the 1930s*, Harvester Press, Brighton, 1980.

Livingston, Dennis, 'The Utility of Science Fiction' in Fowles (ed.), *The Handbook of Futures Research*, Greenwood Press, Westport, Conn. and London, 1978.

Longhurst, Derek (ed.), *Gender, Genre and Narrative Pleasure*, Unwin, Hyman, London, 1989.

Lorenz, Konrad, *On Aggression*, Harcourt Brace & World, New York, 1966.

McLuhan, Marshall Herbert, *Understanding Media: the Extensions of Man*, Routledge & Kegan Paul, London, 1964.

——, *The Mechanical Bride* (1951), Routledge, London, 1967.

McNeil, Maureen (ed.), *Gender and Expertise*, Free Association Books, London, 1987.

Malik, Rex (ed.), *Future Imperfect, Science Fact and Science Fiction*, Pinter, London, 1980.

Maller, Rabbi Allen S., *God, Sex and Kabbalah (Messianic Speculations)*, Ridgefield Publishing Company, Los Angeles, 1983.

Malthus, Thomas Robert, *An Essay on the Principle of Population* (1872) (2 vols), J. M. Dent & Sons, London, and E. P. Dutton & Co, New York, 1958.

Manchester Guardian (see Fawcett Collection).

Marcuse, Herbert, *Five Lectures: Psychoanalysis, Politics and Utopia*, Allen Lane, The Penguin Press, London, 1970.

——, *One Dimensional Man* (1964), Sphere Books, London, 1972.

Marx, Leo, *The Machine in the Garden*, Oxford University Press, New York, 1964.

Mason, Carol, Greenberg, Martin Harry and Warwick, Patricia (eds), *Anthropology through Science Fiction*, St. Martin's Press, New York, 1974.

May, Hal (ed.), *Contemporary Authors*, Vol. 108, Gale Research Company, Detroit, Michigan, 1983.

Mead, Margaret, *Male and Female* (1950), Penguin Books, Harmondsworth, Middlesex, England, 1962.

Meek, Ronald L., *Social Science and the Ignoble Savage*, Cambridge University Press, 1976.

Merchant, Carolyn, *The Death of Nature: Women, Ecology and The Scientific Revolution*, Wildwood House, London, 1982.

Merrill, Judith, 'What Do You Mean: Science? Fiction?' in Clareson (ed.), *SF: the Other Side of Realism*, Bowling Green University Popular Press, 1971.

Mill, John Stuart, *The Subjection of Women*, Longman, Green, Reader and Dyer, London, 1869.

Millett, Kate, *Sexual Politics* (1969), Ballantine, New York, 1978.

Mitchell, Juliet, *Psychoanalysis and Feminism*, (1974), Penguin Books, London and New York, 1990.

Modleski, Tania, *Loving with a Vengeance: Mass Produced Fantasies for Women*, Routledge, New York and London, 1990.

Moi, Toril (ed.), *The Kristeva Reader*, Basil Blackwell, Oxford, 1986.

Monk, Patricia, 'Frankenstein's Daughters: the Problem of the Feminine Image in Science Fiction' in Teunissen (ed), *Other Worlds*, Mosaic, Canada, 1980.

Moore, C. L., 'No Woman Born' (1944) in del Rey (ed.), *The Best of C. L. Moore*, Ballantine, New York, 1975.

Morgan, Lewis Henry, *Ancient Society* (1878), University of Arizona Press, Tucson, 1985.

Morris, Desmond, *The Illustrated Naked Ape* (1969), Cape, London, 1986.

Mowat, Charles Loch, *Britain between the Wars, 1918–1940*, Methuen, London, 1955.

Mumford, Lewis, *Technics and Civilization*, Routledge, London, 1934.

Myers, Robert E. (ed.), *The Intersection of Science Fiction and Philosophy*, Greenwood, London, 1983.

Newton, Judith L., *Women, Power and Subversion*, University of Georgia Press, 1981.

Nicholls, Peter, *The Encyclopaedia of Science Fiction*, Dolphin, New York, 1979.

—— (ed.), *The Science in Science Fiction*, Joseph, London, 1982.

Nicholson, Linda J. (ed.), *Feminism/Postmodernism*, Routledge, London, 1990.

Norris, Christopher (ed.), *Inside the Myth: Orwell, Views from the Left*, Lawrence & Wishart, London, 1984.

Novak, Marcos, 'Liquid Architectures in Cyberspace' in Benedikt, Michael (ed.), *Cyberspace First Steps*, MIT Press, Cambridge, Massachusetts and London, 1991.

——, 'Transmitting Architecture: the Transphysical City' in *Ctheory*, www.ctheory.com/a34-transmitting_arch.html (accessed in November, 1998).

Orwell, George, *Nineteen Eighty-Four* (1949), Secker & Warburg, London, 1984.

Pacey, Arnold, *The Culture of Technology*, Basil Blackwell, Oxford, 1983.

Pagetti, Carlo, 'In the Year of Our Lord Hitler 720: Katharine Burdekin's *Swastika Night*' in *Science Fiction Studies*, Vol. 17, Pt 3, 1990.

Palmeri, Ann, 'Charlotte Perkins Gilman: Forerunner of a Feminist Social Science' in Harding and Hintikka (eds), *Discovering Reality: Feminist Perspectives on Epistemology, Metaphysics, Methodology and Philosophy of Science*, Reidel, Dordrecht, 1983.

Parrinder, Patrick, *Science Fiction: A Critical Guide*, Longman, New York, 1979.

——, *Science Fiction, Its Criticism and Teaching*, Methuen, London, 1980.

Parry, Gareth, 'Virtual Aliyah: Cyborg Theory and Marge Piercy's *Body of Glass*' (unpublished paper), 1999.

Patai, Daphne, *The Orwell Mystique: a Study in Male Ideology*, University of Massachussetts Press, Amherst, 1984.

——, 'Orwell's Despair, Burdekin's Hope: Gender and Power in Dystopia' in *Women's Studies International Forum*, Vol. 7, No. 2, 1984.

——, introduction to 1985 edition of *Swastika Night* (see Burdekin, Katharine).

Pearson, Carol, 'Beyond Governance: Anarchist Feminism in the Utopian Novels of Dorothy Bryant, Marge Piercy and Mary Staton' in *Alternative Futures, The Journal of Utopian Studies*, Winter, 1981.

Pei, Lowry, 'Poor Singletons: Definitions of Humanity in the Stories of James Tiptree Jr' in *Science Fiction Studies*, No. 19, Vol. 6, Pt 3, 1979.

Pfaelzer, Jean, 'The Changing of the Avant Garde: the Feminist Utopia' in *Science Fiction Studies*, Vol. 15, Pt 3, 1988.

Piercy, Marge, *Women on the Edge of Time*, Women's Press, London, 1979.

——, *Body of Glass*, Penguin Books, London, 1992.

Pildes, Judith, 'Mothers and Daughters: Understanding the Roles' in *Frontiers: Women's Studies Program, University of Colorado*, Vol. 3, No. 2, 1978.

Plant, Sadie, 'On the Matrix: Cyberfeminist Simulations' in Rob Shields (ed.), *Cultures of Internet: Virtual Spaces, Real Histories, Living Bodies*, Sage, London, 1996.

Platt, Charles, *Dream Makers: Science Fiction and Fantasy Writers at Work*, Xanadu, London, 1987.

Poirier, Richard, *The Renewal of Literature*, Random House, New York, 1987.

Poovey, Mary, *The Proper Lady and the Woman Writer*, University of Chicago Press, Chicago and London, 1984.

Porush, David, *The Soft Machine: Cybernetic Fiction*, Methuen, London and New York, 1985.

Potter, Allen M., Fotheringham, P. and Kellas, J. G., *American Government and Politics*, Faber & Faber, London and Boston, 1955.

Pratt, Annis, *Archetypal Patterns in Women's Fiction*, Harvester Press, Brighton, 1982.

Rabkin, Eric S., *Science Fiction: a Historical Anthology*, Oxford University Press, 1983.

Radford, Jean (ed.), *The Progress of Romance: the Politics of Popular Fiction*, Routledge, London, 1986.

Radstone, Susannah (ed.), *Sweet Dreams: Sexuality, Gender and Popular Fiction*, Lawrence & Wishart, London, 1986.

Reed, Evelyn, *Women's Evolution*, Pathfinder, New York, 1975.

Reich, Wilhelm, *The Mass Psychology of Fascism* (1946), Penguin Books, Harmondsworth, Middlesex, England, 1970.

Reiss, Timothy J., *The Discourse of Modernism*, Cornell University Press, London, 1982.

Rich, Adrienne, *Of Woman Born*, W. W. Norton, New York and London, 1986.

——, *Blood, Bread and Poetry: Selected Prose, 1979–1985*, Virago, London, 1987.

Ricoeur, Paul, *Time and Narrative*, Vol. 3, The University of Chicago Press, Chicago and London, 1988.

Rigney, Barbara Hill, *Madness and Sexual Politics in the Feminist Novel*, University of Wisconsin Press, London, and Madison, Wisc., 1978.

Roberts, Robin, 'Post-Modernism and Feminist Science Fiction' in *Science Fiction Studies*, Vol. 17, Pt 2, 1990.

Rohrlich, Ruby and Buruch, Elaine Hoffman (eds), *Women in Search of Utopia: Mavericks and Mythmakers*, Schocken Books, New York, 1984.

Rorty, Richard, *Contingency, Irony and Solidarity*, Cambridge University Press, Cambridge, 1989.

——, *Philosophy and the Mirror of Nature* (1980), Basil Blackwell, Oxford, 1991.

——, 'Feminism and Pragmatism' in *Radical Philosophy*, Autumn, 1991.

Rorvik, David, *As Man Becomes Machine*, Abacus Books, London, 1975.

Rose, Hilary, 'Hand, Brain and Heart: a Feminist Epistemology for the Natural Sciences' in *Signs: Journal of Women in Culture and Society*, Vol. 9, No. 1, Autumn, 1983.

Rose, Mark (ed.), *Science Fiction: a Collection of Critical Essays*, Prentice-Hall, Englewood Cliffs, New Jersey, 1976.

Rosenberg, Rosalind, *Beyond Separate Spheres: Intellectual Roots of Modern Feminism*, Yale University Press, London and New Haven, 1982.

Rosinsky, Natalie, entry on C. L. Moore in Watson and Schellinger (eds), *Twentieth Century Science Fiction Writers* (3rd edn), St James Press, Chicago and London, 1991.

Roszak, Theodore, *The Making of a Counter Culture*, Faber & Faber, London, 1969.

Rothschild, Joan, *Machina Ex Dea*, Pergamon Press, Oxford and New York, 1983.

Rowbotham, Sheila, *Women in Movement: Feminism and Social Action*, Routledge, New York and London, 1992.

Russ, Joanna, 'The Image of Women in Science Fiction' in Cornillon (ed.), *Images of Women in Fiction: Feminist Perspectives*, Bowling Green University Popular Press, Ohio, 1972.

——, 'Recent Feminist Utopias' in Barr (ed.), *Future Females*, Bowling Green University Popular Press, Ohio, 1981.

——, *The Female Man* (1975), The Women's Press, London, 1985.

Russell, Dora, *The Religion of the Machine Age*, Routledge, London, 1983.

Sargent, Pamela, *Women of Wonder: Sf Stories by Women about Women*, Penguin Books, Harmondsworth, Middlesex, England, 1978.

—— (ed.), *New Women of Wonder*, Penguin Books, Harmondsworth, Middlesex, England, 1979.

Schiebinger, Londa, *The Mind Has No Sex? Women in the Origins of Modern Science*, Harvard University Press, Cambridge, Mass. and London, 1989.

Schenk, H. G., *The Mind of the European Romantics* (1966), Oxford University Press, Oxford, New York, Toronto and Melbourne, 1979.

Scholem, Gershom Gerhard, *On the Kabbalah and Its Symbolism* (trans. Ralph Manheim), Routledge & Kegan Paul, London, 1965.

Scholes, Robert, *Structural Fabulation*, University of Notre Dame Press, Notre Dame and London, 1975.

Scholes, Robert and Rabkin, Eric S., *Science Fiction: History, Science, Vision*, Oxford University Press, London, Oxford and New York, 1977.

Schur, Edwin M., *Labeling Women Deviant: Gender, Stigma and Social Control*, Temple University Press, Philadelphia, 1983.

Seal, Julie Leudke, 'James Tiptree Jr: Fostering the Future, Not Condemning It' in *Extrapolation*, Vol. 31, No. 1, Spring 1990.

Segal, Hanna, *Introduction to the Work of Melanie Klein*, Hogarth Press, London, 1973.

Shands, Kerstin W., *The Repair of the World: the Novels of Marge Piercy*, Greenwood Press, Westport, Conn. and London, 1994.

Shelley, Mary W., *Frankenstein: or, the Modern Prometheus* (1818), Oxford University Press, 1969 (reprint of 1831 edition containing Shelley's own introduction).

——, *Frankenstein: or, the Modern Prometheus*, Everyman, London, 1985.

Shinn, Thelma J., *Worlds Within Women: Myth and Mythmaking in Fantastic Literature by Women*, Greenwood, New York, 1986.

Shippey, T. A., 'The Cold War in Science Fiction, 1940–1960' in Parrinder (ed.), *Science Fiction: a Critical Guide*, Longman, New York, 1979.

Showalter, Elaine, *A Literature of Their Own*, Princeton University Press, 1977.

—— (ed.), *The New Feminist Criticism*, Virago, London, 1986.

Siegel, Mark, *James Tiptree Jr*, Starmont Readers Guide 22, Starmont House, Washington, USA, 1985.

——, 'Love Was the Plan, The Plan Was . . . : a True Story about James Tiptree Jr' in *Foundation: The Review of Science Fiction*, No. 44, Winter, 1988/89.

Silverberg, Robert, 'Who Is Tiptree, What Is He?' in James Tiptree Jr, *Warm Worlds and Otherwise*, Ballantine, New York, 1975.

Sjöö, Monica and Mor, Barbara, *The Great Cosmic Mother: Rediscovering the Religion of the Earth*, Harper & Row, San Francisco, 1987.

Smith, Jeffrey D. (ed.), *Khatru* 3 and 4, Phantasmicon Press, Baltimore, 1975.

Spender, Dale, *Women of Ideas (and What Men Have Done to Them)*, Ark Paperbacks, London, 1983.

——, *For the Record: the Making and Meaning of Feminist Knowledge*, Women's Press, London, 1985.

Sperry, Roger, *Science and Moral Priority*, Basil Blackwell, Oxford, 1983.

Srajek, Martin C., *In the Margins of Deconstruction: Jewish Conceptions of Ethics in Emmanuel Levinas and Jacques Derrida*, Kluwer Academic Publishers, Dordrecht, Boston and London, 1998.

St Clair, Margaret, 'Short In The Chest' (1954) in Greenberg and Olander (eds), *Science Fiction of the 50s*, Avon Books, New York, 1979.

——, 'Wight in Space: an Autobiographical Sketch' in Greenberg (ed.), *Fantastic Lives: Autobiographical Essays by Notable Science Fiction Writers*, Southern Illinois University Press, Carbondale, 1981.

Stabile, Carol A., *Feminism and the Technological Fix*, Manchester University Press, Manchester and New York, 1994.

Stableford, Brian, 'The Modern Period, 1964–86' in Barron (ed.), *Anatomy of Wonder: a Critical Guide to Science Fiction*, Bowker, New York and London, 1987.

——, 'Feminism and Sf: a Few More Crocodile Tears?' in *Foundation, the Review of Science Fiction*, No. 43, Summer 1988.

Steffen-Fluhr, Nancy, 'The Case of the Haploid Heart: Psychological Patterns in the Science Fiction of Alice Sheldon ("James Tiptree Jr")' in *Science Fiction Studies*, Vol. 17, Pt 2, July 1990.

Stephenson, Jill, *Women in Nazi Society*, Croom Helm, London, 1975.

——, *The Nazi Organisation of Women*, Croom Helm, London, 1981.

Sterling, Bruce (ed.), *Mirrorshades: the Cyberpunk Anthology*, HarperCollins, London, 1986.

Stern, Megan, 'Medical Science and Utopian Bodies: A Comparison of *Frankenstein* and the Human Genome and Visible Human Projects' (unpublished paper), 1999.

Stone, Allucquere Rosanne, 'Will the Real Body Please Stand Up? Boundary Stories about Virtual Cultures' in Michael Benedikt (ed.), *Cyberspace First Steps*, MIT Press, Cambridge, Mass. and London, 1991.

Suvin, Darko, 'On The Poetics of the Science Fiction Genre' in Rose (ed.), *Science Fiction: A Collection of Critical Essays*, Prentice-Hall, Englewood Cliffs, New Jersey, 1976.

——, *Metamorphoses of SF*, Yale University Press, 1979.

——, *Positions and Presuppositions in Science Fiction*, Macmillan, London, 1988.

Swindells, Julia, *Victorian Writing and Working Women*, Polity Press, Cambridge, 1985.

Teunissen, John J. (ed.), *Other Worlds*, Mosaic, Canada, 1980.

Thacker, Eugene, ' . . . /visible_human.html/digital anatomy and the hyper-texted body' in *Ctheory*, www.ctheory.com/a60.html (accessed July, 1998).

Theweleit, Klaus, *Male Fantasies*, Polity Press, Cambridge, 1987.

——, *Male Fantasies* (Vol. 2), Polity Press, Cambridge, 1989.

Thompson, William Irwin, *The Time Falling Bodies Take To Light: Mythology, Sexuality and the Origins of Culture*, St. Martins Press, New York, 1981.

Tiptree Jr, James (Alice Hastings Sheldon), 'The Women Men Don't See' (1973) in Tiptree Jr *Warm Worlds and Otherwise*, Ballantine, New York, 1975.

——, 'A Momentary Taste of Being' (1975) in Tiptree Jr, *Star Songs of An Old Primate*, Del Rey, 1978.

——, 'Your Haploid Heart' in John W. Campbell (ed.), *Analog: Science Fiction Science Fact*, Vol. 84, No. 1, September, 1969 (also (revised) in Tiptree Jr, James, *Star Songs of An Old Primate*, Del Rey, 1978).

Trescott, Martha Moore (ed.), *Dynamos and Virgins Revisited: Women and Technological Change in History*, Scarecrow Press, New Jersey and London, 1979.

Trilling Lionel, *The Liberal Imagination*, Penguin Books, Harmondsworth, Middlesex, England, 1970.

Usborne, Richard, *Clubland Heroes* (1953), Hutchinson, London, 1983.

Valeska, Lucia, 'The Future of Female Separatism' in *Quest*, Vol. 2, No. 2, Fall 1975.

Vance, Carol S., 'Social Construction Theory: Problems in the History of Sexuality' in D. Altman et al. (eds), *Which Homosexuality?* GMP, London, 1989; also in Crowley and Himmelweit (eds), *Knowing Women: Feminism and Knowledge*, Polity Press, Cambridge, 1992.

Ward, Lester Frank, *Dynamic Sociology*, D. Appleton & Co., New York, 1883.

——, *Pure Sociology*, Macmillan, New York, 1903.

——, *Glimpses of The Cosmos*, G. P. Putnam's Sons, New York, 1913–18.

Warner Jr, Harry, *All Our Yesterdays*, Advent Press, Chicago, 1969.

Warwick, Patricia, *The Cybernetic Imagination in Science Fiction*, MIT Press, Cambridge, Mass. and London, 1980.

Watson, John B., *Psychology from the Standpoint of a Behaviourist*, Lippincott, 1919.

Watson, Noelle and Schellinger, Paul E. (eds), *Twentieth Century Science Fiction Writers* (3rd edn), St James Press, Chicago and London, 1991.

Westkott, Marcia, 'Mothers and Daughters in the World of the Father', in *Frontiers: Women's Studies Program, University of Colorado*, Vol. 3, No. 2, 1978.

Whitehead, Alfred North, *Science and The Modern World*, Cambridge University Press, 1926.

Wiener, Norbert, *Cybernetics*, MIT Press, 1948.

——, *God & Golem Inc.*, Chapman and Hall, London, 1964.

——, *The Human Use of Human Beings: Cybernetics and Society* (1954), Sphere, London, 1968.

Wilden, Anthony, *System and Structure*, Tavistock Publications, London, 1972.

Williams, Keith, 'Back from the Future: Katharine Burdekin and Science Fiction in the 1930s in Maroula Joannou (ed.), *Women Writers of the 1930s: Gender, Politics and History*, Edinburgh University Press, 1999.

Wilson, Edward O., *Sociobiology: the New Synthesis*, Belknap, Harvard University Press, Cambridge, Mass. and London, 1975.

Wolf, Deborah Goleman, *The Lesbian Community*, University of California Press, 1979.

Wolf, Naomi, *The Beauty Myth*, Vintage, London, 1990.

Wolff, Charlotte, MD, *Love between Women*, Duckworth, London, 1971.

Wollstonecraft, Mary, *A Vindication of the Rights of Women: with Strictures on Political and Moral Subjects* (1792), W. Strange, London, 1844.

Wolmark, Jenny, 'Science Fiction and Feminism' in *Foundation: the Review of Science Fiction*, No. 37, Autumn, 1986.

——, *Aliens and Others: Science Fiction, Feminism and Postmodernism*, Harvester Wheatsheaf, London, 1993.

Women and Beauty Magazine, *A Collection of Careers Planned for Women*, Sampson, Low, Marston & Co, London, 1946.

Wright, Elizabeth, *Psychoanalytic Criticism: Theory in Practice*, Methuen, London, 1984.

Wysor, Bettie, *The Lesbian Myth*, Random House, New York, 1974.

Zagarell, Sandra A., 'Narrative of Community: the Identification of a Genre' in *Signs: Journal of Women in Culture and Society*, Vol. 13, No. 3, Spring, 1988.

Zamyatin, Yevgeny, *We* (1924), Penguin Books, Harmondsworth, Middlesex, England, 1972.

Zimmerman, Jan, *The Technological Woman: Interfacing with Tomorrow*, Praeger, New York, 1983.

Zoline, Pamela, 'The Heat Death of the Universe' in *New Worlds*, No. 173, July 1967 (reprinted in Pamela Zoline, *Busy about the Tree Of Life*, Women's Press, London, 1988).

Index